ADVANCE PRAISE

"When I began to read, I was absolutely captivated. A marvelous story, and I love the spiritual aspect. I have myself experienced the connection between Native Americans and First Nation's people, and dolphins."

—Dr. Jane Goodall, D.B.E., primatologist and anthropologist, UN Messenger of Peace

"*The Blackfish Prophecy* is a sweeping, emotionally packed book, with a grip-ping tale and a big heart. Rachel Clark has created a fascinating world of smart kids, mystical orcas, and acts of morality that must be carried out, no matter how difficult. Readers of all ages will learn much about killer whales, and why they simply do not belong in captivity. This wonderful story is fictional, but the facts are all too real."

—David Kirby, author of *Death at SeaWorld: Shamu and the Dark Side of Killer Whales in Captivity*

"Rachel Clark has created an entrancing story that not only captures the beauty of the Pacific Northwest and the native and orca societies which make it so unique, but also the potential for deep and powerful connections between human and killer whale cultures in the wilderness environment. I enjoyed it immensely."

—Tim Zimmerman, Associate Producer and Co-Writer of *Blackfish*

"*The Blackfish Prophecy* opens many doors to understanding and possibilities for living as members of the family of life on Earth."

—Howard Garrett, co-director of *Orca Network*

THE BLACKFISH PROPHECY

Terra Incognita & The great Transition: Book One

RACHEL CLARK

Illustrated by
KAREN SAVORY

FAWKES PRESS

permissions@fawkespress.com
Karen Savory, Illustrator
Susan Marie Andersson, Cover Designer
David Kirby & Susan Dente Ross, Editors

Print ISBN 978-1-945419-00-3
EPUB ISBN 978-1-945419-01-0
Library of Congress Control Number: 2016901288

In memory of all those beings who have
Suffered too much or died too soon in the shadow of The Fallacy.

With love to my sons and the generation of the Great Transition:
You are unleashing an epic force for harmony Just by being you.
This is your time.

This book is dedicated to you and to the whales… And to all Earth's life
and ecosystems

With whom you dance across the universe.

The greatest story is that all life is one.
Carl Safina

TABLE OF CONTENTS

BLACKENED BIRTH

TERRA KNELT IN THE PUNGENT GLOOM inside the ancient cedar tree. Huddled in focus, she worked her bow drill back and forth, laboring for a spark. Sometimes she'd use a match, but today was special. Today needed the sacred birth of a coal. A match was so different: the quick unmistakable snap of ignition, the whiff of sulphur, the instant leap of flame. But this quiet work of drawing fire from cool wood, of running the spindle fast against the board, the heat of friction slowly building to a flame drawn up from deep inside her…It was the only way to properly celebrate this news.

Eyebrows knit in concentration, her arm working as sure and strong as any logger's, Terra whispered in sync with her work until it was almost a mantra: "Welcome, little one. Welcome to your dark, cold home. Welcome to the waves washing over you. Welcome to the salmon that will fill you.

Welcome to the sounds that will guide you. Welcome to your

mama, your sisters, your aunties and uncles and cousins and friends. Welcome to your Granny." Lowering her voice even more, her throat tight, she blinked and murmured, "You are so lucky, little one, to be born while your Granny is still here."

Terra's dream came to her again, the way it had almost every day for the last few months since she'd first awoken from it. But now. Now everything was different. As of today the calf she'd dreamt about was real. *Could that mean the rest of her dream was real too?* She shook her head, trying to focus on her work, but took a quick glance at Tiluk, her best friend. Maybe she should tell him the rest of her dream. Maybe Granny *did* need help. Her throat tightened again, remembering. But it was just a dream, wasn't it?

There it is. She inhaled sharply. The birth of a coal was always a miracle.

She put down her bow, bent further and leaned on her palms, her long, otter-brown braid grazing the dirt, and breathed gently into the tiny hole where the newborn orange light lay nestled. Smaller than a match head, it glowed with her breath, an instant response. She sat up, pushing her braid back over her shoulder as she reached for the tinder bundle of dry moss she'd gathered for this fire. Then, tilting her board, she carefully nudged the little ember from its notch into the dry tendrils and whispered, "Welcome little blackened one. Welcome to the Salish Sea. Welcome to Earth."

Terra blew gently on the tinder bundle and a lick of flame leapt up, answering her. She placed the bundle into the ring, and fed it carefully; adding more moss, then the bits of kindling she'd laid aside to dry months earlier. The fire wrapped its arms around the moss and sticks, quickly growing, tripping over itself as it rose higher. Hungry orange light flung back the shadows and the walls came alive. She sighed with satisfaction as she leaned back on her heels; the fire illuminating her pale moon cheeks, her long slender nose, and her prominent heart-shaped face as she looked up at dozens of killer whales dancing across the cave of the hollow tree. She smiled, knowing it was a family tree inside a tree. She and Tiluk had carved every single killer whale of the Southern Resident Community in Puget Sound, all 79 of them, on the walls of their tree cave. The Southern Residents were made up of three maternal family groups called pods—J pod, K pod, and L pod. And now the newest calf of J pod was about to be inscribed here, too. The 80ᵗʰ orca of the endangered Southern Residents. A cause for celebration.

Terra glanced at Tiluk again, her quirky, expressive eyebrows mirroring her quiet smile. Tiluk's black eyes flashed sparks of warmth in the flickering new light. Now she could see Fierce, her kestrel. Fierce was a bird of prey, a falcon, and he was perched on Tiluk's arm, hooded by his tiny leather cap, patiently waiting until it was time to hunt. That would come next...after the ritual birth of fire and carving of the new family member. Like no one else,

Tiluk *got* her reverence for the orca, and now, this calf. Maybe she should tell him everything. She just couldn't believe it was happening. The calf was *real*! She shook her head to clear it. Did that mean she was destined to have a special mission with the calf, as Granny had transmitted in her dream?

Laying a few small logs carefully on her fire, she stood and reached inside her back pocket for her knife. She'd built the fire to last for about thirty minutes, just the right amount of time to carve an orca on the wall of cedar.

Tiluk moved Fierce from his fist to his shoulder and pulled out his wooden flute with its intricate orca and raven-headed mouthpiece. His father Joseph, a native of the Pacific Northwest whose family roots went back about a thousand years, had made the flute for his seventh birthday; and, for Terra, he'd made an elk-skin drum painted with orca and salmon. She realized that was almost exactly seven years ago since their 14ᵗʰ birthdays were coming up. Tiluk's shiny, bone-straight black hair glittered in the firelight, reflecting the etched black ink drawings on his flute. His hair was almost as long as hers, but his was loose, falling around his shoulders like moss hanging from a tree. Terra stared at Tiluk. It felt like they'd always been playing for the whales. Always.

He raised his flute to his lips. Terra recognized the song after the first three notes and flashed a grin of approval, forgetting her dream for a moment.

Simple Gifts was a perfect choice. She sang the words quietly alongside his melody as her knife blade moved deftly beneath and to the right of J-16; also known as Wendy. *'Tis the gift to be simple, 'tis the gift to be free...* Wendy was Granny's granddaughter, and the mother of this new calf. The calf she'd dreamt about. Her parents and Tiluk's and a group of other researchers known as ExplOrca had been studying the Southern Residents here in the Puget Sound for decades. In particular, they followed J Pod. J Pod was a group of 24 killer whales who hunted, slept, swam, and played together. And they were all governed by Granny. *And when we find ourselves in the place just right...* Terra's parents and her "other parents," Tiluk's mom and dad, were marine biologists who'd spent the last 20 years following these whales. It was they who'd helped discover that the Southern Resident families are among the largest, most highly stable family communities of killer whales in the world. And even more important, they'd helped show that long-standing, multi-generational families are the norm for all killer whales. That included another group of related pods known as the Northern Residents who lived in the tidal straits around Vancouver Island, just north of Puget Sound. The whole area was known as the Salish Sea, home to both populations of res-ident whales. And to Terra's family. *'Twill be in the valley of love and delight.*

Then there was Granny. Terra looked up at the etchings as she sang. Granny was at the very top of the family tree. She was the best known and oldest orca ever observed, anywhere. *J-2.* She was over 100 years old and had been with her family for her entire life. Suddenly Terra was face to face with Granny again—as she'd been in her dream—and she felt her urgency once more. The force of her power...and her burning desire to save her family.

She shook her head, confused. Maybe it was all just a big coincidence. That had to be it. Besides, in her dream Granny had said that the new calf and the calf's older brother were destined to work with her as a team. But Terra knew there *was* no older brother. Wendy only had daughters.

That had to be it. The new calf didn't have a brother, so it was just a coincidence. The dream was just a dream. Even if the calf *was* real. Right?

Tiluk played the melody again and this time she joined him in a round until the tree cave swirled with their duet. Terra's hands fell away from the wall as she twirled around, singing upwards, into the hollow tree, towards the whales. *To turn, turn will be our delight, Til by turning, turning we come 'round right.*

"Watch the knife Terra!" Tiluk's quiet but sturdy voice rang out for the first time, his flute silenced. Terra reached for the wall of whales and steadied herself, a slow blush creeping to her face. She smiled sheepishly at Tiluk and tilted her head down a fraction of an inch, acknowledging his care. Tiluk laid his flute carefully in his lap and took Fierce from his shoulder. He stroked the handsome bird as he nodded up at her work. "The calf looks like she belongs there."

Terra exhaled as if she'd been holding her breath. She knew from his reserved statement that he meant a lot more than what he'd said. He knew about her dream, she'd told him about it, and how sure she'd been that Wendy was pregnant. She just hadn't told him everything. He knew she was keeping something from him, but he respected her enough to wait until she was ready to share. That was how they operated.

"Yeah, she does."

The fire was dimming. Terra turned back to her task, chips of cedar flew from her fingertips as the new whale emerged, J-50; Wendy's new calf. To the left and underneath the carving of Wendy were her daughters: J-28 (Beauty) and J-32 (Babe), J-36 (Bountiful), the new calf's sisters, and the ones who—besides her mother, Wendy, grandmother, Eve, great grandmother, Granny, and her adopted uncle Jake…Big Jake— would be nearest her side for most of her life. Wendy was known by the researchers to be an excel-lent mother. Most female killer whales are born that way, but some are exceptional and Wendy was one of those. She was unusually protective and watchful with her calves, and Terra believed it was because Granny and Eve helped her all the time. The researchers knew Wendy was about 43 years old and had raised every one of her offspring successfully; she hadn't lost a baby. Or grandbaby, for that matter. Wendy already had at least two grand-children—Beauty and Babe were both still nursing their first calves. Actually,

Wendy was so old no one had expected her to have another baby. This calf was a *big* surprise to all the researchers, especially since Terra had predicted her birth. She smiled to herself, thinking of the way her mother's jaw had hit the floor when she'd gotten the call earlier today from her graduate student Jason, who'd phoned from the research boat and sputtered something about

Wendy having a new baby. That's when Terra had grabbed her bow drill and knife and bee-lined up here with Tiluk and Fierce.

"I'll be back before paddle watch! Wait for me!" she'd called out as she ran outside to find Tiluk. Because of her dream she was even more surprised than anyone, and had to escape her parents to absorb this news. *The calf was real.*

Terra stood back checking her work in the flickering fire light. Squinting a little, she stepped in with the knife once more, edged the rim of J-50's mouth, nicked a small mark for the blowhole, and nudged the dorsal fin upwards.

Then she bent over and grabbed a piece of old charred coal from the outside edge of the fire. She smudged the new whale carefully, blackening the calf's skin and leaving open spaces for its white and gray patches

There. She's here.

Even though Terra didn't trust *all* of her dream, she was certain the calf was a female. She couldn't shake it. Something was different now that she knew the calf was real. Her brows furrowed. *Is it possible that somehow Granny had really communicated with her?* Because that's how the dream felt.

"Terra," Tiluk spoke into the cedar-smoked air, "maybe some part of you knew Wendy was pregnant because you heard the whales on the hydro-phones." There was a long pause, as if Tiluk and his ultra-quiet nature had to wait a beat before uttering more words. He was just as surprised that the aging Wendy had given birth to this calf as she was. And he'd been thinking about how to explain it, too. "Maybe you understand more of their language than anyone realizes and that's why you had that dream."

Terra knew Tiluk was talking about the live feed her parents had set up before her own birth. The hydrophones just offshore constantly broadcast whale calls up to the main house and the family yurt, where she'd slept with her parents when she was a baby. She'd heard all manner of clicks, squeals, whistles, and rippling harmonic slides since she was an infant. Once she was old enough, she'd moved into her own small yurt and her parents had planted a microphone in her warm, circular room so that she could talk and play music out into Blackfish Cove, the small inlet that was Terra's backyard. One of the reasons her and Tiluk's parents had built their living space and lab— what they called the "main house"—here on Blackfish Cove, was because

J Pod often used the cove as a sanctuary; they'd come to rest and play here. From the day she moved into her own yurt with its two-way live feed Terra had broadcast daily messages to the whales whenever they appeared in the cove. She called them her "podcasts," to the delight of everyone in ExplOrca.

"I just don't think that's it, Tiluk," she slipped her knife back into the leather sheath she'd made. Thinking about her inexplicable sense of connection to this new calf, she shook her head, frowning to herself as she added one more small log to the fire.

Terra sat down next to her friend, shoulder to shoulder as always, and they quietly leaned back against the comforting wall of the tree cave. Fierce rested on Tiluk's shoulder while the two admired the new calf who'd taken her place with the rest of her family on the wall of etchings. Absently, Terra picked up a nearby piece of cedar and pulled her knife back out, the blade finding the soft wood with the same surety of purpose as her bow stick twirling against the board.

Soon more cedar chips fell from her hands. Feeling the weight of his attention, Terra looked at Tiluk and found his eyes resting on her thought-fully. Glancing down at her knife, he nodded towards her hands and said simply, "Maybe we really did make a connection back when we did the Morse Endeavor."

Besides playing their elk-hide drum and flute together for the whales when they were in Blackfish Cove, The Morse Endeavor, was *the* coolest thing she and Tiluk had ever done. They'd secretly called it the Morse Endeavor, and even their scientist parents had practically swooned with anticipation. She smiled mischievously at Tiluk, recalling the time she'd hatched the plan when she was ten to use her whale walky-talky to "teach" Granny's pod Morse code by way of a telegraph. She'd spent day after day, every single time Granny's pod was in the cove, clicking out the alphabet into the live-feed microphone for hours. And she'd always follow the code with her spoken English translation. She'd also speak, and then click out a few simple musical poems, over and over again, hoping her voice would be a grounding rod for the Morse code, just in case the whales could figure it all out. Sometimes she'd use her elk-hide drum and beat out the code with its deep, resonant tones.

Tiluk would help her and take turns tapping, but more often than not, he'd stay closer to the water and play his flute…Terra smiled warmly at Tiluk now as her fingers continued their whittling. He'd always preferred the mystery of music to the more mechanical, scientific approach of her tapping.

He was like his father in that way. Joseph was the boat captain of the crew, and though he always helped the researchers on the team with whatever needed to be done there was also something reserved and unspoken about how he viewed the whales.

Her favorite poem to tap out, either with her drum or her telegraph, had been "One Fish, Two Fish, Red Fish, Blue Fish," by Dr. Seuss, which had been her mom's idea. "That poem might speak to the whales," Claire had said, "if they have any capacity at all to grasp our language through a code."

Terra had agreed, since the first stanza seemed written with orca in mind; the local natives, Joseph's tribe, had called them *Blackfish* as far back as anyone could remember, maybe even thousands of years. Of course, orca were about as similar to "fish" as she and Tiluk were to Fierce. Whales, she knew, are much more like humans…but unfortunately a lot of people didn't realize that for a long time.

The lines came to her—words that, to Terra, managed to embody both her beloved Blackfish and the real fish they depended on. For Terra, it was about the interconnection between salmon and orca. The red fish and the blackfish.

She grinned, thinking of what Dr. Seuss would think of her interpretation of his poem. By now, after all those hours of hopeful tapping, the lines had become part of her, and they rang out in her mind as her knife moved like a wiggling minnow in her hands, the fire flashing in her eyes. And then that last line hit her.

Go ask your dad. She glanced at Tiluk, wondering if maybe she should tell his father the whole story. Joseph, after all, was the one with his quiet native heritage and the one who, when they were very lucky, would tell her and

Tiluk stories about the old ways and the Blackfish myths from long ago. *No*, she thought, scolding herself. *There is no older brother. It was just a dream.* Still… Keeping this new idea to herself, she said, "But Tiluk, we know they never learned Morse. Even after all those months of trying. It was a failed experiment." Tiluk just stared at her, hard. She could almost hear his voice resonate inside her head: *There are no failed experiments*. But she knew better. It hadn't worked.

"I'm taking Fierce out to let him hunt," he said as he stood, nimbly hold-ing the bird while tucking his flute into a leather sheath he'd made for it that resembled a quiver for arrows. Terra understood that Tiluk was annoyed and instead of telling her, he was giving them both some space. He was also making a point.

As Tiluk ducked through the doeskin covering the tree cave's opening,

Terra wondered if he could be right: that their Morse Endeavor had made a connection with Granny's pod. It just didn't seem possible. She was sure it hadn't worked. Even after months and months of tapping, practically until she had calloused fingertips, nothing had changed. There were no magical moments of "short short short short, short short, long, short, short long short, short long short, short long:" *Hi Terra*, clicked in Morse from the cove beyond her yurt's window. Just the usual sequences of clicks, flutters, whistles, and sliding, rippling harmonics. And certainly not a language, as they'd all been hoping. The entire ExplOrca team had been quietly holding their collective breath—the researchers were just as curious and excited as she was about her project. Often someone from the crew would drop in at her yurt to listen with her and see if there was any response from the whales as she tapped into her two-way. But eventually they'd all gone back to business as usual, doing their research and whale observations. They'd given up. It hadn't worked. Disappointed, Terra had resumed her usual Orca DJ routine; only now with Morse code peppering her daily podcasts.

She looked down. *Whoa*. There was the calf, almost finished. Her knife found the soft wood once more, her hands instinctively nicking the finishing touches while she remained heavy in thought, deeply perplexed. She'd never gotten the sense that the whales ever talked *back*. So why now? Why this unexpected connection with this calf? Why the dream? Could it be real? She shook her head again. No. The calf didn't have a brother. Period. But how did she know Wendy was going to have this baby? Would the hydrophones be transmitting something her brain could decode *now*, after all this time?

She knew her parents had planted the hydrophone into her bedroom when she was born on the off chance that a baby human, if exposed to orca song from birth, could develop the brain capacity to understand their language, once and for all. For decades people had tried to teach dolphins to com-municate with humans, and it hadn't ever really worked. Not because the animals weren't smart enough. Many whales and dolphins were at least as smart as humans, maybe even more so. The problem, she knew, was that the whales were just not built to make human sound. Their equipment was wrong. Teaching a whale to use human sounds was like trying to teach a snake to do push-ups.

Loud clanging suddenly rang out from the house down the hill. Terra's head jerked up and her knife slipped. "Ouch!" She'd sliced her finger.

Insistent and dark, the clangs erased everything else. Into her mouth went her bleeding finger as she hastily slipped the knife back in its sheath and stuck the carving of her calf into her pocket. She quickly stamped out the dying embers of the fire and poured the contents of her water bottle on it, just to be sure, then ducked quickly outside, almost crashing heads with

Tiluk. The clanging filled the woods.

"What's going on?" Her voice was off-kilter and high pitched. She didn't expect him to know the answer.

Usually the damp quiet of Pacific Northwest cedar forest and its peaceful stillness soaked into her pores. But now, instead of the harmony of this place, she breathed fear. And she could see it in Tiluk's flashing eyes, too. The heavy iron dinner bell never clanged when it wasn't dinner time. Except in emergencies. Except that one time…

As one, the two friends tore off down the hill towards the main house. Her legs thrashed hard down the trail alongside Tiluk's. *Was it her mom? Her dad? One of the crew, capsized in some kind of boating accident?* Her heart raced and blood pumped against her ears. *What was going on??* The first time she could recall the triangular bell ringing for an emergency was when she'd been two and the twin towers collapsed. Even after all these years, if the bell rang when it wasn't dinner time, she assumed the worst. She'd never forget the ear-splitting clangs as her mother had stood in shock, gripping her tight against her chest with one arm, the other rattling that bell for all she was worth…Summoning her husband and closest friends from their boats and their binoculars.

She skidded on the steep part of the path, nearly tripping over a huge tree root. Tiluk reached out for her. *Get a grip Lewis*, she chastened herself.

"Hey," he breathed sharply, "maybe they're ringing the bell to celebrate the calf. Maybe they're having a party." Immediately she felt better and slowed down. Of course! Her mom was always finding an excuse to celebrate and this was a big deal, especially since Terra had predicted the birth.

"Oh wow, Tiluk, I'm sure you're right. That's gotta be it." They dropped back to a fast walk, and Terra put her fingers to her lips to call in her kestrel who was still hunting. She tasted blood and remembered the cut on her finger. The bell stopped, and they smiled at each other, certain they'd figured it out.

Catching her breath, she whistled again for Fierce, this time leaving her bleeding finger in her mouth and lifting her other arm as she saw him swoop through the branches, a mouse dangling from his small ruthless talons. He landed on her hand as they entered the clearing to the main house. Her folks stood waiting for her on the porch, looking ashen.

Terra stopped. Seeing her somber parents, she knew at once that the bell was not clanging for an early celebratory dinner. *OK, at least they're both okay, that's good.*

But then, she knew. Oh no, it's the calf. The calf!

She crumpled to the ground under the trees, Tiluk beside her, certain that her baby whale had died: the most dangerous time for any wild whale is the first few days of its life. Pulling away from Tiluk, she reached into her pocket and gripped her little whittled orca. Tears sprang up instantly. The carving quietly soaked up her blood as her vision blurred and her parents were coming towards her in slow motion. Her mom, who understood her so well, suddenly knew what Terra was thinking.

"Oh honey, no it's not the calf. The calf is fine."

Her mom and dad sat down in the forest duff, next to them. "The calf is fine Terra," her mom said again, speaking to her daughter's special connection with this calf, hugging her close as her dad quietly took Fierce.

"It's not the calf, sweetheart," her dad said again, gently. Then turning to look at Tiluk, an odd twinge of pain flittering across his face, he added,

"But there is very bad news. It's the calf's older brother at OceanLand. He's killed again."

BLUE FISH

THE ONLY WAY MILES could put up with another stupid trip to OceanLand was if he could do "Lunch with Shantu." His mom, Karen, had wanted to take him and his little sister Aria to the park again and it totally pissed him off. He knew the real reason she took them to places like this was because she felt so guilty about the divorce. "Seriously, Mom?" he'd jumped up from the dinner table, flinging back his chair when she'd brought up OceanLand that night a few weeks ago when Aria was crying again after her dad had dropped them off. "Do you really think Shantu is going to fix this?" He'd stomped out of the kitchen and slammed himself in his bedroom, popping his ear buds in and turning the volume up full blast. Nothing a little Violent Femmes couldn't handle. *Add it up, Mom.*

She'd caved, of course. And so here they were. Dining with freaking Shantu. He could almost tolerate this with *Blister in the Sun* blasting in his ears. It seemed like the first thing his dad had done after he moved out was start showing off his old music collection to Miles…in his spare time; his dad was *always* working. But that was okay. Turns out he *loved* the Femmes. Then it got even better when his dad had hauled off and given him his whole collection of tunes for his 14th birthday a few months ago. If he had his way he'd just sit in his room, game out on his tablet, and crank up Gordon Gano. His mom's lips were moving, and Aria was all excited, pointing at Shantu. The Femmes kept throbbing inside his head while Miles forked up huge mouthfuls of the Swedish meatballs he'd carried off from the "delicious all-you-can-eat buffet." At least he was going to eat well.

He rolled his eyes at his mom when she looked at him again,

imploring him to ditch his ear buds. "Fine," he snapped, pulled them out, stood up and went back for dessert before the show started. He piled his plate with cheesecake and cherry sauce, refilled his Coke, and slumped heavily back in his seat, pulling his hoodie down over his eyes.

"Isn't this exciting Miles?" His mom was too perky; he knew what she was up to.

"Yeah mom, whatever," he grumbled pulling his face and neatly trimmed sandy hair even further into the dark of his hoodie. Peering out into the glaring sun and away from his mom, he stared at Shantu. *That whale is freaking blistered in the sun*, he thought angrily. *Aren't killer whales, like, supposed to live in the* dark *ocean?* Whoa, Miles caught himself. He'd never thought of it that way before…it was the Femmes and zoning out on Blister. *But come to think of it, what the heck? This was freaking Florida. It's like 95 degrees out there and that whale is baking!* Narrowing his eyes, Miles knew he'd noticed something he wasn't supposed to. He'd bet his whole Femmes collection that this whale's black skin was seriously sunburned. He could see it; the top of the whale's back was shedding rolls and bits of skin that looked eerily like this own when he got a sunburn, only a whole lot worse. It looked like it hurt. He knew for sure that the whale's black skin attracted the sun's intense rays, and there was no shade in this restaurant-side pool. Are whales supposed to get sunburned? He snorted. *I seriously doubt it.* He gulped his Coke, *Freaking screwed up whale. Welcome to my world.*

At that instant, Shantu rolled over and pressed his tail flukes hard, whirling immediately towards Miles, Aria, and their mom. "Doodle, he's coming right for us!" he grabbed his sister's hand, and squeezed. Miles caught him-self pressing backwards in his seat while he squeezed his sister's hand a little too hard. The whale stopped, raised his head above water and hovered just in front of them. Even from up here Miles could see that Shantu's body was wider than all three of them sitting at the table. A thread of primal fear snaked up from his abdomen curled in his belly, then slithered up to his throat. *The ocean's top predator*, he recalled from previous shows. *No freaking kidding.* But then he looked into the whale's liquid gaze and sucked in his breath. His fear evaporated. Shantu caught Miles' eyes, and stared. For like a whole five seconds. Miles stopped breathing. Then the whale just disappeared into the deepest part of the pool, his immense dorsal fin draped like a giant deflated balloon over his truck-sized back.

"Oh my word, honey, did you see that? Shantu looked right at you!" his mom gushed at him. *Jeez, could his mom ever give him a little space?* He could hardly enjoy the moment—Shantu *had* looked right at him, and not only that, it was almost as if he'd read Mile's mind, coming over at that exact moment... but now he had to get his mom off his back, again.

"Yeah mom, I noticed," he grumbled. "Whatever." But when he looked furtively at Doodle (he'd given Aria that little pet name a long time ago, you know 'cause she was a *dude* but *not* a dude...she was a *Doodle!*) she smiled at him sweet as ever. She knew it was *way* cool. She crossed her eyes then winked, their little secret society handshake. They'd gotten pretty good at communicating without words. Words blistered. He reached over and gently pinched Doodle's inner wrist. "Here's some cherry sauce. I can't eat anymore." He shoveled the last huge bite of cheesecake into his mouth and stretched back in his chair, letting his long legs unfold in front of him. The blasting music for the show was riling everybody up, including that poor blistered beast of a whale. *Well, buddy, you and me, we're in the same freaking boat.* Miles chuckled to himself. *Killer whale in a bathtub. Kids with divorced parents. Same freaking thing.*

"WELCOME TO OCEANLAND!" called out the disembodied voice narrating their Lunch with Shantu. "TODAY YOU ARE HAVING LUNCH WITH SHANTU, A 12,000 POUND MALE KILLER WHALE." There was an expectant pause, "THE BIGGEST WHALE

AT ANY PARK IN THE WORLD."

I guess they are proud about that, he grimaced to himself. *Biggest whale in a bathtub is more like it.* Miles was having a hard time letting go of the outrage he felt. He glanced at Aria, "That's like as heavy as an overloaded tractor trailer truck!" he whispered to her. Her eyes went wide.

"SHANTU AND OUR TRAINER ARE QUITE A TEAM. THEY WORK TOGETHER EVERY DAY AND AS YOU CAN SEE THEY HAVE A LOT OF FUN!"

Miles watched the tall slim woman working with Shantu almost right in front of their table. She had a tiny whistle in her mouth and long blond hair pulled back in a bouncy pony tail. She had another trainer with her, off to the side, and a huge bucket of dead fish. She wore a slick blue wetsuit with white splashed across it. Blondie was swinging her head back and forth, back and forth, in front of the whale, all perky and hoppy, leaning quickly from one foot to the other. Shantu responded by shaking his head back and forth, back and forth; his precision in reflecting Blondie's exact movements made

Mile's jaw drop. It was like they were two bodies governed by one mind. The audience ooohed and ahhhed in appreciation. *Maybe Shantu did like it here after all…he sure likes that trainer.*

"Miles, honey, isn't that amazing the way Shantu is moving so in sync with his trainer?" His mom was really trying.

"Yeah, mom. It's pretty cool," he had to give it to her, it *was* pretty darn amazing.

"SHANTU AND HIS TRAINER ARE A TEAM THAT PRACTICE EVERY DAY," droned the voice. "WHILE HE PERFORMS HIS BEHAVIORS SHANTU GETS HIS DAILY PORTION OF FISH. CAN YOU GUESS HOW MANY POUNDS OF FISH A 12,000 POUND KILLER WHALE EATS EACH DAY, BOYS AND GIRLS?"

All the kids yelled out at once, Aria included. "100 pounds!!"

"SHANTU EATS CLOSE TO *300 POUNDS* OF RESTAURANT QUALITY

FISH EVERY SINGLE DAY." The audience let out a collective gasp of amazement. "AND YOU THOUGHT YOU HAD A LOT FOR LUNCH!"

The audience loved it. They cheered for the whale. Blondie was throwing a handful of fish into the whale's mouth. Even from back behind the barrier,

Miles' adrenalin surged. *Dude, his mouth is huge. Look at those teeth! Blondie must totally trust that whale.* Miles was fascinated by how close the whale hung to the deck where the trainers worked; he was *right* there.

It was riveting. *Killer whales are just amazing. It's no freaking wonder everyone wants to come to OceanLand!* He glanced at Aria, who was totally enraptured as the trainer sent Shantu around the side of the pool and everybody next to the edge got soaked as he hurled water over the sides with those giant tail flukes of his. Aria screamed with glee, and his mother jumped out the way. Miles sat motionless, letting himself be doused by Shantu.

"KILLER WHALES ARE ALSO KNOWN AS ORCA. *ORCINUS ORCA* IS THEIR OFFICIAL SPECIES NAME. BUT PEOPLE ARE MOST FAMILIAR WITH THE COMMON NAME: KILLER WHALE. THESE WHALES ARE THE OCEANS' TOP PREDATORS. PEOPLE FIRST CALLED THEM KILLER WHALES BECAUSE OF THEY WAY THEY HUNT IN THE WILD. THEY ARE ALSO KNOWN AS 'THE WOLVES OF THE SEA' BECAUSE OF THEIR EXCEPTIONAL TEAMWORK. THEY HERD FISH, TAKE SEALS FROM ICE AND BEACHES, AND TOGETHER THEY CAN EVEN TAKE DOWN LARGE WHALES OF OTHER SPECIES."

Miles' mind clicked into high gear as Shantu went back for more fish, hovering there like a giant puppy begging for treats. *Some puppy*, snorted Miles as he watched the huge killer whale hang in front of the blond trainer with her floppy ponytail. *The top predator of the ocean is doing circus tricks for a cute girl giving him dead fish.* Miles had a sudden unexpected flash of what the top predator would *really* do for fish, out in the actual ocean. Hunt. At high speed. With other whales. An orca team! *Totally awesome!* The trainer rubbed the whale's head fondly, then flung her arm straight out, flipped her wrist in a signal. Shantu swam upside down, spinning into the whale's version of a hand stand. He propelled his huge tail up and out above the water and waved his flukes at the crowd, who were all revved up, clapping madly.

"OUR TRAINERS WORK WITH SHANTU'S NATURAL INTELLI-GENCE. HE LOVES TO WORK AND LEARN NEW

BEHAVIORS LIKE THE ONE YOU JUST SAW. INSTEAD OF
HAVING TO HUNT FOR FISH, HE RECEIVES THEM AS A
REWARD WHEN HE PERFORMS HIS BEHAVIORS CORRECTLY."

"Miles, wouldn't it be amazing to grow up to be a killer whale
trainer?" asked his mom, still trying to draw him out from under his
hoodie.

"YEAH!" squealed Aria, "that's what *I'm* going be to when *I* grow
up!!" as if she'd never considered this possibility before, as if suddenly
her whole world was right.

"Oh sweetie," gushed his mom, "What an exciting thing to think
about!" Miles rolled his eyes. He'd have to talk to Aria, but later. He
didn't want to ruin this one sweet day for her. There weren't enough of
those anymore.

He looked back at this poor sod of a whale begging for his fish.
How can he stand this? Miles asked himself for the first time in his life.
He'd been to at least half a dozen OceanLand shows before, and it never
once occurred to him that the whales were anything but overjoyed to
perform. But now… now everything was different. Now that his parents
were divorced he could R a c h e l C l a r k see things he hadn't seen
before. *I mean, yeah, the trainers say they love the whale, but is he
allowed to be a freaking whale?* Shantu had looked right at him, and
he'd seen it: there was *definitely* someone home in there. He grunted
in angry empathy, and turned his head away from his mom and sister;
he didn't need them reading his mind, too. *Just like my parents think
they're doing what's best for us.*

Miles scowled, looking back down at the table as Blondie stretched
out on the stage lying down, propping her head up with one hand and
waving at Shantu and the audience with the other; an end-of-the-show
farewell. He reached over and grabbed Aria's plate, forking the last of
the cherry sauce into his mouth, pissed off. He was done. *I've gotta get
outta here.* But suddenly the applause tapered off and he glanced back
up at Blondie. *Wait. What the hell?* All he saw were the trainer's feet
thrashing above the water just before her entire body slid beneath the
surface alongside the immense black back of the whale. Miles stopped
breathing. The applause died. *Was this part of the show?* Shantu had
jerked her off the stage and down under the water. It was all happening
so fast Miles didn't know what to think and everything went deathly

quiet. But then the spell broke and someone yelled from behind him, "Hey! Hey! That whale has the trainer!! The whale's got her! HEY!!"

Someone else started yelling, too. "Help her! Please help her! Oh my God, he's got her!"

What the... Miles' heart rate took off like stone from a slingshot. People started screaming. All of a sudden what seemed like a hundred trainers clamored in from nowhere, descending like lemmings to the edge of the pool. They were all frantically slapping the water and whistling, but the whale ignored them. His mom grabbed Aria and yanked her into her arms, pressing Doodle's head against her chest, away from the tank. He'd never seen his mom like this. Wait, there was the trainer. He could see her down there with blood seeping from her head. Her ponytail dangled from her head in a very odd way; her scalp had been partially ripped back off her skull. Miles' stomach rolled. Shantu sat there holding the trainer down at the bottom. He looked like a dog who'd snatched a roast ham from the dining room table and slunk away to where no one could reach him.

Blood pounded in Mile's ears, and he couldn't hear anything but his own throbbing pulse. An invisible weight pressed into his chest and his stomach hissed. He couldn't move. In slow motion, he saw his mom from the corner of his eye speaking to him—her lips moving but his ears hearing nothing. He couldn't look away from Shantu. Karen got up and disappeared with Aria; he was probably supposed to follow, but he was frozen. He was vaguely aware that security had come in to herd everybody out of there. But in the growing chaos he remained, unable to move, watching everything.

Shantu was back at the surface with the panic-stricken trainer, she was gulping for air while blood flowed freely from her ripped-open scalp. The water around her went from a sparkling sky blue to hamburger pink. Shantu let go of her for a moment. The other trainers went into overdrive, dangling dead fish over the edge, smacking the water with their hands, and blowing their whistles as hard as they could. Miles saw the injured trainer treading water as her friends tried to distract the whale away from her. She took that one moment to try to swim to salvation. But the killer whale had other plans. He grabbed her arm in his mouth and clamped down, then hurled with her to the bottom. Miles could see her down there; her panic filled the pool and everyone surrounding it. Then he saw her arm snap in two pieces before a rush of blood surged like an angry red mushroom cloud from the bottom of the pool. The whale and the trainer disappeared inside it.

Mile's stomach heaved against his roiling guts. He clenched his eyes shut and clamped his jaw tight. A violent, all-consuming shudder convulsed his rigid body. Cheesecake and Swedish meatballs hit the back of his throat before splattering against the pool-side glass, blocking the reddened water.

He passed out.

ELEGY

THEY MOVED SLOWLY DOWN the steep wooden steps leading to the dock and kayaks, more like a funeral procession of hunched-over, defeated penguins than a family joyously welcoming a new arrival. The introductory strains of Samuel Barber's *Adagio for Strings* carried across the cove and amplified the melancholy aura enveloping the group. Even the sinking sun seemed dim and drained of warmth behind a thick drape of overcast clouds, the dense forest of evergreens rimming the edges of the cove a somber matte black with none of its characteristic dark emerald gleam. The water, too, was a threatening frigid black. The kids' "four" parents, Claire, Bill, Maggie, and Joseph led the way with Tiluk and Terra trailing behind with the two graduate students. Claire and Bill, Terra's parents, had met long ago in grad school. When they came to the Puget Sound to study orca they met Maggie and Joseph, who were already deeply involved in tracking the wild whales. A quick, intense camaraderie ensued and the four became inseparable. Now, twenty years later, they were family.

Claire and Terra shared a striking resemblance; Claire with her thick, hip-long braid of light brown hair and her kind, open face reflected Terra's youth with a wise and seasoned beauty. But her porcelain skin was quite fair compared to Terra's bronzed complexion as if her brown-eyed daughter had been sprinkled with a light dusting of cinnamon while she was merely sugared. Her pale face, with her warm sea-blue eyes, long straight nose and a well-earned web of grin wrinkles, offered steady humor and acceptance.

It was the magnetic warmth of Claire that Bill had fallen in love with all those years before. But he'd always been the rough one of their partnership.

Prone to losing himself in thought or his scientific pursuits, then occasionally erupting with the hot fire of debate, he'd become softer and more laid back over the years, as if his coarse edges had been polished against a river bottom.

His prominent lion's mane of thick sandy hair was tousled with fringes of gray. He was tall and large-framed against Claire's slender, strong form. He was the rapscallion, she the peacemaker.

While Terra and Claire looked similar, Tiluk appeared to be one of those young men who channeled his father's youth, repeating physical history. Tiluk's likeness to Joseph had recently become so strong, that Claire had already gently teased everyone to be sure they kept track of who was who. "It won't be long before we'll be calling you Joseph, honey," she'd say fondly to Tiluk sometimes. "You already look so much like your dad when we first met that sometimes I have to catch myself."

Like Tiluk, Joseph's hair was bone-straight and very long. But his was a muted silvering black compared to his son's glittering, free-flowing jet-black strands. And unlike Tiluk's, he kept his locks in two tight braids that hung well below his shoulders. Their eyes, too, were black and mysterious; both father and son seemed to see through some kind of veil, their eyes full of unfathomable depth. But Joseph's gaze came set with a force of wisdom that left no doubt as to who was the elder of their group. Like his son, Joseph rarely spoke. But when he did, everyone listened.

And Maggie's unmistakable dark-red mane of curls swept up out of her green eyes every day by a simple bandana, framed a face full of Irish cheer and freckles. Her dark brown skin and corkscrew mop of black-cherry locks were the result of her incongruous mix of Native American and Irish heritage. And though neither deep red curls nor green eyes had appeared in her son, freckles dotted Tiluk's shoulders and chest—a patch o' the Irish—as if to remind him he was connected to more than the generations of native ancestors of this ancient place.

But this evening Claire was no peacemaker. She'd rung the bell. The bell was only for extreme emergencies. Yet when she'd gotten the call from a colleague in Florida about what had happened at OceanLand this morning, ringing the bell was her first response. With that phone call, all the years of hurt and frustration burst, and something broke inside her. She'd known even as she rang the bell that obviously this wasn't a true emergency, but a part of her needed the tolling just the same. Something had to change. He'd killed again. Her heart cringed, thinking of him. She wiped her eyes, again.

Claire shivered inside her parka and glanced back at Terra and Tiluk, hand in hand as they descended the long set of stairs behind her and the other adults. She saw that Terra gingerly held the carved and blood-soaked whale that she'd brought home, her fingers bandaged from the cut she'd given herself. Claire hadn't been surprised to see Terra's carving of the new calf. She knew her daughter felt a special kinship with Wendy's new baby. She took a deep breath of the salted air she loved so much, reminding herself why she and her family were here. But her stomach remained tight with grief and empathy. Now, instead of having the chance to meet the new calf her daughter had dreamt about with a free and easy heart, the news of the killing shadowed everything. And even though she was a scientist, a world-class researcher of the highest order, Claire had asked Terra to broadcast the *Adagio* on the two-way. Just this once. With this latest killing, she felt an overwhelming need to ritualize her sorrow with the whales.

She looked at her husband Bill, taking in his salt-and-pepper windswept tousle of hair and etched face. His grim glance told her he felt as sick with the news and what it meant as she did. Looking back at Joseph and Maggie, she knew they felt it, too. Joseph reached out and clasped her shoulder for a moment, his eyes holding hers.

"Careful Claire," Maggie said, eyeing the narrow, steep stairway. "Mercy, we don't need any more injuries today," she murmured. Claire stopped short, turned all the way around, and leaned into Maggie, hugging her briefly from the stair below.

"I know, honey." Maggie hugged her hard. "I know."

Terra met Tiluk's eyes, puzzled. *What is really going on here?* The adults said they'd explain about the Shantu news later, at dinner. Why was her mom so upset? Terra didn't even know how to feel about what they'd told her. She was too dazed. *The calf has a brother. The calf has a **brother**.* Her mind, overwhelmed by this news—and the killing—had shut down. The words kept rolling around and around her head: *The calf has a brother. But her brother killed a human.* Her brother *killed* someone. It was all she could think of, as if the news itself blocked her from considering its implications. Tiluk had grown even more solemn and quiet than usual. Neither Terra nor Tiluk were ready to know more.

Besides, this was paddle watch: their unbroken daily routine of taking their kayaks into the cove before sunset. Sometimes bidding good night to the sun with the whales, if they came, and sometimes not. Early on in their observations of J Pod, the research team witnessed whales performing sunset rituals that included spyhopping up out of the water as they raised the top half of their bodies above the surface, seeming to peer together at the setting sun, sometimes even mirroring one another's alignment towards it as if they were creating a living orca sundial. Their nightly paddle watch here in the cove had become sacred because Granny's pod so often arrived. It was almost like the whales came here to say good night. Across all these years, the team kayaked into the cove every evening with the precision of a beating heart. Just to watch.

Joseph turned back to look at Terra and Tiluk, soaking up their confusion as if by osmosis. His dark eyes were full of warmth. Tiluk squeezed Terra's hand; they'd talk about it later.

As they reached the bottom of the long stairs, Maggie, Claire and Bill put all their focus into uncoiling the ropes linking the kayaks to the dock, as if by dealing with the coiled ropes they could disentangle the sad mess leading up to the Shantu killing...as if hoping to avoid the conversation that had to come later. Meanwhile, the two graduate students, Gwen and Jason, scanned the cove's inlet for whales. The grad students had become part of their family. They'd been here for the last three summers doing research alongside their scientist mentors. Terra and Tiluk liked having the grad stu-dents around; they were part grown-up and part kid. But right now they were just as confused by the OceanLand news as the kids were. Joseph stood with his son and Terra and the grad students, gazing out over the cove. His was the only peaceful face in their group.

"Uh, Claire?" said Gwen as soon as she'd scanned the cove with her bin-oculars. "They're here already. They're at the mouth of the cove."

Ever the consummate scientist Claire dropped her rope and pulled her own binocs up to her eyes. "They're early," she breathed. "That's odd."

Bill grabbed Claire's kayak before it floated away in the chop.

"Let's get out there, shall we?"

The music Claire had chosen was starting to swell, it pooled and eddied from the speakers on the dock out and over the water as they climbed into their kayaks and started buckling their lifejackets.

"Dad," Terra went suddenly cold. "Are you sure it's safe?"

Terra had been on paddle watch almost every single evening of her life. Never once had it occurred to her that danger might lurk amongst the immense whales they studied. She loved them. She trusted them. But, it suddenly occurred to her that the trainer who'd died today probably loved and trusted Shantu, too.

Bill's eyebrows shot up and he looked to the other adults, connecting to them as if they were a linked web. "Terra, you are probably safer out here with these whales than you are when you build a fire or hike in the woods with Fierce. Put that worry out of your mind." He helped her cast off from the dock as he backed up in his own kayak, making room for the others to cast off, too. Then, almost too quiet for anyone else to hear, he murmured,

"You'll understand soon enough."

"I don't know about any of the rest of you grim reapers, but I'm really excited to see if the pod brings the new calf into the cove!" Jason exclaimed, lifting everyone's mood a little. Jason was the one who'd first spotted Wendy with her new baby this morning out on Haro Strait, where the pod spent a lot of time foraging for fish. He and Gwen were out on the big boat with

Joseph navigating, the way they were almost every day of the long summer, tracking Granny's pod as unobtrusively as possible. Joseph's keen, almost uncanny sense of the whales' movements had garnered him a reputation in ExplOrca as the best orca-tracking boat captain in the world. He could trail the pod without bothering them and somehow, even when they'd disappear for long stretches at a time, he usually guessed right where they were going to surface again. Joseph's whale-tracking skill had brought the team reams of vocalization, foraging, and travel data specific to individuals in J Pod. They were also awash with orca poop, known scientifically as *scat*. Scat gave researchers important data on the whales' hormones and nutrition status. Scat was Maggie's specialty…which, of course, had led to jokes among the ExplOrca researchers over the years.

But it was sun-bleached blond Jason—who looked more golden-tanned-surfer-dude-in-flip-flops than scientist—who'd spotted the new calf swaddled between the enormous backs of its mother and grandmother. First he saw the telltale breathy spout of the newborn, much smaller than any other whales. And then the small little dolphin-sized lump of a baby, a dark bump wedged between the two huge black backs. Jason, stunned, had called up to the main house. Rendered nearly speechless, he'd managed to choke out, "Claire...Terra's dream! Dude! Tell that girl she was right...Wendy's got a new calf!" Click went the phone as Jason hung up on Claire in his amaze-ment. Claire had gaped at Terra over their lunch, and Terra had whooped out loud and run for her bow-drill and knife.

Now, even with the sad news about Shantu, Jason still beamed with his discovery. He hadn't believed Terra when she'd predicted Wendy's pregnancy with a dream, but he'd paid attention. They *all* had. Terra was their special whale walky-talky girl. And, as Joseph had said four months ago, after Terra told them about her dream and suspicion that Wendy was pregnant with a female calf, "You just never know with these whales." Besides, with this calf's birth, his PhD thesis tracking Granny's pod—the whales' long-term relationships and their lives in the Salish Sea—had taken a whole new turn: *Oldest known orca to give birth at age 43, has support from four-generation family.* His thesis might even make it into the venerable pages of the journals *Science* or *Nature*; it was that unprecedented to see an elder animal give birth, let alone track family members of any species in the wild, especially animals as problematic to follow as whales...with *four entire generations* of family members. Jason, in short, was stoked!

"Heads up, people," Bill called out softly to everyone. Granny's large head rose above the water in a classic spyhop just a few dozen feet away. She eyed them for a few seconds then blew loudly and sank beneath the water.

The crew gasped. Even though they saw these wild whales up close fairly often, it never felt routine. It always prompted a mixture of nerves and woozy, volatile joy. Even now...after the tragic news.

"I can see Big Jake out near the edge of the cove. He's patrolling." Gwen said, her 'nocs glued to her face. "I think he's on task to guard the cove."

Gwen, too, was studying this family for her PhD project which was different than Jason's. And even though they were almost always out on the boats together collecting similar data, that's where any resemblance stopped. Gwen radiated farm girl. To this day, she felt naked without her cowboy boots, although she had learned that wearing them inside her kayak was a recipe for ruin. They got wet every single time, and there's only so much seawater that calfskin can take before it chafes and splits. She didn't let go of her cowgirl hat though, along with her more recent accoutrement of choice, her binoculars. Gwen's rolling blond curls fell out of her hat and circled her cherubic round face and rose-tinted hazel eyes. She didn't look like a water girl on the outside, but at heart, she'd fallen for this place. Gwen was particularly interested in the relationships of male whales in the pods; what their roles were, how they interacted, when they socialized with other whales, and how they contributed to their families. She'd been 100 percent spell-bound back in college biology when she'd learned that wild male orca lived in their mother's pods for life. That was extremely unusual with any animal anywhere on the planet. And it reminded her of her own family's farm. Her dad had spent years trying to prep her brother to take over the farm, but Shane remained unwilling. She worried about her dad, and the way he was so filled with the longing for a son to govern their land. Maybe these male orca knew something he didn't. Maybe she'd figure out something import-ant that she could bring home to her dad.

The clincher had been the field trip with that same biology class when— clad in her signature boots and Stetson—she'd taken the ferry from Seattle for a weekend trip to visit ExplOrca headquarters on San Juan Island. She'd fallen in love. It happened the moment she stepped those boots onto her first ferry and felt the salt air whisking her hair off her face, almost seizing her hat, while the city pulsed behind her. She'd left the farmlands of Iowa to attend Washington State University. The dramatic change in the landscape had injected her with wonder—her awe at the immensity of the terrain of eastern Washington and its geologic relief, especially the scablands, came from previously knowing nothing but flat. Iowa flat stretched for miles. Iowa flat pressed down like ironed paper that spread forever. Flat filled with corn and soybeans and rows and rows and rows of tillage made by the huge combines that had been as common to her as fireflies. But the moment she stepped on her first ferry Gwen was home. This was her place. That feeling had been sealed when she saw her first wild orca. She'd known, instantly and without doubt, what she was doing with the rest of her life.

"Gwen put those binoculars down and watch the others," Claire called out gently. "Something unusual is happening here. I've never seen this before." Granny was escorting her daughter Eve, her granddaughter Wendy, and her great granddaughter, the new calf: Eve and Wendy were on either side of the calf with Granny off to the side while the rest of the pod hung on the other side of the cove. The crew let their paddles rest on the water as they watched. In the past, these whales had come to tolerate their presence but rarely acknowledged it. But now, as the *Adagio's* melodic, spiraling phrases swirled upwards, wrapping them and the whales in their somber but angelic strains, Granny circled her family slowly towards their kayaks with clear intention.

"Mom," whispered Terra in a loud hiss, her heart suddenly in her throat, a loud pounding in her head, her mind shorting out on the electric memories of Granny in her dream four months ago and the Shantu killing just today. "What is going on?"

Before Claire could say a thing, Granny disappeared. The *Adagio* peaked in its climactic burst of high-pitched strings, and at the crest of its melodic radiance, Granny rose up and out of the water in a full-body breach just fifteen feet from Terra's boat, drenching her, Gwen, Claire, and Tiluk.

Their collective gasp sounded like a feeble human counterpart to the whales blowing in synchrony. Terra's heart raced, the pounding in her head grew louder. "Mom!" she panted in shallow, quivering gasps. "She's coming towards us!"

Still dripping icy sea water, their boats bobbing in the wake from Granny's splash, Claire and Tiluk glanced at each other, touched their paddles to the surface and swept closer to Terra. Closing on either side of her, Claire said, "It's okay honey, take deep breaths. It's okay."

Before Claire could say another word, Granny brought Eve, Wendy, and the calf to within ten feet of the boats and they swam once around the perimeter of the kayaks, intentionally encircling the crew as if they were herding a school of salmon. Claire fell into a stunned silence softened by the fading resolution of the *Adagio*. As the strings sang out the poignant theme one last time, four generations of orca surfaced together, blowing in synchrony, covering the crew with mist. Maggie and Claire glanced at each other in disbelief. The calf wriggled between its mother and grandmother, captivated by the people in the boats, trying to see them better.

"Mom, mom!" Terra's voice pitched like a raft tossed in a gale. "Granny! Mom! She's coming towards me! MOMMY!"

Granny's dorsal fin slid quietly below the surface just in front of Terra's kayak, her body aimed straight at her. On either side, Claire and Tiluk could only watch as the huge whale descended, her white eye patches visible from above, leaving a wake.

"Mom!" Terra's voice had gone raspy and thin. Granny's huge black body glided beneath Terra's kayak shadowing it from beneath, the precision of her path unmistakable. She passed beneath Terra and Terra only. After she sur-faced behind Terra, Granny swam back around to the calf and other mothers. Then she rolled so that her eye was above water and visible to everyone, but she watched only Terra, who fell instantly silent, instantly transported back to her dream. In that hushed, luminous moment, she recalled something she'd forgotten, something Granny had urged her in the dream: *Be aware for this special connection to come, Terra. Watch for the special connection.* This was it. The calf's presentation. The special connection.

Everyone was riveted. Seconds had passed since Granny's breach. Joseph and Bill inched closer to Terra protectively, and the grad students flanked their small raft of boats. The air was alive, sizzling with a mixture of alarm and curiosity. The adults glanced at each other, bewildered. Nothing like this had ever happened before. But when Joseph looked at Tiluk, the hint of a smile edging his eyes, Tiluk knew that his father understood what the others did not.

As if giving a signal now that she had their attention, Granny bumped

Wendy. The four whales gently slid closer. Then Eve rolled on her side, raising her pectoral fin above everyone's heads, and deliberately exposed the eager calf, her granddaughter, who flanked her side. Wendy nudged her vulnerable newborn up alongside the small raft of boats, so she could meet the eyes of the humans. The calf was rolling back and forth, trying to see everyone. She flashed her belly, and the telltale markings showed that she was, in fact, female…just as Terra had predicted.

A shaft of sunlight broke through the bank of clouds just as the music ended, bathing the group of humans and whales in a sparkling hush. Everyone went silent with the great honor of the calf's presentation. Gwen's chin was trembling in the shade of her Stetson, but she managed to pull her little digital camera out of her pocket and had it trained on the whales. Bill, always so steadfast, had turned white. Jason's eyes darted from the calf, to Wendy, to the other adults, as if trying to make sense of what was happening by watching everyone else. Claire and Maggie, the only other mothers, finally tore their eyes from the calf's eager, wriggling body, and saw tears on one another's cheeks. More than anyone here, they knew what it meant for these whales to trust them enough to present the new calf like this.

Then Granny, Eve, and Wendy brought the calf towards Terra's kayak.

Terra stared down into the water as the three large whales held back, letting the baby swim very close to Terra, her eye coming above water, making contact with the human girl: *the special connection* The calf lingered along-side Terra's kayak, so close that her belly bumped the boat as she rolled slightly to look up into Terra's eyes. The world stopped. Could this really be happening?

Once more Granny slid near Terra's boat, alongside her great grand-daughter, this time staying on the surface, the length of her body sliding alongside the calf, her black skin glistening in the late afternoon ray of sunshine. She blew a misty outbreath, then rolled and made direct eye con-tact with Terra for one more suspended moment.

"Oh Granny…" Terra breathed in, tasting Granny's briny exhalation… then whispered imperceptibly, all her doubts about her dream dissolving in the shared breath of girl and whale. "I will."

THE COVES

"TILUK," TERRA WHISPERED URGENTLY as they reached the top of the long stairs from the dock and the rest of the crew, whom they'd left far below. "Come here!"

Tiluk merely raised his dark eyebrows at her and nodded, quiet as usual. But now Terra sensed his silence had a special weight. He took two steps up and walked next to her, their shoulders touching, heads bent together. "Come to the mews with me," she murmured. She had to get away from the shell-shocked adults. She had to get some space.

Terra glanced at Tiluk, seeing a mixture of wonder and envy. "Granny tried to tell you something." His flat statement startled her. She leaned into him and nodded as they walked into the small clearing on the backside of the house, the side that didn't face the cove. What happened with Granny down there…it was almost like she'd had the dream again. But this time it was real. It was real. Except the news of the killing at OceanLand squelched her awe about the way Granny had interacted with her.

"But Tiluk," she'd barely held it together down there and her eyes started to fill. Blinking, she got to the mews gate, stopped, and turned to look at him. "I can hardly think about Granny and the calf…Even though it was real, what happened with Granny down there," her voice trailed off, and she looked away from Tiluk's penetrating black eyes into the immense cedar and fir trunks standing sentry over the half dozen yurts. "All I keep seeing is that poor trainer," her voice caught, and Tiluk's arms went around her, "and her family."

The trees blurred as the lump in Terra's throat burst. Tiluk held her tight as the tears slipped down her cheeks and into the nook of his shoulder. They stood immobile, the shiver of her shoulders mirroring the pine needles trem-bling in the late afternoon breeze. Finally Terra's swell of shock began to subside, her tears washing away its sharp edge. She hugged Tiluk and took a deep breath. Shantu was the calf's brother. He killed someone. How was she going to live with this? How did it fit with her dream? What just happened out there in the cove?

"Fierce must be hungry, let's take him to the den to hunt before they call us down for dinner," Tiluk said as Terra wiped her cheeks against her sleeves. Before he let her go, Tiluk leaned in against Terra, forehead to forehead as they'd done a thousand times before. Together they took a long breath. Then he stood back and opened the mews gate. Terra donned the leather glove hanging by the door and ducked inside.

She whistled and the falcon swooped from his favorite limb on the enor-mous cedar tree that anchored the mews. He easily hopped aboard her wrist and she gathered up his jesses in her non-bandaged fingers. The jesses were tiny leather anklets that fit snuggly around his legs, each dangling a short length of leather that she could hold or tie onto his various roosting posts.

The jesses allowed her to keep him close; to keep him from flying away. His mews was the same as what any falconer uses as living quarters for their hunting partners. Large and spacious, she'd built it (with Tiluk's help) to make sure Fierce had plenty of room to fly in here when he wasn't out hunting with them. Rabbit fencing covered the entire enclosure and stretched a few feet over her head. The space resembled a very large dog kennel. Her parents had been willing to let her try falconing, but responsibility for the bird fell to her. When she read *My Side of the Mountain* a few years ago, she'd been riveted by Frightful, the peregrine falcon. The idea of hunting and communicating as a team with a bird of prey had consumed her much like the Morse Endeavor. She'd rattled on and on to the crew about falconing for so many months, doing a ton of research, learning everything she could about how to do it—including the huge number of hours she'd have to spend with the bird, and the history of falconing—that finally, her parents had given in.

"If you can commit to doing it well Terra, we'll help you find a young falcon," her dad said solemnly. "But you will be responsible for a sophisticated and intelligent wild animal. It's not something to take on lightly."

She'd known that from her research. She'd also known that falconing was a mutual partnership. The bird was wild; it would never be a pet. At any time a trained falcon could decide to leave. Send it up for a bout of hunting and the bird could simply fly away. Falconers trained carefully for months with a young bird on a leash and a careful regime of feeding and planned, successful hunts, to habituate the bird to the human and to encourage the bird to decide eating was easier when the human was around. By the time the bird would hunt on its partner's command, the falconer could only hope that, to the wild bird, the partnership was more agreeable than freedom.

There was something about working with Fierce. Right now, being in the mews with Fierce, Tiluk standing nearby, she felt better, more normal. She glanced around one more time, taking in the yurts tucked under the huge trees, their shiny metal chimneys belying the way the rest of them blended into the landscape. They looked like large turtles huddling under the trees, their backs covered with a thick layer of dark green moss; serene and waiting for company. She loved the yurts. *Our yurtles*, she thought, a smile fluttering across her face for the first time since the bell rang.

"Okay, let's go." Terra ducked out through the mews door that Tiluk had helped her build.

"Come on," Tiluk took Terra's free hand and they walked away from the small meadow surrounding the mews, and into the woods towards their boulder den. *The den.* They'd played here together since they were toddlers; this moss-covered, green glade only a few dozen feet from the main house.

The boulders, like the yurts and every other spare surface in this temperate rainforest, were inches thick with jade green moss. Rocks were piled up in a giant heap that reached over their heads, and a dozen immense cedar trees stood around the boulders in a circle of respectful silence, as if waiting for the stones to speak. Something always filled Terra when they came here; as if this place were a natural spring, gurgling pure, cold water for whatever was thirsty inside her.

"I'm just so confused about why Shantu would do that," Terra said, staring at Fierce who was still gripping her gloved hand, thinking about another kind of predator, and how no wild orca had ever attacked a human being.

Ever. She recalled her panic at the way Granny had approached her. And how quickly it went away when the whale caught her eyes.

"What's amazing to me," Tiluk said quietly, "is that more of those captive whales *don't* kill their trainers."

Terra's head snapped up and she locked onto Tiluk's eyes. He wasn't much for words, but when he spoke, it usually meant something important.

Fierce squawked and flapped at Terra's sudden movement.

"What do you mean?"

"Terra, you already know this. You just haven't thought about it yet because you've been too busy trying to talk to the wild whales your whole life." He sighed. "And maybe that's a good thing."

Tiluk sat down cross-legged on their special spot—the large picnic-table-flat stone where they'd had countless "dinner parties;" held council; divvied up the treasures they'd discovered in the woods: owl feathers, massive pinecones, coyote scat, giant slugs, edible mushrooms and greens, fallen deer antlers, and once, amazingly, a mountain lion tooth near a mass of old deer bones, which Tiluk still wore around his neck. Here they'd made many weighty decisions about who would guard camp and who would patrol the deep forest. Once, on a day when they were especially lucky, they'd seen an enormous bear tramp through the grove and scratch his back in apparent elation on one of the huge cedar trees. They'd hidden themselves inside the small cave tucked within their den and watched him in frightened awe before he eventually trundled off.

Terra's eyes narrowed at Tiluk as she knelt beside him. Fierce gripped her hand with masterful balance while she settled on the ground. Tiluk waited.

She noticed once again the way he was growing proudly into his native roots.

His smoky, flashing eyes, straight black hair, and hickory-dark skin seemed to glow more and more often with his inner convictions and intense connection to the Earth. She knew from their years of alliance that he sometimes knew her better than she knew herself. He was right, of course. She hardly ever gave a thought to the whales performing tricks for people because she'd been so absorbed by the wild whales. She saw, looking into Tiluk's dark eyes, that she'd let herself gloss over what it might truly mean for these majestic creatures she knew so well to be held in tiny concrete pools. Suddenly, as if releasing a catapult full of built-up knowledge, a force slung itself against her heart. Pain sliced through her: *her whales.*

Oh no.

Even out there in her kayak while Samuel Barber's heartbreaking *Adagio for Strings* played to the whales and they'd all been listening, she'd been numb with shock and grief for the trainer's family and the fact that the calf of her dreams really *did* have a brother. She hadn't even considered the deeper meaning of this news. Come to think of it, it had been the one time her mother had made a musical request, let alone ask that it play on the speakers over the deck so they could hear it out there, too. Still visibly shaken about the OceanLand news, she'd gently asked Terra to play the *Adagio* as they'd headed out for paddle watch. The *Adagio.* Her mother knew.

Oh no.

Between them Fierce screeched. Blinking quickly, she undid his jesses and flung up her wrist. Fierce hurled himself silently into the deep shade of the trees, intent on a kill.

"What are we going to do?" she murmured more to the damp woods around them than to Tiluk. "And what did my dad mean when he said Shantu was the calf's brother? That can't be true, can it?" Tiluk narrowed his eyes at her. His face went stony.

Suddenly the dinner bell clanged, breaking the calm silence of their grove.

Terra jumped and realized that from now on, because of the Shantu killing, every time that dinner bell rang she'd be reminded of each and every orca swimming circles in a concrete pool.

"We're going to eat, Lewis," Tiluk grabbed her hands, careful with her bandaged finger, and pulled her up with a bound.

Shaking her head, Terra could hardly believe this boy she'd known all her life. She remembered him clad in nothing but his little footed pajamas with its herd of blue elephants and purple monkeys, scampering with her into hiding when their parents called, "Bed time!" And how their mothers would hunt all over the main house—searching for them under the desks, in the closets, behind the curtains—never finding their secret hiding place under the stairs. And now, here he was, pulling her up with real strength; so big, and getting bigger almost every day.

Shoulder to shoulder, they walked back to the main house. The smell of food made Terra's stomach grumble despite the afternoon of shock.

"And," Tiluk added under his breath, his voice uncharacteristically aggressive, "we're going to get our parents to fess up."

Before Terra had a chance to ask him what he meant, they were inside and surrounded. Jason was shredding lettuce and chopping tomatoes and pretend-ing not to look at them, his inner surfer dude focused on his knife as if it were the next big wave. Gwen, hatless *and* bootless now that she was back in the house, stood at the kitchen-island with Jason, shaking garlic salt into the oil and lemon juice. She smiled at the kids with her sweet round face and loose curls the color of dried corn. Their dads stood together on the southern porch by the grill, tending salmon steaks. Their mothers were on the western deck over-looking the cove, drinking homemade blackberry mead, deep in conversation.

Terra noticed that they looked more towards the cove than at each other. They were watching the pod, she guessed, and probably talking about the weird way

Granny and the others had showed off the calf. Or maybe about Shantu.

There's so much to think about right now, Terra thought with a dour expression. She felt very tired. Maybe it was the maroon twilight of another late sunset; from up here she could see Haro Strait beyond the deck and cove, and on a clear night, she could see all the way to the twinkling lights of

Victoria. The ceiling to floor windows that stretched from one end of the open living area to the other, and around and back towards the kitchen area allowed for every bit of south-westerly beauty to come in.

Even though it wasn't officially on any map, their family and all of ExplOrca knew the small inlet as Blackfish Cove. Soon after their parents met twenty years ago here on San Juan Island, brought together by chance and their mutual passion to understand wild orca, they'd learned about this cove and how it attracted Granny's family. As they'd been doing their research, following the pods, tracking their movements, marking behaviors, identifying individual whales via their dorsal fins and saddle patches—as distinctive as human fingerprints—

they soon realized that Granny's family visited this cove on a regular basis to rest and play. They'd often sweep through the dense kelp beds that swayed underwater, cavorting and sidling through the thick forest of giant fronds, playing—what looked for all the world—like whale hide-and-seek.

Within those first two years, Maggie, Joseph, Bill, and Claire had managed to chip in together, buy this land on the cove, and build the house…which eventually became ExplOrca headquarters. The house had a large communal space with room for plenty of people—the researchers and friends they anticipated visiting here—with small offices for each of the parents. From the beginning they'd slept in the yurts, never intending for the main house to have bedrooms. Visiting scientists got their own yurt to sleep in. Their parents designed the main house so well that it was featured on the cover of a prominent architecture magazine years ago with the headline, *Great Green Home in the Great Green Woods: Two families + one house = ahead of their time.*

Even when they weren't in the cove, orca were everywhere in here.

Paintings of Blackfish dotted the cedar paneled walls. A hand carved orca mobile hung near the windows, and orca statuary popped up on end tables, bookshelves, and the south-facing windowsill above the kitchen sink. Most striking of all were the two large totem poles bordering each side of the large masonry stone fireplace in the middle of the floor to ceiling western windows. Each pole was slightly different and represented one of the two families. Tiluk's family's totem pole had orca, wolves and ravens carved into it, while Terra's had orca, salmon, and frogs. Enormous fifteen-foot duplicates of each totem pole stood just outside on the deck, facing Blackfish Cove and the sea beyond. Right now it looked as though the totem poles were taking part in Claire and Maggie's intense conversation, standing tall on either side of the two women.

Terra glanced at Tiluk, who looked even more grave than usual. She gave him a silent "*I'll be right back*," then ducked outside the kitchen to the side deck and whistled for Fierce. *I wonder if he found dinner yet?* Her dad and Joseph stopped talking the instant she slid open the glass door. Joseph met her eyes, his long braids of graying black hair swooping over each shoulder and down his chest. Her dad came over and rested his hand around her shoulders. "How are you doing, sweetheart?"

Terra leaned into him, taking in the full measure of her father's solidity and pine-needle smell (he was a woodworker, and Terra adored how he carried the scent of the forest with him). "I'm all right Dad, but I'm worried about Shantu. And," her voice softened, "that trainer's poor family. It's hard to be excited about the calf right now."

Her father looked at Joseph just as Fierce came hurdling out of nowhere, landing clumsily on her shoulder, stumbling before he caught himself and his mouthful of quarry: a very fat chipmunk. They all cracked up. Still giggling, she eased Fierce and his substantial load onto his deck perch, and laced his jesses onto his roost.

"At least you won't have to share your dinner with him tonight, sea squirt," Joseph laughed as he fondly rested his hand on her head for a moment. He'd been calling her sea squirt since before she could remember, ever since her first bath when she'd squirted water all over everybody, according to her parents. And that habit he had of resting his hand on her head? It was part of a timeless ritual that extended back to her birth. They told her that when

Joseph and Maggie had first greeted her, the night of her birth, he'd rested his hand protectively over her tiny head, and said, "Welcome to the world, sweet baby girl. Welcome to the birds who will sing for you. Welcome to the trees that will shelter you. Welcome to the whales who will teach you. Welcome to the sea and the land that will provide for you. Welcome to your loved ones who will guide you. Welcome to Earth, little Terra." And then the four of them—Joseph, very pregnant Maggie, her dad, and her mom carry-ing her new little bundle—had stepped onto the deck beneath a full silver moon. Joseph, channeling some kind of native ceremonial know-how, had taken infant Terra wrapped in softened doeskin, held her gently outwards towards the cove, and concluded with "May the skies and the seas and the lands that rest inside you awaken within you and bring you home." Maggie had even made a beautiful little pen and ink drawing of that night, and inscribed the words of Joseph's blessing below it. Terra had it hanging on the wall of her yurt next to her bed. Tiluk had one just like it near his bed, too.

"Come to the table everyone!" Gwen called from inside.

The dads pulled the salmon steaks off the grill and plunked them onto a platter, Jason brought the salad and a carafe of apple cider, and Gwen pulled a heavy plate from the oven loaded with crisp, rosemary roasted potatoes from the garden. The southern side of the house, just below the kitchen, had a small protected area with enough sun to grow vegetables, and a chicken coop nearby for their flock of a dozen hens. Maggie and Claire, still outside on the now fully dark deck, hadn't heard Gwen. Bill stuck his head back outside and called out, "Claire, Maggie...dinner!"

Tiluk and Terra sat down together at the large table with everyone else as their mothers stepped in through the sliding door on the western windowed wall enclosing the living room and fireplace. Tiluk's smoky eyes flashed at her.

Terra could see he was so wrapped up with Shantu that, just like her, he could barely think about the calf and what had happened down in the cove during paddle watch. She glanced around at everyone. Her mom loved this table. She often reminded them all of how grateful she was that Bill had made it for her early on, when she'd told him she wanted an extra big table, "So there's room for everyone." Terra was suddenly overcome with the raw emotions of the day and felt huge relief that these people, *her* people, were gathered here with her. She clutched Tiluk's knee under the table, and he gripped her hand, hard. How could she face this new insight about captive orca without him?

"So paddle watch was amazing today, wasn't it?" Claire and Maggie had obviously been thick into discussing the pod's odd behavior. But Tiluk slammed his free hand flat on the table. It shuddered.

"No!" he erupted with a force Terra had never seen. "We are not talking about paddle watch until someone explains what the *hell* is going on!"

His mother gaped at him, Terra's mom bowed her head and clasped her hands tightly in her lap, and their dads exchanged a quiet, charged stare.

Gwen bit her lip and looked kindly at Terra; and Jason squirmed uncomfortably in his chair.

"There's something you guys haven't told us, and I want to know what it is. Right now." His voice had gone low and calm, but his eyes pierced the parents, holding them accountable.

Her dad cleared his throat. "Well, Tiluk, you have every right on Earth to know the answer to *that*." He paused, looking around the table, then rested his eyes on Tiluk's. "We had planned to give you and Terra a ceremony that would have explained everything at your joint 14th birthday celebration next week." He looked at Terra then lowered his eyes and exhaled. *Was her dad— her steady, rock-solid dad—feeling it, too?* Narrowing her eyes, Terra realized Tiluk was right. *Something else was going on here.*

"But the whales had other ideas," Joseph said quietly. Claire nodded. "They almost always do," Claire said. "Tiluk, you're right. There's more to the story than what Shantu did today. Much more. I'm not surprised in the least, that you've already figured that out. You two have always been so smart," Claire said, and looked pointedly, first at her dad, then Maggie and Joseph. "Actually, why don't you tell us what you think is going on. I'm starting to suspect you know more than we give you credit for."

Bill's eyes widened, and Terra felt Tiluk stiffen next to her. "Seriously,

Claire?" he spit out, fuming.

Jason cleared his throat, "Uh, hey, not to interrupt but Gwen and I don't mind leaving you guys to settle all this. It seems like kind of a personal moment here."

"No," said Maggie, "Absolutely not. You both need to stay and hear this out. You're part of the family too. Eat. Everybody eat. There's a table full of delicious food here, and mercy, we all need it today." Maggie's dark brown hair flashed red, curls falling out of the bandana she used in an attempt to keep it out of her face.

With her reminder, everyone descended on the heaping plates and the conversation stalled. Awkward now at the idea of telling everybody what he thought was going on, but appeased that the adults were, indeed, going to explain, soft-spoken Tiluk reached for the potatoes and passed them around. Soon, their plates were full and the fresh salmon brought enthusiastic grunts of pleasure, especially from Jason, who tried to change the subject.

"I'm still so excited about seeing the calf! And the way the big girls brought her to see us..." Jason peered out from under his shock of sun-bleached hair, smiling. Jason did *not* like challenging dialogue; he'd rather eat his surfboard than work through interpersonal dynamics. Besides, he was eager to move on to discussing the calf. But Terra looked at him darkly. She could barely focus on eating. Gwen nudged Jason, frowning at him.

"Mom. Seriously." She glanced sidelong at Tiluk, wanting to shield him from her mother's pointed question. "Could you guys *please* just tell us what's going on?"

Just then Fierce squawked loudly from the deck. *Right,* Terra sighed and pushed back her chair. "I'll be right back." *You have to hand it to that bird, he sure knows his routines,* she thought to herself. She went out onto the dark porch, saw the waning moon rising to the south and took a deep breath, calming herself. She unstrung Fierce's jesses, noticed that the chipmunk was mostly gone, and let Fierce settle on her shoulder—his place of choice after his meals, and during hers. She stepped back inside and settled down between Gwen and Tiluk. Fierce, as always, looked once around the table, tucked his head under his wing, and fell asleep instantly.

Terra's dad leaned back in his chair, his plate already scoured. "The truth is, kids, what we have to tell you isn't easy for us. But it's important, probably more so now than ever." He took a deep breath and looked at the two graduate students. "Gwen and Jason, you need to hear this too. We've probably kept it from you for too long."

Now Bill had their attention, Terra noticed. They put down their forks expectantly. He sighed and scratched the stubble on his chin. "Shantu did something today that is terrible. It's sad, it's frightening, and frankly, it's bizarre. Orca don't attack humans. They just don't."

"But Shantu did," Terra said, feeling reassured by Fierce at her right shoulder and Tiluk on her left, "and I want to know why. I can't even think about the new calf until someone explains this to me," her eyes started to well up. "And what did you mean saying he is the calf's brother? The calf doesn't have a brother, just her three sisters."

"First of all," Joseph spoke, "Shantu is not his real name. That's just a stage name that OceanLand uses: it's generic. When a whale dies or gets moved, they can just transfer the name Shantu to the next whale and their audiences are none the wiser. Plus, everybody loves Shantu."

Terra and Tiluk looked at each other; *everybody loves Shantu.* But which whales did they *really* love? They knew as well as everyone at the table that wild orca had distinct and expressive personalities, just like people.

"Unfortunately, this is not the first time this particular whale has killed a human," Terra's mother said quietly. "And if something doesn't change, it won't be the last time, either."

Terra's mouth dropped open and Tiluk leaned closer to her. His jaw tight, Tiluk pushed. "What are you saying, Mrs. Lewis?" He rarely addressed

Terra's mother in the proper form like this. Terra was pretty sure that right now, Tiluk was angry.

"Yeah, Mom. What are you talking about?" Terra insisted. "And why don't we know about this already?"

"You kids know that we've been close friends since before either of you were born," Maggie said, interjecting. "What you don't know…"she pushed her curls back, took a deep breath, and looked around the room as if taking strength from the other adults. "What you don't know is that our friendship was cemented by misery. It was changed forever on a day that even now, after all these years…well, it's still heartbreaking for any of us to talk about." She paused, serious. "On that day, we shared something so tragic that we agreed to dedicate our lives to remembering."

"And to working to make things right," Claire added quietly. "And after what happened today, we have to reconsider what we can do to help." She spoke directly to Terra. "It's why I rang the bell, even though it wasn't exactly an emergency. And it's why I asked you to play the *Adagio*."

Terra was baffled. But Tiluk was tracking like a hungry cougar on a newborn deer. "You guys know Shantu…" Tiluk murmured, understanding dawning.

"First of all," Terra's dad said gently, barely nodding at Tiluk, silently bidding him to be patient a little longer, "we have kept certain things from you. We agreed before you were born that we wanted to let you be kids. To protect you as long as we could. And for everyone's sake, yours' and the whales', we wanted to give you an experience with the wild whales that almost no other children in the world can claim anymore." He added, "It's a big reason we've kept the Internet and television to a minimum around here: we wanted you to be free of those distractions so you'd have real time." His voice trailed off and he looked at Claire, grappling with something Terra didn't understand.

Joseph in his measured way turned to his son and Terra. "Tiluk, you and Terra know from our stories that our people once shared these rich waters with the Blackfish. And that the ancient stories tell of how the whales helped us and fished with us. Our people revered the whales as the wise ones of the sea. Once, not very long ago, it was common for our children to grow up alongside the whales, much as we've made sure that you two have done."

"Of course, in those days, there were no hydrophones," Terra's mom laughed, trying to lighten things up a little.

"True," Joseph's eyes wrinkled in a smile, "but in those days no one needed hydrophones to encounter the Blackfish. Our people lived alongside the orca for countless generations and our elders knew the ancient ways."

The ancient ways? Terra thought, recalling her dream about Granny. *What were those?* In that instant, Terra knew with sudden certainty that she had to tell Tiluk the whole truth about her dream. And maybe... Joseph, as well.

Gwen, rapt with curiosity, spoke almost more to herself than anyone else. "There's so much more going on here than basic science."

Jason snorted and nudged her, "Ya think?" Then he turned to Bill. "I'm not sure I want to hear what's next." Jason, basically, had already fallen in love with this calf, his first, and the one he had discovered. His feelings were strong and fresh, and they made him vulnerable. As of that morning,

Jason found out for the first time that being a scientist didn't inure him to bonding with his study animals. He felt differently, protective and affection-ate, towards Wendy...a whale he knew as a grandmother, one he'd thought was beyond birthing again. That she'd had another calf at her age, well,

Jason wouldn't admit this, but he was seized by admiration. Already he felt more respect for Wendy than he did for many people he knew. And in this moment, Jason *really* wanted to stay with his groovy good feelings.

"Let's talk about the calf," he piped in once more, hopefully.

Bill ignored him with the slightest hint of an eye-roll; he was too focused on the children to respond. "You two also know some of the more recent stories; about the captures and the shootings. The sad stories of what the newcomers to this area have done to local orca families over the last few decades, out of fear or ignorance or greed. We've tried to be honest with you about these things, but we also wanted to protect you until you were old enough. We haven't always told you everything." He sighed, and looked carefully at Tiluk. "And now, with his latest killing, Tiluk has told you for us."

Tiluk's head snapped up, his eyes sizzling. "*What* did you say Bill?" he choked out.

"Dad, what are you talking about?" Terra's voice went thin.

"You were right Tiluk," Bill said reluctantly, looking at his daughter's best friend, his voice thick and heavy, "we *do* know this Shantu. We were all there when he was captured, just before you were born. It happened the day of the Penn Cove Round-Up on Whidbey Island. It was the worst day in the history of the Southern Residents. Every single whale of all three pods was driven by boats and underwater nets up into Penn Cove, which made it very easy to trap dozens of wild whales. Including Granny's family. They caught many of the young whales and took them to be performers, then left many more behind to die." He blinked quickly, and looked to his wife and Maggie. "We were all there, all four of us. It happened when your mothers were both almost nine months pregnant with each of you," he said with clear affection for the women. "I'll never forget it."

"And I'll never forget that they took one very special calf. A calf we'd studied for two years and had grown to love," Maggie said quietly. "Or the way his mother banged her head against the dock over and over again. Screaming. She cried and wailed for days after they took him," whispered Maggie. Speechless, Terra leaned heavily against Tiluk's shoulder. He was holding onto her hand a little too hard. Maggie went on, "He was Wendy's firstborn baby, her son."

Terra's pulse pounded against her ears and her tears welled up. She loved Wendy.

"And *I'll* never forget that his name was never Shantu," said Claire, look-ing at them with caring, gentle eyes. "*It was Tiluk.*"

The table fell silent.

Jason looked like a coyote pup caught in the glare of a logging truck's head-lights, unsure which way to spring to safety. Gwen had her hand over her mouth, trying to blink back tears. Maggie was watching Tiluk and gripping the edges of her chair, trying to let Tiluk have space to hear this news. Her parents, Claire and Bill, were the calm ones, overseeing the disclosure of top secret information. Their quiet presence seemed to keep everyone else from detonating.

When her eyes fell on Joseph and Tiluk, and the chord of raw emotion between them, she saw that Tiluk's jaw was the only part of him that moved. Silently it clenched and unclenched. His eyes, gone black and slick, pierced Joseph with the force of his stare. Terra saw Joseph shudder, but his wizened stare held his son tightly as if he was all that had ever mattered. There was a long moment of total silence as Tiluk's mind spun wildly around this new piece of information, trying to grasp its meaning. He never looked away from his father.

"You named me after that whale." Tiluk's voice was unexpectedly strong.

His flat statement left all questions behind. Joseph answered simply, as if

everyone else had fallen away and the only two left at the table were Tiluk and his father.

"Yes."

"I was there, the day they captured Tiluk, but inside mom's belly." "Yes."

"If she heard the mother's wails and cries, I probably did too." "Yes."

"And Terra was there, also." "Yes."

Tiluk's body creaked with tension. "And the four of you," he finally looked away from Joseph to the other parents, "you were there, and couldn't stop it from happening."

Claire let out a muffled gasp. But Joseph's quick, sharp look silenced her.

"Yes."

Tiluk stared again at Joseph, and once more they fell silent. Terra caught her breath, she was reeling. She could hardly imagine the sadness her family had experienced that day. But the whales... *Wendy. Poor Wendy.* She'd never known that Wendy had a son; that he'd been kidnapped. *Tiluk's name.* The adults would never forget that day because they named Tiluk after the kid-napped calf. No wonder her mom had rung the bell today, so upset that she'd asked Terra to play the *Adagio.* And this proved it: *The calf had a brother... the brother Granny had told her about in her dream.* She could barely wrap her

mind around everything she'd just learned. *The calf had a brother!!*
Maybe, somehow, her dream really was real! Her mother was looking
at her with quiet empathy—she had no idea what Terra was trying to
process—and Terra could practically hear her mom say silently, *I know
this is a lot to absorb Terra. But it's okay, honey. It's okay.*

"I understand," Tiluk took a long breath and sat back in his chair
and looked around the table once more. "I just have one question."

"What is it son?" Joseph spoke with respect. "Why name the calf
Tiluk?"

Maggie smiled gently at Tiluk. She visibly relaxed. Gwen and
Jason both grinned at Tiluk's question, too. Everyone respected how
quickly Tiluk had gone from shock to curiosity. "You ask easy questions,
Lucky," she said. Suddenly, Maggie's rarely-used nickname for her son
took on a whole new meaning. He'd been the lucky one, the other Tiluk,
had not.

"Well, you already know what we've told you."

Tiluk nodded slowly, "That Tiluk means 'to be auspicious or
lucky'." "Yes, and we've let you believe all these years that your name
is a native name of our people." Tiluk nodded once.

"That's sort of true. But there's more to it." Maggie went on, "On
the day of the capture the calf was two years old, I was pregnant with
you, and your dad and I had been making observations of his family for
years before that. When the whale was born we assigned him a number
and planned to give him a name, just like we do for all the newborn
whale calves. He was J-22,

Wendy's firstborn, grandson of Eve, and Granny's first great
grandson. But this calf was special. Every time we went out in the
kayaks he'd spyhop at us and give us the once over."

"What do you mean, 'the once over,'" asked Gwen, who was
leaning towards Maggie, fascinated.

She smiled at Gwen, remembering. "He was intensely curious…
almost from the first day. His mother had barely started to trust us after
the years we'd been out there with them, and she always tried to keep
him close by her side. Her sisters and Eve and Granny would help corral
him, but no matter what they did, he kept trying to get closer to us. We
often had to shut off the engine just to make sure he didn't get hit by
the blades." She looked around the table. "I know we're not supposed

to assign human emotions to animals, but I'm pretty sure his family got exasperated with him more than a few times."

Joseph shook his head and chuckled. "He'd give us the 'once over' every chance he got. When that calf got the best of his mom, grandmother, aunties and his uncle Jake, he'd dart over, get his eye above water, and just stare us down. That kid wanted to know us. He was more curious than a bear cub near a beehive. And he'd get in trouble. The big girls would come get him and push him back under the water and tell him all about it. We could hear them on the hydrophones. Smart family knew better than to let their calf trust humans."

"Yes, they did know better. And look what happened." Maggie sighed.

"Anyway, as you two already know," she looked pointedly at Terra, who had her own special name, "it is a great honor in our native traditions to receive the creation of a new name that is unique to an individual. And that's what our research group decided to do. They honored the calf with a new name when he was just a few weeks old. Tiluk, in English sounds like "to look" which was perfect for this calf, since that's what he was always doing: *looking*. And we learned from a little research that in Hindu "Tilak" means "the mark of auspiciousness." The way this whale was interacting so fearlessly with us we already knew he bore that mark. He was auspicious all right!"

"So we changed Tilak just slightly to Tiluk, and that's how he got his name." She paused, "But it turns out that in this case auspicious didn't mean lucky."

"Maybe, in this case, auspicious means 'success in the future,'" Joseph said so quietly that Terra almost couldn't hear him. "Our people believe the whales are powerful, sacred beings. Perhaps this one has a purpose that we can't know yet."

That's it, Terra thought, *I definitely need to tell Joseph about my dream.* Tiluk spoke at last, almost more to himself than to those at the table. "So I share a name that no one else has, except for a whale that just killed someone." A shadow passed between Maggie and Claire.

"But that's just it," Terra said, "why would he do that? I mean I get it, that he's in captivity and that must be hard on him. But killing a human?"

Tiluk turned in his seat and stared into Terra's eyes. His words echoed in her mind, *You already know this Terra, you just haven't thought about it yet because you've been too busy trying to talk to wild whales.*

She stared back, feeling Tiluk's scrutiny ruffle at her for a long moment... her mind whirled with everything she knew about wild orca, everything she knew about what it might mean for them to be penned in with strangers. Then she understood the answer to her own question.

Terra hesitated, then spoke. "Tiluk hasn't had his family for almost 14 years. That makes him about 16 years old, a maturing bull. He probably remembers his family but doesn't have them around to teach him anything. He must have somehow learned to live with new whales?"

"Yes, honey. It's one of the things we were concerned about from the day he was taken from Penn Cove," Claire said. "In the wild, we never see a whale from one family move into a totally new pod with unfamiliar whales. Orca stay with immediate family members, one way or the other, for their entire lives. We think it would have been extremely stressful, to say the least, for Tiluk to be put into a tank with unfamiliar whales. Tiluk's female tank mates didn't take to him too well, either. They beat up on him a lot," she sighed.

Joseph added quietly, "We think Tiluk's killing was the only way he had of telling us just how bad it is for him. There was nothing else he could do, except maybe kill himself. He's tried banging his head against his gate over and over again, and he's gnawed on the metal bars so much that his teeth are worn down to nubs with the painful roots exposed." Terra's eyes grew large. She couldn't believe she'd never thought more deeply about all this.

"He's spent thousands of hours hanging motionless at the pool's surface, getting a raw mess of a sunburn all over this back," Joseph caught Terra's eyes over Tiluk's shoulder. "That kind of behavior is so strange for a whale that you almost can't even call it whale behavior. The sad truth is that since he was taken from his family, he hasn't been acting like a whale at all; but he *has* been acting depressed. The only place we see that kind of abnormal behavior in Blackfish is in captivity. The amazing thing about Tiluk, and *all* those whales," for the first time Joseph's voice caught and he stopped speaking for a moment, ". . . is that even though he felt so bad, he'd get it together every couple of hours and perform a show for his trainers and his audiences. He loves people. He loved us."

Joseph pushed his chair back suddenly, and went to stand by the fire-place and stare out the window over the darkened calm of Blackfish Cove, his back to the table. *Wow*, thought Terra, *I've never seen Joseph like this.*

"But Mom," Terra said, "you said he killed before. How did that happen? And how could people *let* that happen? And why would you say he'll do it again?"

Gwen, Jason, and Tiluk all shifted to look at Claire; they were all wonder-ing the same thing. Terra snuggled closer and leaned into Tiluk. He put his arm around her, and she rested her head in the crook of his neck. She felt so tired. Fierce squawked in his sleep as she moved.

Terra yawned. Her dad stood up before Claire could answer the question. He came over and gently gathered up Fierce's dangling jesses and took the sleeping bird from Terra's shoulder. "Just like whales, Terra, sometimes it takes people a while to learn. It's only been the last forty years or so that humans have ever—in all of history—tried to keep whales captive for their own purposes. They are still learning." He sighed heavily and looked at Joseph, whose back was still to them as he stared into the darkness. "And now I think *I've* learned that it's time for you two to get to bed. We'll talk more about all this tomorrow."

Terra stood, looked towards Joseph, and said, "Maybe we ought to be learning about the ancient ways, instead."

MILES TO GO

THE KILLER WHALE HAD his foot in his teeth. His heart was racing. He tried and tried to pull his foot away, but it wouldn't budge. The whale just sat there with him at the surface of the pool, holding him like a kid holding a joystick. Gasping for breath he stroked the whale's back over and over, speaking to him, pleading with him to let go. But the whale was in charge, and again he dove down, taking Miles to the bottom of the pool, his arms flailing helplessly. He couldn't breathe! The whale sat there at the bottom, placid, waiting—staring him down— their eyes locked: one set panicked the other resolved. *What is he trying to tell me?* His vision blurred and he felt blackness descend over him. He was going to drown. At the very last second the whale lifted him easily to the surface where he gulped huge mouthfuls of air, sucking it down. *Please let go!* His foot fell free! He could swim to the stage! But instantly the whale's teeth closed on him. His parents were there, on the side of the pool, fighting with each other. They didn't see him. The whale spun around and down they went. He was going to die. Miles began to pass out just before Shantu brought him to the surface and let go. He gulped air. He looked into the whale's eye. Finally the whale turned away. Quickly, he swam for his life, jerking through the water like he'd been elec-trocuted, reaching for the stage where his parents could pull him to safety. But they still didn't see him! And Shantu came back! Mouth open, teeth everywhere. The blond trainer's terrified face shot through his mind, the blood in the water. Her dismembered arm. His parents fighting. Black whale skin engulfed him.

Miles bolted upright in bed, sucking in a lungful of air, his heart ham-mering against his chest, blood pounding hot in his ears. Eyes wide open, blackness enveloped him. *The whale's black skin*! Sucking in another breath, he tried to calm himself. *Get a grip, Frost.* He snapped on his bedside lamp. *Freaking whale!* He sat with the light on and breathed deeply, trying to calm his racing heart. He let his eyes roam the safe walls and floor of his room. *I'm not at the bottom of a pool with some crazy whale.*

Miles pushed both hands through his short blond hair, pulling hard on the roots. It was the second time tonight that he'd had this stupid nightmare. He just couldn't get away from what happened yesterday. He needed to wake all the way up. Again. *I'm not in there, I'm in bed. I'm in bed. No freaking whales here.* His room, in fact, had nothing to do with OceanLand or *any* animals for that matter; not like Doodle who couldn't get enough "stuffties" as she called her stuffed animals. She had like fifty of them, including three Shantus, five dolphins, and a few otters. He didn't know how she even slept in there, since there was practically no room left for her.

His room, on the other hand, was cool. He had his TV, his desktop with its giant screen, his iPod docking station, his DS along with a huge collection of games, and the awesome Bose sound system his dad had given him for his birthday—right after the divorce, by the way…*happy freaking birthday!* His dad had moved into his stinky and dark closet of an apartment, and given him, like, all of his old tapes and CDs. He was pretty sure his dad, just like his mom, was trying to buy him off, too, about the divorce (at least they had *something* in common), but he didn't care. He loved all this old music. He even had his dad's old headphone set, and as long as he knew his friends wouldn't see him, he'd bring it over to his dad's closet and listen to The Violent Femmes, U2, The Cure, and Depeche Mode. His dad didn't care either, since he was always working on his computer. Even when he took them out of his apartment closet to go "spend quality time" with him and Doodle, he'd always be texting or on the phone. *Quality Flippin' Time.* Miles glanced at his poster of Robert Smyth, The Cure's lead singer, hanging over his desk, and was reassured that the Femmes were guarding his door. *No whales allowed.* He'd tacked a poster of them on the front with a sign underneath that said, "*Kiss Off!*" which was one of his favorite Femmes songs. Right up there with *Gone Daddy Gone.*

His eyes came to rest on the xylophone he'd set up on his skateboard.

It was a small one, but it was nice. And every once in a while, he'd beat the heck out of that sucker. There's an amazing xylophone solo in *Gone Daddy Gone,* and the first time he'd heard it, he was totally blown away. From that moment on he'd saved up his allowance, working odd jobs all over the place—which was kind of a pain in the butt, since he could never keep track of whose house he would be in from one night to the next—but he did it anyway. As soon as he had enough dough, he'd gone out and bought the instrument just so he could teach himself to run that sweet riff. He figured it out by playing it over and over again with The Femmes on YouTube, full blast. Then he discovered he could do a lot more than copy the Femmes groove. He could make that xylophone shake with melodies no one else could understand but him. *I'd jam it right now, if it wasn't the middle of the bloody night . . . Freaking whale.*

There was a gentle knock at the door. *Oh cripe, didn't his mom know when to leave him alone?*

The door cracked anyway, and his mother stuck her head in. "Is it that dream again, honey?" She'd come in earlier when he'd actually, apparently, screamed in his sleep. *Stupid flipped out whale.* Like he needed his mom going all gooey on him now. Over this. Like she cared more about him seeing some stupid whale eat someone than whether he had an actual family to come home to.

"I'm fine Mom. Go back to bed. Really." He clenched his teeth with the supreme effort of not being pissy with his mother in the middle of the night.

I've got to figure this thing out. At least I can do something about this, unlike their stupid divorce. With that thought Miles woke all the way up and knew exactly what he had to do.

"Are you sure Miles? I could go and get you some warm milk if you want."

Oh my God, Mom. Seriously? Warm milk is not going to fix this. Just like Dining With Crazy Shantu didn't fix it. Miles snorted quietly to himself, rolling his eyes at his cracked door, disgusted.

"Yeah, I'm okay. Seriously. I'm gonna listen to tunes for a few minutes, and I'll drift right off. No problem."

Whoops. That riled her up. "Miles," she stepped inside the door; her lilac bathrobe clutched against her, and kept her voice threateningly low. "I've told you not to listen to that violent stuff before you go to sleep. It's no wonder you're having nightmares!" She turned to leave and as she pulled the door shut, she murmured so low under her breath she probably thought Miles couldn't hear her, "I can't believe Rob gave you all that garbage."

Whatever Mom. "Garbage." Right. Just shows what you know. It's no wonder you guys had to get a stupid divorce. Even though he gritted his jaw, Miles felt the emotion in his face threaten to spill out. *This is so totally bogus.* He jumped out of bed, quiet as a thief, went over and powered up his desktop.

His screen jumped to life almost immediately. He loved his rocket fast computer. The clock said 3:37 AM. *Perfect, no more sleep tonight.* He shrugged. He searched "Shantu kills trainer." It only happened yesterday, but already he got dozens of hits, including some YouTube links. *Yeah, that's just what I need...to see **that** again.* His stomach clenched. He skimmed the articles.

There it all was:

Shantu kills trainer in Orlando.
Trainer drowns in accident with killer whale. *Accident my jackalope*, thought Miles.
Killer Shantu has deep past. (What OceanLand doesn't want you to know...)
A "Weekly" In-depth Exclusive

Miles' eyebrows shot up. *Now we're talking.* He noticed the upload time on this piece was midnight; it had been posted in the middle of the night—probably while he was having his first nightmare—as a breaking, front-page-feature for today. *Wow, someone was busy yesterday,* thought Miles.

He clicked on the link and glanced at the length of the article by scrolling down. *Busy and super **interested**.* Miles narrowed his eyes. It was almost like this writer already knew a bunch of stuff about this whale and OceanLand, like he'd been tracking the story long before it happened.

"Bingo," he whispered as he started reading.

The Orlando Weekly

Killer Shantu Has Deep Past. (Exclusive: What OceanLand doesn't want you to know...)
June 12, 2013
By Tim Sinclair

When veteran marine mammal trainer Cassidy Dey died yesterday, June 11, in an alleged accident with OceanLand's Shantu, she became the third person killed by this particular whale. But Dey was only one of many trainers who've experienced life-threatening encounters with other captive killer whales, and her death follows another death two months ago at an OceanLand-owned park in Spain.

Dey, who was known affectionately by all her friends and family as "Dusky," died after an incident gone wrong during a "routine Lunch with Shantu event," according to an initial response from OceanLand. First reports suggest that the whale known as Shantu took Dey to the bottom of the pool and held her there. It's not clear whether her substantial injuries (including, what appears to be a scalping and partial dismemberment) or asphyxiation are what actually killed Dey. Killer whales have almost never been known to attack a human being in the wild. Only one such example exists, and that occurred when a whale evidently mistook a black-suited scuba diver for a seal. The diver was spit out immediately, unharmed.

Such "routine events," however, may be anything but normal for these whales. Killer whales—also known as orca, after their species name *Orcinus orca*—live in tightly bonded, matrilineal family groups called pods for their entire lives. The common name "killer whale," originated during the whaling era and was a term of respect from whalers who watched teams of orca hunt down prey like seals, dolphins, and whales. Because of their hunting prowess and food requirements, wild killer whales swim up to hundreds of miles each day.

"Shantu," the whale that killed Dey yesterday, was born into a wild fish-eating family. But the name "Shantu" is used by OceanLand to hide the frequency of whale deaths from their audiences. As a result of this generic name most OceanLand patrons don't know when a whale dies (which is all too common) or is moved to a new park.

Before this particular whale became known at OceanLand as "Shantu," he lived with his mother and extended family. Researchers knew that he was born into a pod with his grandmother, mother, aunts, and uncles. His birth was especially noteworthy, says orca researcher Dr. Claire Lewis, because, "We were only just discovering how tightly bonded wild orca families really are. Our group even published a paper on the calf's birth because it was the first documented case of a three-generation family of orca."

Lewis heads up ExplOrca, a team of respected marine mammal and fisheries researchers affiliated with various universities across the Pacific Northwest, British Columbia and beyond. Shantu's family, says Lewis, is part of the now well studied J Pod, which, in turn, is part of a larger community of whales living in Puget Sound known as the Southern Residents. She said yesterday after the killing, "To us, this particular Shantu was known as J-22, the first great grandson of the governing grandmother whale. But we knew him as Tiluk."

Two years after J-22's birth, some members of the ExplOrca team, including Lewis, her husband and researcher Dr. Bill Lewis, and others, watched the now notorious whale round-up and capture in Penn Cove, Washington. Nearly all the Southern Residents, 100-plus whales, were herded—using blast bombs, boats, and airplanes—into a small cove on Puget Sound's Whidbey Island, just north of Seattle. Over the course of the capture era, nearly *half* the Southern Resident population was either removed or died, impacting the population to this day. Young killer whales were sold to various marine parks including OceanLand, while many other whales died in the net-bound confusion. For months afterwards locals found dead whales whose stomachs had been wrapped with heavy weights in chains by their captors, hoping to hide the whale deaths.

When Tiluk, or J-22, the whale who killed Dey yesterday, was captured at Penn Cove, he was removed not only from his mother (who, according to researchers, wailed and rammed her head against a dock piling for two days after his removal), but also his extended family. Since this whale's capture, scientists have learned that most individuals and families live together for their entire lives. According to a recent paper in the prestigious journal *Science*, wild males of J Pod almost never leave their natal groups and remain with their mother's pod for life. Should a wild male killer whale lose his mother he is far more likely to die himself.

With no legal protection for whales at that time, the ExplOrca team could only watch and record the events in Penn Cove as many of the whales they'd tracked for years were "harvested" or died amidst a pandemonium of screams and tail and flipper slaps that sounded like "a staccato of gunshot-like explosions," says Lewis. "It was the worst day of my life. But it was much worse for the whales." Southern Resident killer whales are now considered endangered and many of their losses occurred as a result of capturing whales for OceanLand to put on display. But, says Lewis, "J Pod and all the Southern Residents face ongoing threats including serious pollution, dwindling salmon populations, rising ocean temperatures, increasing boat traffic, and serious emerging problems associated with fish farms."

While ExplOrca has continued their study of J Pod's wild whales, they've also followed news of captured whales, including Tiluk, from afar. Of the whales captured at Penn Cove, only Tiluk still survives. All the others have died in captivity, much sooner than they would have died in the wild. Of those, Tiluk may have the most notorious story of all.

It wasn't long after his capture that Tiluk killed a trainer at Marine Park of the Pacific, his first captive home. Though details are obscure, most people involved presumed the death to be accidental. Trainer Steve Aaronson had been working daily with the young whale, according to Holly Smith, a former trainer and colleague of Aaronson's at Marine Park. After Aaronson's death Smith left her job to join the Humane Society of the United States where she helped draft legislation for what eventually became the Marine Mammal Protection Act, which now protects all whales in US waters from the type of capture that occurred in Penn Cove.

"Orca are among the most social animals on Earth so they require interaction and are fast, smart learners," Smith explains. "Their capacity for learning is what makes orca, dolphins and Beluga whales attractive to marine parks: they are excellent students and highly athletic, dramatic performers. Using this knowledge and the reward of food, trainers are able to teach whales new 'behaviors,' much as you might teach a dog tricks using hot dogs." One of the ways captive whales get their quota of hundreds of pounds of dead fish each day is by correctly performing behaviors for their trainers.

In captivity, whales must "work" for their food.

"Steve loved Tiluk. And he loved Steve," Smith says. "They'd spend hours playing together and working on behaviors, in and out of the water. Steve even piped in music after hours for him to listen to. One night he called me at home, out of his mind with amazement, to tell me how Tiluk had literally danced a whale ballet all around the pool when he played Beethoven's Ode to Joy. But then it was over. Tiluk would get all excited about music he liked, but just that one time. Steve figured out that the whale never wanted repeats of the songs, even if he loved them the first time he heard them. He *always* wanted something new. He'd go hang his head in the corner if he didn't like Steve's musical choice or if he ever repeated a song; it was his way of saying, 'No thank you, something else please.' We often laughed about this, because it wasn't clear who was teaching who in there. That whale had a lot more going on inside than his audiences ever knew."

"On the day of Steve's death," Smith continues, "Tiluk

was frustrated. Steve was working on a new behavior, a foot push, and the whale was bored. He kept refusing to do the behavior. Steve withheld food, which is what trainers sometimes do to try to get a whale to correctly perform a behavior. Before any of us realized what was happening Tiluk slid up onto the stage with Steve, grabbed his foot, and pulled him into the pool. We thought he'd release Steve quickly, but he didn't. He held Steve out there, and then took him down under water a few times. We tried to get Tiluk's attention with fish and water slaps, to get him to drop

Steve and come to the stage. But he totally ignored us. When a seven-thousand pound whale decides something, there's not a lot you can do. Orca and humans operate at two *completely* different scales—Steve was like rag doll in the mouth of a giant. We could all see his face. He was terrified and he didn't know if the whale would let him go or not. Unfortunately, he didn't. It was the worst thing I've ever seen in my life."

According to Smith, Tiluk was depressed for weeks after Aaronson's death, hanging for hours in the same spot of the pool that he'd recently used to tell Steve, "No thank you, something else please." But he didn't stay with Marine Park for long; the park sold Tiluk to OceanLand despite his known status as having killed a trainer. Marine Park had downplayed Aaronson's death locally, calling it an accident and word never really got out to the public at large. Said Smith, "Those in charge at both parks thought that Tiluk's sale to OceanLand in Orlando—one of the most experienced and well-equipped marine parks in the world— would be the best place for a whale with his past. Since it was supposedly an 'accident,' no one really considered whether this whale might kill again."

By the time Tiluk killed Dey nearly a decade later he'd starred as Shantu in thousands of OceanLand shows for enthusiastic audiences who adored the huge bull, who was, by now, the largest captive whale anywhere in the world. Still, OceanLand had a strict "no water work" policy in place for this Shantu, knowing his unpredictable past, according to Smith, who has tracked Tiluk ever since Aaronson's death and filed Freedom of

Information (FOI) requests to acquire OceanLand's policies on the huge bull. "But," she says, "almost all captive killer whales are unpredictable…these are huge, complex animals with immense brain power and feelings. They can and do exercise their free will, even in these cramped, concrete pools."

One morning after Tiluk had been with OceanLand for about seven years, staff arrived to find a human body in his pool. A fan had snuck in and hidden the night before as the park closed. Evidently, he planned to swim with Shantu. The death of Harvey Mott was downplayed as a freak accident by OceanLand, and most people, including some of OceanLand's own trainers, remained unaware that Tiluk had now killed two people. After Mott's death, Cassidy "Dusky" Dey, one of OceanLand's top, most experienced trainers who knew his past, helped implement what became an even stricter "no water work" policy. In fact, in initial news reports yesterday, some at OceanLand have implied that the reason for Dey's death is that she got too close to Tiluk. OceanLand was unavailable for comment to The Weekly. But when asked by a national news outlet yesterday about Dey's proximity to the whale, Theo Lax a former head trainer at OceanLand, said, "If Dusky were here now, she'd say it was her mistake."

Smith scoffed at this suggestion, calling it insane. "I honestly don't know how that man is going to sleep at night. He knew the risks." She explains: "Whales in captivity are categorically unpredictable, period. They are probably far more stressed on a daily basis than their trainers realize, and that's almost certainly why there have been so many 'incidents' with other trainers and other orca." Smith is referring to examples of various captive orca initiating violent or unpredictable encounters with trainers. These include various trainers being held against their will by whales in the middle of pools, one whale repeatedly leaping on its trainer over and over while herding him away from safety, and, another trainer's death just two months ago in an OceanLand-owned park in Spain. These events are only now coming to light in the wake of Dusky Dey's death, in part, due to Smith's work with FOI to acquire information OceanLand would rather not share publically.

Smith adds, "I'm convinced that Tiluk's severe, unacknowledged stress and suffering are what killed all three of these people." It remains unclear whether Tiluk understands that he killed Aaronson, Mott, and Dey.

Researchers agree that, like humans, young whales have a long, slow learning curve, the eventual success of which hinges on strong family bonds and mentoring—whales teach their young where, what, and how to fish; how to communicate (each pod has distinctive dialects and clearly communicate amongst themselves and with other groups); and what the social norms are within and between families.

"Captive whales experience something diametrically opposed to that," says Smith, who has a doctoral degree based on her years of researching wild orca. "Biologically speaking, they are fundamentally incompatible with captive existence. Beyond all the other harmful fallout of captive life, they are forced to co-exist and attempt to bond with unfamiliar, unrelated whales who have absolutely no genetic investment in a strange whale's future. This is something that never occurs in the wild where orca are intensely committed to and dependent on family. Unfortunately there are many more examples than most people realize of captive whales behaving in abnormal, violent ways with each other and with humans."

Maggie Ravenwood is a researcher at the University of Washington in Seattle, a member of ExplOrca, and the lead author on some two-dozen studies on wild orca behavior and health. Ravenwood, like Lewis, observed Tiluk as a young wild whale prior to his capture. She says, "Wild whales live in an alien world that humans can barely imagine.

Their sound capabilities alone are light-years ahead of human understanding—using echolocation they visualize their entire world in three dimensions. The way they see their world is something humans may be unequipped to understand, ever."

She adds, "Even experienced whale researchers are often mystified when they try to wrap their own minds around what an orca mind is capable of."

Researchers believe that killer whale brain size is related to their communication abilities as well as their social complexity. Their brains are four times larger than the human brain, with complex folding in the higher-functioning neocortex; a telltale neurological sign of the higher thought functions usually associated with humans. The only animal on Earth with a larger brain is the extremely reclusive sperm whale, which was nearly hunted to extinction during the whaling era. Most marine mammal scientists agree that the large brains of all cetaceans— which include dolphins and other "toothed" whales like the orca,

Belugas and pilots; as well as the "filter-feeding," baleen whales like humpbacks and grays—are strongly tied to their social and communication capabilities.

Ravenwood adds, "The complexities and richness of orca culture, which vary enormously between families, more distant pods, and orca living in other parts of the world, continues to surprise us. It's as if they have different and totally separate, learned cultures based on the place they live and the food they eat, much as we see in human tribes. Even their dialects are distinctive between families. What's more, they don't fight. Even populations that co-exist near to one another don't fight. They are highly evolved predators like us, yet they almost never use their built-in weaponry and teamwork for anything but acquiring food. It appears they have sophisticated cultural mores in place that prevent war or even much inter-species aggression. These whales are using their huge brains for something, and we're trying to figure out what."

"The only place we've ever seen them fight," she says, "is in captivity."

When asked about Tiluk's latest killing and why he did what he did, there is a long pause before Ravenwood asks quietly, "I would ask you, if you were him, What would you have done?"

Tim Sinclair is The Orlando Weekly's science correspondent and often reports on OceanLand. He continues to track Tiluk's saga. For updates find him on Twitter @ SinclairOWeekly.

It was the worst thing I've ever seen in my life. The words rang in his head as

Miles sat back and reflexively ran his hands through his hair again, pulling hard on the roots. The clock read 4:58 AM. *Shite-sa!* Miles couldn't take it all in. *I wonder if that Holly lady had bad dreams, too?*

"Whooooa....wait a second," he whispered aloud to himself. "Dude! She quit her dang *job* after she saw Steve get killed. No freaking way. That's huge! I just *bet* she had some crazy bad dreams. Maybe I need to do some-thing different, too." He frowned. *At least with this I* **can** *do something*, he thought to himself as the big *D word* hit him again like it always did anytime he forgot about his parents' split for a few blessed minutes.

He clicked open his Twitter account and typed in Sinclair's tag. He was totally going to follow this guy. *I mean, wow, that's one heck of a story to whip out on the same day that Shantu killed that trainer. Oops, make that Tiluk.* On impulse, he checked Holly Smith, Claire Lewis, and Maggie Ravenwood. "*Yesss*," he murmured. "Hello ladies," he said as he typed their tags into his account. He flashed to *The Princess Bride* and Fezzik the giant's awesome line to Princess Buttercup as he held the four white horses at the end, "Hello lady." And how his dad always used to say that to his mom because it was their favorite movie. Before.

Miles glanced out his window. It was just barely starting to lighten with dawn. *Dusky Dey, huh.* He thought. *So that's Blondie's real name.*

"Hello lady."

More like goodbye lady. He clamped his eyes shut, trying to not to see her again. *Dude, I've gotta get outta here.*

Moving in quick silence, he carefully grabbed his xylophone and skate-board, holding the silver tonal keys tight to his chest to keep it quiet, and tiptoed through the house, pulling the outer door carefully shut behind him.

The humidity, as always, squeezed him like a python as he left the AC for the heavy Florida air. His chest cramping against the pressure, he inhaled, push-ing against the muggy coils. It always took a few breaths to cast them off.

An orange-pink glow barely registered over the hundreds of roofs and thousands of winking street and porch lights, and, even now, like a thousand cars' headlights in the distance, all squeezed together in what could only be called orderly chaos; their Orlando suburb. Home Sweet Home. With no sidewalks anywhere, now was the best time to ride.

He ran quietly down the street a hundred yards to make sure his mom wouldn't hear him, then hurled down his skateboard and jumped aboard. Breathing deeply now, he took in the rich mix of Florida's dank swamps chaffing against the humid wafts of asphalt rising beneath him, the pave-ment still exuding its tarry breath after yesterday's long, hot bake in the sun.

Out…Of….Here…

He sped down the street, jamming his foot hard against the pavement, gaining momentum. He hated the way the road surface rumbled the board, making his teeth shake. He flew around the corner, heading towards the back-end of the development, making tracks towards the smooth sidewalk that lined the outer edge along the swamp. *No freaking sidewalks along the streets, but you can walk the perimeter like it's the outer walls of a prison.* Miles was not in a good mood. The sidewalk ran along people's back yards on one side and what was left of a swamp on the other. Between the sidewalk and the swamp was a substantial fence with signs every hundred yards:

BEWARE
Snakes and alligators DO Attack Humans
Do not approach.

Please report sightings immediately:

Call "G-E-T—O-U-T—H-I-S-S"

He wasn't sure whether the fence was supposed to keep people out of the swamp, or keep the swamp away from the people. The snakes were seriously getting out of control. You couldn't live in Florida and not know about the yellow anacondas, Burmese pythons and boa constrictors. They were a *huge* problem since they'd been accidentally introduced. The snakes loved it here, and they didn't have anybody to eat them, so they were pretty much everywhere. He'd heard rumors at school about snakes that had even eaten little kids. Sometimes he'd just come here and stare over the fence, peering from the concrete stronghold of their subdivision into the dank, vegetation choked, black-watered quagmire. The swamp creeped him out but, at the same time, it pulled at him, beckoning somehow.

The sidewalk was much smoother than the pavement, and he rocketed past all the backyards, blipping from fence to fence at high speed. He veered into the swamp on the fenced walkway that linked the back edge of his massive development to the business district on the other side of the swamp.

There was trash everywhere in here; soda bottles, needles, plastic bags, broken glass. This pathway smelled even worse than plain old swamp; like exhaust and beer mixed with the smell of a dead body rotting in mud. He raced past a couple of sleeping old homeless guys on benches, relieved it was getting lighter outside. He never came here in the dark.

Once he hit the business district, everything clicked. *I'm going to OceanLand.* He hadn't realized it until that very moment. He slowed for a fraction of a second, *Seriously Frost? Umm, Duh! YES!* It was only a couple of miles from their house, which was one reason their mom took them so often—she'd bought a family membership after the divorce. *Broken family membership, more like.* He whipped through the back parking lots of the Taco Bell, McDonald's, Kentucky Fried Chicken, Wendy's and Exxon. When he got to Wal-Mart, he knew he was close. Slowing, he narrowed his eyes and scanned the OceanLand perimeter. First was the gigantic parking area, which is what people saw when they pulled in. It was so big you could plunk down a freaking small town on that lot with room to spare. Behind that was the park itself, which was enclosed by a huge 12-foot-tall solid wood fence that snaked back into thick vegetation. Miles' gaze fell against the trees back there, and instinctively he pushed his board toward them. But this time his foot came down carefully, gently. He'd gone on high alert. He was pretty sure that OceanLand wouldn't want people sneaking around back there, especially after that Harvey Mott guy managed to get himself killed. *Not to mention Dusky yesterday.* The hair on the back of Miles' neck went up as he realized what he was about to do. He pressed his mouth tight in resolve. *I am doing this.*

But the coast was clear, at least way over here on the outer edge of the park. There were some staff over at the entry area, getting out of their cars with their coffee mugs and heading inside, but he was far away and they didn't notice him. He was rolling along on his board one second, and the next he'd easily hopped off into the woods, grabbed up his board, and vanished from the parking lot without a trace.

Instantly the world changed. The trees were thick and the ground was really wet. He stuck close to the fence. *Dude, the last thing I want to do is get lost in the freaking Everglades.* True, the real Everglades were further south, but still. This was Florida, and there were snakes. And alligators. Miles' stomach clenched. He took a deep breath. It was amazingly quiet in here, like he'd stepped through some kind of weird time warp that whisked him away from the familiar comforts of McBuySomething Land. He kind of liked it. But it was freaking different. Dude, his sneakers were starting to squish.

He kept his eyes down, watching the ground. *Don't want to step on a python, Frost.* The fence on his left kept coming in and out of view as he walked deeper into the woods behind the parking lot. *Man, it's thick in here.* But luckily not swampy. Maybe he didn't have to worry about snakes or alligators. *Let them stay in the swamp and we'll all be just fine.*

Miles was heading towards Shantu Stadium at the back of the park. He could tell he was getting close because the fence started veering off in front of him—the whole park bulged outwards to accommodate the huge concrete pools and the giant bleachers—so he had to move towards his right, feeling like a regular bushwhacking pioneer in the deep jungle. He had to duck a lot and keep moving branches away from his face with one hand while he clutched his xylophone and skateboard to his chest with the other. He pushed ahead, his sneakers now completely soaked.

He reached up to push another big branch out of the way. It moved, and a large boa constrictor flew back in defensive posture as Miles' hand recoiled like he'd touched a live wire. He jumped backwards, suddenly seeing the whole snake as it wrapped itself more tightly around the limb it was gripping, staring at him. "Shite-sa," he breathed against the pounding in his chest. "Hello snake." He knew in his head that the snake was a constrictor and wouldn't strike him unless seriously provoked, but still. *Wait a second*, he thought, *I'm on my way to see a killer whale. I can handle you, snake.*

In a rash move, he stepped forward, staring down the snake, who was just above his eye-level, and walked past it less than two feet away, daring it to threaten him. The snake must have been six feet long. It recoiled further, keeping its distance.

Miles walked on. *Dude, what a rush!* He was on fire. *Maybe I'll have to catch one of those suckers and bring it home for Mom.* He grinned, feeling lighter. His fingers started to itch. He was ready to zip the phone; his shorthand for grooving on his xylophone.

Wait a second, isn't that the outer edge of the Shantu tank? Miles wondered to himself when he saw the wooden fence run up against a heavy concrete wall. *Oh, wait... make that the "Tiluk" tank.* Eyeballing it, Miles saw that the concrete was really tall, maybe 14 feet above his head, and it curved in a long, wide stretch through the woods before the stadium rose up and out of the vegetation. Staring, he realized that this one area of the tank bordered the little hidden sanctum of Florida bush he'd just discovered. He wondered if it was the pool Tiluk lived in during off hours. *Maybe he's over there right now.* Miles felt a surge of excitement mixed with dread. *Seriously, that Tiluk really is a killer whale.*

His eyes skimmed the concrete. There was a thick copse of trees pushing up against the wall ahead, as if the trees had grown up from the base of the concrete. Their branches hung high over the top edge of the wall creating what looked to Miles like a little hidden tree cave. It was a small circular area, almost like a fort, enclosed by the bushy limbs and choking vines. He was sure you couldn't see the fort from the other side—where the trainers would be—because the branches and vines were so thick.

Dude, I could totally climb that. Still fired up from his stare down with the snake, he didn't think. He went to the trees, shoved his skateboard roughly into the heavy thicket of trunks, and reached around behind him to push his z-phone down between his jeans and his back. He climbed. This time, he watched carefully for snakes.

Shimmying himself upwards, the small grove of trees were as handy as a ladder. *Wow, something's easy for a change.* Miles realized he better slow down.

Even though it was still really early in the morning, there might be trainers or staff over on the other side, especially after what happened yesterday. Besides his sneakers were so wet they were making little squishing noises.

He glanced down and felt a surge of satisfaction. *He was up high!* Near the top, he came to a stop and ever so slowly poked his head up over the ledge of concrete, keeping his eyes well behind the thick rosette of drooping branches. He was camouflaged and wanted to keep it that way.

He had guessed partially right. The concrete was flat here underneath the tree cave fort…he might even be able to safely sit inside it so no one could see him. But past this tree fort, the concrete stretched onwards for some distance—maybe 20 feet—before it dropped down into a pool. It was the large performance pool that sat right in front of all those bleachers, which were over to his right. Near the bleachers was a small out-building, the place,

Miles figured, that the trainers kept food and gear for the performances. Way over on the other side of the big show pool, he saw a gate. On the other side of that gate was the large "Lunch with Shantu" pool. *Ugh.* Miles' stomach twisted. A third pool was off to the side of that.

So the pool is a little farther away than I thought. That's ok. Tiluk won't be able to hop up here and snatch me. There was no way he was going to make the same mistake that Harvey Mott guy had made. He knew firsthand how tiny and helpless a person really was compared to a 12,000 pound killer whale. By now he was a full grown, adult male bull. Miles was actually pretty relieved about how far away the pool was. Giving a quick glance in all directions, he couldn't see a soul. Slowly, as quietly as he possibly could, he scaled the last few feet of his "ladder," pulled himself silently into the tree fort, and hunkered down cross-legged. Tree branches and vines encircled him, letting the filtered light of dawn inside. It was actually kind of pretty.

Well Mom, Miles stifled a snort, *You don't have to worry about me lying in bed listening to violent music. I'm just over here hanging out with this killer whale.*

Or am I? Where the heck is he? Miles narrowed his eyes, suddenly on alert.

What the heck? He realized he hadn't heard any whale breaths or seen any hulking black whale. There. Over in the "Lunch" pool there was a patch of black, partially hidden by a bend in the pool. *I bet that's him. And I bet he's over there hanging out next to the third pool where they keep the other two whales.* Miles was pretty sure that OceanLand had a total of three Shantus right now, and he thought they were keeping Tiluk away from the other two because the girls beat up on him all the time. That meant the huge show pool in front of him was empty. *That's pretty much just fine with me.* Miles was very relieved.

Baaawhooooosh. There it was. A quiet, slow blow billowed above the black back hanging in the pool around that bend. Maybe they were all napping. He knew from what they said in the shows that killer whales, like dolphins and Belugas, rest with one half of their brains at a time. They have to be awake enough all the time to remember to breathe. *Pretty darn weird.* Miles couldn't imagine keeping half of his brain awake while he slept. *But maybe then I wouldn't have that stupid nightmare.*

Baaawhooooosh. Baaawhooooosh. Two more long, quiet blows sounded at almost exactly the same time, and Miles could just see two clouds of spray coming from the direction of the third pool. *Yep. Just like I thought…Two more whales.*

With one more furtive glance around Shantu Stadium, Miles reached behind him and carefully pulled out his z-phone, holding the keys tightly so they wouldn't vibrate their tones. Handling it like a ticking bomb, he used utmost caution to lay the xylophone down on the concrete. He wanted total radio silence. He didn't want to alert Tiluk to his presence until he was ready.

Miles grinned at his own vigilance: trying to set down a xylophone without making a sound is like playing the deluxe reverse version of Operation. One tiny bump and the whole thing tinkles a rainbow of tones.

Miles pulled the two small wooden mallets off their handy clip-in spot on the instrument, and sat cross-legged again. Enclosed in the little tree fort, he could see out, and was pretty sure no one could see in. No one else was around. *I better hurry up and do this though, 'cause I bet someone's gonna show up soon. It must be almost six-thirty.*

If a xylophone can whisper, that's how Miles played it. He wasn't sure whether Tiluk would hear much if anything, but still. Maybe he'd be able to sense the vibrations through the concrete. He had to try.

The first song Miles thought of to play for Tiluk was Dueling Banjos. He'd heard it for the first time last fall when he'd been watching David Letterman. Some guy was getting a fifty-thousand dollar music award from Steve Martin (whom Miles' *adored*)…for playing the banjo. The banjo! Miles had never heard of Dueling Banjos before. But when Steve and that prize-winning-plucker twanged off together, his blood hopped. He stayed up all that night listening to the song over and over on Youtube and taught himself to riff it on his z-phone. It was one of his all-time favorites. Now, ever so gently, Miles tapped out the first nine tones of the song. *Bawhoosh!* Tiluk blew instantly, a short, clipped burst. Before Miles could blink, he dove and reappeared at the gate that separated him from the Lunch pool and the show pool. He was about 50 feet away.

Da, da, da, da, da, da, dee dee, da… Miles tapped out the same phrase again, louder this time. Dueling Banjos was so awesome, and this phrase…. this phrase was *sooo* cool. It was such a question!

Tiluk dove again and smacked his tail hard on the water's surface.

No way. Miles tried to stay calm, but holy banjoes, Tiluk could hear him! *Bawhoosh!* The whale's blow reverberated around the stadium. He had the whale's full attention!

*Da, da, da, da, da, da, dee dee, da…*Miles dinged out the next phrase, five tones above the first, same exact phrase. Another hopeful question.

And Tiluk spyhopped. His entire head emerged on the other side of the gate, his white eye patch glinting at Miles. *Tiluk is giving me the once over*. Miles shivered. *I wonder if he can even see me.*

*Da, da, da, da, da, da, dee dee, da…*He played the repeat of the second phrase right away. *Maybe he can hear me better when his head is out of the water like that.*

Tiluk dove again. He tail-slapped mightily, then jetted around the small pool pushing a large wave of water over the edge. He reappeared behind the gate with his head slightly above the water now.

DA, DA, DA, DA, DA, DA, DEE, DEE, DA…Tiluk squeaked out his own version of the phrase through his blowhole.

Miles' jaw dropped. *No. No. No.* He shook his head fast and hard, clearing his mind. He did *not* get enough sleep last night. This wasn't happening! No way was that whale over there piping out Dueling Banjos with him. No. Freaking. Way.

Tentative, he played the first phrase again. *Da, da, da, da, da, da, dee dee, da… DA, DA, DA, DA, DA, DA, DEE, DEE, DA…*

Holy smokes. Miles sucked in his breath. *I have got to be dreaming again.* The whale's tones sounded different, much more airy and raspy, but there was no mistaking he was imitating Miles music. It was almost like he already knew the song. But how could that be?

Miles went on with the answer to the first question. *Da, da, da, dee, da… DA, DA, DA, DEE, DA…*

"Hello whale," breathed Miles.

Da, da, da, dee, da…

DA, DA, DA, DEE, DA…

Miles stopped playing. His mouth hung wide open. Tiluk hung there. *Bawhoosh!* He rose up again, spyhopping, looking over the pool towards Miles as if to say, "Well? Come on already. Play some more!"

Just then two people in OceanLand garb came out from a door near the Lunch pool. They each had a bucket. They had no idea what was going on. Seeing Tiluk still spyhopping, they stopped, put down their buckets and watched the whale. After one more long stare in Mile's direction Tiluk low-ered himself back underwater.

BAM! Tiluk rammed the gate between the Lunch pool and show pool. Hard. The trainers forgot their buckets and started blowing the thin pipe whistles around their necks.

Uh oh. I better get outta here.

Tiluk took off around the pool at top speed.

BAM! He hit the gate with full force, ignoring the trainers and their whistles. This time the whale pulled back from the gate, spyhopped once more, and looked towards Miles. Then he sank back into the water, rolled sideways and slapped his ten-foot long pectoral fluke hard on the water so that a large spray of water rose up and sloshed the edges of the pool. He dove and sped once more around the pool, coming to a stop in front of the gate.

DA, DA, DA, DEE, DA...a question directed to no one other than Miles. The trainers dropped their whistles and gaped. *Oh boy, I really need to get outta here now...Next time, whale.* Hastily he picked up the z-phone and shoved it back inside his pants. It tinkled a few tones. The trainers' heads snapped in his direction, both peering intently across the pool towards his fort.

Quickly Miles scuttled backwards over the concrete wall, climbed down his ladder, grabbed his skateboard, and ran-walked as fast as he could back through the brush while trying to stay silent. He remembered the boa. Geesh. He didn't know if he could handle any more surprises. Not today.

"Please," he found himself saying to no one, "no more snakes."

GRANDCHILDREN OF EVE

From: Terra Incognita Lewis <terralewis@explorca.org>
Date: June 12, 2013
To: Dr. Jane Goodall <jginstitute@jgi.email.org> Subject:
Orca Breakthrough & Question

Dear Dr. Goodall,

My name is Terra and I talk to orca whales. I mean, I don't
exactly talk to them, but I've been trying for practically
my whole life. I have a hydrophone in my room that lets
me listen to the whales, and a microphone I use to play
"podcasts" out into Blackfish Cove where I live on San Juan
Island in Washington. Anyway, a long time ago my best
friend Tiluk and I tried to teach the orca Morse code and we
spent about six whole months tapping for them. But nothing
ever happened. We never heard any reply.

Until this morning. See, my parents are marine biologists
and we study J Pod here in Puget Sound, which I bet you
know about since you study and try to protect so many
animals everywhere. Did you know J Pod is governed by
this one ancient whale we all call Granny? She's over 100
years old!

Anyway, at dawn this morning I did my first podcast since
Shantu killed that trainer at OceanLand yesterday...Did

you hear about that? When Cassidy Dey died during an "Lunch with Shantu" event? I just bet you know about it. But I bet you didn't know that "Tiluk" is the whale's real name. He is Granny's great grandson. His mother and sisters and aunts and uncle are here, living without him. Which is pretty screwed up since in the wild, the whales live with their mothers and families for their entire lives. But I guess the people at OceanLand didn't know that when they first captured all their Shantus.

Anyway, I guess his family misses him, because when I did my podcast this morning, I tapped out a message about Tiluk for the first time ever. I never really thought the whales actually understood me since they never responded, but I always talk to them, and use Morse code, just in case.
So anyway, I knew the whales were down in the cove, I think they rested there last night. I had my message all ready to go so I could make sure I got it right. First I said "Good morning whales," like I always do, then I said each sentence into the microphone, and then tapped it out in code. Here it is:

Wendy's son Tiluk is alive. He lives in a small human pool and works with humans to make other humans happy. We do not know if he is happy. Yesterday Tiluk killed the human he works with. We are all worried about him. We all feel sad for the human's family. I think you should know he is alive. I promise to do everything I can to make Tiluk happy again.

Jane, it was incredible! After I tapped out and said that first sentence, all the orca vocalizations coming from my hydrophone just went dead. That's never happened before. The whales were totally silent the entire time I broadcast my message! Then, the loudest, strongest wavering wails came through! They were so loud I had to put my hands over my ears! I've never heard these sounds before. Then the whole family raced out of our cove, which is also pretty weird. I'm worried about them.

Do you think they actually understood me? I think most scientists would think I'm crazy, but maybe you'll get it. I haven't even told my parents about this yet. If the whales really can understand me, I don't want half the world coming here to study them like whale ETs. They need their privacy, especially now.

I know you must be super busy and more famous than some movie stars, but I feel like you are the only person who can really understand my problem. My friend Tiluk knows about this, too. He's been helping me with everything so much. But he's not Jane Goodall.

If you were me, what would you do?

Sincerely,
Terra Lewis

PS. Just so you know I'm sending a letter about this to Dr. Janet Carson at NOAA, too. Wow, this might get confusing... two Dr. J's!

Terra was on fire. She hit send on her first e-mail and started the next one immediately. Being the daughter of biologists was good for a few things, including knowing who to track down in times like these. She was worried if she didn't write these letters and only told her parents about what hap-pened that they'd just reassure her and tell her everything would be okay. After hearing about the secret they'd kept for so long, which she could sort of understand, she was worried that they'd just say, "Let us be the parents, Terra. It's okay for you to just be a kid."

She was *so* done with that. She knew what would happen then: They'd write up the Morse Endeavor in another one of their tons of research papers, and either, the world and the Navy would descend on her whales, or the whole thing would get buried in paperwork. And she'd get to be a scientific author at the age of 13. Like *that* was important.

I don't think so. After what happened during her podcast this morning, she had to do something that was going to make a real difference. Terra's brows knit in concentration.

From: Terra Incognita Lewis <terralewis@explorca.org>
To: Dr. Janet Carson <jCarson@noaa.email.org>
Date: June 12, 2013
Subject: Orca Breakthrough & Question

Dear Dr. Carson,

We met a long time ago when I was about eight. You came to visit us and we had a dinner party. You and my parents (Claire and Bill Lewis) used to work together in marine biology when you were a professor at Oregon State University, and my parents were graduate students. You did paddle watch with us that night, and met Granny's pod. I bet you remember.

Anyway, I know that now you are in charge of the National Oceanic and Atmospheric Administration, and you were picked by the President to be on his "science team" (I think that is AWESOME, by the way, congratulations!), and now I have an important thing to tell you.

I just sent a letter to Jane Goodall, too, which I copied for you below. It explains everything. Basically, I think the orca whales we are studying can understand Morse code. But I'm not totally sure yet, and I don't think it's a good idea for anyone to know. I'm writing to you for advice.

What should I do if I find out they *do* understand Morse code? I know if it's true, word will get out fast, and I don't want the Navy using killer whales for whatever war operations or defense stuff that they do. I know that they've used bottlenose dolphins for that kind of thing, and the idea of tearing apart families of wild whales again makes me sick. Since you are a marine ecologist who really knows how important orca are in their marine system, I thought you'd have some good ideas. Especially since you are so high up in the government now.

If someone in the government *is* going to find out about our Morse Endeavor (that's what my friend Tiluk and I call it) I want you to be the first to know.

Sincerely,
Terra Lewis

There. She felt better. Much better. Terra took a deep breath and sighed.

She looked around her bedroom. Her yurt was so beautiful. It was a 12-foot circular space, the walls, a cross-hatch of wood lattice with a hefty green canvas draped around the outside. There were three "windows" and a door. The windows were strong plastic sheeting, with screens, which she could open, and the door was made of solid pine. The simple cedar planked wood floors had burnished over the years to a rich, soft hue that shone like a flickering ember. A large sheepskin rug covered the floor between her bed and her super cozy woodstove. The rug was her favorite place to sit—snuggled with hot tea in front of the fire—when she wasn't at her desk doing podcasts or sitting on her bed drumming.

She loved this bed. Like their huge dining room table, her dad had built one for her and one for Tiluk when they were both two. It was right after the twin towers had fallen, actually. He'd told her once a long time ago when she'd asked about that, "Life is short. I wanted to make sure you and Tiluk had a beautiful and comfortable place to sleep as you grew up. The towers just reminded me of what was most important at that time in my life. I could spend more time modeling salmon on my computer, or I could go into my shop and make something that would last you both forever." He'd grown quiet for a moment. "Besides," he'd pulled on her braid grinning, "It was time for you to leave our bed anyway, sea squirt. You were starting to kick in your sleep."

Like it or not, her entire family had adopted Joseph's nickname for her.

Only Tiluk used a different term of affection, "Lewis." She knew that was because Tiluk—with his native blood—had a love-hate relationship with knowing that Terra was descended from Meriwether Lewis. Lewis and Clark, and all they represented, were part of the reason his people had lost so much, including like, thousands of their ancestors to terrible diseases, and a ton of their old ways and culture, not to mention so much of their homelands and waters. Terra knew that for black-haired Tiluk, the boy who breathed the forest and felt a connection to the Earth that was even stronger than hers, it was a harsh reality to live with. But she also knew he loved her like his own sister, and without Meriwether Lewis they wouldn't have each other now.

She glanced around again feeling that sense of fulfillment she always got in here. Her collection of falconing books, birding and tree guides and keys, and her other favorites, including, of course, all of Jean Craighead George's books, were lined up neatly on the nook of her bed's headboard. Above them and hanging around the perimeter of the yurt were all her treasures— pinecones, animal skins, beautiful stones, deer antlers, about a hundred awesome bird feathers, and the bones. She loved finding bones. She even had keys to help her identify the bones and feathers she collected. It was like a never-ending reverse scavenger hunt: the woods would offer up all these amazing things and she'd have to figure out just what they all were and who they'd come from. Once she'd figured out the answer, she penned a neat label and displayed the item in here, her little museum; the place that was her very own turtle shell, the place she retreated when she needed comfort or rest. Her refuge. Like the whales in Blackfish Cove. That's *their* sanctuary. But if they did truly understand her message of death and loss, she wondered, would their sanctuary ever be the same again? *I hope so,* Terra thought to herself as she gathered her things together.

Tiluk would be here any second. Knife? Check. Bow drill? Check. Water bottle? Check. Compass? Check. Not like she'd ever need that again. She and

Tiluk knew the lush forest of this island as well as they knew each other. Still, they'd learned from strict adherence to the survival skills their parents had taught them: You never go into the woods without a compass. Period.

She pulled the dark brown wool sweater that Maggie had made for her over her head and grabbed her light rain jacket; it was still cool outside in the early morning damp and you never knew when it would start raining. She stopped short when she saw the blood-stained orca whale she'd carved yes-terday sitting on her nightstand. Fingering it, she gently packed it, too, and noticed that her cut had already started mending. Then she stuffed the jacket and the rest of her gear into her fanny pack, clipped it around her waist, and stepped outside just in time to see Tiluk heading to her yurt from the mews with Fierce perched on his wrist. The early morning light cast through the trees and mist, backlighting her friend and the kestrel so they were wrapped in an otherworldly cloud. She shivered, either from the sudden cool outside her door, or the way Tiluk looked... a swirling halo of yellowish light danced around his entire body as he moved silently though the wispy fog.

"Hey," she said.

He nodded at her, a slight tilt to his head pointing the direction he wanted to go: his wordless language. She fell into step, shoulders touching, and they headed to the tree cave. *First things first*, thought Terra to herself. They both knew what had to happen before they hiked into the woods. The walk back up to the tree cave this morning was filled with the ruckus of bird calls and squirrel chatter as the forest awoke, bustling with energy and purpose.

Everyone who lived in here had things to do, Terra knew. The animal games of morning were all about finding food, settling territorial disputes, calling in mates, and a thousand other little things she'd never see, playing out every moment between birds and beetles and squirrels and frogs. The pandemonium of this time of day always electrified her; just by being out here she became part of something much bigger than herself. Plus, this morning's walk with Tiluk was nothing like yesterday's scramble down the hillside in the wake of the clanging bell. Today, they knew about the other Tiluk. Today, everything was different.

Terra took a deep breath with the weight of that knowledge as she looked up at the huge tree. It was ancient, waiting for them. Its arms spread out, round and round, as if twirling in a standstill, stretching high above their heads, mosses and vines covering its dozens of limbs. Despite its great hollow trunk, it continued to thrive with the water and nutrients it drew up deep from the ground. Still silent, they ducked inside.

"He's yours," she said to him, as they entered. This time it was Terra who sat quiet in the dark, holding Fierce, while Tiluk knelt down with his bow drill. He knew exactly what they were here for, of course, and after he had fire, he went immediately to Wendy's spot, found Babe, Bountiful, and the new calf, and pressed his own knife into the wood near Wendy.

The calf's older brother. Wendy's first born son, Eve's grandson, Granny's great grandson. Tiluk.

"I can't believe Wendy lost her first calf that way," Terra murmured, as she watched Tiluk carve his namesake into the family tree.

"It's why she's such a good mother to her other babies." He said it so matter of fact. She knew instinctively he was right, and her heart swelled in understanding, knowing what Wendy had lost and why she protected her other children so fiercely.

As the shadows flickered on the walls of her cave, Tiluk the whale emerged and took his rightful place beside his mother and family. *I wonder if there's any way he can come home?* Terra thought to herself as she watched

Tiluk's nimble fingers fly.

"Tiluk? Do you think they really understood the message this morning?"

Even though she'd written to the Dr. J's, and even after the way the whales had acted, she was still having a really hard time believing they could actually understand Morse code. They'd never responded before and she'd been 100 percent positive that the Morse Endeavor hadn't worked. It was just so…unbelievable.

He stopped carving, pulled his knife away from the wall, and turned to look at her in the flickering light.

"Terra, you have to start trusting those whales. They aren't just research animals." The frustration in his voice was thick and it startled her. He turned back to finish carving Tiluk, and etched in the immense dorsal fin, the sign of full sexual maturity in orca bulls. In reality, of course, Tiluk's dorsal fin slumped uselessly over his back, the same way all captive male dorsal fins did. Like a sorry-looking deflated black balloon instead of the ramrod tall signal of health and virility it was meant to be. But here Tiluk carved it erect and strong, towering above his sisters' dorsal fins. His appearance in here with his family made his absence from their everyday lives stark and unavoidable. Tiluk was shaking his head quietly to himself, and muttered under his breath, "Poor guy is busting his seams to go hang with the girls in the superpods, and they've got him trapped like a rat in a sinking ship. Christ, it's awful."

Miffed she watched him finish up. She *did* trust them, didn't she? Narrowing her eyes, she stared at the long black hair draped around Tiluk's back and shoulders. *What was he talking about?*

As if reading her mind, he turned to her again. "Hasn't it ever occurred to you that those whales *did* learn Morse code back when we did the Morse Endeavor?" his eyes flashed at her in the dark light. "And then decided not to let on?"

He turned back to his work, "It's not as if they have any reason to trust humans."

They're more than research animals.

Terra's hand found its way inside the fanny pack she'd put down on the floor beside her, and she pulled out the carving she'd made of the new calf and stared at it. She suddenly went white as everything came together, spinning and swirling in her mind like the branches twirling high above her head. She'd spent her entire life following her parents' scientific approach of tracking, observing, and recording data on the whales. Even the Morse Endeavor was a kind of experiment. If I do "A," then "B" should happen. And if B doesn't happen, then nothing has changed. She never once stopped to consider that the whales had actually learned the code, and then—and this is what was washing over her like flood water—that they might have the wisdom and intelligence to keep that knowledge hidden. Maybe, in fact, there was an extraordinary "C."

She looked down at the baby in her hands, recalled her dream, and leaned back against the tree, feeling as if she might faint. Fierce gripped her arm and squawked. Her breathing went shallow and there wasn't enough air. The way the pod had introduced the calf last night flashed through her mind. And Granny's long stare…She'd been so wrapped up in her scientific expectations—not to mention her shock over Tiluk's killing—that she was just now facing what was right in front of her. The doubts that would otherwise keep her from helping the whales vanished: The whales knew more than she'd thought. A lot more. She felt woozy.

"I've gotta get out of here," she gasped as she stood shakily and stumbled into the fresh air outside.

Tiluk sheathed his knife, ducked out of the tree, and was beside her in a flash. He gripped her arms, saw her white face and round eyes, and pulled her into a ferocious hug. Fierce squawked again and hopped off of Terra and onto Tiluk's shoulder; his jesses tangling in Tiluk's long black hair. Tiluk held his friend tight. She was a caterpillar wrapped inside the snug cocoon of his arms.

"I need to tell you about my dream," she finally managed.

"I know." He dropped her arms, stepped back and stared fixedly into her eyes. He handed Fierce back to her, ducked into the tree, smudged out the fire with his foot, poured some water on the embers, and grabbed her fanny pack.

"Come with me," he tried to take her free hand but found the orca baby there. She held the carving up between them; her blood stain had darkened the wood so it looked like black whale skin.

"She's special." Terra's voice rang clear with wonder, as if the flood waters had washed away her doubts and skepticism, leaving behind all that was strong and true inside her. "And so is her brother."

"I know." He wrapped his fingers through hers so the baby was nestled safe between their palms.

"Come on."

Together they walked into the primeval forest. Tiluk looked over at her as they walked, studying her face. She felt different somehow, but she couldn't quite figure out why. It was as if she'd been wearing a veil over her eyes all this time and suddenly, with Tiluk's question—and her realization that the whales must have learned Morse code but then kept it a secret—it got swept away and she could finally see clearly. Only she'd never realized before that the veil was even there.

As they hiked deeper into the woods, they went up a series of switchbacks. She knew where he was taking her. It was their other favorite place besides the tree cave and the den of rocks. *So if Granny and her family had known Morse code all this time,* she speculated, *Wouldn't that mean that they had made some kind of pod-wide decision not to let on?* And wouldn't that mean some kind of sophisticated language or understanding that could lead to…she couldn't think of the word…was it consensus? Yes that was it, like in her and Tiluk's little island school. She recalled when the whole school voted to make a decision to ban soft-drink and candy machines after her and Tiluk's class had done a big research project showing the impacts of sugar on kids' health, and then presented it to the student body. Yeah, kind of like democracy.

Terra stopped to catch her breath; they were almost to the top after nearly a mile of gentle switchbacks through the heavy drapery of ancient cedar trees and Douglas firs. She let go of Tiluk, handed him Fierce, and reclaimed her fanny pack, strapped it back into place, and took a long swig of water. Tiluk, meanwhile, stood back, let go of Fierce's jesses, raised his arm upwards towards the immense majestic trunks towering all around them, and whispered, "Go."

Fierce hurtled out of sight swooping into the maze of large trees. Terra and Tiluk looked like miniature dolls against the colossal giants that stood silent all around them. The forest floor here was thick with shade-loving ferns and dozens of fallen trees that had turned into nurse logs—the trunks barely recognizable anymore as they lay beneath a deep layer of moss and many younger trees growing up from the moist, rotting wood of their once living bodies. This place was a cathedral; the majesty of the trees surrounding them, their trunks wider than most cars, their boles rising well over a hundred feet about their heads always stilled Terra's mind and filled her body with a peace she never felt anywhere else. It was one of the few places left on their island, and across the entire Pacific Northwest for that matter, where humans had let the ageless trees stand. She wondered, for a moment, as she always did when she came here, whether that was enough. She knew that with climate change and pollution, these particular trees as well as her beloved garden of rainforest stretching all around them and beyond, were seriously threatened. Already she and Tiluk had noticed dieback on some of these trees, a withering of their lush, opulent branches; branches that were home to plants, mosses, fungi, lichens, and animals. Even in this relatively untouched old growth, the forest community was changing too, just as many others already had in response to warming temperatures and the widespread logging of Pacific

Coast temperate rainforest. Terra frowned, thinking an unbidden question.

If you fall from grace in a rainforest, does anyone hear the sound?

She caught her breath and looked at Tiluk, who met her stare. He probably knew exactly what she was thinking. They were both well aware of what has happening to their Eden. Then she capped her water bottle, stuck it back into her fanny pack, and walked on ahead of him. Still holding the baby whale, rubbing it like a worry stone, she headed up and over the crest of the hill and towards the thicket; the gurgling stream calling to them as they walked down into the miniature valley.

As she walked, she found herself wondering about her beloved forest and the whales, her mind making connections it had never made before...this forest and the whales had something in common: They were both being badly harmed by human activity. But many people didn't seem to understand that, and she wondered why. Was the thing that drove people to capture wild orca the same thing that leads them to pollute the air and water and ignore the peril of climate change? Her mind wandered a little further, to Tiluk and his heritage. Could "it" be the same thing that had let European settlers believe it was acceptable to drive native people from lands they'd lived on harmoniously for thousands of years, committing horrific acts of genocide and war that Americans continue to excuse as Manifest Destiny? Could "it" be what caused slavery and rape and murder?

Were people just being human?

Her stomach twisted with the thought, she just couldn't believe that was true. Then her dream came to her again, Granny telling her she had a mission with the calf and her brother...and for a moment, her doubts about it faded again. *There's something about that dream*, she thought. *Something that will make sense of all this.* If the whales knew Morse code, maybe Granny really had some-how contacted her in her sleep. They were almost there: their super-secret counsel cliff. This, of course, had to be where she told Tiluk the whole truth.

She scrambled down with Tiluk right behind her towards their outcrop, grabbing onto bushes and saplings to slow down her slide. Ever since they first took this hike, years ago, they'd always stayed quiet during the hike through the cathedral of trees, as if by unspoken agreement, to honor its grace. But here; here was different. Terra slid the last few steep feet down on her bum, stood up quickly on the massive jutting boulder, turned around and gave her empty hand to Tiluk as he slid down behind her, the gurgling stream and waterfall behind her filling the silence with a wild voice.

"She's his sister, you know," Terra looked at Tiluk as they stood together above the waterfall, a thread of sadness unfurling in her heart.

"I can't even imagine what my life would be like if someone had stolen you away when you were two. I would miss you every single day."

Tiluk nodded, his eyes full of understanding, and the two locked their arms around each other, taking a long look around. Their counsel cliff was a miracle of exuberant life scraping hard against rigid geology. They were standing on a boulder the size of an inverted tractor trailer truck, a huge column of rock that blocked a pushy stream of water on its path through the little valley behind them. But the stream would not be stopped, and a few feet below them, it muscled its way with great force around the corner of this boulder to find the descent it craved. With similar three-story-tall rocks on the other side of the stream, the water found empty space between hunks of granite and with all its built-up roiling energy, it burst over the edge, flinging itself down to the rollicking pool far below. At the edge of that pool grew one of the largest red cedar trees Terra and Tiluk had ever found in this forest. Its trunk measured a full fifteen feet at its base (they'd brought a tape measure one day) and rose up alongside the boulder on which they now stood, its first limbs jutting out over their heads, sheltering the large room-sized flat space of rock that was their counsel cliff. They could sit on this rock, up high, next to this incredible tree and at the same time be, at least a little bit, perched in the canopy of the forest.

"At least his younger sisters don't know him," said Tiluk as he pulled Terra into the tree's refuge and down next to him onto the thick nest of fir needles that cushioned their favorite sitting spot. "Maybe that's easier for them, at least." He looked down at the whale carving in Terra's hands. Somber.

"It's not easier for the rest of his family, or Wendy," murmured Terra, handing Tiluk the whale. "Or for him…"

He just shook his head, keeping his eyes down, turning the whale over and over in his hands, studying it. Terra looked at him and saw he was blinking hard. He rubbed a hand back against his eyes. She had to remind herself that here was the boy who shared a name with the calf's brother. But *he* had been there to see the new baby while her very own brother, the *other* Tiluk, was trapped in a pool 3,000 miles away. And this was the boy who understood what his people had lost, who'd grown up touched with his own kind of grief. Tiluk shared more than a name with this whale. She took a deep breath. Exhaled.

"It was almost like Granny called me," she began, hesitating at first. "I didn't tell any of you guys about the details. I figured you'd just think I was crazy, or that it was just some weird dream. But it felt more real to me than eating breakfast after I woke up."

Tiluk looked at her, his black eyes glistening and shadowed. She saw something there. Suddenly Terra felt a pit of insight open inside her: Tiluk *needed* to hear her dream. Maybe more than she needed it herself. Why hadn't she told him already? She'd been holding onto it like it didn't matter. But maybe it mattered more than anything.

Closing her eyes, she leaned against him and recalled it once more, this time, trying to explain something to her friend as if it might be powerful medicine for his wounds. Her voice joined the rushing stream below as she told him how it was unlike any she'd ever had before. He already knew she'd been dreaming orca forever, hearing their music on many nights while she slept. But this dream was otherworldly, almost like it wasn't a dream at all. Almost as if it were real.

"I was in the tree cave and it was early morning, the break of dawn," she began. "I was dozing while the forest got loud." Terra often had sleepovers in the tree cave. She loved waking at dawn to the bird song swelling around her. But that morning, amidst the chirps and chatter of the wakening forest, the warm, cedar-smoked grotto wrapped around her, suddenly something changed.

"I knew I was half asleep and listening to the sounds all around me, and suddenly I felt this huge pull, almost like a magnetic force. Right at that moment, I woke up..." she looked at Tiluk. "I woke up in my dream. I was awake but asleep."

Tiluk nodded at her, his eyes reassuring her that he didn't think she was crazy.

"Then the force pulled me away from the tree cave. I shot outwards, very, very fast, and flew up above the tree to the top of its canopy and I could see everything." She grew quiet, remembering. She'd flown out of her tree and up over masses of the green treetops of cedar and Douglas fir where she could make out every fine needle sparkling in brilliant yellow sunshine: the radiant gold light rippling across the landscape of her dream was more dazzling than anything on Earth...but oddly familiar, as if she already knew this place.

"It's so hard to explain this in words. It was the most brilliant, beautiful place I've ever known, but it was right here. And I felt like I'd seen it before... or knew it all along." She looked at him again. "Isn't that odd?"

Tiluk just watched her, waiting. She sighed and relaxed. His eyes said to her, *No way am I calling you crazy, Lewis. This is what I've been waiting for.*

She closed her eyes, letting the dream come back. "The force pulled me out, way out over Blackfish Cove and then down into the water," she said.

Underwater was a shimmering, liquid realm full of its own greenish light and rich, three-dimensional landscape.

"It was amazing Tiluk, the water." She grew quiet. The cove and its under-water world, so full of shapes and terrain and fish and kelp, was nothing like the black, cold, flat world she'd imagined her whole life. It was a boisterous underwater *nation.* Was she still on the same planet? Sound was *everywhere...* it permeated her entire spirit. It hummed and bounced and echoed, and she knew without knowing how she knew, that a lot of what she was *seeing* was because of sound.

"I got to experience it, you know? Really see and hear what it is like to live down there. And it was so different than what I'd expected." She struggled for words, "It was this majestic rumpus of life...and we are totally, one-hundred percent blind to it."

She paused. "All this time I really thought it was just some crazy dream!" She shook her head, glancing at him again. Her voice shook a little, "But now the calf is real and she has a brother." Her voice came out in a whisper, almost reverent. "And our whales understand the code."

He glanced up into the tree above them, and reached for her hand. "Tell me the rest."

Terra looked up, too, taking a measure of calm from the great tree's steady presence. The tree made her think of how she'd felt with Granny.

"It was Granny, the force that pulled me out there. She was waiting for me in the cove, and she was like this huge, powerful magnet. I knew she'd drawn me out there from the tree cave." Terra took a deep breath. "Granny summoned me. "

Tiluk clasped her hand, reassuring her. She added, "This is why I didn't tell you guys all the details. It sounds totally crazy."

"Not to me, Terra," he looked at her, something alight in his eyes that hadn't been there before. Tiluk almost never called her Terra. When he did, it was a piercing term of endearment.

"It was overwhelming; she was so powerful, but so unbelievably kind and gentle. Just being next to her, I felt like I was getting a thousand hugs from all four of our parents at the same time." Her voice gentled with her remembering. "And she was so so wise."

"I couldn't believe she called *me*!" She'd felt overwhelming, humbling awe to be summoned by this immensely central and powerful matriarch. The joy

Terra had felt in Granny's calm, wizened presence was indescribable. Her black rubbery skin and her deep, peaceful eyes radiated so much warmth. "I mean, why me Tiluk? Why me??"

Tiluk didn't answer her, but looked down again, staring hard at the whale carving he still cradled in his other hand...the calf.

"She looked into me. I could see her eye, and she just looked *into* me...like, into my heart. She saw everything." Terra shivered.

Terra closed her eyes in concentration, recalling. "She didn't have to speak, but I knew everything she wanted me to know. Her mind linked with mine. And she told me Wendy was expecting a baby girl and that there was something special about her. Granny had chosen her—even before her birth—to help save the pod. Her family can't survive unless people wake up."

She opened her eyes. "Granny summoned me because she needs us to join forces with the calf."

Tiluk nodded and looked at her, serious. "Why the calf? Why not Granny herself?"

Terra stared at him, her eyes watering. "That's the hardest part. She's old. She's going to train this calf to receive her wisdom. She's leaving Earth soon." She wiped her eyes and took a deep breath. "She told me to pay attention, and to be ready for the connection to come... the connection with the new baby." She recalled the calf's presentation last night and felt her pulse quicken.

"After the dream, I basically put the whole thing out of my mind. It was just too weird...but after the way they showed us the calf last night, the way she came to my boat...and the way they brought the calf over and when

Granny stared at me..." Terra's voice trailed off. "It was exactly what she told me to watch for…that special connection."

She pulled hard on her long braid, the doubts threatening to surface again. "I just don't know anymore," her voice fell flat and brusque like a stone against granite. "It's just too weird and crazy to believe."

Tiluk stared at her, his eyes impenetrable but loving. "There's more," he said, validating her experience. "Tell me." He handed the baby whale carving back to Terra.

Looking appreciatively at her friend she said, "Just as the dream was ending she told me the thing that made me think the whole thing really *was* crazy. It's why I was so sure it was just a dream." She swallowed. 'Until yesterday that is…"

Tiluk's eyebrow went up, his face calm, his lips tilted in a rare half grin; as if he already knew what she was going to say. He squeezed their hands around her carving.

"She told you that the calf has a brother…and that you and her brother and the new calf have a special mission together."

Terra smiled at Tiluk's instincts. It was exactly what Granny had impressed on her. And it was why she'd doubted the entire thing…. because she'd believed there was no brother. Just as she'd believed the whales didn't understand Morse code. She felt her doubts fade away again as she savored what was happening.

"But now we know this calf really does have a brother," she murmured, holding up the little whale between them, staring at it. "Which means…"

Out of nowhere, Fierce arrived, flying up over the edge of the boulder where he knew he'd find them, a little shrew dangling from his claws. He found his favorite perch, a spot looking directly out over the cliff's edge down to the waterfall below, and began ripping the shrew's body into chunks, eating with gusto.

Remembering his own hunger, Tiluk reached into his pocket and pulled out the bag of dried apples and nuts he'd brought along for their snack. He handed some to Terra, raised a handful to his mouth, and looked up into the branches of the magnificent tree standing over them, a mixture of peace and trust set-tling over his face, as if its grand life force could seep into him once again.

Then Tiluk stared at her. For a long time. Even for him.

"Which means," he said finally, "you need to talk to my dad."

TIL NOW

"AND WHERE WERE YOU TWO off to this morning?" Claire called out from behind her laptop as Terra and Tiluk trundled in from outside, their clothes ruffled and damp from their hike. Claire's heart warmed seeing the softness in their two faces; she knew right away that together they'd sorted through some of the difficult emotions of the big news. She eyed Maggie and saw the same relief on her best friend's face. Not a day went by that either woman didn't feel a moment of fulfillment with their decision to combine their families and live in this sheltered, fertile place together.

"Just hiking with Fierce, Mom. Where's Joseph?" Terra stood in the entry-way and pulled off her muddy boots, leaning on Tiluk. Then she turned and did the same for him. They'd left Fierce out in the mews, but his meal was evident on Tiluk's sleeve where little stripes of blood from those talons had imprinted on his jacket.

"He went off island first thing this morning," said Maggie, poking her head up from behind the refrigerator door as she scanned for lunch. "He said something about seeking counsel from the tribe's elders."

Tiluk's eyes darted instantly to Terra's, his eyebrows raised. *See?* He said silently to her.

Disappointed, Terra's shoulders slumped. Now that she and Tiluk had talked she *really* wanted to spill the whole thing out to Joseph and hear what he thought about it all.

"He should be back later this afternoon, sweetie," Maggie said to Terra, reading her body language as well as her own mother. "Is everything okay?"

"YAW Mom," Tiluk did a deadpan Harvey the Dinosaur.

"Everything is just FINE. There's a dead TRAINER, a kidnapped SON, and a pod of wacky whales acting weally WEIRD. Everything is just GREAT! HA-HA!"

Everyone knew Tiluk loathed Harvey. He'd despised him from the first time Claire had brought home a DVD from the library, when the kids were two. Then, later on in school, where he couldn't get away from what he called the "Pointless Purple People Eater," the teachers would sometimes use in lessons and sing-alongs, he'd coped by impersonating Harvey, who now, on occasion, showed up when Tiluk was exasperated or annoyed. This meant a great deal to everyone who knew Tiluk, since he was usually so quiet and reserved. He *really* abhorred that dinosaur.

Claire and Maggie both laughed at his unexpected outburst, and Jason, who'd been sitting unnoticed on the couch working behind his laptop suddenly clipped it shut and stood up. "I'm with you Tiluk. No kidding man." Terra looked at Tiluk, grateful. She didn't want to talk about Joseph and he'd distracted his mom for her. She wasn't going to talk to anyone else but Joseph about her dream, and now she was itching to do so.

"Well, we want to talk to you two about all that," said Claire as she shut her own laptop, looking at Jason then Maggie. "Why don't you get some-thing to eat and we'll circle up at the table in ten minutes for a family meeting. Jason, you too. Gwen is out on the boat, but I'd like you here for this. You can fill her in when she gets back."

Jason raised his eyebrows with a quick nod and impish, handsome smile. "Sure Claire, I guess after last night's news I can take anything you can dish out."

Claire blushed and flashed him an appreciative grin, feeling a moment of light-heartedness. The grad students kept things around here so lively even in the face of this difficult news. Lord, she loved her work and her people. Again she felt that familiar sense of fulfillment sweep through her as she stood up from the large dining room table and took her laptop back to her office; and even though she was still smiling and shaking her head at Jason's comment, she realized she was also uncharacteristically nervous. Tapping lightly on Bill's office door she called, "Time for a break honey, the kids are back."

Late last night, after Terra and Tiluk had gone to bed, she, Maggie, Joseph, and Bill had all agreed that today they were going to have to fess up. Her stomach twisted a little and she leaned against the wall. She'd never been sure they'd done the right thing. And it had definitely gone on for way too long. Now she was jumpy. She realized her heart was racing. Just then the door swung open and Bill came out into the hallway. Meeting Claire's eyes and her concern, he wrapped his arms around her.

"It's okay honey. We did what we thought was best for the kids. They'll understand that."

"It's just….I just really wish we'd told them sooner. I feel remiss."

"Honey, we're all busy, and things slip by sometimes. Maybe, especially, this…you know?" Bill asked.

She nodded. He was right. "Well let's go get it over with then, shall we?" She took his hand and turned back towards the living room. "I can't imagine doing any of this without Joseph and Maggie." As an afterthought she said, "I'm glad Joseph went to talk to the elders today, but I do wish he were here for this, too."

Bill frowned a little. "I've never understood why Joseph puts so much stock in those silly native stories. I wish he'd accept that for what it is: a dying way of life. And get back to living in the real world."

Claire stopped short, dropping Bill's hand. "And I've never understand why you've been so resistant and unaccepting of his culture, Dr. Lewis," her eyes flashed. Claire only referred to her husband by his professional title when she called him out on his over-bearing skepticism. "Can't you see how much Joseph has brought to this family?" She walked ahead of him down the hallway. "Sometimes you can be so blind," she muttered, shaking her head.

"Claire, wait," Bill said, and Claire stopped, turning to face him. "I'm sorry. You're right. I lose patience with things that aren't rational, and frankly, I wish he were here right now, too. It would be a lot easier to talk to the kids. He's a source of strength and wisdom for our family."

Claire softened at Bill's words and smiled her easy smile. "It's okay honey, we're both just jumpy about this. Let's go talk to the kids."

Hand in hand, they walked back out to the big room and sat down with Terra, Tiluk, Jason and Maggie who'd put together a quick spread of fruit slices, cheese, and crackers. The sun was bright today and the room felt warm. Claire stepped to the big windows overlooking the cove.

"The pod is still gone," she said. "They must be out foraging for fish. They sure acted oddly last night. And the way they showed off the calf," she looked at Maggie and Bill first, then her eyes settled on her daughter. "It was just amazing…"

Terra fiddled with her napkin then looked at Tiluk. They knew why the whales had left the cove this morning. But they weren't going to tell these three about the podcast, or the wailing whales, either. They were waiting for Joseph. Jason saw their shared glance, and looked at them pointedly, one eyebrow peeking up beneath his sun-bleached surfer hair, as if all of a sudden he suspected they knew something. He had a whole new level of respect for Terra after discovering the calf she'd dreamt about yesterday— and a hunch that she might know more than she was letting on.

"We're going down to play for them after lunch, Mom," Terra said quickly, trying to distract Jason away from asking questions. "Maybe they'll hear us and come back in for paddle watch later."

"It *was* amazing, wasn't it Claire," piped in Jason. "I don't know if there's an example of that sort of behavior anywhere in the literature. I think it might be a first." He was still staring at Terra, like a hound dog sniffing a hot trail. Terra squirmed in her seat, uncertain.

"SO," boomed Bill, totally unaware of the subtle inquiry going on between Jason and Terra. He stretched back from the table and pushed his emptied plate away. "We have something to say to you both."

Terra breathed out in relief and let herself focus on her dad. But she could see Jason still peering at her and Tiluk with a look on his face that said, *I'm watching you two.*

She ignored Jason and rolled her eyes at her dad. "Seriously Dad, I can't take any more surprises. Last night was hard enough." She smiled a quick furtive glance at Tiluk. "Unless you're going to tell us Tiluk is coming home from OceanLand."

"First things first," Maggie said quickly, then addressed the kids. Claire left the big windows and came around to stand behind Maggie's chair, rest-ing her hands on her friend's shoulders. "There's something you both need to hear from us," Maggie said, and took a deep breath. "It's an apology."

Terra and Tiluk looked at each other, surprised. This was not what they were expecting. Even Jason dragged his focus away from Terra and Tiluk and looked at the women with open curiosity. "What are you talking about Maggie?" Terra asked.

"Well, first off," continued Maggie, "there's the way Tiluk learned the truth about his name last night." She reached over and took Tiluk's hand briefly. "We never meant for it to happen like that, honey. It broke our hearts to have to tell you not only that your namesake had been captured like that in Penn Cove, but then…" her voice trailed off. "That he'd killed people."

Tiluk nodded at Maggie thoughtfully. Jason snorted quietly, "Yeah, let's have Harvey try *that* one on for size and see what he'd have to say."

Tiluk almost smiled. He liked Jason a lot. They understood each other. "Uh, Oh-KAY kids, today we're going to sing about the HUGE killer whale who ATE his trainer, oh-KAY? Oh KAY!!" said Tiluk, unable to help himself in the face of Jason's inspiration.

"So why *didn't* you guys tell us about Tiluk?" Terra asked, rolling her eyes again, this time at Tiluk and Jason. This was too serious to joke about, didn't they get that? Besides, there was her dream… She needed to figure all this out, like, *now*! What if Granny really was depending on her? She needed to talk to Joseph.

Bill turned to Tiluk and Terra. "We want you both to know we made a decision, a long time ago shortly after your births, that we would keep certain things—*adult* things," he peered measuredly at Claire and Maggie, then at Jason, "from you. Like I said last night, we'd planned to give you both a transition ceremony for your 14th birthday celebration… when we'd tell you all about Tiluk."

"And a few other things," added Claire, staring at Terra.

"What do you mean *a few other things?*" Terra scowled, a sour taste rising in the back of her throat thinking of last night's news. Besides, right now, with Joseph gone, all she really wanted to do was get down to the dock with her drum and Tiluk and his flute, and call in the whales. She had to see the calf again. And Granny. Everything was different now.

Tiluk spoke. "She means that they are going to full disclosure mode now. Right Claire?" She smiled gently back at her beloved and wise "other" child, and nodded gently.

"We realized yesterday that maybe we waited too long," said Bill.

"Or maybe we didn't," said Maggie firmly. "The point is, as your parents—and as biologists—we decided to try to shield you from certain…. *issues* while you were young children."

"The time has come, the walrus said, to speak of many things…" Terra cracked a grin, as she quoted from *Alice in Wonderland*. "Come on, give us some credit. You're going to tell us about the captive whales and climate change and overpopulation and all the ways we humans are basically screw-ing up the planet, right?" She folded her arms over her chest. "You guys might have *thought* you were shielding us from all that, but we know more than you realize." She glanced around at the three parents. "I mean, seri-ously, you guys gave me a name that never lets me forget any of this stuff."

She'd known since she was a little girl that her given and middle names, Terra Incognita, were meant to symbolize a unique time in human history.

Terra Incognita they'd told her was a term from long ago when the first cartographers explored the world on big wooden sailing ships. If they had to draw an incomplete map, they'd roughly sketch in the mysterious part—the area they couldn't fully explore—and label it "terra incognita:" *unknown land*.

"We are all living in an unknown land," their parents' had said. "This is the first time in Earth's history that humans are mixed up with so many changes. It is our *terra incognita*," they told her and Tiluk. "And you two, and *all* the other children of the world, are about to inherit a changed planet. One that is different than human beings have ever known."

Claire seemed to watch her daughter's thoughts. "You're on the right track, honey, but there's more. What we *haven't* told you is more disturbing than any of that. Until now, we've behaved as your guardians…your protectors." She was struggling for words.

"What we haven't told you kids is just how bad it really is," Bill's voice hit the table like a gavel.

"And honestly, it was easier not to tell you," Claire mumbled, as she stared downwards, not meeting anyone's eyes. She took a breath. "There was never a good time, and this is just so…"

"So basically you're apologizing for the state of the world then?" Jason jumped in, his groovy inner-surfer-dude swamped by an angry wave of frustration. "'Cause I'd sure as hell like someone to do that for me, and then get themselves off their asses and fix the problems." He glanced at Claire, his trusted mentor. "*I* sure as hell didn't ask for a dying planet." He went dark and smoldering. "How much longer are kids even going to be able to be kids, at the rate we're going?" Jason gripped the edge of the table, his jaw tight. "We've got it so good in this country, and we're so freaking blind to what's happening out there!"

Bill looked respectfully at Jason and sighed, running his hands through his salt and peppered hair. "I know Jason," he said, the women across the table nodding quietly in agreement. "I know… It's not easy. It's kind of like knowing the Black Plague is coming while wanting to shield the children not only from that knowledge but also from the disease itself."

He paused and Jason nodded. "Yeah," he said to Bill. "That's it. Only it's more like the Black Plague, AIDS, and World War Three, all wrapped into one big juggernaut of greed, ignorance and apathy," he grumbled. "And every living thing on this planet stands to lose." He shook his head, glancing at the other adults, his anger rising. "Hell, they already are." He looked at Tiluk and Terra, "You two have no idea what most kids on the planet are dealing with right now."

Jason stood up suddenly; unable to stay still, pushed his chair back violently, and walked to the large window overlooking the cove. "It would serve those bastard oil companies right if the whole damn system crashed!" Claire said one hushed word. "Jason." He just looked back over at her, his face a snapshot of rage and grief and powerlessness. Then he spun his head back, away from Claire, out towards the cove, staring.

"The point is," Bill said, turning back to Terra and Tiluk, "that— whether it was a good idea or not— we decided to let you be kids for as long we could. But you are old enough now, and mature enough," he looked steadily at them, "for us to start treating you like the adults you are obviously becoming."

Terra felt a blush, her blood rising in response to her dad's acknowledgement. At the same time, she was confused and startled by Jason's outburst and this business about the plague. Jason and her dad had made it sound like the world was coming to an end. She looked at Tiluk to see if he felt it, too. He was just staring at Bill, his eyes smoky, trying to make sense of what he'd just heard.

"So, here it is," said Claire, all in a rush. "Terra, your name is a testament to this exact conversation. We are *all* in unknown territory. There's not an adult on this planet who knows how to talk to their child about what is happening." She took a breath and squeezed Maggie's hand. "Most of them ignore it or, for many reasons, don't even really know about it themselves."

"Or they deny it," Maggie said, "because it's much easier to deny what's happening than to accept the enormity of it and then have to do something about it."

"The river is called de Nile…" said Jason from the window, his voice still tinged with anger. "And it is deep and wide."

"But the truth is," Maggie said, "what is happening right now, in your generation, has never—not in all the history of life on Earth—happened before. No species has ever ravaged this planet, or its own members, the way we are right now." Maggie looked at the kids, her jaw tight and cheeks aflame against her dark red hair. Terra had rarely seen Maggie this fired up. Her voice sizzled. "Change is one thing. Destruction is another."

"The human ASS-steroid," quipped Jason in Harvey singsong. "Try that one for size *Harvey*," he spat out.

Claire shot Jason another look, asking him to tone it down. Then turned back to the kids. "We wanted to protect you from all this as long as we could," said Claire quietly, she sat down next to Maggie. "Until now…Now it's time to tell you the truth."

"And the truth is," Bill said, somber. "The truth is…that J pod, and all the Southern Residents, are in serious trouble. We've been watching the signs for years now, and what's happening to them is very disturbing. As you know, they've lost 30 percent of their population just since you were born, and they'd already lost a lot before that because of the captures and killings. What you don't know is that it's starting to look like the whole pod and others around the world may be headed toward extinction."

Tiluk's eyebrows went straight up at Terra with a silent, *See?* Her dream.

Without realizing it, her dad was affirming exactly what Granny had said in her dream: *her family can't survive unless people wake up.* Terra's heart rate started to increase.

Bill pressed on, clueless to his daughter's revelations. "And the prob-lem is we don't even know for sure why they are in trouble. It could be the pollutants..." Terra knew wild orca have some of the highest levels of cancer-causing contaminants, like PCBs, on Earth because they live at the top of the ocean's food chain. "Or it could be the huge drop in the salmon populations they feed on..." This was Bill's area of expertise. He studied the impacts of the dams all over the Pacific Northwest; dams built just a hundred years ago that blocked salmon migration, causing severe declines in the orcas' primary food source. Salmon can't swim upriver with dams in the way, and the fish ladders people had built on the dams were a mere Band-Aid: they helped a little, but with the dams in place, the massive salmon runs of the past that fed the orca were gone. "Then there are the sea lice and the damned fish farms..." he said, rubbing his hand roughly against his forehead, trying to wipe away his scowl. Fish farms had sprung up like invasive weeds every-where in the Salish Sea and north into British Columbia as people tried to raise ever more seafood for others to buy, at the same time that natural fish populations all over the world nose-dived. Sea lice and diseases which can kill the fish had exploded in the cramped, dirty fish farms where tens of thousands of fish lived in confined sea pens. And now, what was left of the wild salmon, showed signs of both lice and disease.

Jason piped up again. "And hey, let's not forget the hottest milestone of all." They all turned to look at him, still standing at the window. "Last month carbon dioxide topped out at over 400 parts per million! WOO-HOO!!" He banged his chest five times with both hands as hard as he could, looking like a pissed off gorilla. "First time in five million years, baby! Now *that* is some-thing to be proud of!" They all knew what he meant. Climate change was the biggest unknown of all, it overshadowed everything else; and it was already dialing up the world's ocean temperatures, melting hundreds of millions of tons of glacial ice, and changing fish dynamics around the world, including the orcas' salmon, which thrive only in very cold water. Even now, starved polar bear carcasses were washing up on Alaskan shores, graphic evidence of global warming's consequences. Everyone at the table knew that climate change threatened the world's orca populations, too. Not to mention human populations everywhere.

"And now, on top of everything else, there's what happened with

Tiluk and the trainer," added Claire quietly. She looked around at everyone. "The orca need our voices. We can do something about this." She stopped, blinked.

"We can do something about *all* of it," Maggie said firmly. "It's a choice." Terra's eyes were filling quickly and she felt herself slipping down some kind of rabbit hole. This was all *way too much*! How would they know how to help in the face of all those terrible problems? How would they know what was causing the orca to die? How could they stop it? Her stomach tightened and she croaked, "Um, can we go down and drum on the dock now, please?" A slight whine edged her voice and she was blinking fast. She had to get out of here. She had to see Granny.

"Wait," Tiluk murmured to her. He looked up and spoke to the adults, "There's a reason you are telling us about all this now."

Bill nodded. "You are quite right son," he said, looking appreciatively at Tiluk, praising his insight. "We're telling you now because it's time we tell you the truth. But it's also because we're going to take some action." The whisper of a smile flitted across Bill's face, erasing his scowl for a fraction of a second. "And we want you two to help us."

Tiluk raised an eyebrow, and Terra's desperate urge to leave the table evaporated like mist on the dock in a sudden splash of sunshine. Air filled her lungs. Action?

"We've tried for years to help those whales the best way we knew how, by studying them and trying to inform the world about their amazing families, behaviors, communication, and, just..." Maggie paused, "how special they are."

"We thought that by studying the wild whales, we could help protect them and also somehow help the captive ones." Claire leaned into Maggie, her composure failing her, her voice thin. "But after hearing about Tiluk's killing yesterday..." she took a shaky breath, "we have to do something different."

Terra stared at her mother, her *scientist* mother. Her mother, who was among the most famous and well-respected orca biologists in the world. What did she mean *different*? And what did her dad mean by *action*?

"It was bad enough studying orca in captivity back when I was a grad student," explained Claire. "I spent a long time recording their vocalizations, and I saw what happens to captive whales. It was heartbreaking. But to know what Tiluk must be going through that he did what he did yesterday, and to have known him as an *individual,* to have seen his mother grieve…" she blinked again. "We have to do something."

In that moment, seeing her mother's empathy, Terra understood much more about why she'd rung the bell yesterday: her mother had had enough.

"And let's all remember that our years of doing basic science *has* done something," Maggie said hugging Claire's shoulders. "It's helped us understand so much about the Southern and Northern Residents and the transients. Without our science, the wild whales might not have the legal protection they do today. And we might not have the leverage to help them in other ways." Maggie's next words were the pivot they all wanted. "And now… just maybe, we do."

"What do you want us to do?" Tiluk was watching Claire and his mother carefully, with total concentration, as if he'd been waiting his whole life for someone to race up and hand him the baton so he could *run.*

"We're putting together an official proposal for OceanLand to retire Tiluk to his family and Blackfish Cove," said Claire, to sudden whoops and grins erupting from both kids. They jumped up and grabbed each other's arms, bouncing up and down and hugging. Jason smiled at the adults, sharing the kids' surge of empowered hope. Light poured through the room, dispelling the gloom.

"And we're going public with it. It's time people woke up to what's really going on," Claire added once the kids calmed down. She sat straight in her chair, chin raised, eyes flashing. "We want you to help us gather information about life for orca in captivity. And we want you to brainstorm some clever ways to let people know the story of wild whales." Her voice grew fierce making the kids' smiles get bigger. "We know a few more things now than we did twenty years ago." She banged the table with the palm of her hand. "It's about time that OceanLand, and the *real* world, did, too."

"You got it Claire," Tiluk's voice rang with strength. "We're *on* it!" He raised Terra's hand in his, showing the adults their clasped fingers. And there, as if it had become part of them, was the tiny wooden calf, her nose and flukes peeping out from between their clasped hands.

"Uh, mom, I think you just activated the wonder twin powers," Terra grinned at Tiluk's unbridled energy. Maybe things weren't so bad after all. Maybe they *could* do something to help. Her dream swept through her. It was happening! She hadn't even seen the calf again yet, and here they were, finding a way to help Granny's family. Her heart fluttered. She couldn't wait to get down to the dock. Maybe Granny and the calf would come.

"That's good Terra," said Bill, still serious. "…'Cause we're damn well gonna need it."

DRUM ROLL

MILES WAS BUZZING like a yellow jacket, even now, hours after the Dueling Banjos duet with that whale. At least a dozen times today, he'd had to stop and ask himself if he'd been dreaming. Having that Tiluk whale freaking *answer* him? It unleashed some kind of serious jolt of electric energy in him that wouldn't stop. After this last bout with Aria, he'd decided he needed the one-man band treatment. He'd spent three hours after The Duet just skateboarding all over their subdivision, back and forth, back and forth, around and around, and still he couldn't calm down...or even think straight. Finally, his mom had yelled for him and he'd come in dripping with sweat, and she'd said, "Shower young man," giving him The Eye as she took in his wreck of an appearance. "You need to take over with Aria; I've got to get to work."

"Whatever Mom."

Stepping into the shower, Miles almost slipped. He was shaking so hard his teeth were chattering. *Seriously? I'm shaking?* he marveled at himself. Then immediately he thought of the Femmes, *All Shook Up.* He held his quivering hands up to his face, recalled that dang snake, and everything else, and said to himself, *Yeah, I'm all freaking shook up. All freaking **messed** up, too.*

Finally he'd made it to his room alone. But that was after he and Aria had to watch yet another stupid movie off Netflix—it was one the perks of being her babysitter while his mom was gone, they got to watch all the

G-rated movies they wanted...*G flippin' movies*, Miles *hated* G movies. Aria had looked at him, all dewy eyed when Ariel becomes human for good, leaving the sea behind forever. Miles saw a whole different thing going on as he'd watched *The Little Mermaid* for the bazillionth time—all he could think about was Tiluk being stolen from the sea. When Aria swooned at the end, gazing up at him with that gooey smile, and said, "She's so happy to live on land!"—well, he wasn't proud of it, but he'd lit into her like a Hummer cutting down an innocent little Florida Key deer.

"Aria, don't you know this story is a load of elephant dung? Just because people think mermaids might want to become human and leave the ocean, doesn't mean they actually WANT to!! Disney made it up to make you feel good," he'd hissed. "But bloody helicopters!!! That movie makes people feel like it's a good thing to take smart creatures from their homes and never let them go back again!"

Her sweet little eyes had filled with tears, of course, and he instantly felt like the most evil-green-eyed-monster in the whole wide world, and he'd tried to apologize. But the damage was done. Aria just looked at him; she went all quiet, and her little mouth trembled, but she hugged herself tightly, and nodded vacantly at him when he tried to explain. She'd gone somewhere else. That's what she did when things got rough at home. She checked out and went deep inside herself, and you couldn't get her back. And it maddened him. He knew it was all his parents' fault. So it broke his heart to see her check out today because he'd been such a jerk.

So here he was. It was time for the one-man band. He'd left Aria to watch *Phineas & Ferb*, gotten her some milk and cookies, and tried to say he was sorry one more time—but she was wrapped up in the show now, and he'd been totally cut off. And so here he was.

Miles had accidently discovered Bobby McFerrin on YouTube while exploring different xylophone performances back when he was teaching himself to play. Bobby McFerrin was all his. He hadn't come from his dad or anyone else. He was one thing Miles had found him for himself. He smirked as he turned his speakers up full blast. *Well, okay, maybe **two** things…then there's this whole **whale** situation.*

Even the xylophone didn't calm him down the way this did…he was pretty sure the one-man band is what had kept him sane during his parents' split. And still did. But no one, *and that meant no one*, was allowed to know about how he'd beat on himself, turning his whole body into a drum, his hands becoming mallets, and how he'd strike the rhythm out all over himself. Thank God for Bobby McFerrin. And thank God his mom worked all the time so he could come in here and rock out.

Miles claimed the beat, matching Bobby, knocking his palm flat and hard on his chest. Singing along as Bobby sang. He *loved* this song, he loved the way it made him feel so free.

I'm gonna hop in my car…. Bum bum dee-dee bum… Drive away… Bum bum dee-dee bum…

He thumped alongside Bobby…over and over. *I'm gonna go so far… Bum bum dee-dee bum…*

Miles took a breath and launched into his own version alongside Bobby. He rang his hands down on his thighs, back up on his arms, syncopating the rhythm and creating new, tinnier sounds than McFerrin's chest beat. He spun around, singing even louder…his Dueling-Banjo-yellow-jacket energy rising.

Man, what really happened out there?
Who could ever catch me? Catch me? Catch me?

* * *

Terra went back to her yurt after lunch. She said to Tiluk on their way out of the main house, "I'm going to play into the microphone for a while. They're more likely to hear me underwater. I can't wait to see Granny…" She figured the fastest way to do that was to start drumming, calling them in. "Will you keep watch?"

He just glanced at her, a quick nod, and kept walking alongside her. Tiluk was deep in thought after their parent's announcement that they were drafting a proposal to OceanLand to retire Tiluk. When they got to her porch, he turned to face her, and clasped her arms as he did when something important was coming.

"Your initials, Lewis. They're no accident." He gripped her tightly, dropped her arms, and walked towards his yurt, calling over his shoulder, "I'm off to go muckraking."

She smiled grimly at his reference to those journalists they'd learned about in school, the ones who, back in the early 1900s had exposed the terrible problems with things like the meat industry and other issues with the industrial revolution and its factories and smoke and terrible working conditions for so many people. Tiluk the muckraker. Their parents had just given Tiluk the perfect place to focus his passion.

But then her mind returned to his comment about her initials, Terra Incognita Lewis. T.I.L. She and Tiluk had grown up knowing they sort of shared the same name, he was *Til*uk, and her initials were *Til*. They'd always believed their parents had intentionally given them that honorable recognition of connection.

Terra and Tiluk: Til and Til. But now? She reached out to the doorway where she stood to steady herself. "Whoa," she breathed. "They named me after the whale, too." Suddenly the interconnection between her, Tiluk, the whales, her family, and this place blew through her like a wind gusting into a great sail. It swept through her, spilling over in a shudder, her body shaking all of a sudden.

"Whoa…" her voice was thick. She stood still, facing down the shudder while letting the unusual sensation swell through her. She took a deep breath through her chattering teeth. *Better get my drum*, she thought.

Inside, her yurt was still warm even after the hours she'd been gone. Before she'd left this morning she'd stoked the wood stove, and now, even though the fire was out, it was still toasty. As soon as she stepped inside, she felt more normal again…except for the chattering teeth. She was going to drum, but then she noticed her computer and realized there was one thing she had to do first.

She opened Facebook and quickly made a new page called Blackfish Cove, then dumped a bunch of ExplOrca's research links onto it. It was time people understood the wild whales of J Pod. She thought about her dream again, and her parents' plans for a retirement proposal. People needed to know about Granny and her family, and how they'd lost Tiluk. Then she added a short post and highlighted it so any visitors would see it first:

> Welcome to Blackfish Cove, a place to learn about the wild
> orca of Puget Sound. This page was started on June 12, 2013,
> the day after Dusky Dey's death at OceanLand, in honor of
> both Dusky and Tiluk (who most people know as Shantu):
> the whale that went crazy and killed her. Please use this page
> to learn more about wild whales and what it means for these

smart, social, and very family-oriented creatures to be held in captivity. I'll post more soon.

That's better, Terra felt more satisfied. She knew Tiluk's muckraking research would go right to the Blackfish Cove Facebook page, too. She sent him a link to it, feeling like she'd done something proactive for the whales.

And now there was this. She checked her microphone out to the cove to make sure it was on, then took her drum onto her bed. She thumped it once, and a deep, resonant thrum shuddered through her and the yurt. Her own shakes gave way against the power of the taut elk skin. The way those vibrations passed through her always made Terra feel a little mystified. The sound waves tickled parts of her insides with their vibrations. Sometimes while she was drumming she'd pretend she was an orca, surrounded by the sound waves of echolocation. But until her "Granny dream" she'd never realized what it must really be like for them. The closest she could come to imagining it would be sitting in the very center of a hundred-piece orchestra with a blindfold on, just letting the music penetrate her every cell.

She thumped the drum in a slow regular beat. This always helped her settle her mind and feelings…but now…now everything was so different.

She thought of her initials as she began drumming, and all she could hear as she thumped was *Til… Til… Til… Til… Til…*

She recalled that line her mom had said over lunch, that line that said everything. "Until now…Now it's time to tell you the truth."

She claimed a double beat, eyes closed, losing herself. Everything else falling blessedly away.

Til now… Til now… Til now… Til now…

* * *

Miles let go. Where Bobby had the acoustic genius of a nightingale— the way his voice warbled and trilled and moved everywhere, and made every sound known to man—Miles went percussive. Bobby supported his voice with that simple chest beat, palm flat against himself, but Miles kept up an easy hum while his hands took off like a flock of starlings, a *murmuration*, he knew it was called. He'd seen one once, over at the nearby marsh; like a giant school of fish in the air, he'd thought at the time. Thousands and thousands of starlings together, turning and dipping, splitting and rejoining, swirling and swooping as if governed by one mind. In the moments he saw it, his heart had swollen like a raging river, and there'd been a voice in his head, "You will never forget this."

And now, totally lost in the music, his hands were like those starlings.

They fluttered and moved and beat and found their way up and down his body; his legs, belly, torso, neck, shoulders and arms. The way his body moved, twirling and swirling, leading the murmuration.

Bobby was bridging; there were no words now, just the humming of his voice box into the microphone he held against his own throat. And the sustained deep chest beat. But Miles was flying. His hands and body were everywhere, adding a whole new dimension to what was on his computer screen. It was as if Miles was doing with his hands and body, what Bobby was doing with his voice: The one-man band.

* * *

"Terra. You there? Over," the two-way radio crackled to life.

She reached over to her bedside table and grabbed the walkie-talkie with-out missing a beat.

"Here. Over." She kept thumping the drum. *Til now...Til now...*

"I think I see fins outside the cove." *Til now...Til now...*

Oh, that was *excellent* news. Terra felt relief wash over her. Tiluk's yurt had a slightly better view of the cove, and especially of the Strait beyond.

"Meet you on the dock. Bring your flute? Over." *Til now...Til now...*

"Done. Over." *Til now...Til now...*

She increased the strength and rhythm of her drumming for another few minutes, hoping the whales would hear her through the microphone, entic-ing them into the cove. The beats were words now, she couldn't shake them. As she closed, she pounded harder and harder, faster and faster. Calling the whales. Calling Granny and the calf. Everything that had happened in the last two days ripped through her and spilled onto the elk skin drum.

Til now...Til now...Til now... Til now...TIL!

Terra picked up the drum, grabbed her mallets and headed for the dock.

Tiluk was already there, his legs dangling over the side. When she realized what he was playing she had to stop. It was *Last night I had the strangest dream...*That great Simon and Garfunkel record they'd heard over the years when their parents had cranked out on hippy music. Her face broke into an enormous smile with Tiluk's honoring of her dream, and the way this song somehow wrapped the entire conversation they'd just had with their parents, too. There was great power in this song. She sat down with her drum, dan-gled her legs over the side with Tiluk's, picked up the beat, and began to sing.

Last night I had the strangest dream I'd ever dreamed before...

The native tones of his flute embodied her best friend. It was as if he was sharing a part of himself that he never revealed in words. She loved holding the beat beneath his melody.

She sang. And drummed.

I dreamed the world had all agreed to put an end to war...

Terra thought of what her parents had talked about earlier as she sang the words. Put an end to war. *War. War against the planet. War people didn't even realize they were fighting.* She scanned the horizon. She needed to see Granny. There were no fins in sight in the cove, but she could make out a group beyond its mouth—just a few blows, the clouds of their breath drifting over the waves.

Til now...Til now...Til now...

This song, those words. A mighty room. Filled with people. People coming together once they knew the truth, and the stories of the orca, as her mom had suggested. If only people could know how she felt every time she sat on this dock with Tiluk while they both played to the whales. A kind of wordless communion and harmony filled her that always pressed her heart open. No one else but she and Tiluk could possibly understand the magic. Except, maybe, Jane Goodall. Terra smiled quietly to herself. She knew how to communicate without words with intelligent wild animals. *And hardly anyone else on Earth gets it anymore.* Terra thought of Joseph and how he'd explained bits and pieces of their native heritage to her and Tiluk over the years; how he'd told her that once, long ago, all the native tribes understood the wild creatures as their brothers and sisters, and that the intelligent ones, like the orca, were revered as wise leaders of life on Earth.

Her beating strengthened, bolstering the melody and those potent words of the song.

Til now... Til now... Til now...

Never fight again. The orca never fought. They foraged for fish. But there was no war. How did they do that? Not fight. Terra fell into a drum-beat reverie, lost in the rhythm and Tiluk's perfect melody as she recalled her dream and the whales' response to her coded podcast that morning. But what if there was even more to Joseph's stories of the ancient ways than she'd ever realized? What if the whales really *were* leaders, somehow? What then? Would humans be able to learn something from *them*?

She looked at Tiluk, wondering where Joseph was. What had Maggie said? He'd gone off island to see the elders. Her beats quickened, realizing what this meant. She'd been too distracted before to think about it. *Oh wow. He went to find the **elders**. Oh. Wow.*

Til now... Til now... Til now...

The song. The words. The dancing. Round and round. Such ecstatic danc-ing. This song was bringing it all together, her parents, their full disclosure of what was happening, the plan for action, the hope she'd felt as her heart fluttered upward, thinking of sharing the orcas' amazing stories with people, thinking of bringing poor Tiluk home to his family. She looked at Tiluk, and a bubbling smile split open her face. Something was taking her. Her voice rose in song as she drove her mallets down and the sun caught the flickered reflection of the sparkling black water dancing in her eyes.

And guns and swords and uniforms were scattered on the ground.

The breeze pushed her wispy hair backwards as she blinked, buoyed like Fierce on a sudden updraft. She beat harder. She needed more; more strength to call the whales. More power. The way they'd left earlier, wailing, at high speed. She squinted towards the edge of the cove. *Granny where are you?* she called out with her mind. She couldn't see fins anywhere.

* * *

Silently, the door to his bedroom cracked open. Little Aria peeked in, saw her brother, wild, ecstatically dancing, slapping his hands hard all over his body, like he'd stepped into a nest of yellow jackets. He was spinning, spinning. She moved in, back pressed against his wall, gaping. He whirled and twirled. Eyes still closed. Hands still beating and running up and down, up and down, and all over his body.

Gonna drive so fast... Bum bum dee-dee bum... Who could ever catch me? Catch me? Catch me?

The song was ending and with a last aggressive roll, Miles poured every-thing he had into the finale. His eyes tore open as he flew to a stop, saw Aria, and there she was: Cindy Lou, the little Who girl who caught the Grinch swiping all the Whos' presents...looking at him like he'd stolen everything.

In the glint of her trusting eyes, the yellow jackets vanished and he knew what he had to do.

* * *

Tiluk watched Terra over his flute. His eyebrows rose. She knew he couldn't keep up anymore. Her beat was too strong, too fierce for the melody; it needed its own space. She hammered harder and faster with her mallets, like a soldier on a snare drum, and shrugged at Tiluk. Tiluk understood, and dropped the melody. In its place, he shot out mighty trills alongside her drumroll. Something was happening, and she was going to figure out what it was. She scanned the outer edge of the cove, looking for the whales. Their fins had disappeared. *Did they leave? Granny where are you?*

As Terra's arms started to give out, weak with the aching fire of her muscles, an eruption of whale blows sprayed her and Tiluk from a few feet away, sounding almost like gunshots they were so loud. At the exact same moment, Joseph put his hand on Terra's shoulder and she startled, nearly dropped her drum in with the whales. The entire pod had come in secretly, swimming underwater from off shore to the dock, then announced themselves with their huge bulks and startling expulsions. Terra smelled their fishy breath, they were so close. Her stomach dropped. The calf was right there, nestled between Eve and Wendy, looking at her. She rolled and showed Terra her belly.

Heart racing, she watched Granny sidle up next to the dock just below her, making unmistakable eye contact with her once again. *Was this really happening?* Joseph squeezed her shoulder gently, and Terra jumped.

"I think it's time we talked," he said.

CAPTIVATED

FB Private Message
To: Blackfish Cove Facebook
From: Miles Frost
June 12, 9:36 PM EST

Hi Blackfish Cove,

I saw Tiluk kill his trainer yesterday. At first it was awful. I had nightmares twice last night…could barely sleep at all. But then I got online to try to find out more about what happened. That's how I found you. I know he's Tiluk and not Shantu, and I know he came from the Penn Cove roundup near where ExplOrca does its research. Which is why I'm writing. You people seem to know your killer whales.

I found out that captivity is pretty bad for killer whales, which is not good news since all these kids everywhere—including my little sister— think OceanLand is awesome and that the whales are happy there. I think Tiluk killed that trainer yesterday bc he's, like, seriously MESSED UP!!!

Also, there's something else. And I can only tell you this bc I saw Maggie Ravenwood of ExplOrca quoted in this one news story from the Orlando Weekly; she seems to "get it" and I hope whoever reads this can pass her this note. I haven't told ANYONE yet since it's, like, UNBELIEVABLE. See, the thing is, I live near OceanLand and I snuck in there early this morning, and I hid near Tiluk's pool and played

Dueling Banjos on my xylophone.

And it was freaking AMAZING! Not only did Tiluk hear me and start swimming around, and popping his head out of the water, and acting all excited, he also ANSWERED me!!! I mean, he seriously answered me! He "sang" the same phrase back to me, after I played the opening notes. I couldn't believe it was happening! But then the trainers heard him, and I had to get the heck outta there.

Now, all I can think about is going back there and playing some more for him. He was acting desperate for me to keep playing, banging his head as hard as he could against his gate. I think he's pretty miserable and he likes the music. But that doesn't really seem like enough, does it? Do you know if there is anything else I can do to help that messed up beast of a whale?

Thanks, Miles Frost.

PS. I have a lot of time on my hands since my mom is divorced and she works all the time. If I do play for him again do you want to know what happens?

PPS. My email address is "milesfrost@gmail.com."

——

To: Miles Frost <milesfrost@gmail.com>
From: Terra Incognita Lewis <terralewis@explorca.org> Subject: Tiluk
June 12, 7:03 PM PST

Dear Miles,

Wow! You saw Tiluk??!! And you *played* for him???? AND HE ANSWERED YOU??????????????

I don't even know what to say!! WOW!!! You'll never ever believe this but I play music for whales, too…for Tiluk's *family*!!! We—our family

I mean—actually study the family of whales that Tiluk got stolen from 12 years ago. And I've played for them ever since I was little.

HE SANG BACK TO YOU??? That is SO AMAZING!! Especially since, this morning, I think maybe my whales understood me and my Morse code message about Tiluk! Maybe all these whales are way smarter than we realize?

I bet Tiluk would LOVE it if you would go back there and play more music for him. But you have to be super careful since the trainers probably wouldn't want anyone in there…plus, I guess you'd be extra careful, too, since we know Tiluk has killed people. You would stay FAR away from his pool, right?

You're definitely not the only one who wants to help Tiluk. I'm so glad you wrote, since the whole reason I started Blackfish Cove today on Facebook is to try to help him and other whales in captivity. This morning, I also emailed Jane Goodall and Janet Carson (she's in charge of NOAA and my parents know her from when they were graduate students). They BOTH wrote me back already… I got their messages just before yours!!! Can you believe that??? I guess they think this thing with Tiluk is pretty important.

Anyway, I'm forwarding you their messages. Plus, you can read the letters I wrote to them, too, (they're below), then you'll be all up to speed on what's going on here. I think I'll call them The J Squad for J Pod ;-) Oh, and YES, I'll show your PM to Maggie and to my mom, Claire Lewis (she's pretty famous in orca circles bc she's studied their vocalizations for like twenty years…you are going to ROCK THEIR WORLD with this Dueling Banjo thing…).

I'm glad you wrote Miles. I'm really glad you are down there with Tiluk. I just feel so sad for him since he hasn't had his family in so many years. Did you know that wild male killer whales never ever leave their mother's pod for their whole entire lives?

Terra

PS. I'm sorry you saw the killing. That must have been horrible. I'm also sorry to hear about your parents. I can't imagine that since I pretty much have four parents who are around me and Tiluk like a whale pod. It must be hard for you and your sister.

———

Forwarded message:

To: Terra Incognita Lewis
From: Jane Goodall
CC: Janet Carson
Subject: Re: Orca Breakthrough & Question
June 12, 6:37 PM EST

Dear Terra,

Your story moved me. It certainly does sound as if your pod of orca whales may well understand your coded messages. The world's creatures continue to amaze me, even after all these years. If I were you, I would talk to your parents about what you've told me if you haven't already done that. From what you shared, it is evident that they are wise, compassionate, and much more knowledgeable about orca biology and behavior than I can ever hope to be. Trust their guidance. If there's one thing I've learned, it's to know when to learn from others—whether human or non-human. The chimps certainly taught me that.

And now I have a question for you. Would you please keep me posted on what you and your parents decide to do? The story you shared of Tiluk and his family, and their possible capacity to understand your tapped code, is one of the saddest but also most hopeful things I've heard of in a long time. I will think about whether there is something I can do to help.

Warmly,
Jane Goodall

———

Forwarded message:

To: Terra Incognita Lewis
From: Janet Carson
CC: Jane Goodall
Subject: Re: Orca Breakthrough & Question
June 12, 6:39 PM EST

Hi Terra,

It's so nice to hear from you. You must be almost 14 years old now? You are right...I'll never forget paddling among Granny's pod and watching the sunset with them. It's one of the most special memories of my life. I've never seen anything like that before.... the whales definitely appeared to have a sunset-watching ritual, just as your parents had tried to explain to me. But until I saw it, it was hard to believe. I'd like to come back some time and do that again when I'm not so busy.

That surprising experience is why I am taking what you've told me very seriously. It seems possible that it is true. If Granny's pod really can understand Morse code it would show that genuine two-way, cross-species communication between two highly intelligent—arguably *equally* intelligent—sentient beings is really possible. What you've described to me, suggests that this may go well beyond anything we've been able to achieve with the ape species, like the chimps or the bonobos. That would make it one of the greatest scientific occasions of all time. You have my word. I am grateful to know what you've shared, but until we know more, your story is safe with me. Do keep me updated, however. You are correct to worry about how the information could be used by the Navy and others.

Please give your parents my best. I so enjoyed working with them both as graduate students. You have special parents, my dear. It is wonderful to see what you are making of your life. You may not understand this now, but you are fortunate to be using the gifts they have given you to grow, explore, and learn about who you are, even at this young age. And for that, I'm certain, they are so very proud.

Sincerely,
Janet Carson

———

To: Terra Incognita Lewis
From: Miles Frost
Subject: Seriously?
June 12, 10:47 PM EST

Terra,

You *talk* to the whales? Seriously? And you personally know Tiluk's family??? That is just crazy AMAZING! I'm just, like, FLOORED by your email! It's so much better than anything I could have hoped for (which is kind of a nice change for me right now, but that's another story).

Anyway, Wow. I'm not sure where to start! It's freaking INCREDIBLE that you got a letter from Jane Goodall. DUDE! That is like, SOOO cool! She's like practically the most famous woman in the freaking world! And I don't know that other Jane, but she sounds super important. She was picked by the freaking PRESIDENT?? You must be doing some pretty top notch kinda stuff, to get those letters from The Jane Squad (sweet name, btw).

OK, here's what I think. I know what it's like to have your family all broken up, so I really want to make Tiluk feel better as soon as I can. That's, like, all I can think about. And I could totally tell that my xylophone "said" something to Tiluk…you know what I mean, Terra? I mean, there he was just bored out of his mind, hanging in his pool, and the SECOND I tapped out my tune, he came to life. And the way he kept banging his head over and over on his gate, DUDE, it was like SERIOUSLY a major BUMMER to have to leave so the trainers wouldn't catch me. I just want to go back there and play Tiluk about a thousand different songs—did you know he only likes to hear a song once, and then he wants to have a new one? I learned that from my research about where he lived right after his capture. Freaking SMART whale! He must've been super desperate to "answer" me…

Anyway, I'm super tired. But after tomorrow, I think I'm gonna start going over there like every morning at 4AM. That gives me like two whole hours before the staff start to show up. And yeah, you wrote about being careful and never forgetting that Tiluk has killed people. I get it. But DUDE, why the heck did he DO that? I mean, yeah, no wild orca has ever seriously attacked a human. Yeah. So why Tiluk? Because he's freaking TRAPPED LIKE A RAT. Pisses me off. And all those kids everywhere who think Shantu is happy? NOT! They should start telling OceanLand:

Keep Shantu? Shame on You!

I better get to bed, I feel kinda woozy.
I'm really glad you wrote too, Terra.

Later,
Miles

PS. It is awful.

———

To: Miles Frost
From: Terra Incognita Lewis
Subject: Trapped
June 13, 6:32 AM PST

Good morning Miles,

So I told my parents (all four of them!) and Tiluk about you at dinner last night, and I showed Maggie and my mom your first PM. DUDE (as you like to say, although, nudge, nudge: I am not a "dude"…), they are all AMAZED by your whole story. Maggie, that's Tiluk's mom, even got kind of choked up when she heard that not only did you see Tiluk kill someone but that your parents are divorced. My mom wants me to write this to you: *Tell Miles we are all thinking about him.* Miles, she is so blown away about the Dueling Banjos Duet that I don't think she really believes you yet. (I do!)

And you know what else? My dad had a pretty good point. He said, "Miles might want to be extra careful about what he chooses to play for Tiluk the next time he goes in. If OceanLand catches on—and that's only a matter of time—it might be the last time he gets to play anything."

I hadn't thought of that. But Miles, what if you only get one chance to "talk" to Tiluk again? What do you think you should play?
Over, (that's what Tiluk and I say on our two-way radio)
Terra

PS. Do you ever want to talk about it?

PPS. Oops, I almost forgot to tell you. On the same day that Tiluk killed Dusky Dey, Wendy (that's Tiluk's mother) had a new calf… she'd be his little sister. Kind of weird and sad, if you ask me.

———

To: Terra Incognita Lewis
From: Miles Frost
Subject: TwoLuks!
June 13, 9:50 AM EST

OK Terra, PLEASE tell me your friend has a nickname because I'm getting way too confused trying to know when we're talking about my whale or your friend!

Could you do me a favor? Don't tell me anymore about that calf. I have a little sister too, Aria (I call her Doodle, since, like you, she's not a "dude") and she's like the only person in the whole world who really understands things at home. My mom and dad sure don't. Anyway, it's just too cruel to think about Tiluk having a new sister that he'll never even know.

Your parents sound unreal. Tell them I'm fine. They don't need to worry about me.

But your dad is right. What if they catch me the first time I go back? I had an idea about that. You said you have a way to listen to Granny's pod when they are in the cove, right? Well…what if I brought my cell phone to Tiluk's pool and we Skyped him to your cove? We could set up a two way between him and his family!! What do you think about that Miss Terra Incognita Lewis?

Yo, what's with your name anyway?

Over,
Miles

PS. No.

———

To: Miles Frost
From: Terra Incognita Lewis
Subject: RE: TwoLuks!
June 13, 7:05 AM PST

That's BRILLIANT, Miles! I LOVE that idea. Can you imagine if they can remember each other's voices? Oh, it gives me shivers just to think about it! Let's do it. When? We'll have to remember the time difference, too. I'm going to talk to the "moms" about this at breakfast in a few minutes.

You don't sound fine, Miles. Just so you know, Tiluk (oops, let's call him Lucky, that's what his mom calls him sometimes) hardly ever talks. He's just a super quiet person. I'm Miss Chatterbox, (why do you think I'm the one with the whale walky-talky?), and I have to say, I really, really like emailing with you. You TALK! Plus, you are doing some amazing things…I mean, I can't imagine what a big surprise you gave Tiluk when you played for him. That probably was the highlight of his year!

Anyway, I can tell that something's bothering you, so fess up when you're ready, Frost. You'll feel better once you do. I should know. I feel SO much better about everything now that I talked to Joseph (Lucky's dad) about the calf and my dream. Oops. Um, I don't know how I can NOT talk about the calf, since she's like the biggest deal right now besides Tiluk (the whale!). My parents even told me last night that I get to NAME her!! Which is like the BIGGEST honor around here. It's because I dreamed about her way back when, before anyone knew Wendy was prego. I haven't told the others yet, even Tiluk, (oops, I mean Lucky)...but I think I'm going to name her Hope.

What do you think?

Look up my name and see if you can figure it out. I'll give you a hint: my parents' are the world's geekiest biologists.

Over but not going anywhere,
Terra

PS. I'm patient.

———

To: Terra Incognita Lewis
From: Miles Frost
Subject: Hope, NOT
June 13, 10:23 AM EST

Terra, Now that I think about it, even if we do a live feed and Tiluk and his family get to hear each other again, what good is that going to do? I mean, it's not like he's ever going to see them again, and it might just remind him of everything he lost.

No way.
Over

———

To: Miles Frost
From: Terra Incognita Lewis
Subject: Hopeful
June 13, 8:45 AM PST

Hey Frost,

Get a grip. You know what? I've been there. But it's time to *do* something. Are you in? Or not?

You know what Maggie said when I told her about your last note? She said, "Miles has to decide that there is always hope, no matter what he's seen or gone through." She also gave me a message for you. It goes like this: "Miles, I'm a child of divorce, too. It *is* hard.

No other animal but humans breaks up the secure nests of their offspring like we've started doing very recently. It's not good for kids, and I think we as a society are not honest enough about that. I wish I had known that when I was your age."

So, anyway, she thought your idea for a live feed to connect Tiluk to his family might give him hope…something he hasn't had in a very long time. It sounds like you've started to give him hope with your music. Don't piss me off, Miles. -til

———

To: Terra Incognita Lewis
From: Miles Frost
Subject: Skyping Whale Nests
June 13, 12:01 EST

Date: TONIGHT (June 14)
4:00 AM Eastern (1:00 AM Pacific)

Tell Maggie she's freaking WEIRD. And you bloody well better "hope" that Tiluk doesn't go off and kill himself when we play live feed from

Granny's pod...

PS. Do I need some kind of special equipment? I've got a cell phone and speakers…

PPS. Good luck with the one o'clock in the morning thing. Maybe staying up that late will be "unknown territory" for you, Miss *TIL*.

TIES THAT BIND

CLAIRE WATCHED HER DAUGHTER and marveled once again. For all her years of studying these whales, devoting herself to science and the careful observations needed to understand them, Terra's desire to make direct contact sometimes startled her with its intensity, even now. As Terra continued drumming, in an attempt to call in the whales for what could be a historic two-way live feed between Tiluk and his family, Claire's eyes circled Terra's yurt. It was just after midnight and the wood stove radiated its heat and light among her family. All of them—even the graduate students, whom she loved, too—were here… watching her daughter work some kind of magic. Her eyes met Joseph's and held; he'd been watching her. He'd seen it too. There was something unusual about Terra's connection with these whales, and for the life of her, Claire could neither put her finger on it nor understand it. But she knew Joseph had some ideas. And she trusted his wisdom. It's just that it wasn't *science*. And when it came to understanding how the world worked, she respected and trusted science almost more than she trusted herself. She knew that for all these years together, sharing their families and lives and children, Joseph had kept a lot of his native wisdom and intuition to himself—out of respect for the groundbreaking work the

ExplOrca team had done for so long. But as they held one another's gaze, Joseph's dark eyes penetrating hers, she nodded at him, her wordless message: *I know*. Something un-measurable was going on here.

From the very beginning, of course, she'd hoped for it. It's why she and Bill had set up the hydrophone feed to Terra's bedroom since practically before her birth. It's why they'd supported Terra's podcasts and the Morse Endeavor, as she knew they secretly called it, though she never let on. But it was her daughter's intensity of focus, her unflagging passion to reach out to these whales that sometimes just...mystified her. Because for all these years the whales simply didn't respond. She recalled all the times when she'd stand outside on the deck, watching Terra and Tiluk play their duets down on the dock as the pod rested along their beach at the far side of the cove. But the whales had never reacted; either to the duets or to Terra's daily podcasts.

Until now.

Terra's drum beats filled the yurt, entrancing everyone. They filled the mic and traveled out over the cove. She thrummed in code: long, pause, two short, pause, short long short short, pause, short short long, pause, long short long, followed by a four beat pause. Then the whole sequence began again: long, pause, two short, pause, short long short short, pause, short short long, pause, long short long. She was spelling out T-I-L-U-K, over and over again. Claire knew that Terra was hoping to call Granny's pod in from wherever they were, even though it was the middle of the night. This was a first. Absolutely something they'd never tried before. And she'd been certain it would never work.

That is, until Terra and Tiluk told them about the coded "Tiluk podcast" the morning before, and the way the whales had raced out of the cove at high speed, wailing.

"They did *what*?" Claire had said, slamming her coffee mug down so hard on the table it splashed over the edge.

"It's true Mom, they did. It took me a whole ten minutes to tap out the message about Tiluk, and they were, like totally silent, which never happens, and then they just started this pandemonium of cries!" Terra took a breath. "It was so loud coming through my speaker that I had to cover my ears!" Terra shivered and said, "I wonder if they had to leave the cove because all those giant wails were hurting their own ears!"

Terra's drummed code filled the yurt. BUM...pause...bum-bum... ...   pause...bum-BUM-bum-bum......pause...bum-bum-BUM   ... pause... BUM-bum-BUM...

Tiluk.

Claire looked at her husband; they exchanged a glance of wonder. Neither could believe all that had happened in the day and half between

Tiluk's killing and the calf's birth...and what Terra was attempting right now. Terra also told them earlier about The J Squad, showing them the letters from Goodall and Carson. Maggie had dropped everything and started making calls; she reached colleagues at the University of Florida and arranged for a special delivery of high-quality hydrophone equipment to Miles' house that afternoon. Within hours, Maggie had him all set up and they'd exchanged a few direct emails, gotten one another's cell phone numbers, and had the whole two-way live feed all planned out. Now it was up to Terra and the whales.

Could this really happen? Claire wondered as she watched Maggie speaking quietly on the phone to Miles, helping arrange the final steps of turning on his equipment. If it did, it could make their proposal to OceanLand become an international news sensation.

Terra's drum beats were soothing. *Would the whales respond?* BUM… pause…bum-bum… … pause…bum-BUM-bum-bum…… pause…bum-bum-BUM …pause…BUM-bum-BUM...

Claire thought again of Miles.

Everyone had been worried about Miles. Tiluk had killed a person. More than one. Claire could hardly bring herself to consider that this young boy she hadn't even met would put himself in harm's way, and without his own mother's knowledge. This had been their biggest hurdle today in deciding to act on his idea.

She'd said it one last time at dinner earlier, "Doesn't anyone else here think we ought to stop Miles? I mean, sneaking into OceanLand at four o'clock in the morning with hydrophone gear hardly seems like a good idea for an adult let alone a 14-year-old boy."

Bill looked at her, and said, "We all agreed, right honey? We've been over this a hundred times. Miles will never be close enough to the pool for Tiluk to grab him. He's going to follow our *exact* instructions, throw the mike into the pool, get back to his little fort at the edge and broadcast from there."

They were all pretty sure Miles hadn't told his mom about the plan. He'd dropped Maggie a line shortly before dinner that said, "Goods received. Mom was at work. We're a go."

Maggie said, "This might be just what Miles needs right now, Claire. And think of what it could mean…"

Claire had nodded and grown quiet. They all knew what it could mean.

Which is why she was letting herself go through with this...and why they'd all gathered here tonight.

BUM...pause...bum-bum...   ...   pause...bum-BUM-bum-bum......pause...bum-bum-BUM ...pause...BUM-bum-BUM...

Claire checked her watch. It was 12:35 a.m., about twenty minutes since

Terra started drumming. Gwen stood up from her spot by the woodstove and walked quietly around the small space, filling everyone's hot cocoa mugs. Her Stetson and boots somehow suited the yurt, as if two old ways of life had met up and revived one another. Jason, with his surfer's mane and hard cut muscles, sat on the sheepskin with Terra and Tiluk. He shook his head no to cocoa; he was too busy twiddling sheep's wool between his fingers, oblivious to everyone else in the room as he listened. Gwen smiled at Claire as she poured the cocoa, her cherubic Iowa farm girl face pure and curious. Claire's mouth turned up in a slight grin at the unlikelihood of Gwen and Jason, so very different from one another, yet here for the same reasons all of them were. She knew her grad students wouldn't miss this for the world. Maybe nothing would happen. But then again...This could be the biggest moment of their career.

Wait. Claire cocked her head. There. Jason stopped twiddling and looked up at her. She looked to Terra, then Tiluk. They'd heard it, too.

A distant whistle. Then another. And another. The sound and number of whistles amplified fast, as if the whales had hurried to get into the cove.

Claire's jaw dropped.

"What is it honey?" Bill asked quietly. Everyone knew that Claire was the

Master of All Things Orca Vocalizations. She'd been the lead author on more than two dozen important scientific papers; all related to orca sounds. Claire *knew* her killer whale calls.

Everyone stared at her, the whistles now filling the yurt with quivering urgency.

Claire could barely speak, and tears started rolling down her cheeks, unbidden. Joseph came over next to her, put his arm around her.

"They're calling Tiluk's name," she managed to say. She took a deep breath, "That's his signature whistle they're repeating."

Claire had been studying the pod's vocalizations since she'd moved here, well before Terra's birth. She'd charted and mapped thousands of different recordings, and she knew Tiluk's defining whistle as if it were own child's name. The night of his capture, only a month before Terra's birth, she'd stroked her swollen belly and listened to his whistle over and over again, alone in her office, committing it to memory even though he'd been lost. In her grief, she'd recorded the day's events at Penn Cove in great detail in her journal. She hadn't known what else to do. While she'd listened to his whistle play over and over again, she'd drawn up notes for a paper examining the long-term impacts of capture events on pod dynamics. She'd never forget that whistle. Ever.

She took another deep breath and wiped her cheeks, trying to contain her emotion. She looked at her daughter, overwhelmed. "Terra, at least one of those whales understands your code for Tiluk, because that's the first time in nearly 14 years that we've heard them vocalize his specific whistle.

They're hearing your drummed code and responding with their own language for Tiluk."

There was a collective gasp from the adults in the room; the whales had just proven that they understood Terra's coded drumbeat. A major scientific breakthrough.

"Jesus," Jason whispered.

Terra nodded, her drumbeats growing softer in response to the whales' calls, letting them take over. It was the first time they'd ever responded to her. But she wasn't surprised. Tiluk stared at Terra, a slight smile on his face, the two of them lit with comprehension. They were both sitting cross legged on the sheepskin next to Jason, while the other adults sat or stood around them. His face told her everything. He might get to hear Tiluk, his namesake, for the first time in his life. And he was part of this plan to give Tiluk a message from his family. His black eyes flashed at Terra. She saw satisfaction. *No place else in the world I'd rather be, Lewis*, she could hear him saying in her mind.

Claire's eyes narrowed. "And it's not just that, there's layering to those vocalizations. There's a lot more information coming through than just his signature whistle."

Claire's mother bear kicked into high gear. "Maggie, Tiluk needs to hear this. That's his mother doing most of the calling. I recognize

Wendy's whistles. Tell Miles to turn on his feed right away," she checked the mic and sound system, making sure for the 100th time that their recording equipment was on. This *definitely* needed to go into their proposal.

The whales' calls for Tiluk were growing louder by the second. "They are venting all the love and grief they've pent up all these years," Joseph said, dropping the statement like a secret key that could explain what was hap-pening. "It was Terra's drum code, and her message yesterday that triggered it. The code reminded them of Tiluk and now the pod is calling out to him with everything they couldn't say all these years."

Maggie spoke urgently into her phone. "Miles, the whales here are vocalizing Tiluk's name. Turn on your live feed so he can hear them, and please watch carefully. It's really important that we know what happens when he hears his family for the first time." Maggie spoke with the quiet clarity that Claire had come to love about her. "Something unusual is hap-pening out there."

Maggie nodded, and closed her eyes, listening with total concentration for long seconds to the pod's vocalizations, loud and urgent. Then Maggie's eyes opened wide at something Miles said to her. The vocalizations from Granny's pod stopped sharply, almost as if their feed had been cut. Everything went still. A tremulous whistle carried from Tiluk's pool so far away, into the yurt and out into the cove. Tiluk put down his hot cocoa mug and grabbed Terra's hand. "That's him," he whispered staring at the sheepskin, listening as hard as he could. "That's him. He's heard them."

They all listened, spellbound, as the sound of Tiluk's whistle came through. The pod stayed silent at first. Then one voice joined Tiluk's, a reply.

His signature whistle followed by a long series of trills and slides.

"That's Wendy," Claire breathed, tears spilling over again. "She's calling to her son."

Then he joined her. Everyone in the room went rigid with awe as Wendy and Tiluk called to each other, singing a mother-son duet for the first time in 14 years. Tears started to slip down Terra's cheeks, too. "I'm so grateful to Miles," she whispered, her voice thick. "I can't believe this is happening." She grabbed both of Tiluk's hands, blinking hard.

Overcome, Gwen knelt down on the sheepskin next to Jason and he put his arm around her. "Well, this is something for our notebooks, huh cowgirl?" Claire suddenly cocked her head. "Oh no..." she breathed. "This isn't good. I'm hearing distress calls from Tiluk." The duet went from trills and whistles to strident, harsh slides. "He's telling his mama how bad things are." Maggie's expression went dark. "Miles says Tiluk is starting to get agitated. He's swimming in circles around the pool."

In response to Tiluk's distress calls, the rest of the pod, quiet until now, erupted in a deafening chorus of calls, whistles, slides, and harmonics. "They're trying to reassure him," said Joseph darkly, "even though there's nothing they can do to help."

"Oh no," Maggie whispered, gripping the phone and closing her eyes. Then the yurt shook with vibrations. "BAM!"

Now Maggie was crying. "Tiluk just rammed the gate, he's losing it." The pod went wild. Their calls got even louder and more chaotic. "Wendy knows what that means, she knows that sound." Joseph spoke quickly before the rest of them even clued in. "It's exactly what she did over and over the day they stole her son."

Then again. "BAM!"

"Miles doesn't think Tiluk is going to calm down. He's lost it," Maggie said, holding the phone away from her face. She looked at Claire, anxious and confused. What should they do now?

Then "CRASH!" A huge sound wave surged through the yurt, shaking the floor as if an explosion had gone off. Claire dropped her mug, the hot chocolate spilling over Terra's sheepskin. Maggie cried out as Jason leapt to his feet and said, "Wendy, NO!"

"Mom, *Wendy*!!" shrieked Terra, panic grabbing her. They all knew instantly that Wendy had rammed the dock in her helplessness. Terra flung herself outside, running hard. Despite the dark, she took the stairs two at a time. The stairs shuddered again with another ram from Wendy and she had to grab the railing to steady herself against the quivering wood.

Finally she reached the dock and ran to the edge, breathing hard, squinting into the dark. She could just make out the starlit waters and the black shapes of the whales. Granny and Eve were taking Wendy out of the cove.

She saw the three dorsal fins, all in a row, Granny and Eve a little below Wendy's motionless form. "Oh no, oh no, oh no" the panic pressed hard against her insides. Was Wendy dead? Did she crack her skull open?

The dim shapes of the rest of the pod followed the three matriarchs out of the cove. There were no breathy blows. There was only silence.

Terra heaved violently over the edge of the dock, retching into the water, tears slick on her face. It was welling up inside her, all of it. It was too much. She felt like she was heaving all the horrors of the last few days right into Blackfish Cove. Suddenly Tiluk's arms were around her, grabbing her middle and pulling her back from the edge, holding her like a vice.

Sobbing, she fought him at first, flailing against him, fighting reality. He held on, tight and hard, and finally, as the pod disappeared into the black night at the edge of the cove, she stopped fighting and let him hug her. Her jolting cries shook her against him and she couldn't seem to breathe.

"Terra, look," her best friend's voice was tight in her ear, his arms gripping hers. "Look…"

Tiluk gently turned her back towards the water and she looked into the cove one more time, broken and afraid to see. A small black shape rose and blew from the middle of the cove. It was the calf. She swam quickly towards the dock, just as the rest of the crew arrived. She stopped, blew spray all over them, spyhopped right below them, and stared straight at Terra.

Then she dove and sped for her family.

SOME ARE VERY, VERY BAD

MILES SNAPPED HIS PHONE SHUT. Tiluk was still ramming the dock, methodically, as if he were a gigantic metronome, keeping some kind of sick and twisted slow-motion beat. Miles stared at his phone. He wasn't sure he believed Maggie. Not sure at all. Something snapped inside him tonight. Watching Tiluk hurl himself against that gate right after he recognized his family's voices? After 14 years? Fourteen YEARS!!?? Well, let's just say that Mile's life started crashing up against his own gates. He had things pretty bad with his parents' split. But this… "Dude, I am sooo doing something about this," he'd murmured as he watched Tiluk, blinking against the lump in his throat. *This is so so wrong.* "Maggie," he'd whispered into his cell phone, his voice cracking, "We have to fix this."

"I know honey," she'd said to him and he'd known in that moment she was crying. "We are. What you just did? Helping Tiluk hear his family again? You *are* fixing it. Don't forget that."

Then, after Tiluk crashed his gate for the third time, something happened way up there in Washington State. He'd heard a distant booming sound and Maggie cried out. Then the line went dead. Just dead. He had no idea what happened. Now he had to ask himself, Was he really helping Tiluk, like Maggie said? Were they helping the rest of his family by letting them hear each other? What the hell just happened up there?

Miles shoved his phone into his pocket and started to pack up his gear. It would be dawn soon. Last thing he needed were trainers showing up while the hydrophone was still in the pool. He'd have to trust the rest of the team to handle whatever was going on with the Tiluk's family. He had enough to deal with here, with this crazy, battered beast of a whale.

He pulled the contraption in, trying to ignore Tiluk's crashes, hoping the whole time the whale wouldn't kill himself. *I wish he'd stop that.* The way he was heaving his entire body weight at top speed into that gate, Miles was worried he really would sustain lethal injuries. *Uh-oh…maybe that's what happened. Maybe his mother crashed against something, too*, Miles thought. Understanding dawned. He stared at Tiluk and spoke quietly into the dark-ness. "That would explain why Maggie hung up on me."

Miles stopped what he was doing. He couldn't move. It was as if, for a split second, he *was* the whale. Both trapped away from their families. Shaking his head aggressively, Miles said, "I'm gonna help you."

Wait a second. In a flash of recall he thought about that story he'd read by that journalist Tim Sinclair. What was that song that guy Steve had played for Tiluk all those years ago that he'd loved so much he'd danced to it? *Right, that's it.* Miles got all his gear stowed and ready to go…*I've gotta be ready to bolt.* Then, in a last ditch effort to calm Tiluk down, he pulled out his z-phone.

I wonder if I can get it on the first try. He hummed the opening phrase. Then tapped it out, loud and strong.

Da, da, da, da, da, da, da, da, dum, dum, da, dee, DA, da-da!

Yes, that's it. He'd managed to play the first phrase of Ode to Joy from memory. *Not exactly joy he's feeling out there in that jail cell of a pool, but I bet he felt something like it when he first heard his mom.* Miles squinted through the early morning darkness from inside his little tree fort. The crashing stopped. "Good boy," he whispered. "Thatta boy."

He played the second phrase quickly, wanting to keep the whale's atten-tion away from crashing against the gate again.

Da, da, da, da, da, da, da, da, dum, dum, da, dee, DA, da-da… Then Tiluk sounded.

DA, DA, DA, DA, DA,DEE-DEE, DA, DA, DA, DEE-DEE, DA, DA, DUM DEE DA…

"Oh bloody helicopters" he exhaled, "he remembers." Tiluk hadn't just repeated Miles; he'd sung the next phrase, anticipating it.

Miles was prepared this time. He wasn't going to flake out on Tiluk ever again.

He played the next phrase and Tiluk sang with him. "How the heck can this be happening?" Miles whispered. Who would ever believe it?! He reached over, pulled the recording gear up out of this backpack and snapped on the hydrophone. *Maybe it'll record this even though it's not underwater anymore.*

He zinged out the rest of the symphony's opening phrases, and Tiluk sang the whole thing with him. Their duet was an odd mix of metallic chimes and watery breathy tones. When they were done Miles looked up, shivering in the warm air. His teeth were chattering. The darkness had lightened to a fierce breaking dawn, and Tiluk erupted. He rose straight from the water as if standing, and used his powerful tail flukes to propel himself backwards across the pool.

"No way...he's dancing, just like that guy said," Miles whispered, wide-eyed, as he sat watching Tiluk, spellbound. It was almost as if the song they'd played together had helped the whale remember the good part of what happened, and forget about his horrid predicament for the time being. *Aced it, Frost. He's not crashing anymore*, Miles thought, relieved. But this? Tiluk erupted again in a full-body breach, crashing down and pushing huge waves of water over the edges of the pool.

"Holy smoke...That is one big whale."

That voice, the one that came when he saw the starling murmuration long ago, came again. "You will never forget this." But there was more. "Brother."

In that instant, Miles felt a permanent bond with Tiluk. The mesmerizing breaches kept coming. *Maybe, hearing his family, he finally felt happy for a change and this is how he shows it,* he thought.

Riveted, Miles stood up, out of the tree fort, and watched; consumed by the connection he felt to the whale...and how they'd sung together... and how, Miles blinked fast...how much he identified with Tiluk. He couldn't move; he was transfixed by the whale's dance. Tiluk was still breaching when the trainers appeared a few minutes later. As soon as they showed up, Tiluk stopped breaching, went immediately to the side of the pool and hung there, motionless, as if there'd never been a song or dance. Then Miles remembered the article again, "Whoa. He's saying, 'No thank you.'"

"Well brother, I'm with you. No damn thank you. Let's get you the hell outta there." And Miles bolted.

* * *

After Terra and her family made their way back up to her yurt the clock read 1:11 a.m. Her mom kept hugging her and asking her over and over again if she was okay, like she didn't know what else to do. Finally Terra said, "Mom, seriously, I'm okay, but we have to do something!"

Her dad looked around at them, his face grave, then his scrutiny came to rest on Terra. "Let's all remember that we—and especially you, Miles and Tiluk—just *did* do something," he said. "What you kids just arranged and managed to pull off is history, pure and simple." He looked over at the recording equipment that now contained hard evidence of Tiluk's plight and his family's love and great distress for him. "Whatever happens to Tiluk and Wendy now," he sighed and rubbed his hands over his bleary eyes, "they've heard each other."

"I just hope she's not dead," Maggie said.

"We won't know that until at least tomorrow," Bill said quietly. "Everyone's tired and stirred up, and the best thing we can do for *all* these whales right now is get a good night's sleep. We can't help them if we're at half-mast."

Terra crossed her arms over her chest, miffed. Her dad could be so.... *reasonable*. "But Dad!"

"Let me talk to the sea squirt for a minute," interrupted Joseph. "You all go on to bed." He looked at Bill as if to say, "I've got this." Terra knew that look from the thousands of times one of the four parents would do exactly that; the old good cop, bad cop routine. She rolled her eyes and looked at Tiluk. *At least it's my dad*, he said to her silently with his expression as he came over to her once more. They locked arms, holding each other's fore-arms, foreheads tilting together, and inhaled, eyes closed. They *had* done something to help. Terra was thinking of Miles. He was already part of their team. And even though he was watching dawn break in Florida, she knew that he was part of their hug, too.

"'Night Lewis," Tiluk murmured.

"Thanks for keeping me from falling in down there." She smiled a little. "It would've been pretty cold."

"Anytime."

Terra noticed that Gwen and Jason, so quiet for most of the night as they'd witnessed the "family reunion" were staring at her a little, apprising her, as if they'd suddenly discovered she was some kind of mystic. As a result of what happened, they'd instinctively become much more her allies, and somehow more similar to each other than a cowgirl and surfer-dude could ever be. The live feed had been one of the biggest moments of their careers as biologists. And the way they both watched her now…she felt vulnerable and shaky and brave, all at the same time. Gwen reached for her, and Terra walked into her arms. They hugged and Gwen kissed the top of her head, while Jason rubbed her back a little. Awkward but determined.

"That's some big stuff, Terra…you gave us a hell of a lot to think about tonight," Jason said quietly. "I'm gonna start calling you our whale girl." He pulled on her braid with evident affection.

Terra flushed and Joseph started herding them all out of her yurt. "That's all everyone. Time for bed. We'll talk more about everything tomorrow."

Her mom gave her one more hug, and so did her dad and Maggie. Then everyone was gone and she was alone with Joseph; her dream— and what she and Joseph had talked about earlier—feeling about as far away as Orlando.

"I know what you said about the ancient ways," Terra said as she sat on her bed and fiddled with her braid, staring at her drum. "And I think that's really cool. I really do." She looked up at Joseph finally with a pleading look. "But how's that going to help them now?" Terra curled her knees up and hugged herself tightly as she sat on her bed, her throat still raw from retching. "They need help *now*."

"We don't always know the answers, sea squirt," Joseph said as he settled heavily into Terra's rocking chair and opened her stove, adding a log. "The thing about the ancient ways is that they work in mystery. For thousands of years our people knew this. And we worked in harmony with the Earth and her creatures."

He poked the logs. "As a people we've nearly forgotten not only that the ancient ways exist, but how to trust them. I'm as uncertain about what to do next as you are," he said, looking at her thoughtfully as he leaned back in the rocking chair. "But I know for sure that something is happening with you and these whales." He glanced at her nightstand, at the blood-stained carving of the calf she'd made and picked it up, rubbing it thoughtfully.

"The dream you told me about yesterday on the dock, Terra. There's more to that dream than you realize." He stood up, putting her whale back on the nightstand. "Trust the process." He rested his hand over her head the way he did so often, in a good night gesture. "Something is happening that we haven't seen in many generations. Do your best to trust that, sea squirt," he gave her shoulder a squeeze, then walked to the door.

"But Joseph…" she said once more, still on fire. "How am I supposed to sleep?"

He looked at her with a smile in his eyes, "Sleep for your dreams Terra, it is more important than you know."

Then he walked into the deep night, closing the door quietly behind him. She didn't know what Joseph was smoking because there was no way she was going to sleep. Dreams were all fine and good but these whales needed *action*! Suddenly she knew exactly what to do next. "Ancient ways," she muttered. "Whatever."

She booted up her computer.

I'm going to fix this, she thought pulling on her braid, her face serious.

I'm going to find information on what captivity really means for these whales, and I'm going to make sure people know about it. No one will ever pay money again, once they realize these animals need their families as much as we do. She frowned, thinking of Miles' parents and of Wendy hurling herself at the dock. *Maybe even more.*

She smiled a little when she saw that Miles had sent an email:

I guess you lived up to your name tonight, Miss Terra Incognita Lewis.

She wrote back:

Feels more like being buried under it….

And there was a note from Tiluk. It was a list of links from his muckraking yesterday. He'd simply written "OceanLand Muck" in the subject line with a bunch of links to articles and YouTube videos. "Thank you, Tiluk," she whispered, grateful for the head start. "Maybe this is all we'll need."

On a whim, she sent the links to Miles, copying Tiluk. She wrote one line:

Wanna help us rake this muck?

It was 2:04 a.m. She brought up her Blackfish Cove Facebook page so she could drop any of these stories into it as she went. She wanted to use that page to give people information about what real life was like for wild orca *and* information on what life was like for captive whales. Then people could see for themselves how captivity basically makes it impossible for whales to be whales.

A flag popped up. *Who's tagging me right now?* she wondered. *It's the middle of the night.*

She clicked on it and there was an incoming Facebook call from Miles Frost.

Miles, she smiled again. She accepted the call, and suddenly, there was Miles, his lightly distorted image appeared before her, and she noticed his trim blond hair and earnest, handsome face immediately. She felt herself blush before she even had a chance to say anything. She noticed a fleeting feeling of relief that her blush would not be visible on Miles' computer screen. *Get a grip, Lewis,* she thought to herself as she reached up and smoothed her hair. *It's just Miles.*

"Terra?" Miles' voice came through from 3,000 miles away. "You there?" "Right here, Frost," she said. "It's nice to see you."

There was a pause as the two stared at one another's images, both smiling in that somewhat dorky way that happens when you are trying to have a conversation through a computer.

"It's nice to see you too, Terra." Miles said. "Look, I called because I didn't want you looking at all those links by yourself in the middle of the night."

Terra's eyebrows went up. This was the last thing she'd expected to hear. "Miles, what are you talking about? How is Tiluk? Did he stop ramming his gate? What happened after the live feed ended? I need to tell you about Wendy."

Suddenly Terra's pent-up concerns flooded out and she started shivering.

"Terra, stop. Listen to me for a minute. I'll answer all your questions, but I need to tell you something first."

Terra stared at Miles' image: it had that little herky-jerky quality, but his voice had been clear and strong. She caught her breath as she realized how much she already trusted this boy. She felt herself relax a little.

"Okay Miles. I'm listening. What is it?"

She heard Miles sigh, and caught a glimpse of his hands rubbing up over his face. "Miles?"

"Yeah, I'm here Terra. It's just that I…" he got quiet again. This time Terra just waited, unconsciously pulling on her braid as she stared at her screen.

"You have a braid," she heard Miles say, more to himself than to her. "Dusky Dey had a ponytail…"

"Oh Miles," she paused, thinking about what he'd said about not wanting her to see those links by herself.

"Terra, there are some things you can't un-see. What happened to Dusky…I…" Miles' voice cracked and he got quiet again.

"I just wanted to make sure you didn't see anything like that by your-self," he said after a moment, his voice stronger. "From what I've seen these whales have it a lot worse than OceanLand lets on. And some of those links might be hard to look at, especially for someone like you, who only knows them in the wild. Let's just check together, okay?"

Terra blinked. "Okay," she said, so moved by his emotion and care that she found herself unable to say anything else. She thought of Wendy ramming her head against the dock. Her stomach churned. *Some things you can't un-see.*

"First one's first, then?" he peered at her.

She nodded and murmured, "Yeah," while thinking to herself, *Who is this guy, where did he come from, and what did we ever do without him?*

"Thank you, Miles." She wondered if he could hear the thickness in her own voice.

"Hey, the first link is by Tim Sinclair," Miles had already opened the first story. "That's the guy who wrote the amazing article I read the night after I saw…well, you know. He's the reason I contacted you in the first place."

"Okay, I've got it up now."

Sinclair had published another story in the *Orlando Weekly* called, "Follow

Up to Penn's Round Up: Captured Orcas Mostly Dead a Decade Later."

"Thank you, Tim," she murmured as she clicked the link, steeling herself against that headline.

"Miles," she said more loudly. "That's the round-up that my parents saw. It's the one when Tiluk was stolen from Wendy."

"I know, Terra," Miles said. "This stuff totally sucks. I can't believe I went to OceanLand all those times and never realized any of this bogus fecal matter." Terra could hear the strain and anger in Miles voice. "Shantu is a sham... *Sham You* is more like it."

One corner of Terra's mouth twitched up in a grim smile at the truth of Miles' bitter insight. She started reading:

> With Tiluk's killing of Cassidy "Dusky" Dey, just a few days ago, questions once again arise on the suitability of keeping killer whales for captivity and performance. The *Orlando Weekly* has learned that Tiluk is the only surviving orca of the 12 captured in Washington's Penn Cove, nearly 14 years ago. We now know that females in the wild can live well into their eighties (some researchers even suggest they can routinely live to be one hundred), and some males until their forties and fifties. Most captured whales die at less than half the age they would in the wild. So we now know that captivity itself is associated with very premature death for whales.

Terra skimmed the rest of the article but her stomach churned again with the news about how all the whales that had already died so much younger than they would have in the wild. *No more time for puking,* she thought, swallowing against rising bile. She learned that the whales had died either of infection, some weird disease unheard of in the wild, or because they'd been beaten up on by the other whales in the tank. One had even killed himself by smashing his head over and over again against a steel gate.

"Miles, how can people not know about this stuff?" Terra stuffed her braid into her mouth and started nibbling on it, staving off the intense sadness she was feeling.

"Maybe they don't want to know," he responded, his voice still gruff. "But this guy Tim is on it."

OceanLand maintains that such deaths are "normal" and that their captive whales enjoy the best medical care in the world. They suggest that these deaths are within the natural range for wild orca mortality and said in a recent press release, "these are deaths that would have occurred in the wild, perhaps even sooner than they did with us, where the whales receive the best diet of fish, the best veterinary attention, and stellar quality of trainer care and social engagement. Killer whales face increasing threats in the wild such as rising levels of toxins in the water, and falling populations of prey."

Terra shook her head in disgust over the brazen misrepresentations. OceanLand was implying that wild whales were better off in concrete pools than in the oceans.

"I can't believe OceanLand would say that! It's no wonder people don't get it, they're not hearing the truth," she said out loud in frustration, her braid falling to her shoulder.

Sinclair went on, as if he'd read her mind.

But OceanLand has not caught up with what orca researchers have learned: Wild orca live much longer than OceanLand has so far admitted. To suggest that the "wild" is less safe for a whale than a captive pen appears to demonstrate a willful attempt by OceanLand to mislead its fans. When one understands that OceanLand has trademarked the name "Shantu" while parading a series of sick, stressed, and dying animals through its facilities to appear as "Shantu" the question must be asked: Why keep whales at OceanLand at all?

The biggest argument for captivity that OceanLand (and all other captive facilities) makes is that orca and other highly intelligent and social cetaceans are "ambassadors" for their species; token animals who give humans the chance to become educated about them by observing and interacting up close and personal. But human ambassadors willingly volunteer for their positions. Whales do not. Given what we have learned since the Penn Cove capture, one has to wonder whether OceanLand has either its audiences or orcas' best interests at heart.

OceanLand makes almost two-thirds of its money from of its Shantu programs: in the first nine months of 2012 it pulled in nearly $90 million. OceanLand is owned by the publically traded Nightshade group, whose net worth is $580 billion. The Nightshade group is the largest alternative investment firm in the world. When OceanLand went public on Wall Street early this year, it had some of the world's largest banks assisting. Even

OceanLand admitted in its first public offering of stock that there was a risk to their investors, since their "product" may not behave as they wish (and that trainers may be injured or killed) or that audiences may decide it's inappropriate to hold sophisticated and intelligent wild animals as captive performers. Clearly, the biggest reason OceanLand keeps whales on display is its own bottom-line. And that bottom line is far more massive than any whale.

Imagine what that kind of cash could do to protect the real seas of this world. Not to mention the now endangered populations of orca that live there: populations that are threatened to this day, in part, as a direct result of OceanLand captures…Captures that have led to early death for almost every one of the whales taken from their homes and families.

"Terra, a big part of the reason your family of whales is in trouble now is because of all the captures from before." He looked at her through the computer. "I read another story yesterday about the Southern Residents, and how almost *half* of their entire population was either killed or kidnapped during the capture era." He paused. "I can't even wrap my mind around that! I also read that even now, all these years later, the wild whales who didn't get caught never ever go back to the places where the captures hap-pened. They avoid 'em like the bloody plague."

Terra stared at Miles. "Wouldn't it be great if OceanLand did the right thing, now that they know how big their role in the problems really is…?"

Her voice trailed off.

"Yeah and there's so many 'right' things they could do..." Miles agreed. "Like retiring all their whales *tomorrow*. When I think about those incredible animals swimming around and around and around in those tiny isolation chambers, I can barely take it. It makes me wonder if Tiluk did what he did, just to wake people up to how bad it is for them. It's no wonder the guy went bloody crazy."

Wake people up. Her dream. Granny's message. Miles. Tiluk. The whales.

Terra yawned, she was finally starting to feel tired. Her clock said 2:58

AM. "Miles, what happened after the live feed. Is Tiluk okay?"

She heard him snort. "Okay? He's not dead, if that's what you mean..." She could almost taste Miles' frustration. He got quiet. "But you know what? I think when he heard his family it really meant something to him. I got him to stop banging that stupid gate by playing him a song, and he did it again Terra..." Miles' voice went soft. "He did it again."

"He sang back..." Terra whispered, startled by Miles' proactive thoughtfulness and the way he'd decided to play a song for Tiluk even as he was crashing against his gate. All *she'd* been able to do when Wendy rammed the dock was puke over the side of it.

"Yeah, he sang back. And then he started dancing...he breached over and over again, like he was happy. It felt like I was watching a joy dance."

A joy dance. Terra marveled at the idea of this, recalling times she'd seen the wild ones do much the same thing as they cavorted outside while feeding. She loved watching them when they leapt and played like that. The majesty of them, the huge release of their breaches. "Joy dance" was the perfect description. She stared at Miles' image. This boy. What was it about him?

"What about Wendy? Was that awful noise I heard the sound of her ramming your dock?" Miles asked.

"Yeah, she lost it as soon as she heard Tiluk ramming his gate. I ran down there and Granny and Eve—that's Wendy's mom—were on either side of her, taking her out of the cove. It looked like she wasn't moving or breathing. We're all worried she might be dead." Terra's head tilted down, she felt overwhelmed.

Miles went quiet for a moment, watching her through the computer before he said, "No Lewis. She's not dead. No way would Wendy off herself like that right after hearing her boy for the first time in 14 years. Sad, yes.

Upset, yes. Helpless, yes. But dead?" He stared at her. "No way, Terra. She's too smart for that. Besides, she has the new calf." She heard him take a long breath. "If anyone is going to kill himself, it's gonna be our guy Tiluk down here in Orlando."

Terra giggled. Something about what Miles said hit her with its black-truth absurdity. "Thanks a lot, Frost. I feel so much better now."

"Anytime, Lewis." She saw him reach up and pull his hands through his hair and noticed his room had grown brighter. It was morning in Florida.

"Hey, Miles. Let's sign off so you can get some sleep."

"You too, whale girl. And speaking of sleeping, you haven't told me about that dream yet." Terra felt a little jolt at being called "whale girl" for the second time tonight...this time by Miles.

"I thought you didn't want to hear anything else about the calf," she said, recalling his email.

"Changed my mind." She could see him smiling. "But you go have some sweet dreams for now...and tell me about it next time."

Next time. She liked the sound of that. A lot.

"Terra, listen. Before we sign off, I skimmed these links you sent while we were reading Sinclair's article. I'm about to email you a short note about what each one is. Some of it is pretty upsetting, just like I thought. Especially the videos. Do me a favor and don't watch any of this stuff before you got to sleep."

Terra stared at Miles, a question, unspoken, on her face.

"Just trust me on this, okay? Watching a whale leap over and over again onto his trainer isn't the same as counting sheep."

"What are you talking about Miles?" Terra asked, confused.

"Seriously, Terra. It's one of the links you sent. It's a video. Watch it tomorrow if you have to, but not now. Think about our whale's joy dance instead, and have some sweet dreams, okay?" He sounded so earnest. "And then tomorrow you can decide which of those links you actually want to look at, after you read my notes on what each one is about, okay? Just remember what I said." He got quiet again.

"Some things you can't un-see, right Miles?"

"Yeah." Miles said, solemnly. "Right." Terra felt a poignant surge of affection. She wanted to hug Miles, knowing what he'd seen, knowing what he'd already done to help.

"I hope you get some rest too, Frost." It almost hurt to say good-night.

"I promise I won't look at any of that stuff until tomorrow, okay? I know it would make me too sad tonight anyway." She thought of Wendy again. There was too much sadness for one day already.

"Thanks, Terra."

"Night, Miles."

"See ya," Miles said, then his image clicked off and she was alone. She yawned again and glanced at the clock on her computer. 3:23 a.m. At least she had a chance of getting a little sleep. She wondered if Miles would even try to sleep since it was past dawn where he lived. *Miles.* She shook her head, feeling her face grow warm. "Focus, Terra," she said to herself. She reached over and picked up the carving of the calf, looked at it, rubbed its belly and tail. She glanced around the yurt again: her drum, the microphone, the spilled hot chocolate on her sheepskin. So much had happened tonight. And she was so tired. But there was one more thing she had to do.

"Okay, Miles, I promised not to look at the links, but I want to see what you wrote," she said as she checked her email.

And there it was, his note, just like he said. It was long enough that she realized he must have been making these notes while she was reading the first news story. He really cared.

Hey Earth girl,

That's what your name really means, right? *Terra*. And that's pretty much the truth, from where I sit anyway. I get the sense you are connected to more than just your whales…

So, here are my notes. Tiluk (your friend) must have already watched and read all of this if he's the one who sent it to you. Thank him for me. It's muck alright…

Link #1: The Tim Sinclair story we read tonight (that was cool, I liked seeing you and doing that together) Link #2: Trainer killed by an orca at OceanLand-owned park in Spain. Two months before Dusky died. Pisses me off. WTH was OL thinking? Using "Tiluk-Shantu" for performances after what happened in Spain? WTH? (It's a news story, not a video. Thank God.)

Link #3: Seriously injured killer whale at San Diego OL. Naku is the whale's name and half his freaking JAW is MISSING. (Terra, you do NOT want to see this before going to bed...if ever). Naku was trying to avoid getting beat up by the other whales, but oh boy, they got him anyway. Never happens in the wild. Totally screwed up. These whales are not family, and they can't escape each other. This just happened last week, and they aren't sure he'll survive.

Link #4: VIDEO. Counting sheep? Seriously, this is unbelievable.

Killer whale doing a show with a trainer in Texas. Whale leaps out of the water and falls down on top of the trainer... over and over again... trainer keeps ducking underwater to save his sorry neck from breaking. Whale *totally* doing it on purpose. The guy tries to escape, swim away, and the crazy beast just keeps herding him back out into the middle of his prison-tank, and leaps on him again and again. Seven minutes of hell. He got out alive. Barely.

Link #5: VIDEO. How many dang OceanLand's are there? In this one, at yet *another* OL... in Ohio...a whale grabs the trainer with his teeth and goes to the bottom of the pool for like a minute, then surfaces, then takes him down again. Trainer tries to calm the whale down. But whale just takes him down over and over.

The video lasts for like twenty damn minutes. He finally gets away, by swimming over a net and up on stage, but the whale tries to come after him!! Just like I saw Tiluk do to

Dusky. Freaking crazy. Luckily this guy had friends right there who dragged him up and away from the whale.

Link #6. VIDEO. More of the same. Trainer working with orca at some OTHER OL somewhere. Puts her foot on his mouth a few times. He grabs her and takes her down. She is so damn lucky, another trainer let one of the dominant female whales into the tank with her, and the big guy holding her under let her go. Her arm was BENT THE WRONG WAY when she got out.

These last two reminded me of the nightmares I had the night Dusky died. Ughh.

So, what are you guys going to do with these links besides posting them to Blackfish Cove? Does ExplOrca have plans? What can I do to help?

I guess I'll try to get a little nap before my mom wakes up.

'Night Terra,

Miles

"'Night Miles," Terra whispered. "Don't let the whales bite." She squeezed her eyes shut tight against a current of emotion pushing up against her throat. Wild whales would never do these things. For the whales to do the things she'd just learned about…she swallowed hard… they must be dying inside. They must be going crazy-berserk-insane with stress in every tank all over the world.

She squeezed them shut even tighter, until she saw red. Red like blood. "I swear Granny— on everything I love—we're going to fix this."

FREETHEM

WENDY RAMMED THE DOCK and blood spurted from her blowhole and there was nothing Terra could do, her arms and legs paralyzed. She could only watch, sobbing in horror. "Wendy, stop!"

"Terra, wake up." A voice looped around her, pulling her gently away from the bloodied whale. "It's a nightmare, Lewis. Wendy's okay…I saw her a little while ago."

Tiluk's voice. She rose slowly to the surface, and felt a gentle tap on her cheek. She opened her eyes and there, sitting on her chest, head cocked side-ways as he peered into her eyes, was Fierce. He tapped her cheek again with his tiny, sharp beak. Gentle.

"I thought you could use a little Fierce energy this morning," Tiluk said.

"He's already had breakfast; I took him down to the cove to hunt… the pod was out there and Wendy looks fine."

The small falcon walked forward on her chest until he was sitting squarely on Terra's throat, and stared at her. Then he spread both his wings and fluttered them mightily in her face, batting her chin and cheeks with his rumpus. A few feathers ejected off his wings and floated down onto Terra's bed.

She broke out in a huge grin. "Hi Fierce. It's nice to see you, too." Terra pushed herself up, forcing the bird to walk backwards, down her sloping torso so that he ended up sitting on her belly. His head cocked upwards, still watching her.

"Are you sure she's okay? She was definitely not fine in my nightmare,"

Terra reached under the bird's feet, let him walk onto her hand, and sat all the way up. Tiluk, who was sitting at the foot of her bed, was still smiling at Fierce's little performance.

"This time your dream was just a nightmare. She's really fine. I could see the calf with her, nursing and playing with kelp fronds. They were tag teaming each other with the kelp. Looked like they were playing Keep Away."

Terra raised Fierce to her cheek and nuzzled him. "What a relief." She looked up, away from the bird, at Tiluk. "Maybe that's her way of dealing with last night…maybe she needed a little special down time with her new baby. I wonder if her head hurts after all that ramming…"

Tiluk shrugged. "She's going to be okay…at least for now. It's Tiluk I'm worried about."

Miles. Last night's call shot through her abruptly. All those links. Tiluk must have seen them all since he's the one that researched them in the first place. *Some things you can't un-see*. No wonder he was more worried about Tiluk-Shantu, than about his mother Wendy, relatively safe in her wild home.

"You saw those videos, didn't you?" Terra asked him.

"Yeah, and a wish I hadn't. I should have warned you not to watch them," Tiluk said with an apologetic grimace. "They're just so wrong."

"Tiluk, I didn't watch them. Miles warned me." Tiluk's eyebrows shot up in a question.

"I couldn't sleep last night after everything, so I decided to do some more research. I forwarded your list of links to Miles, and he called me through Facebook before I had a chance to see any of it."

"Good," Tiluk replied, a look of thoughtful respect on his face. "Miles has seen way too much…I'm glad he warned you. But lots of other people need to see that stuff, even if it is hard to watch. *Especially* because it's hard to watch." He swallowed and took a breath as if he'd spoken too many words at once. "Hardly anyone realizes the truth about those captive whales."

Tiluk stood up and walked to the door. "Which reminds me, everyone is down at the house putting together the proposal to OceanLand to retire Tiluk.

I already sent them those links, and they've found even more. After this, I don't see how OceanLand will be able to justify keeping *any* orca captive anymore." "I hope you're right Tiluk," Terra said as she absently stroked Fierce's soft belly.

"Your mom has something to tell you. Come down soon. Besides, it's almost lunch time, Lewis." He grinned at her as he opened the door, then turned into the sunlight, his black hair glinting, and disappeared.

On a whim, Terra reached over to her nightstand and picked up her whale carving; its burnished sides felt cool and smooth. She held the little calf up in one hand with Fierce in the other hand, and brought her two hands together. "Fierce, meet the calf. Baby whale, say hello to Fierce."

Fierce nudged his head against the carving and squawked. Terra smiled.

"You're happy here with us, aren't you little bird?" It was much more a statement than a question. She knew Fierce was content. But Tiluk-Shantu? He was another matter altogether.

"Let's go find out what Mom wants to tell me," she spoke to Fierce as she put him on his perch and hastily got dressed. "Maybe she's going to make me an author on this proposal or something," she said, thinking about last night and how the whales understood her Morse code drumbeat for Tiluk. "That *was* pretty amazing…"

She pulled the brown sweater Maggie had made for her over her head, anticipating the damp chill outside, and put the calf carving into her pocket. She reached for Fierce and he sidestepped up her arm, onto her shoulder. Then she walked into the cool sunshine and down to the house, almost for-getting to notice the way the sun shimmered through the thousands of pine needles, casting elfin-green sparkles of light everywhere. But halfway across the yard she stopped and looked up. She opened her arms wide, feeling Fierce tighten his grip for the ride he knew was coming. She twirled, round and round, head back, the lengths of the enormous trees soaring over her head, filling her vision. Fierce squawked and flapped as she spun.

She stopped and took a deep breath. "Okay, that's better. Now let's go."

As she stepped into the mudroom she heard her dad's voice. "So, any of you ever see a whale out here sit motionless for days on end, never moving, never vocalizing?"

Terra stopped, listened. They must be in the middle of writing up the proposal and tossing ideas around. Her dad's question was startling. She peeked out of the mudroom and into the living area, glimpsing Jason and Gwen who'd been brought up short by her dad's query. Their faces were blank. Everything they did as graduate students was about recording behaviors and actions and swimming patterns and vocalizations. Their entire lives revolved around capturing data on the varied activities of the wild whales, including how they often swim up to 100 miles a day. Trying to imagine an immobile orca would be like conjuring up a human toddler who sat for hours on end in a corner, unmoving and silent.

"Didn't think so," Bill frowned. "Way too many of these animals are showing clear signs of depression and severe stress. They've got the elevated stress hormones to prove it." He held up a wad of research papers he'd been reading. "Tiluk, in particular, hangs frozen in his tank most of every day, except for the damn performances. And other whales respond like this, too. They almost don't have any other choice, confined like they are to those tiny pools."

Terra leaned against the doorway and listened. No one knew she'd come in, and she didn't want to interrupt. Thank goodness her folks— and ExplOrca—were making this proposal. She swallowed.

Next she heard Maggie's voice. "Some animals are naturally suited to domestication, like dogs, cows, horses, cats, turkeys, and rabbits. Their size, scale, and social behaviors allowed them to move from being wild animals into the human world fairly well, even joyfully. These are the animals that have lived and evolved with humans for *10,000 years*. Cages and fences simply help us and the domesticated animals define a closeness, a *relation-ship* that already exists between us and them. But eight-ton whales are not domesticated and never will be. They need their family and culture to learn *everything*. They are totally incompatible with captivity. Without their family and the ocean to sustain them, they can no longer be whales. A cage does to a whale the same things it does to a human, maybe more so. Cetaceans were never suited for the human world. Period."

Terra could hear the fast typing of someone else as Maggie spoke. She guessed it was her mom, the speed-demon typist. She couldn't quite see the dining table where her mom and Maggie were probably working together.

Maggie was on a roll. "It would be like aliens abducting a bunch of humans to make them 'ambassadors' to their planet 30 light years away, and keeping them caged in a brick closet for the rest of their lives with no hope of ever doing what fulfills them or seeing their families again. And they'd only be able to get food by doing sit-ups, hand stands, jumping jacks, and jogging in place, while a bunch of aliens watched from above. Some of these humans might grow a little fond of their alien captors because, like whales, we are predisposed to bond tightly with other social beings. But those alien friends would never hold a candle to the humans' own lost family and friends."

"Not to mention their freedom." Bill said heavily.

Terra could hear Claire typing Maggie's words as she'd vented. "Got it. Bravo, Maggie. That's our conclusion. We've spent most of our professional lives being scientists, and trying to avoid any form of political action, but at some point, I guess we have to decide that action isn't political when it's just what needs to be done."

"It's time," Joseph murmured. "There are signs..."

"Personally, I think those captive humans might want to kill their alien abductors," said Terra loudly as she walked into the room. "I think I'd go pretty darn crazy if all I could do every day was hang out in my cell, do some calisthenics, and eat nasty food that was nothing like what I liked to eat before they caught me."

"Well, well, well. Speaking of signs, good morning sweetheart," Claire said as Terra came over and sat down at the table next to her mom, Fierce still perched on her shoulder.

"Yeah, Terra, our whale girl. She's a sign, all right," Jason piped up. "A sign that these whales know a lot more than we realize."

"Hi everyone," Terra smiled over at Jason. "I'm really glad you all are working on this. Mom," she turned back to look at Claire, "did you guys put stuff into the proposal about what was in those links that Tiluk found?"

"We did honey. And then some. I'm afraid there are now plenty of examples of captive whales doing things that absolutely contradict wild whale behavior and biology. Especially their shortened life spans. But also the way they treat one another in the tanks...unrelated killer whales would never live together in the wild. Some of these parks even have different subspecies together, like transients and residents. There's a lot of brutality going on in these tanks that the parks like to say results from 'normal' dominance hierarchies."

"What a load of garbage!" Gwen exclaimed, all riled up. "The only 'dominance hierarchies' these animals have are about their mothers and grand-mothers. They live with their families their entire lives. They rarely associate with unrelated families, and when they do, it's part of a social gathering…and everyone has the option of swimming away if things get too intense." She took a breath. "Plus, you'd never ever see transients and residents engage socially in the wild. They have some kind of cultural boundary in place."

Joseph left the window and came over to stand behind Terra, resting his hand on her head. Fierce tilted his head up and stared at Joseph for a moment, then turned and tucked his head under his wing.

"Speaking of cultural boundaries," he said, looking at Gwen, "I think we need to remember that OceanLand just doesn't know a lot of what we have learned about the wild ones. Maybe that's the key. There is OceanLand culture—that says keeping marine mammals to educate people is beneficial and can be done in a healthy way for the animals. Their whole approach and all their literature underscore this culture: OceanLand and its community, so far, truly believe that they are doing right by the animals."

Jason snorted and rolled his eyes, exasperated. "That's not a culture, that's a delusion," he grumbled.

Joseph nodded briefly, acknowledging Jason's point, but went on, "At this point, many of them probably *have* to believe they are doing right by the animals. Or else they might not be able to live with themselves."

"So *that's* why they call it The Belief show," Jason said loudly, dope slap-ping himself. "Now I get it!" Tiluk, who'd been sitting on the couch next to Jason gave him a high-five.

Everyone laughed, but it was grim humor. The Belief show was one of the most famous and popular things OceanLand did. It revolved around the captive orca and their tricks. Joseph smiled at Jason, and continued. "But then there is another culture, a culture outside of OceanLand. The ExplOrca culture: one which cultivates a scientific understanding and respect for the biology and social dynamics of these wild whales in their true homes."

"I think you are giving them way too much credit, Joseph," Bill declared, voice raised with anger thick and simmering. "Like Jason said, that's not a culture at OceanLand, it's a delusion. And I seriously doubt they really believe they're doing right by the whales. They *believe* they are doing right by their *company*...And they're willfully ignoring evidence they don't want to admit. So, it's more like a parent-child relationship. OceanLand is very naïve—and almost intentionally ignorant—in its understanding of killer whales, which is potentially dangerous for everyone in the family...so it's high time someone wiser came along and taught them some lessons. Just like any competent parent would teach a misguided child."

"Do we get to use corporal punishment?" Jason quipped under his breath.

"Either way," Maggie interjected, "everyone will benefit from sharing what we've learned about wild whale biology and behavior. Speaking of which," she looked over her computer at Claire. "I'm going to send this proposal to the J Squad. I'd like to keep them posted on what's going on."

"Good idea." Claire replied. "And let's send it along to Miles, too. He's part of this now, and I imagine it will be more satisfying to him to see this proposal than we can imagine...given what he witnessed."

Miles. Suddenly Terra had an idea.

"Mom, let's send the proposal to that journalist Tim Sinclair who writes for the Orlando Weekly. Maybe he can share it with his readers in Florida. I bet they'd want to know about this stuff."

Claire turned in her seat and grinned at her daughter. "See honey, this is exactly why we asked you and Tiluk to brainstorm with us and get involved.

That's brilliant." She reached over and squeezed Terra's hand. "I'll copy this to you, and you send it to him yourself."

Terra smiled with her mother's acknowledgement. "Besides," Claire went on, "Maggie and I need to pack. We get the ferry in an hour."

Terra's eyebrows went up. "You're leaving?"

Claire looked over at Tiluk with a question on her face. "Yeah, I didn't tell her Claire. Too busy getting rid of her nightmare this morning," Tiluk said.

Joseph stepped away from Terra and came around to sit on the other side of the table, so he could face her when he spoke. "We all stayed up late last night talking after I said good night to you, and we agreed to put a rush job on writing this proposal today so your mom and Maggie could fly to

Orlando tonight and hand-deliver it tomorrow morning."

Terra stood up so fast her chair fell over backwards with a crash. "Mom, I have to come with you!" she yelped, as Fierce woke up, startled and screeching. He flew off Terra's shoulder, flitting around the room squawking, until he saw Tiluk who reached out a hand. Fierce landed there, still protesting and shook himself. If birds are capable of annoyance, Fierce was the picture of irritation as he nearly scowled in displeasure at the insult of his rude awakening. He stared at Terra, shook himself once more, stepped closer to Tiluk's long hair, and put his head back under his wing.

"Sorry, Fierce," Terra offered, somewhat calmer as she reached down and picked up her chair. "But I have to go!" She looked at Joseph, her urgency bristling, sensing this decision was already made and she wasn't going to like it. "Tell them Joseph, I *have* to go. I need to help explain why Tiluk needs to come home." Her eyes welled up and she looked at her mom and Maggie, reading their expressions of soft understanding.

"I'm not going, am I?" She crossed the room to Tiluk and sat down next to him on the couch, sullen. She crossed her arms in front of her as she blinked through her emotion. "This sucks."

"We knew you'd want to go sweetheart," Bill said as he reached over

Tiluk and squeezed Terra's knee. "But the OceanLand officials need to hear this from Mom and Maggie right now…they are two of our most respected scientists. The best chance we have for retiring Tiluk is to bring the folks at OceanLand some hard-core professionalism, serious research, and rational arguments." He squeezed her once more before he stood up. "We know you're a serious scientist like the rest of us, but all OceanLand will see is a 13-year-old whale hugger…" He grimaced. "And I'm afraid that would be last thing on Earth that would convince them to retire a whale who makes them millions of dollars."

"Soon, honey," Claire said as she stood, picking up her laptop. "Soon you'll be able to come and speak to them, too. We need to do it this way first, though. Besides," she smiled at Terra, "I have a feeling you can do a whole lot more to rally support for this proposal from here, what with your Facebook page and your idea to send our proposal to the journalist in Florida." She smiled. "OceanLand won't know what hit them."

"It still sucks," Terra grumbled. "Joseph, what about the ancient ways? This doesn't seem very mysterious to me... I should be going with them."

Maggie looked at the clock and stepped towards the door, "I'm sorry honey, your mom and I need to get ready or we'll miss the ferry. I hope you'll understand." She put her arm around Claire, "Come on. We need to go. Let the dads handle this one."

"Wait Claire, Maggie," Joseph said from his place at the table. He turned and his full, potent look fell on Terra, his black eyes seemed to sharpen and his whole demeanor shifted into warrior mode.

"Now you've done it," Tiluk said under his breath to Terra, who shrank into the couch a little under Joseph's scrutiny.

"You are being given a lesson, Terra. Remember, trust the process." His eyes held her so tight she forgot everyone else in the room for a moment. *Trust the process.* That's what he'd said last night. But she knew she wanted to go with her mom and Maggie! She stuck her hand into her pocket, taking hold of her whale carving as if it could give her strength and comfort.

"What can you learn from this lesson?" Joseph asked her, quiet but forceful. She stared back at Joseph as she rubbed the whale. Suddenly she understood.

"Mom, you guys will see Miles, won't you?" her voice thin.

Claire smiled at the almost visible shift in her daughter. "Clever girl. Yes, we plan to take him to lunch tomorrow after our meeting at OceanLand. And his mom, too. It's time she got up to speed on all this."

Terra stood up and walked to Claire. She pulled the whale from her pocket, grabbed her mother's free hand and shoved the carving into it, pressing her mom's fingers tight around the calf.

"Take her to Miles. He needs to see her. Tell him thank you."

Then, blinking hard, Terra fled.

AMENDS

IT WAS ONE THING TO ESCAPE into the woods while her mom
had to catch the ferry with Maggie—she'd done that today, she'd been
so upset about their decision to go without her. No way was she coming
out to say goodbye, even if they *always* said goodbye, no matter what.
Her mom had left a note tacked to her yurt door:

> I understand, sweetie.
> I love you, Mama

But this was different. *Really different.* Terra buckled her life jacket
and pulled the straps tight, then climbed into her kayak. It was pitch
black and moonless, just like she felt inside. Her mom would probably
kill her if she knew what Terra was about to do. Well, probably all four
of the parents would. She shook her head. She didn't care. Then she
was rowing with all her might. Her kayak sped quickly from the dock,
out into the cove towards Haro Strait. The lights of Victoria twinkled
from a great distance away across the water. They looked like a cluster
of stars against the horizon, a luminescent huddle of children beneath
their starry family. Ever since she was a little girl listening to Joseph's
stories, Terra had always thought of Victoria's lights as the brood of the
Pleiades. In deep winter months with no moon, you could see the Seven
Sisters move down the horizon reaching towards the city lights as if to
gather their lost babies into their arms. But they could never touch each
other before the mothers disappeared below the horizon.

Now all she saw was her own fury. Victoria's lights were just
another ugly reminder of why she was so mad. She was *so* mad! Terra

pulled harder on her paddle, ripping through the black water of the cove at top speed, the dark moonless night enveloping her. As she moved beyond the mouth of the cove, the chop grabbed her, insistent. The Strait, one part of the large Salish

Sea, was a main artery of the Pacific Ocean. Its waters forced themselves between land masses into a roiling, unpredictable channel of lurking and angry currents. The parents all referred to Haro as Harrowing Strait, and after their many years of research spent navigating its unpredictable cur-rents, they weren't exactly joking. She was forbidden to be out here alone.

She didn't care. The chop just echoed her own anger, and she rowed right out into the Strait, pulling further from Blackfish Cove. Her kayak bounced hard through the waves, the bottom shuddering each time it came down, making her teeth rattle. Freezing spray hit her hands and face. She didn't care. The icy shock felt good…as if the jolt of the drenching needles brought her closer to the ones her heart ached for.

She *had* to find the whales. Somehow she had to tell Granny that she understood. She had to apologize. It wasn't bad enough what had happened last night during the live feed when Tiluk and Wendy both freaked out and started ramming themselves. Terra recalled puking over the dock and felt her stomach churn again. And the links that Miles warned her about, even they weren't as bad as this. She just couldn't take it anymore. The only place she wanted to be right now was by Granny's side, trying, somehow, to say how sorry she was…for everything. She had to find the whales.

As she paddled Terra flashed back to this afternoon after the moms left and she'd crept from the woods back down to her yurt on the sly, still so pissed off about not being allowed to go with the moms that she'd had to spit every few minutes. Her face had been red and saliva kept pooling in her mouth, teaching her that the saying, "I'm so mad I could spit," was, in fact, true. Once inside, she went immediately to her Blackfish Cove Facebook account to post those horrible links that Tiluk had found, and that Miles had warned her not to watch, to her newsfeed. First she typed this comment:

Warning: Graphic and disturbing images and information follow in this and the next five posts. Even though these are hard to look at, they are super important to see and know about. The whales need us to know.

Then she tracked down Tim Sinclair at the Orlando Weekly and emailed him ExplOrca's proposal. Her note to him said:

Dear Mr. Sinclair,

My mom is Claire Lewis at ExplOrca, and my new friend Miles Frost saw Tiluk kill his trainer last week. We all are super worried about Tiluk (and we all feel horrible for Dusky's family). Please feel free to share this proposal to retire Tiluk with your readers. Miles lives in Orlando. I'm copying him on this so you can contact him if you want. Maybe your readers want to know what it was like for a 14-year-old boy to watch a killer whale eat his trainer.

I'm really glad you are covering the whales. Thank you.

Seriously,
Terra Lewis

As she hit send, her computer chimed, alerting her she'd been private messaged. She clicked back to her Blackfish Cove page and read the message:

I'm a former OceanLand marine mammal trainer. I worked with the orca for years. I knew Dusky and worked with Tiluk. There's a lot more you don't know about. I quit a long time ago because of it. Did you know that the whales gnaw on their steel gates and break a lot of their teeth? To "prevent infection" the vet would drill their teeth out, basically remove the roots, and then we trainers would have to hose down the whales' mouths a few times every day. Just to keep the holes inside their teeth clean. Some of us think the whales die so young because of infections in the drill holes in their teeth. It must be incredibly painful for the whales. Here's a video of the tooth procedure...you can see the drilled teeth compared to the whole teeth. Let me know if you want more information. There are so many things I didn't know while I was a trainer. Now I'm trying to let others know the truth. Dusky's death was 100 percent avoidable. These whales should never be held captive. I'm glad ExplOrca is starting to talk about this issue, too.

Sincerely, Joanna Burns

Terra was getting further from land. She glanced back. She could barely make out the mouth of Blackfish Cove. Her kayak was plowing through the waves, but her arms were starting to tire. She didn't care. She didn't care if she was a tiny dark speck out here in the middle of this enormous sea. She had to find them.

She hadn't told her dad or Joseph about Joanna Burns' message. She hadn't even told Tiluk. She'd been so sickened by the former trainer's note she didn't reply at first. She couldn't talk about it all afternoon or at dinner. Claire had called after dinner to let them know she and Maggie had landed in Orlando, and Terra refused to get on the phone. She couldn't.

During paddle watch the sunset had been fiery orange riddled with brilliant sapphire blue streaks across the sky and all Terra could think about was someone taking a power drill to the tenderest parts of Wendy's son... because he'd been gnawing at the steel bars holding him prisoner and breaking his own teeth. Immediately after everyone docked their kayaks she went up to her yurt, mumbling something to her dad about needing to go to bed early because she was so tired. He'd given her a squeeze and kissed the top of her head, and said, "I'm not surprised honey. I hope you sleep well."

"Night Lewis," Tiluk had said quietly, his caring tone letting her know he understood she needed to be alone.

Tiluk. What would he think of this? Of her paddling out here by herself? What would he think of the drilling? She paddled harder. What would he think of what she'd discovered in her mom's office just a few minutes ago?

Terra spit into the waves.

She had to find the whales. Even if she struggled against these waves and icy waters, it was nothing compared to what the whales had gone through. She had to tell them she knew. *Some* human had to make amends. Somehow.

Back in her yurt after paddle watch, she'd replied to Joanna Burns:

I'm glad you wrote. I had no idea. It's unbelievable. Please send whatever information you have. We need to get this stuff out to as many people as we can.

Thank you for quitting,
Terra Lewis

She spit into the waves again. There was still no sign of the pod, despite rowing so far out. She looked up and back. She could barely tell where Blackfish Cove was anymore. Everything was black. The never-ending body of saltwater glimmered by starlight, as if she were paddling across deep space, compared to the opaque solidity of the land so far behind her. She was starting to tire as the kayak bounced against the hard waves, the frigid spray showering her with every bounce. And she was freezing; the water had penetrated her sleeves despite her sturdy raingear and wool underneath. *Where were they?*

She scoured the waters, her eyelashes and cheeks wet with salty spray. Suddenly she had an idea. She raised her paddle high over her head and slapped it down flat against the waves, as hard as she could. She did it again.

And again. Three dots. Her gloved hands were blistering, but she didn't care. She raised her oar, and walloped the water, this time waiting a beat longer than before. And again, and again. Three dashes. Then a pause. Then another whop, a longer one, and a shorter one. A dot, a dash, and a dot. Then that set repeated again. Her arms were burning fire. Whack. Pause. Whack. Whack. Pause. Whack. Pause.

There. She'd spelled it. What she'd come out here to say. S-O-R-R-Y. Maybe if they heard her, they would come. Maybe they didn't even know what that meant. But she had to try. She started again. Whack. Whack. Whack. Her arms were screaming with pain against the beating they were taking.

She recalled her mom's journal and her energy boiled up, keeping her going. Whack. Pause. Whack. Pause. Whack. Pause. She kept whacking. After she'd replied to Joanna Burns she'd tried to go to sleep. But all she kept seeing were drills and whale teeth and whales biting gates and bloody blowholes and whales turned into battering rams. It took less than five minutes of this before she'd thrown off her covers and took up her drum. The drumming calmed her after a while, and then, suddenly, she'd known what to do. She'd grabbed her headlamp, and crept down to the main house to her mom's office.

Her mom and Maggie were in Orlando, her dad and Joseph and Tiluk and the grad students, fast asleep in their yurts. It had been nearly midnight when she'd crept in there in the pitch black with her headlamp on. She didn't want to wake anyone with lights in the main building. And she'd just sat down in her mom's chair and looked around the darkened office, wondering.

What else had her parents hidden from her?

It was a room she'd been in hundreds of times. There was the dark wall of glass before her; in daylight it gave her mom an eagle's view of Blackfish

Cove. In front of the window was a beautiful cherry-wood table, one her dad had made for her mom years ago. "For you to think and dream at," he'd said to her. Her dad always kept something from the forest in here on her mom's table, surprising her with something new every now and again. A pinecone, a piece of fragrant fir bark, a bouquet of cedar boughs, antlers. Her mom refused to get rid of any of those gifts so the edges of the windows were crammed full of nature goodies. Kind of like in her yurt. There was a coyote skull, about hundred different bird feathers, random pieces of bone, huge dried leaves, and sitting on the floor beneath it all was her mom's prized object: the ancient and powerful-looking orca skull that had washed up on the pebbly beach on the other side of the cove.

The table was crowded with papers and magazines. The piles further from her mom's seat were covered in thin dust. What was she looking for anyway? Something had drawn her in here.

She slunk off her mom's chair and crept over to the cupboards to the right of the desk. She'd never opened them before. Inside were more papers and about three hundred yellow-spined magazines—*National Geographic*.

So that's where she keeps these, Terra smiled to herself. *National Geographic* was such a staple in their lives. It nearly equaled salmon and orca in status. She moved over to the other wall of shelving and cupboards. There were dozens of old black-and-white composition notebooks to the left, and then towards the right, they were replaced with sturdier moleskin journals. She pulled one of the old black-and-white comp books. It was dated "Oct-May '91-92." She flipped through her mom's handwriting filling the pages.

"Whooooooaaaa, Mom. Your diaries," Terra breathed.

She shut it quickly and reshelved it. *No way Terra, No way! You **cannot** go reading mom's private journals.* She looked down and clenched her fingers together, shaking her head. *I should really just go back to bed right now!* But what if there was something in those journals that could help her help the whales? What else had their parents hidden from them?

Suddenly, Terra overcame her reluctance. It didn't matter at all. Finding the information was way more important than whether or not she got it from her mom's diaries. She knew exactly what information she wanted: the year leading up to Penn Cove. Why had her mom and the others been so affected by that round up that they'd name Tiluk after the whale? And why had they named her Terra Incognita, for that matter? What was so urgent before Penn

Cove that made them want to devote their lives to studying these creatures?

I mean it is super cool and everything being whale biologists, but is there more to it?

She found the journal she was looking for and flipped it open. There in her headlamp's beam was her mom's choppy script, as if she couldn't write fast enough for her own thoughts. Terra skimmed the entries, most of which tracked her mom's day-to-day observations and recordings of two orcas at

OceanLand in San Diego. Terra knew her mom had gotten a big break there as a graduate student. She'd been given permission to come in and basically eavesdrop on the whales with her brand-new hydrophone gear as part of her groundbreaking efforts to begin understanding the complexities of orca vocalizations and communication. So she and Bill had packed their gear and flown down to California for a few months— leaving Joseph and Maggie behind to keep tracking the wild whales. The first entries were pretty standard, just her mom jotting down the hours she recorded the two whales—a male and a female named Korky and Storky. She learned Korky had been pregnant – and her mom was also pregnant with *her* at the same time.

"Wow, that must've been kinda weird," Terra murmured as she'd hunched over the journal, cross-legged, her braid in her mouth. In one entry she read, "Baby moved a lot today, right while I was recording some of the strongest vocalizations between the whales. Almost think the baby could hear them, and responded."

Terra warmed at this idea. *I was hearing them even before birth. Wow.* She closed her eyes, trying to assimilate everything she'd found out over the last couple of days, including, now, this. She'd been connected to orca from before she could breathe. *Maybe that's why I dreamt about Granny. Maybe Granny knows somehow that I'm one human she can trust because my connection is so deep.*

Terra kept reading. Her mom often slept out by the pool, recording day and night, slumbering with a big pillow to cradle her growing belly and wearing headphones while she slept. Bill would join her most evenings after a busy day of graduate work on salmon. He'd bring her dinner, and they'd sit by the pool, listening and watching. Then they'd cozy up together on the thick camping pad they'd slogged in, and watch the two whales do a sunset ritual. Terra's eyes grew wide at this. Even those two captive whales had bid the sun good night every evening, just like Granny's family does sometimes. *Whoa.* They'd spyhop together at exactly the location where the last bright rays of sun hit the edge of the pool.

Terra knew that not all orca get along so well in captive pools. Korky and Storky were lucky that they liked each other. As she skimmed, she read about her mom's growing belly and her difficulty's with sleeping but never once did she consider leaving her awkward sleeping arrangements for the cozy bed at their apartment. She wrote in one spot, "Feel so blessed to be here. Who else has the chance to study these whales' vocalizations so thoroughly? I feel very privileged and grateful to OceanLand for giving me this opportunity. It's something we can all benefit from. Humans and whales. Basic science on orca vocalizations is so new!"

But then her mom's entries took a different tone as Korky approached her delivery: "Worried about Korky and her baby. Last time there was a captive birth, baby was lost because it imprinted on mom's eye patch instead of her belly patch. She never learned to nurse. Hope this one is different. It's Korky's first calf. How will she know what to do?"

Then a few pages later: "What's it like for Korky, knowing her baby is coming, and not having her family around to help her? Hard to think about. I'll have everything I need when my baby comes."

Terra started gnawing on her braid as she read these last two entries. She'd *been* there! This was almost too much to believe. She'd been there as Korky approached her own birth. She'd grown in her mother's belly alongside Korky's growing calf. Practically feet away from one another. Their mothers listening to each other, watching each other. *It's no wonder I like drumming for them so much.*

Terra had to stop and look up into the dark of her mother's office, the ring of light from her head lamp coming to rest on the huge orca skull. A dizzy feeling came over her and a sense of whooshing; the world started to spin a little with her sudden sense of interconnection. *Maybe Joseph is right…Maybe there is something going on between me and the whales. Maybe it started before I was born.*

And then she'd read the two last entries:

"Korky gave birth yesterday. Had false labor a week ago. Tonight it finally happened. Calf...BEAUTIFUL. Bill was here, too. We watched together. Eerie experience we'll never forget. Our baby moved a lot while Korky was calling. She struggled with the labor. But she did it. She fell in love with the calf immediately, nuzzling it so gently. But there were no other whales to help,

(Storky sure as hell didn't know what to do), so she had to lift the calf right away so it could breathe. That was it. It was all over. The calf imprinted on her white eye patch, and from that moment on, she tried to nurse from her mother's eye. Heartbreaking. Was unable to nurse. Staff had to take the calf away from Korky, and they are now trying to feed it with a brew of other milks and vitamins. Very hard to watch."

Terra knew from their wild observations that mother whales get a lot of help from the family during birth. Other adults gather around and basically "catch" the new calf. They have to. Without their help, there would be no way for mom to teach her baby to nurse. The other adults carry the new calf to the surface to breath air for the first time and then guide it to the mother's mammary slit tucked inside the white patch on her belly; that's when the baby instantly imprints on the mother's white belly patch. With her family's help the mother is able to squirt the hot rich milk right into the calf's mouth. And from then on the calf knows exactly where to go for milk. Knowing that spot is life-or-death-critical to a baby whale living in the dark ocean. Terra could see, reading her mom's words, how easy it would be for a calf in a concrete pool—since there would be almost no help—to accidentally imprint on the mother's eye patch. *Ughhh*, her stomach clenched again. A mistake like that almost couldn't be avoided in a captive pool without family there to help.

Then, the final entry:

"I quit. Every day after calf's removal, Korky was constantly at the gate separating her from the baby. She called nonstop. Calf responding. I got it all on tape. The staff tried everything they could. But it didn't learn how to eat. A week after its birth, it died. Korky knew. She saw its removal. She spent that first day crashing against the gate, over and over. Then she started hanging below the water in front of the gift shop, which she can see from her pool. She stared for hours at the display of killer whale stuffed animals. She stopped vocalizing. Storky spent a lot of time by her side, nudging her and rubbing her. Nothing worked. Last night I needed a break. Went home to sleep and get away—feeling her grief. When I came in this morning, the pool was cracked and half the water gone, it was sluicing all over everything; even the gift shop was flooded. Everyone was crazy, trying to fix the pool and refill it before the whales were grounded. I stayed out of the way, but overheard one of the trainers explain what happened. Korky tried to get to those little stuffed animals because they made her think about her dead baby, and she crashed so hard against the tank that she cracked it."

"I can't be part of this anymore."

Whack! Terra threw everything she had into her whacks. She'd spelled out S-O-R-R-Y at least five or six times by now. And still no whales. *Granny, I need to tell you I understand.* That moment in her mom's office had changed everything. Korky's baby had died and *she* had lived! All because Korky's mother was in lockdown while her own mother was free. She knew instantly and without doubt that she was forever linked to Korky's loss with a responsibility—no, a *mission*—to make things right. She *had* to find Granny. There was suddenly nothing more important than apologizing and fixing this. *All* of this. Whatever Granny wanted her to do with the new calf and her trapped brother Tiluk…she was ready! The dream was real.

"I UNDERSTAND!!!" She shouted over the rush of waves.

In extreme frustration, she brought the oar up with a surge of adrenalin-driven force and slammed it down once more. Tears streamed down her face mixing with the salty slick of freezing spray that now glazed every part of her. She could hardly see through her frozen lashes.

But this time, her arms strained and exhausted, she misjudged her stroke. The wave caught her oar and pushed it backwards, wrenching her grip from the handle and catapulting it into Terra's face, crushing her nose. The blow knocked her out. Blood gushed down her chin, soaking the neck of her shirt and dripping onto her raincoat. Her body slumped over. The paddle floated away as her kayak listed into the hungry waves.

"BAWOOSH!"

"BAWOOSH!"

"BAWOOSH!"

All in a row, three orca surfaced nearby as if they'd been hanging below the surface listening. It was Granny, Eve, Wendy, and the rest of the pod. The calf clung close to her mother, uncertain. But the adults knew the taste of blood, and they knew what an oar meant for a human paddler. Terra was seriously injured and stranded in dangerous waters. Each of them felt a special affinity for this particular human, and so, as orca have done throughout history, they helped her.

BROTHERHOOD

MILES KEPT FIDGETING with his napkin. They were at the IHOP down the street from OceanLand and he could hardly believe he'd managed to convince his mom to come here without giving away the surprise. It was Saturday, so she was off work. *She was probably just so happy I asked her to do something with me, that I could've asked her to take us on a trip to Timbuktu and she would've said yes.* He would never have asked his mom anything like this in like a million years 'cause he was still so mad about everything—he'd rather crank out in his room with his z-phone and the Femmes for-freaking-ever, than ask her for anything unless it was to change history and zip their family back together again. *Like that would ever happen!*

"Miles, this is never going to change. Your father and I both love you, and that will always be true, but we don't love each other anymore."

Whatever. The way he figured it, if they could stop loving each other, then they could stop loving him and Aria, too.

He reined in his thoughts when his mom returned to their table with Doodle, who'd had to go "code two." He crossed his eyes at her and winked. He was ready to eat a mountain of pancakes.

"So sweetheart, what's going on? What did you want to talk about?" He could tell his mom was just, like, gaga over his request to talk to her about something important. She was practically gushing at him. That was a good sign. He needed her to say yes, though he was pretty sure he'd do it anyway, even if she said no. Hitchhiking would work just fine. And running away from home. He thought of Terra. Meeting her would make it all worthwhile.

"Well Mom," Miles started carefully. "You know how I had that bad nightmare about that whale killing that trainer?'"

"Oh I do, honey. Is it still keeping you up? I've been worried about you ever since it happened, but I haven't' really known what to do. Maybe I should call a counselor…" She trailed off. He could practically hear her having some angry thought about his dad along the lines of, *If your father were a better man we would still be together and we could figure this out and help you. But I don't even have time to think now; I'm so busy working so hard to make enough to keep the house, put food on the table, and get you two to school every day and yada yada yada.*

"Mom," he said loudly, cutting off her obvious line of thinking—and her gushing. "Chill. It's okay. I haven't had the nightmare since that first night," he fingered the cell phone in his pocket, getting ready.

"Oh Sweetheart, that's *wonderful!*" She reached over and took his hand, which he tolerated for exactly one nanosecond before sitting back, and pulling away. "What a good idea sweetie, coming here to celebrate!"

"MOM! Seriously, would you listen to me?" Miles' voice got loud enough that people turned and looked at him, and then at his mom and sister. His mom looked back at him, surprised. He probably hadn't said this many words in a row to her in, like, a whole year.

"There's a reason I'm not dreaming about Tiluk anymore," he said firmly, but his stomach did a flip-flop. He pressed the cell phone instant dial to

Maggie's cell. The signal she and Claire had been waiting for from the lobby of the restaurant. They would give him two minutes from now.

"I haven't dreamt about him, because I'm *with* him at night."

His mom put down her glass and began coughing. *Oh bloody helicopters.* She was coughing so hard she could hardly breathe. She was choking on her water, and tears were coming out of her eyes. Now the people across the table *really* had something to look at. *Great. Just great.*

Doodle looked alarmed. Their mom's face was getting red as she hacked away. He knew she was okay because she put her hand up at him, and shook her head no, like she was saying, "I'm okay, leave me alone for a minute."

He could tell she was embarrassed but also, like, *super* pissed: her eyes pierced him over the napkin she held to her mouth. *Oh great, here it comes,* he thought to himself.

Finally, taking in a long catching breath, his mom stared him down like the Sphinx deciding whether or not he could pass, or if, instead, she'd blow him to pieces.

"What on *Earth* are you talking about Miles?" her voice a raspy whisper that scared him with its intensity. He knew it was extra bad when she *didn't* use a pretend curse word.

"Don't be mad Mom, this is all really good. Just hear me out." Miles sat straight up and stared back at his mother, willing her to stay calm. She stared back menacingly, apparently deciding to wait before speaking again. Doodle had shrunk; she'd squirmed into the corner of their booth, trying to become invisible.

He took a deep breath. "See, I couldn't sleep, the dream was awful, so I got up and did research on killer whales. I had to figure out why that whale killed his trainer."

His mom rolled her eyes aggressively, and harrumphed, "Oh please Miles, they're *killer* whales. That's what they *do*! That trainer just did something she shouldn't have. Give me a freaking break! I'm so angry right now I can't see straight." Her mouth clenched and Miles could see the bones moving beneath her temples. "You better have something better than this. Thank *God* he didn't get you, too."

"Mom, *stop!*" he hissed at her, glancing around. "That's just it! They're

NOT killers. Not of people anyway. Wild killer whales have never attacked a human. The reason Tiluk killed his trainer is because of what happens to these whales when they're in captivity."

Doodle piped up bravely. "You mean Shantu, Miles."

His mom glanced down at Aria, remembering she was there. She wrapped an arm around her, and pulled her close.

"No Doodle. His real name is Tiluk. OceanLand calls a lot of their whales

'Shantu' so no one realizes when they die and a lot of them do, because living in a concrete pool when you're a 12-thousand-pound whale kind of *sucks*," he spit out. He glanced at his mom trying to get a read on her, then back at Doodle. "Tiluk was kidnapped from his mother and the rest of his family when he was only two years old. It'd be like if someone you didn't know came along and took you away from Mom and me and Dad, forever."

Aria cringed against their mom's side, her eyes wide. "Really Miles? How can they do that? How can they take babies away from their families?"

Miles watched his mom's face carefully. This was getting a little close to home for her. *I mean, it's not all that different from taking us away from one parent or the other, when we really need to be with* both *of them.*

"That's enough Miles; you're scaring your sister. I don't want to hear any more about this. You're not going back there. Whether or not he's a troubled whale because he lives at OceanLand, he still *killed* someone." Her voice went low and thick. "And there's no way you're going back there. Period." "Actually, Miles has been a huge help to our orca research program," Maggie said as she and Claire walked up to the table. Miles' mom looked up at the two strangers, bewildered.

Karen sat back, totally caught off guard by the appearance of two women she'd never seen before in her life. They stood next to the table, smiling down at her.

"Uh, Hi Mrs. Frost. We're from ExplOrca, a research team that studies wild orca. We know it's incredibly awkward to drop in on you like this but now that we know about Miles' OceanLand trip, and what he's managed to accomplish there," Claire glanced fondly at Miles, greeting him for the first time with open affection, "it seemed really important to come and talk to you."

Miles felt a surge of relief. Finally, someone who could explain every-thing to his mother. Maybe she'd actually listen to them.

"Could someone please tell me what's going on here?" Miles' mom snapped right before breakfast showed up. Claire and Maggie stood back while plates of pancakes, eggs, sausage, and bacon made their way around the table. Miles' mom fixed him with her eyes, accusingly, as if she were saying, *What in the world is this about?*

But she managed to choke down her confusion and buck up. *Go Mom*, thought Miles. "Please bring us two more cups of coffee?" Karen requested as the waiter finished up. With a nod he disappeared.

"Would you two care to sit down and tell me what's going on here?" She peered with suspicion at the two other women. "I'm at a total loss. And I'd really like to be brought into the loop," she shot Miles another reproachful look.

"That would be wonderful, if you don't mind too much," said Claire smiling gently.

Wow, that must be Terra's mom. Dude, she is like seriously beautiful. He couldn't help noticing both women's striking appearance. Claire was tall-ish and slender. But she looked powerhouse strong, like maybe she bench pressed the whales instead of studying them. Her face was so kind he had to fight the urge to ask her to sit next to him. But her hair. It was bone straight, caught in a simple long braid that hung nearly all the way down her back, a glowing luminous brown. And Maggie. He sucked in his breath as she pressed in next to him. *Miles these are mothers,* he reminded himself. *Mothers*!

But holy smokes, they were so pretty.

Miles pulled his breakfast over to the far edge of the table, squeezing him-self up into the corner, making way for Maggie and Claire.

"It's really very wonderful to meet you Miles," said Maggie, reaching out her hand to shake his. Her phenomenal dark cherry and hazelnut hair, a mop of curly squiggles pulled off her dark-skinned, lightly freckled face with a simple red bandana, made him swallow his tongue. He nodded at her and tried to smile.

Claire leaned over Maggie, sticking out her hand, too. "We can't thank you enough for what you've been up to," said Claire. "All of us at ExplOrca are just so grateful you got in touch with us in the first place. And we're still reeling from what happened the other night."

"Uh, hello over there," interrupted Miles' mom, tapping her fingers lightly on the table. "Still waiting here." Doodle caught his eye and raised her eye-brows at him with some glee. He winked at her. He could tell she was having a great time watching this "surprise" unfold. It was pretty hard to shock their mom about anything anymore. Right. He shook himself out of his Boy Meets Superwomen reverie, and started talking.

"Mom, I want you to meet Dr. Maggie Ravenwood and Dr. Claire Lewis."

The two women reached across and shook hands with Miles' mom, who graciously responded, stifling her anger. "Um, it's nice to meet you both, I guess? I'm Karen Frost, single parent, teacher, and extremely confused mother."

Miles saw them both smile kindly at his mom. He barreled on. "I found them while I was doing the Internet research I told you about on wild killer whales. They've been studying orca for like, 20 years or something. And they know Tiluk. They've been studying his family ever since he was taken from

Puget Sound in Washington."

"Actually," Claire explained, "Miles found my daughter Terra. She's the one who first heard from Miles when he wrote to her a few days ago about seeing Tiluk's killing and," she glanced over at Miles, clearing her throat, "...and about how he'd gone into OceanLand the night after the killing and played his xylophone for the whale."

"You did *WHAT*?" His mom's voice went thin and reedy, like she'd lost the lower registers. Her bass was gone, only the high pitches were left.

"Mom, you said you didn't want me listening to that 'violent' music any-more. I had to do *something*, and after I learned about that poor sorry whale, I had to go see him. I *had* to."

Miles slumped back against his seat, arms crossed in front of his chest, as if to say, "If you don't get me, then too bad for you."

"But Miles it's a killer whale. A *killer* whale! You took your life in your hands without even *telling* me first!"

"I didn't though mom. Seriously. I never even got close to him. I kept like fifty feet away from his pool. I stayed totally safe. Believe me, I didn't want to end up like that Dusky Dey lady. Give me some freaking credit..." Now it was Miles' turn to trail off.

His mom relaxed at this. "Well I guess *that's* reassuring. But what on Earth did you think you could do once you got in there? I mean you're 14 years old, and he's a whale, Miles. A *whale*!"

Cripe, this was tedious. He hadn't had a conversation this long with his mom since he was like 10 years old and she actually had time for talking.

"I played for him," he said, sulking. He bent over his plate and shoveled in the rest of his pancakes.

"The thing is, Karen" said Claire, wrapping her slender fingers around the steaming coffee mug in front of her, "Tiluk sang back."

Karen's eyes widened. "Excuse me?"

"Mom, if you would ever stop and listen to me, this is what I've been trying to tell you." His head still down, his face shadowed, Miles shot his words across the table like darts. There was so much more to this conversation than a flippin' whale.

He looked up at her finally, his voice thick. "I played Dueling Banjos for him, and he sang the song back to me."

"Oh," she said softly, understanding finally dawning. "Oh."

Doodle looked at him in rapture, her pancakes totally forgotten. "The whale sang for you Miles?" she whispered.

At least his sister could get it. "Yeah Doodle, he did. It was unbelievable. Not only that, he sang *with* me."

Doodle's jaw dropped.

He swallowed...might as well get this part over with. He looked at his mom, his eyes flashing defiance, and said, "And I'm flying up there with

Maggie and Claire to make sure his family can hear him singing again. The night before last, I got him on tape, and they need to hear him.

"Let's not rush this Miles," Maggie jumped in. She looked at Karen, "One thing at a time."

Karen took her opportunity, totally ignoring what Miles had just said.

"First of all," she softened for the first time looking at Miles but her words were still strong, "Miles, you are in serious trouble for doing what you did.

We'll have to talk about consequences later. I can't begin to *think* about what those could be. I might even have to consult your father about this. You are never, *ever* to do something like that again. You could have been killed. You're lucky OceanLand didn't catch you and press charges. *Big* trouble young man." His mom pinned him with her stare like he was a bug.

Miles sighed and nodded, slumping in his seat. His mom's reason had returned. He bit into his bacon. *Bacon makes everything better*, he thought.

"Second of all," she looked first at Maggie and Claire, then back to Miles.

"You've obviously done something quite important—*and you're still in big trouble for it*—but I'm willing to give you credit where credit is due."

She looked at the two other mothers, "I'd like you two to tell me the details of what happened and why you are here in Orlando. We're a long way from Puget Sound. Obviously, you wouldn't be here talking to me if this wasn't a big deal."

Miles breathing grew shallow. *Maybe she was finally paying attention. Maybe she could hear this out. Maybe he could go!* He looked at Doodle, who grinned mischievously and leaning backwards so she was in her mother's blind spot, she put her hands together like she was praying, her cherubic eyes sidling sideways towards their mom. Miles knew she felt the same flicker of hope that had just sprang to life in his belly. He could feel Maggie stifling a smile beside him when she saw Aria's antics.

The two researchers spent the next few minutes filling Karen in on what had happened: Miles' idea for the live feed, how Wendy and her family recognized Tiluk's voice and vice-versa, how mother and son had sung to one another, and how the whole thing had ended with the two whales turning themselves into battering rams. Miles watched poor Aria's eyes fill as she listened. By this time their mom had nearly forgotten she was sitting there.

"You mean to tell me that Miles helped a whale who hadn't heard or seen his family for 14 years make a phone call to them?" Karen asked, the anger in her voice still simmering.

"That's exactly what he did," said Claire. "And that 'phone call' is the reason we're here now in Orlando." Claire got quiet even though every-one could tell she still wanted to say something. "That phone call your son helped to make was one of the most moving things I've ever witnessed in all my life. I'll never forget it," she said, her voice thick with emotion. "And we just couldn't have done it without Miles."

Karen looked at Miles, plainly taken aback. "You make it sound like Miles was instrumental in restoring hope in a war zone. Surely it's not so bad for these whales. I take the kids to OceanLand a lot, and we love the Shantu show. The whales always look happy and do all kinds of amazing tricks.

They wouldn't be cooperating so well, if they were as unhappy as you make them out to be."

"Unfortunately, that belief is a widespread mistake and it's perpetuated by OceanLand itself," said Maggie, taking over from

Claire. "These whales are among the most social animals on Earth; they work with humans because there's no other choice. OceanLand capitalizes on that intense sociality, and they make huge profits from it. But," she stared pointedly at Karen, "make no mistake, those whales bond with their trainers because they are desperate for the families they lost. Trapped in those pools, it's the only thing they can do."

Miles cleared his throat, reminding everyone that he and Aria were still there.

"The point is," Maggie said, keeping them focused, "What happened on that phone call two nights ago is what brought us down here to Orlando.

Our research team put together a scientific proposal to retire Tiluk to his wild home, to his family. We presented the proposal to OceanLand officials just before we came here to meet you."

Karen's eyes widened as she nodded almost imperceptibly. "Okay, I get it. I understand this is a big deal. For you...and for the whales. But," she narrowed her eyes and glared at Miles, "this is also a big deal for me as Miles' mother. I'm incredibly angry about this. I can't believe Miles did what he did without informing me, and I have to say, you two must be good people and respected researchers, but I'm pretty damned pissed off that you'd let my son do what he did without my permission."

Claire nodded and sighed. "I completely understand Karen, and you have every right to be angry. I almost didn't let him go through with it.

About a thousand times that day I came this close to shutting the whole thing down." She was staring down into her coffee, swirling her mug. But then she lifted her gaze to meet Karen's and Miles saw tears in her eyes.

"The only excuse I have for you is that we've waited our entire professional lives for an opportunity like this, a chance to prove—and literally get hard evidence for—the whales' severe emotional distress at being held captive, away from their families. Miles gave us that chance, and I'm truly sorry my own hopes for the live feed got in the way of our being totally honest with you from the beginning." She wiped the corner of one eye. "The whales are our family, too."

Karen just stared at Claire for a long moment, her food forgotten. Then

Miles watched his mom do something he never expected. She reached over to Claire, took her hand, squeezed hard, and said, "Claire, if all of us could be as good at apologizing as you are, the world would be a different place."

She took a shaky breath, visibly moved. "Thank you for telling me that. I understand what happened a lot better now."

She smiled a little. "I'm even starting to think that maybe you all are one the best things that's happened to Miles in quite some time." Karen looked at her son, "Things have not been easy for him lately."

Who is this woman and what did she do with my mother? Miles fidgeted with his napkin, uncertain about what had just happened, and asked, "So what about OceanLand this morning?" The last thing he needed was his mom going all gooey on him, but she did seem more agreeable, so maybe now was his chance. He looked at Doodle who crossed her eyes at him. She sensed things lightening up, too.

"Good question Miles," Maggie said. "First thing this morning we made a presentation on behalf of ExplOrca, left the paperwork with the head honchos, and told them we're taking legal action. Tiluk is the only captive whale from the endangered Southern Resident orca community who is still alive. All the other Southern Residents who were captured in the past have died in captivity...much younger than they would have died in the wild. Our proposal will also go to NOAA and the National Marine Fisheries and basically make the case that, because of what we now know about his mental and physical state, not to mention his capabilities, Tiluk's captivity is in total opposition to the Marine Mammal Protection Act *and* the Endangered Species Act...and that OceanLand is therefore holding him illegally." She paused, and turned to look at Miles. "We'll be including the recording of the reunion Miles helped set up ...you can't hear that and not realize that Tiluk is devastated by the absence of his family."

Karen nodded thoughtfully. "And Miles wants to go up there with you and help."

So she had *heard him!* Miles' belly flamed up again in a mixture of anxiety and anticipation.

Claire turned to smile warmly at Miles then looked back at his mom. "He and Terra have a lot in common. Both of them are doers. They've seen the injustice here, and they are both taking some strong actions. Miles with his xylophone and his 'phone call,' and Terra, well," Claire shook her head, her face soft with fondness and admiration. "Terra's already managed to get ExplOrca in touch with Jane Goodall and Janet Carson, the head of NOAA."

Then she looked at Karen seriously. "Bringing Miles up to Blackfish Cove for a week right now would give us a huge boon. Imagine the press this proposal would get if people realized that a young boy who'd witnessed

Tiluk's killing was working hard to reunite him with his family, or, at the very least, retire him."

Miles' eyes got big and his jaw fell open. He'd never even thought about this. *Wow,* he breathed to himself, *Claire's so totally right! I could so totally help Tiluk! And it might even work!* He looked across the table at Doodle, who was just sitting there gaping. She still hadn't touched her pancakes; she was so spellbound it was as if her whole collection of stuffties had come to life right in front of her and had spent the last few minutes dancing on the table.

"And speaking of Terra, I almost forgot," Claire spoke again as Karen, still silent, contemplated all she'd just heard. "I can see how close you are to your sister, Miles," she said, turning towards Miles as she reached into her pocket. "Terra asked me to bring you this. She made it."

She pulled the carving of the baby whale from her pocket and held it up, then reached across Maggie and placed it into Miles' hands. He cradled her gently, as if he held a baby bunny rabbit, and stroked the darkened, burnished wood. "That's a carving Terra made of the new calf. The calf Wendy gave birth to on the same day Tiluk killed his trainer," Claire said quietly. "It's his sister. None of us ever thought he'd ever have the chance to meet her."

Karen's eyes went wide and she covered her mouth with both hands. "Now, thanks to you, maybe he will."

VIGIL

THE MOMENT CLAIRE STEPPED past security and locked eyes with Joseph, she fell apart. They'd gotten the call in Orlando while the plane was still on the tarmac. Miles had been sitting between the two women—about as giddy and excited as a squirrel on steroids—and he'd been telling Claire and Maggie about Tiluk's "joy dance." He was so animated as he described his xylophone, the Ode to Joy, and the way Tiluk kept breaching, that the people in front of them had turned around, smiling, and started listening to his story, wide-eyed. Everyone loves a good airplane moment.

His mom had decided to let him go…he was pretty sure it was the whale carving that had done it. And the way she'd seen him fight back tears when

Claire had said that maybe—because of him—Tiluk might meet his sister. That carving had gone into the pocket of his hoodie and he hadn't let go of it since. Except for when he'd hugged Aria goodbye, he'd let her hold it, and she'd said,

"Miles, try as hard as you can. They need each other." She squeezed him super tight. "I'll miss you, but I'm glad you are going to help them."

He felt so sure he could help, too. As he told about the "joy dance," it seemed like everything was finally starting to go right. It was the first time in ages that he felt so enthused and confident. *And* he was going to meet Terra, this girl he felt like he already knew. But then, as the last passengers filed past to the back of the plane, Maggie's cell had rung, and she'd gone absolutely white as she'd listened.

"Claire, there's been an accident," she said, clipping her phone shut, and standing to switch seats with Miles, then leaning in to her friend, her voice hushed and urgent. "I'm not sure what happened… something about Terra rowing out onto the Strait, alone. She's had a head injury and she's hypothermic." Maggie gripped both of Claire's hands. "Honey, she's in a coma. Joseph's going to meet us and take us right to the hospital."

It was like the lights went out. Claire went totally dark. Miles could feel it.

The whole plane felt different. She couldn't speak, she just let Maggie clutch her hands and stared. "Breathe honey," Maggie said. "Breathe. She's going to be okay. We're on our way."

Then Claire had gone somewhere else. Neither Miles or Maggie could reach her, she just sat immobile and silent the entire flight. Except that half-way through the flight Miles heard her say one thing: "I didn't say goodbye," and he saw her knuckles, white, tightly gripping the armrests on either side of her. And Miles? He'd just zippered the whole thing off. Like he had to do all the time now because of the divorce. He managed by pushing it all away.

Now, after de-planing in Seattle and getting past the security gates to where Joseph stood waiting with his son, she stopped dead, her bags slid to the floor, and she stared at him, white-faced and frozen. She couldn't move. Or breathe.

Then Joseph moved to catch her, his arms pulling her against him, and she began shaking, her silent sobs eerie. Maggie stood back as her husband ministered to her dearest friend. She needed him now. Tiluk and Miles found each other, and held a respectful silence together as they watched Claire's shock open enough to let her begin to confront what had befallen her daughter.

Her knees buckled and Joseph gripped her, gently coming down to the floor with her, right there by security with dozens of people swirling and walking past them. Some slowed to watch, their eyes filled with empathy, while others moved past as if nothing was happening. Maggie put her arms around Miles and Tiluk, and pulled them close in front of her. Joseph just stayed with it, swaddling Claire against him as if she were a colicky baby, riding out her uncontrolled spasms, her silence finally breaking open with huge wracked inhalations.

Tiluk moved closer to Miles, let their shoulders touch. A silent acknowledgement. "So you're the one who's got our whale's back," he said under his breath.

Miles took in Tiluk's long shining black hair, the way it cascaded around his face and shoulders. "And you're the one who's got Terra's." He leaned even closer to Tiluk. "How bad is she?" he whispered.

Tiluk looked back at him and Miles noticed a depth to those black eyes he'd never seen before.

"Hush you two." Maggie pulled them against her, "We'll find out soon enough."

Joseph met Maggie's eyes. "Let's get her to the car. She needs to see her daughter."

Claire was still buried in Joseph's embrace, her eyes pressed tight into the crook of his neck, her arms locked around his back, her knees pulled up under her own chin like she was a little girl. Joseph cupped her face, pulling her out of herself. "Claire, I want you to stand up now. We're taking you to Terra."

Another spasm shook her, and suddenly her tear-streaked face lit with comprehension. "Where's the car!?" she cried, and she was on her feet so fast that she knocked Joseph over backwards. Tiluk and Miles, as if with one mind, stepped in and offered their hands to Joseph, who stood, his eyes giving them each a silent thanks, his eyes giving Miles a special crinkle of warmth, their first greeting. Maggie stepped in and locked arms with Claire,

"Come on honey, Joe's got it right outside."

Joseph put his arm around Claire's other side, and he guided the five of them through the airport. And somehow, taking those steps with Maggie and Joseph supporting her through the chaos of SeaTac, Claire began to come back to herself.

In the car the steel of her voice overrode her usual gentleness. "Tell me everything." She glanced over at Joseph as he pulled out of the parking garage, "I need to understand."

"We still aren't sure what Terra was doing out there," he began cautiously, concerned about how much Claire could actually bear to hear, "but because of the nature of her injury, we're pretty sure she paddled out into the Strait.

Whatever was going on, she'd been out a long time. Her body temperature had dropped, too." He kept his left hand on the wheel and reached over to Claire, trying to get a read on her. "It looks like her oar must've gotten wrenched by a wave, and slammed back up into her face. There aren't waves that strong in the cove. For some reason she decided she needed to go out on the Strait…in the middle of the night."

"But she's forbidden from going out there alone," Claire's voice went black as she fought the choice her daughter had made. "She *couldn't* have done that." Joseph squeezed her shoulder, looked at her briefly, then put both hands back to the steering wheel in Seattle's heavy traffic. "What was she thinking?" Claire croaked. Her right knuckles went into her mouth, and she bit down, hard.

He sighed heavily, "The doctors think it's just a light coma and that she'll come out of it soon, but we won't know for sure until she wakes up."

Miles noticed he said "until" and felt a thick drape of darkness fill his mind. She *had* to wake up. He glanced at Tiluk, determination on his face. He'd just found this girl, he sure as hell wasn't going to be saying goodbye to her before he could say freaking *hello*.

Claire's head fell forward, her hands fisted like baseballs tight into her eye sockets. Maggie reached forward and squeezed Claire's shoulder from the backseat. "Don't keep beating yourself up, honey. She's going to be okay. How could we know she'd do something like this?"

Claire turned in her seat, looking forcefully at Tiluk. "Tell me exactly what happened this morning."

Tiluk leaned forward, closer to Claire from the back seat where he was wedged between Miles and his mom. "When I woke up I went over to Terra's yurt to wake her up."

Miles had no idea what a yurt was, but he kept quiet. He had his hands shoved into his hoodie pockets, gripping the whale, reminding himself why he was here. His cheeks had grown warm with envy, seeing the great trust Claire held for Tiluk. His mom never looked at him like that, and Claire wasn't even Tiluk's mom! *What the heck is a yurt, anyway? And who the heck **were** these people?* They were like that Little House on the Prairie family—the freaking Ingalls, which he'd seen in its G-rated entirety on Netflix. Aria *adored* that Laura Pipsqueak girl. And *Pa*. And *Ma*. People like that don't exist anymore. Do they? His dad's voice suddenly boomed in his mind, "A *what*? What the hell is a *yurt*? A regular house isn't good enough for them?" He could imagine his dad snorting with derision. Miles breathed against the contempt he'd learned at home, and forced himself to keep listening to Tiluk.

"Usually she's awake before me, calling on the two-way to wake *me* up. So

I figured she'd just overslept since she hadn't slept much the night before."

He looked down at his lap, hesitant. "But she wasn't there. Her bed hadn't even been slept in. But the whales were really churned up, the hydrophone was on and all I heard were tail slaps, over and over again."

Tiluk swallowed. "Claire, the slaps were code."

It was obvious that Claire could no longer speak, but Maggie whispered, "What did they say?"

Tiluk met Claire's eyes in the mirror. "They said 'Very bad.'" He grimaced. "I knew right away it was Terra so I got Bill and dad as fast as I could, and we all ran down there, and there she was

Miles got the distinct sense that this was more talking than Tiluk had done in the last year, so he wasn't surprised when Joseph stepped in. "She was out in the middle of the cove in her kayak, unconscious in her boat, surrounded by Granny, Eve, Wendy and the calf." He looked over at Claire again, "I've never seen anything like it, Claire. It was like they'd been waiting for us. As soon as they saw us, they made a life raft around her and brought her right to us at the dock." He checked the rearview mirror, catching Tiluk's eye, then over at Claire again. "Seeing them surround her so quickly, like they were teammates taking position around their boat? Those whales brought Terra in from the Strait after her accident." He reached over and wiped Claire's wet cheek with his thumb. "Claire, the whales saved Terra's life."

He pulled into the parking lot at the hospital and stopped briefly at the Visitors Entrance. Claire was out of the car before he even pulled to a stop. "Room number?" she called out over her shoulder as she ran, and Joseph yelled, "304" at Claire's back.

That was the worst moment for Miles, he felt like a total trespasser. *What the heck I am doing here?* he was thinking as he watched Claire's mother-bear energy carry her at a dead run into the hospital, nearly crashing through the sliding glass doors that didn't open fast enough for her. He found himself wondering whether his own mother would run so fast.

Maggie looked over at him like she'd read his mind. "Miles, we want you here. It's not how we expected things to go, but it's the way things went. And regardless, we are really glad you came and that your mom trusted us to bring you out here. Please don't worry anymore." She took a deep breath, "After what you did for Tiluk," and he knew she wasn't talking about her son but the whale, "you're one of us now." Her eyes filled with tears. "You two boys..." she said, then stopped, unable to finish.

"Come," said Joseph as he parked, and they headed for room 304.

The room was warm when they filed in, silent. There was a constant hum of medical machines, the blip of Terra's heart rate traveled across a screen in limelight green, the drone of the heater set on high to bring her body temperature back to normal, the monitor scanning for brain waves.

Claire had disappeared again. She was sitting by her daughter's side, holding her hand, 100 percent unaware of anyone else in the room. Bill, exhausted and unshaven, stood in greeting. His tired eyes found Maggie's and he began to crumple. She walked into his arms, and they held each other. Miles stood with Tiluk once again, in silent respect. Bill's shoulders shook silently for a moment, as if he could let just a tiny bit of his worry out for his friend to help him carry. Then he pulled back and looked at Maggie, "I don't know what the hell she was thinking."

Maggie put her palms flat on either side of his face, solemnly meeting his eyes, and said firmly, "We're going to find out as soon as she wakes up."

She kept her hands on his cheeks, and stayed locked into his stare with a fierceness Miles hardly recognized. *What is that?* he wondered. The word "solidarity" came to him, but he didn't really know what that was, other than hearing the word during those boring history lessons at school about the suffragettes rallying for the vote and blacks for civil rights…something about standing together. *Whatever.* He couldn't stop looking at Terra, she looked…dead.

Her body lay limp and small beneath the hospital-green bedspread covering her, and the little bit of skin he could see was the color of elephant tusks, ivory and hard with no depth or life. Her face was almost totally hidden beneath a metal nose frame meant to help shield and mend her broken nose. Tape stretched across her cheeks and up her forehead. Her eyes were frozen shut.

Shit. Miles heard himself say inside his own head. His breathing went shallow and his own heart started racing. *Shit.* He felt dizzy and unconsciously leaned against Tiluk.

Bill looked at him then, and Tiluk moved even closer to Miles, giving him wordless support. Bill nodded at Miles, and Miles dipped his head in reply, trying to express all his hope and concern in one silent gesture of empathy and greeting. Then Tiluk drew him close to Terra, on the opposite side of Claire, and they stood for a moment, the IV machine so close that Miles could hear the drip. Joseph came up behind them and stood with them for a long while. Silent. Finally, he took the boys over to the couch under the window, and they sat. And sat. All of them, Claire, Maggie, Joseph, Bill, Miles, and Tiluk dripped sweat with the heat of the room but none seemed to notice, or care. Terra's skin, however stayed dry as a sunbaked bone.

Every half hour or so, a nurse would come in and check Terra's vitals: her body temperature and heart rate. Then scribble something on a chart hanging by her bed and leave again. The quick, efficient sounds of the nurse overrode the room's whirring and it was as if the group came up for air every time one appeared. Everyone but Claire would look from one to another, checking to see they remained clustered nearby one another in these dark waters, then, when the nurse left, they'd submerge again into the whirring.

Once a doctor came, and the adults—even Claire, who had to be drag-led— stepped outside with her, leaving the two boys alone with Terra.

Tiluk spoke. "She's going to be okay." "How do you know that?" Miles asked him.

"My dad asked the elders to see our shaman. The signs are good." *Shaman? Elders?* Suddenly a thousand questions jammed in Miles' throat, but the door opened and Claire walked back in with new purpose, tall and direct. She looked at Miles and Tiluk as the others followed her in.

"Help me."

She stood at Terra's bedside and showed them what to do. They pulled her covers back, and both put their arms carefully underneath her, then heaved her over gently towards them, carefully, just a little bit, so there was more room on the bed.

"Thank you," Claire said to them as she eased herself up into the bed next to her daughter, stretching herself long, cradling her body around Terra's like a cat with a kitten.

"The doctor seemed to think it would be a good idea for Terra to have some human body heat next to her now that she's stabilized," Maggie explained. "She thinks Terra's been in a kind of torpor after being so cold for so long, and she wants to try this and see if it helps wakes her up."

Tiluk asked what Miles wanted to, "Is her brain okay? Does it look like she *can* wake up?"

Maggie joined the boys and hugged them to her once again. "The doctor thinks it looks pretty good. But we won't know for sure until she wakes up."

Just then the door opened a crack and Gwen's head appeared, peeking in respectfully. "I made sandwiches for you all, just in case you decide you're hungry." Miles glanced at the clock. It was already 10:30 p.m.—which made it 1:30 a.m. Florida time—and he wasn't even close to tired. *Was I really at IHOP this morning?* "How's she doing?" Gwen asked.

In a flash, Claire's head swiveled towards the door, not disturbing her daughter in the slightest. "Gwen, it's good to see you. Come in. Both of you." Gwen and Jason tiptoed in carrying a picnic basket. It was as if Claire had walked through some valley of darkness and returned. Her voice was quiet with strength. "The doctor thinks it was a good thing she got so cold for as long as she did. She says that sometimes that sort of cold-spell can stave off the worst problems with concussion. She's pretty sure this is just a light coma, and she could wake up at any time."

"Oh Claire, thank God," said Gwen, her voice wavering. "I've been so worried." She looked at Jason. "And Jason, too. He almost drove me nuts pacing the house all day. Neither of us could work or concentrate on any-thing. I finally had to send him out to split wood while I made these."

Jason looked sheepish, then started passing sandwiches around. Miles suddenly felt ravenous. Apparently everyone else did, too. They fell into the sandwiches without speaking. Everyone but Claire, who ate nothing. The smell of PB&Js floated across the room, the essence of comfort, and Miles was surprised that he had never realized once in his whole life that jelly could taste like hope.

As they finished up, Joseph quietly filled them in on the rest of the details from the doctor, and they listened gravely. Gwen was clearly having a hard time keeping her tears in check. Finally, Tiluk broke in. "What's going on with the whales?"

Gwen looked at Tiluk as if he'd hit a nerve, her head jerking towards him. "Uh, yeah, I almost forgot about that," she looked back at Terra. "I've been so worried about her." Her voice trailed off.

"Gwen?" Tiluk asked again, curious now. "The whales?"

Jason finally spoke. "We were around the house all day, so we kept an eye on them. We thought that once you guys found Terra this morning, that they'd leave to go forage like they always do. But they didn't."

"It was pretty weird. The whole pod stayed in the cove all morning, even though that's prime foraging time," Jason said. "Then, around lunchtime— right after I remembered Fierce and went out to feed him, half the pod was gone. Big Jake, Bountiful, and Eve had left, while Granny, Wendy and the calf stayed behind with the rest of the pod."

Miles rubbed the whale carving in his pocket as he listened. The calf. "Claire," Gwen looked at her friend and mentor, "I think Granny sent them out to forage. I saw them return this afternoon, and it looked like there was food sharing going on…they brought back fish. I've almost never see the pod split up like that."

Joseph cleared his throat. "They are holding vigil for Terra."

Everyone stared at Joseph and the whirring room spun down to silence.

He went on, "Our elders have told that in the ancient times some Blackfish had special bonds with certain tribe members. Those connections were real, but in today's world almost all of us have forgotten. And we know from the stories that sometimes whale families would stand by their human friends in difficult times." He looked around the room, "Just as Granny's pod is doing now."

His eyes came to rest on Claire, and he spoke to her directly. "They will stay in the cove until Terra comes home." He looked around the room. "Up until now they haven't trusted humans enough to let on so much." He shuddered. "But up until now, they've had lots of reasons not to."

Gwen gasped. "Joseph, that reminds me." She dug down into her large leather bag and pulled out Claire's diary. "I found this on the floor of your office today," handing it to Claire. "It struck me as odd, since your journal shelves are usually shut. But they were wide open and this was on the floor…"

She asked the question everyone in the room was suddenly wondering. "Maybe Terra found it last night, and that's what sent her out into the Strait?"

Claire sat up in bed next to Terra and began flipping through the journal, her face draining of color. "I wonder which entry it was…" Her voice went thin. "Oh no…." She shut her eyes tight, her face contorted in pain as she gripped the journal to her chest.

"I already I know."

CONTACT

WHEN TERRA LEFT HER BODY she slipped into a current of electric joy, letting it lift her up and away. She knew this feeling. It was like before, only *much* better. The brilliant fizzy effervescence was like sunlight streaming bliss. She could see the hospital room and all four of her parents, and Tiluk, and even Miles, whose dampened spirit she recognized immediately, as if she already knew him. All of them, and the walls, and the equipment, and her bed, and her sheets, shimmered with an undercurrent of intense vibrating energy suddenly made visible to her. It was everywhere, linking everything. It *was* everything. How could they be asleep to this joy?

None of them saw her; they were all looking down, gathered around the bed where her body lay. Wait, Joseph. He looked up. He looked at her. He *saw* her. He knew. And there was someone else, someone who also saw her. Someone dark and glistening and strong. Freedom swept through her like wind, lofting her up and away from the room, spinning her out the closed window and above Seattle, a still-glistening butterfly on her first flight. She danced across the sky, tumbling through the rippling energy; it connected her to everything. She *was* the energy. How could she not have known this before? This unity? This joy?

Her heart swelled to contain the bursting radiance she suddenly under-stood, it opened and opened, unfurling to let in all this golden brilliance. She was her heart, she was everything. She was spinning; spinning and spinning in complete rapturous abandon, the joy sweeping her up in a spiral dance. Love took her like an ocean reclaiming a raindrop, erasing every hurt and doubt she'd ever had.

She saw the Space Needle: it glittered, glowing a deep, warm light. And the rest of the city shone like burnished platinum. But at the same time, it all looked different. She was "seeing" not with her eyes but with something much more ancient. It was Seattle but it was the fluid energetic soul of Seattle she saw through her own specific lens of individuality. What she saw was tempered by who she'd become. Terra's perception had shot outwards in its web of connection, suddenly freed from the physical constraints of her body. What she observed as *beyond* herself was wholly linked to her own capacity to "see." And so she was seeing Seattle not as a physical place but as energy.

Energy coursing like blood through veins. Energy that had a story, a history, a link to the past, to the future, and to everything else on Earth.

Terra's spirit-mind stretched with this freedom, entering the river of energy, letting itself be transported across a great swath of the immense grid she'd tapped. In a split-second eternity, she tumbled across the sky above

Seattle losing herself to the unifying field; the urge to join, undeniable. But the power of her individual intent was likewise fierce. There were specific things she needed to do. She called herself back, the voice of her own making a unique twinkling star of sentient intelligence in the vastness of space.

"Granny! Granny! Where are you? I'm here!" Terra called with her spirit-mind, making the glimmering web around her quiver as if she'd taken hold of it and shook it. The radiant threads shuddered with directionality and Terra was both pulled and guided instantaneously, at high unearthly speed. It was less like traveling fast than it was a sense of staying still while everything else raced by. Her call had localized in Granny's mind, arousing their bond, and the magnetic link swept Terra's perception towards Blackfish Cove.

And suddenly they were together, Granny and Terra. But this was nothing like before. When she'd met Granny in her dream, the whale had been quiet, simply staring at her, conveying through her eyes with her deep soul-penetrating regard all Terra needed to know about her special connection to the unborn calf and the calf's brother. Granny had been regal and Terra had been humbled, privileged to be summoned. And she'd thought it was only a dream, doubting its reality for so long.

But now...*now*! This was no dream! This was more real than life! The radiance of their connection consumed them like flame, fiery ripples spreading outwards, illuminating the entire Cove and bathing it in flashing pulses of orange yellow light. With it, Terra suddenly understood the significance of this moment: their intense, collaborative willpower had brought them together. Their bond, its purpose, was blinding. This was more real than any-thing else she'd ever known. Even their communication was more real—an ancient spirit-mind connection that relayed thoughts and images and emotions, giving each the other's true experience.

"Greetings whale dreamer," Granny's own rising joy swept through Terra with her welcome. She felt the great whale's magnificent force—her vast memory banks and history and wisdom—as their two perceptions merged in union. In those first moments, Terra, though consumed by the brilliant flash of their bond, sensed the whale's twinge of wonderment. She sensed Granny's surprise. In that moment she understood that her dream, the dream so different than this, had been orchestrated by Granny. The whale, in a time of great need, had used her spirit-strength and dream capacity to bring Terra into her dream world. But this. This was different. Terra was here on her own terms, under her own directive and willpower. Terra could feel Granny marveling.

"Greetings ancient mother," Terra offered in return. And instead of humility like before, she was filled with ecstatic unity, the joy of their connection.

In an instant of mutual understanding—of perceiving their common ambitions—Granny became a partner, a revered matriarch with whom she could work to fulfill their joint mission. She suddenly understood that all those years of hearing the whales through her hydrophone had primed her for this; that her brain had, in fact, been altered. She had been tuned to hear

Granny's far-ranging frequencies, and her heart filled with appreciation for her parents and their hopeful foresight. Granny grasped Terra's insight and her feelings. She moved closer, holding Terra's flighty perception with gentle firmness, like Terra so often held Fierce.

"You are close, young one, but there is more. You must acknowledge your own power. Although they have helped, you never needed our songs or your parent's hydrophones. *It is your own drive to connect that attunes you to us.*" Terra sensed Granny's wonderment once again, and with it came the whale's astonishment at Terra's unexpected appearance.

"It is what makes you a whale dreamer, the first for us in thousands of moons." Terra felt

Granny's hope and shuddering relief as if they were her own. "Until this moment, I did not know that a whale dreamer once again walks the land." Love and tenderness enveloped her as Granny's gratitude swept through her, expanding her twinkling light of perception for an instant across space and time. With its flash, Terra knew peace.

"That it is you, Terra, makes all things possible. The prophecy is true after all." Something deep inside her clicked. Yes. Whale dreamer. As if she already knew. But she was uncertain. What did that mean?

Granny sensed Terra's wonder. "The whale dreamers were once very common and came to us, and to *all* the whales of the Earth, throughout the Great Ages Past…before the Great Sadness." Granny's experience of The Great Sadness spilled through Terra, and her light dimmed with understanding.

"The Great Sadness….it is why I am here now," Terra realized.

Granny flickered agreement, but still Terra felt her surprise and with their intermingled spirits, she understood it. It was as if this magnificent being, through sheer force of will, had staved off her own and the pod's hopelessness at the kidnappings, the loss of Tiluk, the dwindling salmon, the starvation, the diseases, the oil spills, the warming waters of Salish Sea, the pollutants and their cancers. And now, with Terra's arrival, Granny's world changed in the dazzling flash of their bond. Hope. Relief. Something about a prophecy.

Terra felt resolve wash through her. The whales really *did* need her, they needed her dreaming. Especially now. "But Granny, why did the whale dreamers vanish during the Great Sadness? Why would they leave when the whales needed them the most?"

Granny's light dimmed. Quiet for a moment, she responded, "The Great

Sadness belongs first to the people and The Fallacy. In their grief and repression and denial, most have forgotten to be dreamers." Granny shuddered slightly, as if caught by a deeper unpleasant insight. Then she turned to Terra, who felt resolve once again, but this time it was Granny's. It was as if, with Terra's question, she suddenly understood what she must do.

"Come, young whale dreamer. There is no time to waste. You

shall soon see." And suddenly they were flying. The spirits of whale and human soaring together across the immense golden grid of space-time, Granny's life-force holding Terra's close…the whale a seasoned traveler of this place. Terra felt extreme velocity with no force.

And then they arrived. Wait. WAIT. Terra tried to flee. To pull away from Granny. But the whale held her close. "You must know, whale dreamer. You must understand."

She'd felt the joy, the unity. They seemed everywhere at first. But this place. It was blocked from the grid of light by pain. And terror. And a con-fused overwhelming mixture of desperation and despair. The light here was severe, it scratched across her spirit from every direction, beating her with its harsh insistence. Hot. Inescapable. And he was there, waiting for her. *Tulku*. His true name, *Tulku*. Not Tiluk. The name he carried across many lifetimes.

Tulku. All this she knew in an instant. And she shrank before his extreme power, his splendor. His complexity and pain and grandeur.

"I did not mean to kill her," his spirit entered her awareness like a sharp blade. She felt his remorse cut her.

"I loved her."

No, it wasn't remorse. It was potent awareness. "My third sister arrived that day. I dreamed of her birth. But I could not be there." Terra sensed the outrage and grief that had poured through him that day, the day Dusky got too close. "Three sisters I have missed. And this sister. This one. My earth-mind went crazy. I could not stop." He grew quiet for a moment, and Terra saw a flash of Dusky Dey in his spirit.

"I loved her." Tulku's spirit reached for Terra's and she held back, cowering against Granny's gentle wisdom. Granny, Tulku's great grandmother.

"Go to him, young whale dreamer. He is safe here. He is not earth-bound in this place. Let him teach you. He cannot harm you."

He waited, not coming closer. "I loved her, and I knew she loved me. She believed all was well for me and for the other whales." Terra stayed with Granny, still uncertain.

"I loved her in her innocence." Terra felt herself being pulled towards Tulku, felt herself start to relax into his tremendous wisdom. "I killed her in my earth-bound anguish. My earth-mind snapped…as it had before." His spirit swirled hot with this difficult truth, and Terra sensed him, gripped by his own earthly weakness, venting his accountability. "We taught one another many things."

Terra's curiosity rose alongside a growing sense of trust. Tulku. Why did his spirit cause hers to tremble as if together they made some inexplicable harmony? Why had she suddenly lost all her questions, as if the answers were already given?

"Let me show you, young whale dreamer. You are safe here. I've known you across lifetimes. I've expected you."

With that, Terra felt Granny move towards her great grandson. "You knew?" "I could not tell you, Great Mother, or else she might never have come."

He reached again for Terra. An invitation. "She had to choose to find you, to accept her own power. To be who she is."

"So the prophecy is true?" Granny asked.

Terra let herself move to Tulku as he replied, "The prophecy is true." And then they were together, Terra and Tulku. Her guide. "Welcome, whale dreamer. Welcome." Tulku's spirit rushed through hers, then settled…she felt him separate but within her at the same time. This was different than what she felt with Granny, as if Tulku were holding parts of himself away from her. And instead of the almost overwhelming joy and surprise of her bond with Granny, this was a link she somehow already knew…it felt as if something too-long-missing had slid into place, as if she'd always known this magnificent being.

"I must show you my earth-mind now. Be strong." And they were descending. The light of this place grew harsher, hotter, glinting off a million water drops and glaring white walls. The sound of whale hearts beating and whale blood pulsing, thrummed through her and bounced off all the walls. Such a wrong sound. The confinement amplified it, consuming them. Where was the flow of water, the rush of waves? Where were the sounds of snails, and kelp, and fish, and the scrape of sea urchins and starfish against boulders? Where was the symphony of the tides, of the whole ocean moving and breathing? Where was the sound of their families? The sound of their pods, calling their names, clicking their language? Where were these sounds? In here, the sound of their own voices drove them crazy—the way they bounced and bounced against the walls and echoed in all directions.

The walls were everywhere. So many walls. The hot light, the sense of scratching, constant pain, the light overwhelming everything. The walls. The beating hearts. The pain in their mouths, their broken teeth. The rakes across their backs from the other whales. The other whales. Some, hanging so still, immobile. Waiting, waiting for the next show, even with its mind-blasting clatter of voices and shrieking tones, waiting for something different, for relief from lethal monotony…for food, for love. Love that only the trainers could offer now…a distorted, tainted love, so unlike their wild legacy it was unrecognizable. It was something else. Some darting around and around, swimming constantly in circles. Always the walls, always the hot light glinting into their eyes, their skin. Always the echoing, inescapable sounds ripping through them…their intensely sensitive hearing and bodies constantly abraded by the strident cacophony caused by the walls. Some swimming up, down, around and around, popping above the water, over and over and over, looking…trying to escape the bedlam for a few seconds. Has anything changed out there yet? Can we go home now?

The horror gripped her and she felt her own earth-mind begin to instinctively darken and shut-down in self-protection, pulling its own shutters against the foul pain and injustice of this place. Night, Terra understood, was a relief, the darkness a drug to numb them, to let them imagine, for a few hours, the dark ocean.

And she understood something else. Their profound tolerance. Their constant faith that the humans who held them here must love and need them. This is why they gave so much. This is why they didn't act out more often on their distress.

But all of them trapped. By the walls, by their earth-minds. None of them saw Tulku or Terra. "Only a few of us can use the dream world, whale dreamer." She felt Tulku's explanation before she thought to ask the question. "When I am here, even I need my great-grandmother's help to rise above my earth-mind, to find the dream place. This is why I hang for so many hours, waiting in my tank, hoping she will come and dream with me. It is impossible to escape to my dreams without her wild call."

Tulku pulled Terra back a little, away from the distress and insanity of the pool. And despite her great relief at rising up from that place, she found she wanted to stay, to help. To tell them she'd seen and understood.

Tulku continued. "She came to me that day, and brought a dream of the birth of my sister. My third sister. She's the next carrier of wisdom, the one chosen by my great-grandmother to receive her ancestral map. Another dreamer. The one I was destined to protect and support throughout all the years of my life, making sure she could safely lead our family." He paused. "I was to be her Great Protector. But I am not there."

"When I returned to my earth-mind the day of my sister's birth," Terra felt Tulku shudder under the weight of his burden, "it was time for another show. I did all she asked, but my heart was sick, knowing my sister had arrived and she was not to know me, to receive my brothering." For only an instant, Tulku allowed a flash of his mental state that day to penetrate Terra's awareness. Horror and panic seized her, the whale's misery and outrage and loss. Her spirit darkened as she felt what he'd felt. In that brief moment, Terra learned that "brothering" was a designation just as urgent to orca as mothering is to humans.

"Together my sister and I were to have grown together and fulfilled our destiny as the guides of our pod: she the Keeper of Life, me the Great

Protector." Terra got a split-second vision of Tulku and the grown calf swimming wild with their family in Puget Sound, leading J Pod into an uncertain and perilous future. A future even more difficult for J Pod to navigate with-out the pair's wisdom and guidance. But Tulku added solemnly, "Now, it seems that is not to be." Terra thought of her dream and Granny's vision of the calf and her brother working together with Terra. She thought of the proposal. Maybe she really could help. She was here with the calf's brother after all! She reached towards Tulku, within her but beyond her. "And Dusky knew nothing of this," she expressed herself for the first time in the great whale's presence.

To let him know she understood. "She did not."

There was silence between them as Terra projected her own mental snap-shot, forgetting the proposal as she felt, once again, his anguish. She flashed to her paddling out onto the Strait, the urgency she'd felt to make amends, to apologize to Granny—to all the orca—for the suffering people had brought to them, even if they'd been unaware of the pain they'd caused, as Dusky had been. She'd felt feverish with determination to express her regret. Now was her chance to give that apology to Tulku and Granny. They could both hear her now.

"Now *I* know," Terra shared with Tulku. "Now I can apologize for the people who didn't know better."

"You do know, whale dreamer, but there is no need for an apology, as you call it." Tulku pressed this knowledge to her, as a gift. "Your connection is what we need more than anything."

At this, Granny expressed once again to Terra. "It is your drive to connect that attunes you to us, whale dreamer. Humans are unrivaled in their capacity for feeling empathy and immediacy in the presence of others, both human and non-human. People, like whales, can sense the grandeur and interconnection of all that is. If they allow it. If they know who they are."

Tulku added, "The trainers and the audiences are there because they all have the same drive to connect, they sense the magnificent potential for the force of our bonds," Tulku went momentarily radiant, "but they mistake and defile their desire to connect with their dangerous habit of domination. That habit, born of The Fallacy, is *not* who they are."

Terra was confused. But Granny continued, explaining. "The human capacity to connect with others has been one of the greatest forces for both good and brutality ever known on this planet," the ancient grandmother went on. "When they lose the connection, when they disallow their own relationship to others, when they forget, as so many have now forgotten,"

Granny quivered with the sadness of what she was relaying, "they are capable of inflicting the most terrible suffering."

The experience of the whales in the pool cut into her, and she understood.

It was so simple. People had forgotten their connection to the wild ones, for-gotten to honor and respect these beings for who and what they are, because they'd forgotten themselves. People had chosen domination, and in so doing, they'd cut themselves off from their own brilliance. For an instant, Terra grasped the terrible loss and madness of this for the people themselves…a psychosis of separation. When we trap the whales, we trap ourselves.

"In the Great Ages Past, human cultures around the world revered these interconnections. It is why we had whale dreamers for hundreds of generations. There was such joy between us…" Granny grew quiet. "And such power." "The ancient ways," Terra shimmered, as she took in

Granny's wisdom and felt the truth of what she was learning.

"Yes, whale dreamer. The ancient ways, as you call them, are what account for the long periods of peace and harmony on Earth, before the Great Sadness." Granny went on. "Most humans have so deeply forgotten, that they now assume war riddles all of human history…that war, itself, defines humanity." Granny surged towards Terra, her rising power aflame with her ancient knowledge of harmony. Her authority boomed through Terra. "I know this to be false."

Tulku moved towards Granny. "Let us go now, Great Mother. The prophecy." He turned inwards to Terra, their connection still binding them. "There is much more that you must see, whale dreamer. The pools of captivity are merely a symptom."

And they rose up, away from the pool, flying across the grid of space-time once again, this time Tulku's magnetic force directing them. Faster and faster, the extreme speed whipping by even as they seemed to be still. Terra felt the horror of Tulku's place—his confinement—melt away as she rejoined the grid of light and unity. She knew now why he would wait for hours in his tank, hoping Granny—the great ancient dreamer and grandmother—would arrive and help lift him to this dream place…away from his earth-mind. Tulku's power here, in this place, was magnificent. She wondered what he meant, that the pools were a symptom. As Tulku sensed her thoughts, Terra felt a shift, as if the Earth moved, and he allowed her a glimpse. Something much, much bigger was going on here than what she thought. Something way beyond whales trapped in pools. And Tulku—her guide, her teacher—knew what it was.

And then they stopped. Tulku disappeared and Terra was alone with Granny. Alone in a place she already knew.

THE BLACKFISH PROPHECY

THE TRIBE IS GATHERED for the young boy's dreaming ceremony. They are circled together on the pebbly beach of Blackfish Cove as it appears five thousand years ago. The drums fill every member of the tribe with the same pulsing energy of the golden grid of light—and even though they cannot see it, they all know it, deep in their souls. The drumming brings them to the other world. The boy is central, leading the beats from the middle of the gathering as he sits facing the cove. From birth, the tribal elders recognized this boy as a dreamer and have fostered his gifts. The tribe reveres the orca of this place—the great leaders of the sea. They have seen the power of the bonds between human and whale.

The boy drums. The elders drum around him. Warriors, bent over with great carved dorsal fins on their backs, dance and circle him. Women painted black with large white eye patches chant with him. The children rattle and drum beside him. The boy enters trance. He looks up, into the spirit place…...*and locks in with Terra. It is Tiluk! The boy is Tiluk!*

"Granny!" Terra's spirit burned with surprise. "Granny, it is Tiluk. It is *Tiluk*!" "Yes, whale dreamer." She radiated light into Terra, enfolding her with reassurance. "You must watch what happens next. No matter what you see, even if you are shocked, try to stay present."

"I understand." Terra was so stunned at seeing her friend here, his face different, but his soul unmistakably the same—that she forgot to ask Granny what happened to Tulku. She turned back to the scene on the beach.

The boy's gaze passes through her into the cove beyond. Does he see her? He looks outward, drumming, beckoning to the dorsal fins in the cove. A pod of Blackfish rests nearby. As she watches, Tiluk's trance frees his spirit from his body, and he floats up and over the cove while his hands continue drumming. A great bull whale, resting but his spirit free like Tiluk's, rises above the water, joining the boy dreamer. The two greet, they know one another. It is the whale Tulku.

Tulku! He was here He was living in the body of the great bull whale! Terra was so startled by this, by the possibility that Tiluk and Tulku once knew each other eons ago, it nearly undid her. She slipped and Granny held her. They remained. They watched.

Whale and boy join in a brilliant orange-yellow flash of communion, their swirling spirit energies mingling, the ripples of their bond gliding outwards into the golden grid of light linking all that is. The tribe—though their eyes are blind to the spirit joining—feels it in their hearts; the women grow quiet, the men calm their dancing, the children bow their heads, touched by grace.

Together boy and whale remain for an eternity within heartbeats. They fly.

They cavort. They play, and the boy, as always, absorbs great wisdom from the whale. Then they grow still for many moments and his light sparkles and grows brighter. The light fills him and his people. The whale and his dreamer once again share with them the experience of unity.

"What you are seeing, whale dreamer, was once commonplace and is now long forgotten." Terra received Granny's wisdom from her vast and ancient storehouse of experience. It was her ancestral map. She, the chosen leader of her pod, had received her ancestral map from her own great-grandmother, who'd likewise received hers, backwards for countless generations. "The whales and dolphins were the first dreamers on the Earth. We were the first to experience the unity of all that is with conscious awareness. It changed the course of our evolution, and brought us indescribable joy and peace." She paused. "Our dreaming began millions of years before humans walked the Earth." Granny's perception expanded outwards, focusing Terra on the brilliant connection she was witnessing between Tulku and Tiluk.

"When the first humans began to awaken in their dreams, the whales reached for them...as I once reached for you to tell you of my granddaughter's calf. Orca, especially, felt a kinship with these emerging leaders of the lands."

Granny's spirit billowed, wrapping Terra in that same peace she'd experienced earlier, and the ecstatic, joyous feeling of their bond. "When the first humans responded, when they awoke in their dreams and found the orca—it was their powerful and innate drive to connect with us that brought us together. And it was the first time on Earth that two sentient intelligences experienced one another in the dream world…in the place of unity. The force of bliss that arose from their union cannot be described. The resulting bond between us changed everything. We revered one another and learned together for hundreds of generations after those first connections."

She pointed Terra's perception back to the tribe. "What you are seeing is one of the ways that people experienced that bliss and wisdom, through their whale dreamers." She paused once more, giving Terra a moment to absorb what she was receiving. "Not all have the same drive to connect, so not all are dreamers." She shifted her expression deeper, so Terra felt a weight of significance. "Yet all of life depends on the dreamers. It is no mistake that your brother-friend Tiluk is here."

Terra felt a whooshing sensation sweep her awareness down, down, into a swirling depth of recognition. As if Granny's sharing had lit a long fuse that was snaking its way towards igniting a world of light. What was happening?

"Know this, young whale dreamer. What you are about to see, is one of the most vital pieces of orca-human history ever experienced. It is the reason I have chosen to stay on Earth for so many years, and it is the reason our kind have not given up." Granny wrapped her wise, gentle energy around Terra. "It is the key to Earth's salvation." Then she touched Terra's spirit with grateful tenderness and added, "It is no mistake you are here, either. We've been waiting for you."

Terra felt the light spreading, warming her across a great expanse of time.

As if a pure brilliant wildfire was spreading across her soul, illuminating parts of her she hadn't known before.

"Watch now." Granny drew Terra close and pointed them back towards the scene from so long ago.

The boy awakens from his trance. Turns to his elders with an expression they have never seen before. The drumming and chanting are silenced. All wait to hear his learning. He looks around, glances towards the cove, then back at his people. His face, drained a little of his usual dark color, registers an unexpected strength and seriousness that keeps them hushed. Something is different this time for the whale dreamer. Something has happened.

"The ancient one, Tulku, has given us powerful medicine." He pauses, trying to put into words what he has seen and experienced. "The ancient ones foresee a time of great sadness," says the boy finally, to the startled gasps of his tribe. "The people will forget our bonds with the whales. We will forget our bonds with one another. We will forget our interconnection. The pain of this forgetting will cause us to do terrible things to each other and to the whales and to the rest of life. It will cause us to burn and damage and forsake the very Earth herself."

A shocked murmur moves through the tribe. How can this be? The Earth is mother of all life. People are the brothers and sisters of all beings. And people are the great leaders and stewards of the land, their bonds with each other among the most powerful and capable of caring and compassion on all the Earth. How will people ever forget this? How could they walk away from their sacred privilege of honoring the exuberant beauty of life? How could people ever harm the ancient ones, the whales, so full of wisdom and love?

The boy dreamer continues. "But the ancient ones understand. And more than anything else, they want us to know they will never stop loving us no matter what happens, because they know the truth: that we will forget. And they will know, when the Great Sadness arrives, that it is we who will be in such terrible misery and pain that we will inflict suffering upon them, our greatest allies."

The people shake their heads and begin to whisper amongst themselves, unable to imagine ever forgetting. Or ever imposing such suffering on the

Earth and her children. This is impossible. How can this be? Confusion moves through the tribe, and angers begin to rise. Perhaps this boy is lying. It is inconceivable that the people would ever fail to revere the whales or the Great Mother Earth.

The elder sitting nearest the boy dreamer stands up. He is the shaman, his long wooden staff hewn of red cedar and crowned by a carved raven's body with outstretched wings. His long gray hair courses around his shoulders and torso in a cascade of old growth, the skin of his face wizened by wrinkles and his piercing eyes, black and hooded.

He raises his staff and brings it down heavily, commanding. He looks around, pinning the crowd with his dark eyes, silencing them. Then his heavy gaze falls back across the boy, serious. "If what you say is true, you must explain yourself."

The boy dreamer looks back towards the cove, his eyes rest on the dorsal fins rising from the black waters, especially that of the great bull, his partner whale, Tulku. "Tulku brings us wisdom from the field of Oneness…it is wisdom from beyond the Earth." He looks back to the tribe again, and then up, into the eyes of the shaman. "The ancient ones have received a message from the wise ones of other worlds. It is a message for us."

The tribe utters a collective gasp and the people rustle in wonder and confusion. Other worlds? This has never happened before, a whale dreamer speaking of other worlds. What is he saying? Maybe this boy really is lying.

The shaman stares into the boy's eyes, looking for answers but seeing only Tiluk's virtue. He must either trust the boy, or ridicule him and lose something precious forever. "What is this message, whale dreamer?" his voice steady and believing, deliberately leading the shaken tribe to respect the boy's words rather than mock them.

The boy smiles. Quiet. He looks at the shaman then lets his eyes move around the circle of his people, their confusion still evident, but their love for him more so. With the shaman's questions, they've grown curious.

"The Others are the ancient ones from other worlds. They have long known of the whales dreaming here on Earth. Now they know of us. They have knowledge for us."

There arrives a nervous eagerness among the tribe. Others? Ancient ones from other worlds? Could this really be true? That the Earth is not alone in the vastness of the star land? That the myths and stories of the star people are real? They look at one another. Is it really possible that there exist leaders of other worlds? And that they can communicate through the whales?

The shaman speaks. "What is this knowledge, whale dreamer?"

The boy dreamer stands. Moves to the water's edge. Raises his arms and calls out, "Tulku, I ask you to speak with me."

Then he kneels down on the pebbles, the small waves lapping his knees. His head falls forward, and he is instantly in trance. The people gasp and marvel at this. The dreamer entered trance without his drum; they've never seen this before! Suddenly, as one, the tribe comprehends their privilege and the power of what is happening. Now the whale dreamer has their full attention and respect.

The shaman sits down once more, takes Tiluk's drum to him, and begins a gentle, quiet beat, supporting Tiluk's trance and beckoning the tribe to deepen as well. All eyes rest upon the whale dreamer at the water's edge, the pod's dorsal fins moving slowly in the cove. Then, the large bull, Tulku, turns about, and swims toward shore. There are more gasps. The whales almost never approach. His towering black dorsal fin comes closer until the massive bull rests in the deep waters a few feet away from Tiluk, the two aligned, facing each other.

"The Others send you their love." The whale dreamer's voice is low and resonant, changed. With reverence, the people nod and listen quietly in wonder. The great Tulku is joined with the dreamer. For the first time, they are speaking as one.

"We thank you ancient one," responds the shaman. "We are ready to receive your wisdom."

"The Others want you to know the Great Sadness is inevitable for those like you. When intelligent, social beings can manipulate and control their resources, there is always a Great Sadness. When highly evolved beings like you discover how to make fire—and then more tools that release vast, unforeseen stores of energy—there is always a Great Sadness.

The people are shaking their heads in confusion. What is the dreamer talking about? Why would there always be a Great Sadness? The shaman strengthens his drumming. "Explain this to us, whale dreamer," the shaman's voice rings out over the tribe's confusion. "What do The Others know of how to avoid a Great Sadness?"

Tiluk/Tulku responds in a voice deep and grave. "The Great Sadness is unavoidable. It is a universal law. With fire-starting comes the release of great energy. Populations feed on this energy and grow, some more than others. More tools are created that release more energy. Right now, you cannot even begin to imagine the tools that will come to you on Earth. Right now, all you have are tools to make fire. But eventually, on every planet where those like you arise—huge masses of sleeping fire energy, long dormant underground, are released by *new* tools. The vast fire energy burns, heating the planet. And certain populations feed upon that energy and explode. It is those populations who have succumbed to The Fallacy and they impact every other being on their home planet. There is no avoiding this."

The boy dreamer straightens, raising his head to gaze at his partner whale, and adds, "What is unknown is the outcome of Earth's Great Sadness."

"How might we influence that outcome? What is The Fallacy?" the shaman asks, eyes burning with intent. He wastes no time with frivolous questions. If The Others are here to offer a message, this is the greatest, most important moment of his life. He knows the people can only benefit from such a message if it is received.

"First, know this. Not all populations explode as they release the new fire energy. Some quickly learn how to integrate the energy to sustain them-selves in ever more harmony with their local world. Many cultures on Earth know this and have lived with harmony for tens of thousands of years. Yours descends from and maintains such a culture."

Every tribe member nods at this, as the shaman scans his community. Yes, they recognize this truth in themselves, it is so obvious. How could it be otherwise? Even in disputes with other local tribes their primary goal is to reach accord with communication and mutual respect. Fighting is always a last resort.

"But," the boy/whale goes on as if anticipating their question, "there shall be those fire-tool cultures that are infected by The Fallacy. They are the ones who will forget. The Fallacy is a feverish sickness that poisons some cultures with a terrible idea. An idea that is highly contagious: it is the idea that one is separate from another. That all are not connected. It is this falsity that makes it possible for some to dominate others. Such cultures make terrifying tools designed only to kill and dominate others, or to hoard resources."

More than anything they've heard so far, they are most alarmed by this: that anyone could forget. How could people ever forget? The tribe is dazed.

But the dreamer speaks again, explaining. And as the shaman begins to under-stand the profound significance of this visit, he opens his mind to receive this information in his deepest memory banks. He must remember everything.

"The first time this happens on Earth—as on other planets—is when those like you discover how to grow and store food crops. With the help of cook fires, the sun's energy is unleashed, and there are those who mistakenly think they will benefit from hoarding and controlling food resources. Their fallacy leads to greed, jealousy, arrogance, domination, war, and—most toxic and damaging to their spirits—fear. These, in turn, cause brutality, terrible suffering of others, and grave damage to the resilience and resources of their natural home. This Fallacy is driven by ignorance. Ignorance of what is truly happening. Ignorance of interconnection. Ignorance of the universal law."

Tiluk/Tulku's voice booms: "The Fallacy is not innate to human behavior, or to *any* sentient behavior on other worlds. It is a short-term obsession with a dangerous idea that justifies the release and hoarding of energy at all costs."

The dreamer pauses. Then speaks more loudly. "And if not seen for what it is, it can only result in domination, terrible suffering, and death."

Then his voice softens. "Unfortunately, in many cases we have observed, the fear, the hoarding, the greed, the arrogance, and the jealousies worsen over these generations while the population does not realize it is exploding.

Then The Fallacy grows stronger as it is adopted by populations touched by its ever expanding stranglehold while it marches with its armies and invasions across entire planets where those like you arise."

The boy laughs and his voice echoes across the cove, "But it is just an idea! And it is wrong!" Tiluk/Tulku straightens and pulls his shoulders back, his voice ringing out even louder now. "But the most dangerous time of all—for Earth and for all planets where those like you arise—is when those who believe The Fallacy discover sleeping fire energy. For when too much ancient sunlight is released, it is only a matter of time before the planet's resilience and much of its Life will begin to perish."

The people go mute with shock. Even the shaman is momentarily lost. This is a terrifying fate. Is it possible to lose an entire planet to The Fallacy?

The dreamer turns to gaze fixedly into the shaman's black eyes. They connect, soul-to-soul, and the shaman takes in a lungful of the sea's exhalation, gaining strength from her breath, and nods his readiness.

The dreamer speaks directly to the shaman. "Now take heed, and give this to your storytellers to pass from one generation to the next, and onwards into a future in which your Earth will find itself in the grip of her own Great

Sadness. It is at this historic moment—in the worst and most terrifying times of the Great Sadness as Earth finds itself fevered and approaching irrevocable tipping points, that many humans will mistakenly believe that The Fallacy—and its hoarding, greed, domination, and war—are the result of normal human behavior. Likewise some will come to believe that the rising temperatures are normal, too."

"Know this!! Such behaviors and rising temperatures are *not* normal! They are warning signs! They are symptoms of dwindling resources, a looming population crash, and a fevered planet!"

The tribe murmurs together, confused about what they are hearing, yet recognizing the intensity and value of it to those in the future. They are deeply disturbed. It is frightening, this knowledge. It means that other populations who share the Earth with them may come to dominate and destroy them.

Finally, the shaman speaks again, his mind alive with his deep listening, and his inner pledge to retain this knowledge and pass it forward. "Honorable Tulku, what have The Others shown you of those like us on other worlds who survive their Great Sadness? What may we learn from them?"

"The Others have seen those like you either destroy their world as they know it as they are lost to The Fallacy, or they recall wisdom and unity. Those who survive their Great Sadness must understand it. With that discernment, they remember the truth. They heal their culture and the sickness of The Fallacy, as they come to revere, honor, and learn from those cultures who never succumbed to its toxic notion of separation. Together they create a thriving new world." There is a long silence as Tiluk/Tulku allows his words to fully settle over the people.

The shaman speaks with respect, working to understand his tribe's role in this decisive moment and committing all he's heard to memory. "But we already know unity, ancient one. We revere the Oneness and the interconnection of all that is."

The boy dreamer laughs, and says, "We know! It is why we are here with you. We come to you now because you must be forewarned. And because you play a role...Those who are drugged by The Fallacy must wake up, see what is happening, and remember their connection to all that is if your planet is to survive as you know it. They must remember who they really are. Those who know unity are instrumental to this, the Great Transition. It is true on Earth as it has been true throughout the universe."

The great bull exhales a loud BA-WHOOSH, turns and circles quickly into the cove then comes around sideways to shore at high speed, sending a series of strong waves quickly up onto the beach, sloshing the whale dreamer and capturing the tribe's attention as the dreamer responds.

"Know this, children of Earth. The force for harmony on your planet is very strong. This force is always present on worlds that survive their Great Sadness. The extreme compassion and love and intelligence of your species, and that of your sentient partners such as the whales, allows for many pathways for humans to know unity, and to see the Great Sadness for what it is...and thus to heal it. This force is innate to humans and Earth itself, and it is infinitely more powerful than The Fallacy's desperate response to shrinking resources."

"We have great hope for humans. We are here because of one of these pathways. Your bonds with the whales allow us to share with you as we are doing now."

The shaman nods and sees others in the tribe slowly nodding, too.

They understand. They trust the orca's great wisdom, they know the power of the bonds between human and whale.

"Since their emergence on Earth, a few humans have always remained aware of their connection to unity. Some of your most revered and respected leaders tell of their connection to all Life, and teach others of this connection. Other people glimpse the Oneness through the pathways, including science, religion, social relationships, music, art, storytelling, meditation, dreaming, and drumming. Tragically, many times in your world as populations begin to explode, there are some who insist that their beliefs are the only way for everyone. But this is always their misguided attempt to control resources. This is also a terrible mistake that will lead to immense suffering and subjugation on your planet."

The great whale expels again, BA-WHOOSH! And the dreamer laughs. "*Of course*, humans are always connected to all that is. The greatest question is whether they will arise to witness this consciously, as a global family."

The shaman notices the tribe is absorbed. They are as one, listening to the whale's message. He asks, "So, are you saying that to survive the Great

Sadness, humans—in the time of their worst despair and suffering, the time of The Fallacy—must awaken to know unity?

"It is only then, in their worst times of despair, that the whole human family will be ready to awaken and to ask for help. Help that has been there all along," responds the dreamer.

Tulku spins around, lowers his great head and body, and raises his huge tail above the water before bringing it down fast and hard, splashing the boy and some of the tribe with its spray. Drenched by the cold water, the dreamer erupts in laughter. "It will be a rather more momentous occasion than when you discover your planet does not spin at the center of the universe!" The dreamer laughs again, a great hearty booming chortle that carries out to the pod and beyond.

Still laughing, he says, "Once the evidence of unity is discovered by the scientists, it will be easier for so many. Hearts will open...and then we shall see..." The tribe looks to their shaman. This is so much knowledge. How can they hold it all? Is it their responsibility to bring this wisdom to the whole of Earth? How can they do this?

As if sensing the tribe's concern, the whale dreamer chuckles again and offers an answer. "This is not your job. There are many others, including us, bringing these messages to the people of Earth. We have great hope for humans. It is why we are here."

Tulku rolls on his side and lets his eye come above water, gazing at the boy. The dreamer pauses and looks up, staring at the great whale before him. "We have endless gratitude for the whales, who allow us to share with you now. Their hearts are immense and very powerful."

The shaman stops drumming. He is consumed by an insight.

"You *are* The Others. You are speaking to us through the boy dreamer and his whale."

The boy erupts with the great, reverberating laugh once again.

"YES! Greetings, brother," the dreamer shakes with laughter, "Greetings to you all: sisters and brothers of Life." He grows quiet again, and looks to

Tulku. "We are not the whale or the boy, but we come to you because of their bond. You are among the fortunate ones in the universe who have partners like the whales. They have gained far more spiritual power in their evolution than humans…they are much older. Humans are very young."

Then the dreamer turns and looks back at the shaman and the tribe.

"Which is why we bring you this message: Those like you can halt their own destruction and heal their planet when they understand the Great Sadness and awaken to their interconnection with all that is."

"For when beings like you realize that you are born of stars, that you are the universe looking at itself, that you are linked in the deepest parts of your souls in more intimate relations than you'd ever dreamed, that you, and all Life, are forged from the mingling of star dust across billions of years of space and time—that is when the magnificent diversity on your home planet Earth becomes a hallowed, sacred reminder of your privilege, and your responsibility. That is when each being, each life form, every species, every ecosystem, is known and revered as a singular phenomenon of the powerful exuberance of Life itself. And it is only the tool-wielding sentients—beings like humans—that are capable of either the glory of its witness or the tragedy of its destruction."

"We tell you this from other worlds, other worlds that have awoken from their own Great Sadness before it is too late. The joy and passion and brilliance and creativity unleashed by such self-aware sentients on other worlds like your own, erases all fear and causes a tide of healing and harmony and peace to sweep across the land and seas. Inflicting any kind of suffering on another, or on the Mother planet becomes unthinkable. Then comes a permanent peace and an enduring harmony."

"This is what happens in other worlds that survive their Great Sadness.

Such worlds are precious beyond measure, and they are filled with joy, laughter, love and creativity you cannot yet imagine. The iridescent states of such planets are revealed and the great coherence of their nature thrums across the universe itself. We come to you now on those same harmonic waves. Such planets hold a force for harmony more powerful than anything else in the universe."

The tribe is silent with awe. They are starting to conceive the true magnitude of what is happening. This is more than just serious medicine. This message could shift the entire history of Earth. The shaman stands on the tipping point of his life and the lives of so many others, and his drive to protect the people and the Earth is overwhelming. He, like everyone in his tribe, would now give his life to ensure Earth survives her coming sadness.

"Is there anything you can tell us about the Great Sadness that will help the people to awaken even in their worst times of misery?"

The whale dreamer shudders. "There is one thing we can tell you."

The boy pauses and the tribe is alert to the coming revelation. "In their terrible forgetting and their frenzied quest for resources, those on Earth in the grip of The Fallacy make the most grievous mistake that any world any-where, ever makes."

The tribe murmurs, uncertain they want to know of this mistake.

But the shaman is insistent. Perhaps, somehow, he can mitigate its harms if he knows what is to come. "What is this mistake?"

"As the fire-energy is released and populations begin to explode, some become so obsessed by their hoarding, that they take the Keepers of Life as property." Tiluk's voice rings out without judgment. "One half of the world's beings are seen—for many generations—as a resource to be con-trolled and kept by the other half. And in so doing, they *all* come to believe it is acceptable to keep other cultures, people, and countless animal allies, as property. The suffering that comes from this is unspeakable."

This is too much. Of everything they have learned so far, the tribe is aghast. The women reach for one another, the men shake their heads, some of them even stand up, their faces contorted by bewilderment. This, they cannot understand. They protect and revere the great Keepers of Life. Just like the Blackfish do.

"Such worlds right themselves when the Keepers of Life achieve freedom: for they hunger for justice and truth. Once they understand what has happened and why, their magnificent power to restore harmony in their world is beyond your imaginings."

The dreamer claps his hands together and bellows in laughter once more, "It is so simple! They are the Keepers of Life!!" He turns to the shaman, holding his belly in rollicking delight. "You want to know how to help the people to awaken in their worst times of misery? Give the women their freedom! Then you shall know harmony!"

The dreamer is shaking his head from side to side, his smile open wide, thumping his chest in delight. His merriment is contagious, and the tribe relaxes. This is an easy mistake to fix! This they know!

The shaman is less confident, for he comprehends that if a people can take others as property, they must be severely disturbed. Still, he is thankful for the wisdom from The Others. It is in this moment that the shaman comes to a realization.

"You have come to us now with a purpose."

"You are wise, brother. YES! And it is the most important thing we bring you, children of Earth. But you had to receive our knowledge first. Without it, the prophecy would mean nothing to you. The whale, Tulku, will give you this prophecy. His wisdom is great. You already have the bond. Trust it with all you have….Remember it into the future."

The dreamer looks to Tulku. "The prophecy must come from the whale." "Before you go, I have one more question." The shaman speaks with urgency, his powers of foresight awakened by the knowledge he has received.

"What happens to those like us who do not survive their Great Sadness?" The dreamer turns serious, his light and merriment dim. "Darkness and loss prevail. The loss of highly evolved planets such as yours, so full of life, so awake with sentient beings, so precious in the universe…it is a grave and terrible loss. A permanent silencing of a world unique and extraordinary beyond measure. But the souls learn.

They will have another chance on another world. Yet the loss is so terrible it takes them much longer to achieve harmony and peace and love. It is not a desirable outcome. You will know if this begins to occur on Earth if the whales and the other sentients decide to leave. They love Earth, but they are tired."

The shaman looks out at the darkening waters, the cloak of immense cedar forest, the reddening cloud-streaked sky, the brilliant sliver of the rising moon, the beauty of his people, and the whales in the cove. He hangs his head heavily for a moment, hearing a fate too painful to imagine. Then he lifts his eyes to the dreamer and the whale, raises his staff and brings it down, seeing his tribe's significance. "We shall do whatever we can to help our Great Mother Earth survive the coming Sadness. Thank you wise ones for the gift of your knowledge...We are ready to receive this prophecy."

The dreamer roars in laughter once more, "We know! We know you! It is why we are here. It is why you are to receive the prophecy. Farewell!"

Tulku dives and swims away at top speed, out to the center of the cove, before erupting in a great breach, up and up, all the way out of the water, his immense black body glistening in the setting sun for a full second before splashing down in the midst of his family.

Tiluk stands and turns to face his people. He raises his arms, his jaw tight with rising strength. His vanishing childhood of dreams, love and nourishment visible in the young man standing before them now. "Tulku and his kind have picked us and our people because we revere the bond. It is true that the dreamers will fade away during the Great Sadness, but they will return. They will return first to people like us— the ones who honor the

Earth's wisdom, the oldest cultures on the Earth, the ones who have survived the domination and the Great Sadness, the ones who know the power of the bond. But then the dreamers will rise from the growing populations of Earth, too. They will awaken in their dreams. They will awaken from The Fallacy."

"The dreamers will come to the Blackfish once again. That is the prophecy... Tulku is giving us this prophecy because the first dreamer to return shall come to our people, many generations in the future." He stares hard at his tribe, then turns to the shaman.

"She is here with us now."

And Tiluk looks straight at her. Terra flames bright. Tiluk! Everything that has happened before has been leading to this moment. She was born for this. Tiluk's spirit, like a sunbeam, pours through his eyes, linking with hers.

Terra's wild flaring connection to Tiluk leaps like fire and the only thing that keeps her steady is Granny's potent stabilizing force.

The tribe erupts with a collective gasp of wonder. She is here now? Where? A whale dreamer from the future? Such a one as this must be very powerful! They look to the boy dreamer, then the shaman, wondering what happens next. The shaman simply watches the boy. His face filled with absolute trust.

His life has changed forever.

The boy dreamer looks to Terra, nodding towards her and Granny, beckoning them. *Come now. It is time.* Before Terra's astonished mind can ask any questions, her spirit, still linked with Granny's great force, flies to Tiluk, her unshakable trust in him fueling her acceptance of what is happening.

The boy lets his gaze travel among his tribe, threading their cohesion as if weaving a basket of many reeds. Then he looks to Granny and Terra, though they are invisible to the tribe.

The brilliant force of Tulku rushes once again into Terra, filling her like a blast of wind. Tulku: great and ancient brother of the new calf. From within the dazzling swirl of their spirits she hears the great Tulku tell the prophecy through the boy dreamer as he speaks aloud, the tribe staring in open-mouthed wonder.

"You are this dreamer, Terra. The first to return to us from the future. We welcome you. You will help the Blackfish, as we shall help you and your people. You, and those like you, will awaken in your dreams to receive our wisdom and to help heal the Great Sadness. With the return of the dreamers, a tremendous power and force for harmony will be unleashed across all the Earth."

The tribe utters a collective gasp of joy. This is it. This is why The Others came. This prophecy. This prophecy will be the link that holds them to one another and the Earth in ages to come, as The Fallacy dominates the great land and the first peoples. With this prophecy, they regain their trust in all that is. Even after the frightening things

The Others foretold. The Earth can one day rise far beyond the Great Sadness. Now they know what is possible.

And they know that the dreamer from the future walks among them. They will do anything to support this dreamer. The children rustle in their mothers' laps, as if something inside each one of them has shifted. They begin quietly drumming on their own legs and laps with their little hands.

The mothers look down at their children, then at one another. Something is happening here. The children drum louder and the mothers and warriors join them. They are all drumming now.

Suddenly Terra feels her heart pierced by the calf—her presence glows within Terra's energy field. She, too, has been called by her great brother,

Tulku. Then Terra feels the small wooden carving of the calf—stained by her own blood—appear in the center of their swirling fire-white connection: in an instant, the calf becomes the center of their union. Stunned by her appearance, Terra looks to Tiluk in shocked wonder, and only Granny's presence holds her steady.

"Welcome whale dreamer. Now is the time! Wake up! Wake up!" cries Tiluk.

The tribe begins to chant, seizing up the boy dreamer's energy, the great Tulku's power filling them through the ring of spirit fire that has formed all around them. *Wake up, wake up, wake up*, they chant with the potent beat of the drumming. *Wake up wake up wake up.*

Terra's spirit, already swirling with Granny's, the calf's, and Tulku's, merges and she forgets everything, everything but what happens next. What happens when she releases her identity and flashes outwards, radiating into everything. It is the shaman. He stands in the midst of the chanting. Now, with the growing ring of spirit fire connecting them, the shaman sees Tulku's spirit hovering offshore, his raven-sharp eyes mirrored by the piercing black raven atop his staff. He sees Tulku, and he sees Granny, and he sees Terra, and he sees the calf, and as his awareness joins with theirs he raises his mighty staff once more. And as the tribe chants, he crashes the staff down; the light of his connection to them pours through the raven's eyes, to the quiet, peaceful eyes of Terra's little wooden carving of a baby whale—now the blood-stained heart of this blazing human-whale connection. And a brilliant white light splits worlds open, linking the spirit world to his people, making the fiery ecstatic connection visible in the blinding flash of an exploding star over Blackfish Cove. And in the shuddering explosion the shaman thunders,

"Wake up, young Terra, so that we might rejoice!"

Terra becomes the universe. Then everything goes black.

BEFORE I SLEEP

IT WAS LIKE THEY WERE STALLED. The tribal elder—scratch that— the *shaman*, had arrived after midnight. Joseph and Tiluk, watching Claire snuggled in trying to warm-up Terra's cool body, had exchanged a few quiet words; it had been Tiluk's idea to get her drum and Joseph's to call the shaman. Joseph had made a call (who knew shamans had cell phones?) and the elder had arrived two hours later, drum in tow. Miles still felt like he'd walked off a space craft into another world. *Who were these people?*

He looked again from Terra's limp form up to Tiluk, who sat across from Miles with her drum in his lap, gently, methodically beating. A heartbeat. Quiet. Miles mirrored Tiluk as if they were two sphinxes stationed on either side of a warrior, waiting for her to answer their riddle. Only in this case the warrior was cradled by her mother. Claire, too, was awake but caught in a netherworld of isolation. Once she'd realized what had sent her daughter out on the Straight, her face had gone rigid and pale, and she wouldn't talk or respond to anyone. He was certain she was blaming herself for Terra's accident. It made him wonder, about five times every minute, what the heck he was doing here. Even though he felt so welcomed, he kept on doubting it. Why would they want him around, anyway? Maybe he was a huge bother right now. That's when he'd remember the carving in his pocket. And tightened his fingers around it.

Miles caught Tiluk's shadowed glance for the hundredth time that night; Tiluk's wordless calm had become a constant source of reassurance that Miles had already come to rely on...even though the kid was younger than him. Back at home, the kids were either worried about who had the coolest X-box or how to avoid getting bullied. Miles loathed school only slightly less than he hated being home dealing with everything that had come after the divorce. The only place he felt okay anymore was alone in his room with his computer and z-phone, or playing Chutes and Ladders with Aria in her room full of stuffties. But all that had fallen away when he'd stepped off the plane earlier, with Tiluk and the others treating him as if...well...as if he were part of their family. And now it was still their warmth and wordless understanding which kept him from simply bolting out of the hospital room to find the first bus to the airport. It was like they were one huge magnet and he was a thousand bits of iron shavings, pulled to them, coming back together again.

He looked over at the couch below the window where Maggie, Bill, and Joseph were all huddled together, also awake. Maggie peered at Miles through the shadowed room. Miles still couldn't get over it. *Geesh, I only get one parent at a time and she gets four, all at once?* The room was cast in a half-twilight, a greenish artificial glow coming from behind the bathroom door just behind him. The dark behind the windows felt permanent. He was starting to think this night would never end. They were stalled.

Stomach clenching again, Miles forced himself to look across Claire and down at Terra. He'd had the hardest time with Terra. He'd been in here all these hours, and aware of the accident, but at the same time, trying not to think about this girl being in an actual coma. *God, I wish she would wake up.* Every time a nurse had come in, which, by now, had tapered down to about once an hour, he'd watch like a hawk: peering at the equipment, the readings the nurse took, the way she'd take Terra's pulse and blood pressure—but then, every time she'd fill in Terra's chart, every time—his stomach boiled and his face went stony against his emotions. The lump, now on permanent loan from his belly, pushed harder against the back of his throat. He squeezed his eyes shut tight, gripped the little whale in his hand, and willed

Terra to wake up. Tiluk's drumbeats—*wake up wake up wake up*—repeated over and over and over again.

Wait. Of course. Why hadn't he thought of it before?

Miles reached over Claire and put the little whale carving into Terra's limp hands. Tiluk whispered over the drumbeat, "Good idea

Miles. She needs the calf while she's journeying."

Journeying. Whatever *that* meant. Miles had given up trying to understand what was with these people, and was just going with it. If Terra weren't so out of it, he'd probably think the whole thing was seriously cool! Her hands were so limp. *Come on Terra*, he said silently. *Come on.* He reached over again and carefully threaded her fingers around the whale so that it was clasped within her palms. Tiluk looked at him, nodding as if to say, *Yes, that's what she needs.*

And then there was that shaman guy. Whoever heard of a shaman named Dave? Seriously. He didn't act like a freaking shaman. *Dave*, kind of a middle-aged geezer, if you asked Miles, had claimed a spot behind Tiluk when he'd walked in hours ago. And then he'd just stood there all this time, like a big lump of smelly denim and flannel, not doing a thing. Oh wait, he *was* chewing on freaking tobacco, and spitting it into a cup every few minutes.

Seriously disgusting. Miles could smell the tobacco; a slight woody sweet-ness that was actually pleasant had overridden the hospital smells. But still. He was *spitting*. Tobacco! Miles looked at Dave now, and his heart skipped a beat. The glittering eyes shining at him looked like a pit vipers'…then they were normal again and Dave just smiled at him, his long thinning hair falling in greasy gray locks around his shoulders. *He's about as scruffy and rough as they come*, thought Miles to himself. *Shaman my buttookiss.*

As if reading Miles' thoughts, Dave took his cup and spit again, staring right at him, his smile widening to show the yellowing teeth in his mouth. He was beaming. Miles looked down and rolled his eyes so no one could see him. *What a kook. Why was this weirdo even in here?*

"Dave, what do you think?" Claire watched the exchange between Miles and the grizzled man, and it was as if his grin had calmed her and allowed her to break through her own silence. "What's happening?"

"Claire, she's just under. Period. She'll wake up when she's ready," harrumphed Bill from the couch. "It's a nice gesture that Dave brought in Terra's drum, but it's going to be her own will power and the *doctors* that get her up and running again. Not some drums and tobacco." He glanced at Miles and rolled his own eyes, with a pointed look at Dave's back that said as clear as day, "*That* crazy guy is not helping my daughter."

Claire shot a look at her husband, silencing him. "I don't care *what* gets her back again Bill, and if the drumming and tobacco and Dave help, even a little,

I want them all." She glared at him in disbelief, as if stunned by his outburst. "She's busy," Dave smiled openly at Claire, a sing-song voice answering her and ignoring the exchange. Miles noticed a couple of teeth were missing. *Busy? With what?* Miles wondered. Dave's quirky smile grew even bigger. "The best thing we can do," interjected Joseph, "is to stay calm and keep the circle warm." His eyes went first to Bill, then Claire, "She needs us to stick together."

Glancing around the room Tiluk strengthened his beats a little in agreement. *Wake up wake up wake up...*

Speaking of warm, it was *hot* in here. Everyone was glazed in a thin sheen of perspiration. But Terra's skin was still cool and dry as bone. *Wait.* Miles looked again. *There.* A single tiny bubble of sweat had popped out at Terra's hairline, just behind the metal face mask protecting her nose. Miles looked around. Had anyone else noticed? Did that mean she was warmed up again? Was she coming back?

Dawn's rosy fingers were curling through the cracks in the blinds and the room had gone from bruised black and blue and purple, to flushed indigo, almost imperceptibly. Dave, still standing behind Tiluk put down his tobacco cup and placed both hands down, gripping Tiluk's shoulders tightly while he continued drumming, and locked eyes with Miles again. Whoa. The glittering pit viper eyes were back. What was going on?

Wake up wake up wake up... Tiluk's beats rose another notch in strength. And as if Dave were shedding an invisible skin, he rose and broadened, power surging through him, even his limp hair went suddenly full and gray-black and shiny, like those eyes. Those eyes that were still staring at him. He couldn't look away. Did the others see what was happening? What was going on?

The new, viper Dave took his stare downwards, to Terra, drawing Miles' eyes with him. Miles couldn't shake the feeling that Dave had become more animal than human, like a snake, head reared, quietly hissing. Together they stared at Terra, and Miles knew everyone in the room had felt the energy shift in here. Something was definitely happening. What the heck was it?

Then, the shaman raised his arms, and Miles got this incredible mental visual of a huge raven standing over Terra and Tiluk, both sheltering them with his wings, and guiding them with his immense power. That was it, *raven*. Not snake. Transfixed, he took Claire's hand. The others, as if guided by one mind, stood and came to Terra's bed, circled her, and took one another's hands. Terra, Tiluk, and raven Dave were in the middle of the circle while the others linked together around them. Maggie stood next to Miles, holding his other hand. Even Bill seemed intent with focus now.

*Wake up wake up wake up...*Tiluk kept beating the drum quietly, his glittering eyes flashed, mirroring the shaman's razor-sharp stare above him. *Wake up wake up wake up...*

There. He saw it. Terra's hands, wrapped around that little baby whale carving, they trembled and squeezed. She moved! Tiluk looked at him, he'd seen it too. "Come on honey," Claire said, tightening on Miles hand, and the whole group was instantly squeezing hands around the trio. "Come back to us."

Dave rose even taller, his arms still held up like wings, and he spoke. His voice was a low, potent force, the exact opposite of his earlier slap-happy sing song. The air went electric with an almost audible crackling energy.

Miles got a whiff of ozone, the odor of high voltage. "Rise up young Terra.

Return from your journey." Arms outstretched, he faced each person in the circle, locking eyes in a hard stare before moving to the next person. Then he looked to the window, at the splashes of brilliant sunlight peeking into the blinds. "Wake up, young Terra," he turned to faced her, his eyes on fire as if taking the light from the dawn and beaming it like a laser down at her limp body; his arms outstretched above her, "so that we, too, might rejoice."

The ozone smell blasted across Miles with a tremendous flash of light that shot between all the slits of the blinds, and a split-second of blinding whiteness flared throughout the hospital room. As if lightening had struck. A surge of energy coursed through the group like a ring of fire.

Claire cried out, dropping Miles' hand. Then everything went still. Very still. Miles noticed two things at once. One, Terra's whale was gone. Her hands had fallen to her sides, palms raised, arms flat on the bed. No whale. Two, geezer Dave was back, but rickety as a street sign in a hurricane. Joseph silently grabbed a chair and pulled it close, just as Dave sat heavily into it, eyes closed, head bowed, one hand gripping his chest tightly, tiny streaks of wetness at the corners of his eyes.

What the heck just happened? Where was the freaking whale carving? Was that flash thing real? Is geezer Dave having a bloody heart attack? Miles' questions poured through him as if he were a sieve with nothing underneath to catch them. He looked around. Maybe it was just some weird sunlight glinty thing. Maybe the light refracted on some deformity in the window glass, and it just happened to flash into the room at that exact moment? Wait. Everyone else was looking around, too. Mystified. Silent. Staring at Terra. And her open, empty hands.

What. The. Hell?

"Tiluk?" At the sound of Terra's raspy voice Miles lost it. The tears broke and two tiny rivers spilled over, silent. Maggie put her arm around him, and hugged him to her as they watched Terra's return.

Tiluk had put down the drum and scooted closer to the bed, taking one of her hands, leaning close, while Claire, still cradling her daughter, found her other hand. "I'm right here Lewis," said Tiluk quietly. "I'm right here."

Miles could see her eyes were still closed and she was groggy. Claire's cheeks were wet, too. And she was just waiting, following her daughter's lead, letting her awaken however she needed to. *They have so much respect for each other*, the words rang in Miles mind as he marveled even now, about how differently this family operated compared to his own. *What is that like?*

"Tiluk. I need to see Tulku. Take me out to him Tiluk. Granny, I need to see Tulku…Granny?" Terra's head moved back and forth, her eyes still closed, as if looking around. "Granny, where are you?!"

"Shhhhh, honey, you're okay," Claire glanced around at everyone. Her eyes as curious as everyone else's. *Tulku? Who the heck was Tulku? What was Terra talking about?* Claire sat up and leaned back against the bed's head-board, Terra's head carefully cradled against her shoulder. She gently put her free hand on Terra's forehead. "Granny's okay too, sweetheart. She's at home in Blackfish Cove waiting for you."

"Tiluk, Tiluk!" Her eyes were still tightly closed. "I need to tell him

I understand. Tell him I understand, Tiluk. Tell him we are coming. Tell him we will end the Great Sadness! Tulku? Do you hear me? Granny, where are you?" Terra was getting more agitated. She was obviously still half out of it and had no idea where she was.

"It's okay sea squirt," Joseph stepped forward and cupped his hand over Terra's head, glancing down at his son with admiration, then over at Dave, with some kind of inexplicable satisfaction. "It's okay," he said again. "He already knows. You did it. You can come back to us now."

What the heck was Joseph talking about? Miles was getting more con-fused by the second. He didn't know how much more of this bizarre stuff he could take. Was she going to wake up, or not? He wiped his eyes with the sleeve of his hoodie, Maggie squeezed him again and he felt her reach down and kiss the top of his head, her relief plain as day. Miles suddenly realized that Maggie didn't give a hoot whether Terra was talking nonsense or not, she was *talking*. She was coming back. That's all that mattered. Miles saw

Claire look up at him, then at Maggie above his head, the look on her face so full of relief and friendship for Maggie, he almost shuddered. Maggie just tightened her grip around him even more.

But Bill clearly felt frustrated about the strange things his daughter was saying. He stepped in now, and put his hand down on Terra's arm, letting his own arm rest over his wife. "Terra, you've been in a light coma, you had an accident, and now it's time for you to wake up," Bill said, ever the voice of reason.

"You're here with us…in a hospital." He glanced around, then locked eyes with

Joseph, almost challenging him. "Wake up now honey," he said firmly.

An enormous whooshing went through Miles, like a wind that only his soul could feel, blasting through him with a force of magnificence that brought him to his knees as he slipped from Maggie's arms. He *knew* this being! He leaned against Terra's bed looking at Tiluk. He saw the same force sweep through Tiluk, too. Their eyes grew wide. *Tulku*.

Terra's eyes flew open, "Tulku!"

Whoa, Miles could see that she'd felt him too. Gaping, she looked around, a distance edging her focus, as if she wasn't even in the room with them. Then she saw Miles and Tiluk. "He's here. He knows," she whispered to them, her chin trembling. "Thank God," she croaked as tears began streaming down her cheeks on either side of her metal mask. She squeezed her eyes shut again, pulling her hands away from her mother and Tiluk and clasping them in front of her face, her head bent forward, her shoulders quivering.

"Honey, who's here? It's just us. Everything is fine," Claire was starting to look concerned. What had happened to her daughter? "You're awake now and that's all that matters."

Geezer Dave stood up, as if he'd waited for this moment his entire life. Still squeezing his chest with one hand, he cleared his throat and looked at

Joseph, who smiled at Maggie and Tiluk; his glimmer of satisfaction even stronger now. *That force.* Miles was spellbound. Whatever was happening, he'd instantly understood that he was instrumental to it all. *Tulku. Brother.*

"Long, long ago, our people tell of a time when the Blackfish spoke to us through their chosen ones," began Dave in his smiley-toothed sing-song, oblivious to how odd he sounded as Claire and Bill struggled to make sense of what was going on.

"Dave, please just sit down and let Terra wake up. The last thing any of us need right now is more woo-woo," said Bill, grimacing in annoyance.

Claire looked down at her daughter, whose shoulders were still shaking, her hands still clasped in front of her face, but who'd peered up at Dave, expressing fully awake curiosity for the first time since she'd been under.

"Let him speak, Bill," she urged, looking pointedly from her husband to their daughter, her eyes saying, *See, she's listening, she's paying attention to Dave's story.* Bill shrugged, resigned.

Geezer Dave reached for his cup with his free hand, the one not clutching his chest, and spit. *I guess it's not a heart attack*, Miles thought to himself.

"But the stories are very very old, very very ancient," Dave warbled, smiling at Terra, whose tears had stopped. She was calming, hanging on his words. "Our people even lost faith in the prophecy. When the whites came and smothered the land and the native peoples…and the animals and plants, our brothers and sisters…our people lost faith. Their sadness was too great." His gaping, yellow-toothed smile looked so out of place with what he was saying that Miles felt an inappropriate giggle forming deep in his belly.

"But the shamans, like the great Blackfish leaders, knew the truth." He nodded, confirming himself, still smiling. He rocked back and forth on the balls of his feet, reached for his cup, and spit again. Miles had to stifle the urge to laugh. He pressed his face against the blankets on Terra's bed, hiding his grin from the others. But Tiluk saw it, and he passed a tiny smile back to Miles. *Tiluk. Brother.* Mile's humor faded into gratitude, a weight of alliance settled across him, and he knew his life was starting. Now.

"The ancient ones passed down the secret knowledge…and the relic."

Dave's smile widened even more, until everyone could see the four or five black spaces that should have had teeth. He was rocking more quickly on his feet, in time with his hand, which was thrumming on his chest, against the pocket. He reached out for his cup with his other hand and spit again.

Miles' eyes narrowed as he zoomed into Dave's chest thumping. It reminded him of the one-man band.

"So," he said, still patting his chest, "We shamans did not lose faith, even as our sisters, the Blackfish leaders, began to weep." He looked right at Terra, and those pit-viper eyes flashed again. "We've been dancing for our sisters, holding faith for them, even as they began to doubt the prophecy in their grief."

Terra stared at Dave. His raven self was emerging, he radiated strength and his eyes penetrated hers. All his humor had vanished. Miles could practically see black feathers and a strong beak appear as he locked with Terra. Joseph reached towards Dave, put a hand on his arm, respectfully, as if to remind him everyone was watching.

"It is time," Joseph said to Dave gently. He glanced around the room catching everyone's eyes but Terra's, whose head he still cradled gently with his other hand. "We were not sure until this moment… until now." He looked at Dave, then down at Tiluk. "Now we know the prophecy is true." "The relic." Terra said it calmly, but the strength in her voice made her mother look down at her in surprise. She reached her hand out towards

Dave, open. Waiting.

Dave stopped patting his chest, reached into his pocket, and pulled out a small orca whale carving that looked like it belonged in a museum. It was so ancient—cracked, worn, burnished and darkened—that it was almost unrecognizable. "Our relic descends from many generations before me.

From thousands of years ago. Her destiny, *their* destiny, as it always has, lies with you." He looked forcefully at Terra, then down at Tiluk and Miles, "And with those like you."

Dave stretched out his huge, black-feathered arm-wing that Miles could practically see—his face so regal and piercing—and handed Terra her little whale carving, the one she'd made to honor the new calf, the one that had somehow, with the fierce passion of her spirit, traveled back in time to anchor a brilliant vital connection between humans and orca. A little carving that had stayed there, in the Great Ages Past. Only to be passed down, hand to hand, shaman to shaman, storyteller to storyteller, all through these many generations, all through the times of the Great Sadness, all through the terrible losses of the whales and the people, and the grief of so many…only to be placed back in her hands. Now.

"*What the hell?*" Bill went white and spoke before anyone else had a chance. "What the hell are you playing at Dave? That's enough of your hocus pocus," he hissed as he leaped up, snatched the carving from Terra, and shoved Dave quickly up against the hospital room door before anyone could stop him.

Miles' dad flashed through his mind…this was more like it. Maybe these people *were* normal…sometimes.

Joseph turned, glanced at Dave and stepped to Bill. He put one hand on Bill's arm, and stared at him. Silent. Eyebrows up. *Yeah*, thought Miles, *normal except for this part*. No one ever intervened when his dad was a jerk. Ever. The two men sized each other up, Bill still pressing poor old geezer Dave into the door while he let his friend hold him accountable with his stare. But Bill's eyes were still sizzling. He was firm about this, he wasn't backing down.

Then Claire spoke. "William Sebastian Lewis. Enough. You do not want to regret this later," she said calmly, eyeing her husband with a quiet ferocity. "Let the man speak. Your daughter woke up for him. Do the details really matter?"

Bill looked from Claire to Joseph, then, with some contempt, to Dave. "I don't want him filling her head with nonsense," he sounded defeated and his grip on Dave loosened.

"Give me the whale, Dad," said Terra, who couldn't turn around to see the three men clustered at the door. "You don't know what you're talking about," she said firmly as she put her hand out once more, palm up, waiting. If she'd been standing, Miles was certain she'd be tapping her foot in impatience. Bill looked once more at Dave and Joseph, then over at Terra's waiting hand, then down at the little worn carving hidden inside his fist.

"Give her to me," Terra beckoned with her open hand, emphasizing her words, "and I'll explain."

There she was. His daughter was back. He let his grip on Dave loosen and stepped away with a piercing look into the old man's face, as if to say, "I'm watching you." Dave just grinned at him and moved to sit on the couch as Joseph stepped back to Terra's bed, and rested his hand once again on her head. Bill sat down next to Tiluk, pulled the chair close to the bed, and put the little ancient whale back in Terra's hand, wrapping his own hand around hers and taking a ragged breath.

"Terra, sweetheart," he shuddered as he exhaled, "I'm so happy to see you up." He squeezed her hand and reached out to caress the little bit of cheek visible from underneath her protective face mask. "We're just so happy you're awake. You were out a long time…" He glanced at Claire. "There's nothing you need to explain."

"I do though, Dad." She looked at him and reached her other hand to his, clasping his hand in both of hers, the whale nestled within. "And you are going to hear me out." She gave him a hard look, then looked around the room for the first time now that she was fully awake, reaching one hand instinctively for Tiluk, who was still kneeling at her bedside squeezed against Bill's chair. They exchanged a look that held years of their friendship and, now… so much more lay in Terra's eyes. *Tiluk, the boy dreamer*. Did he know his own role?

Then she saw Miles, still kneeling at the foot of her bed. Her breath caught, "Miles?"

"Terra." His voice sounded gruff, and he squeezed her blanketed feet tenderly. Blinking quickly as all the feelings of the night before swept through him, he said, "It's really good to meet you."

She let go of Tiluk and reached towards him as he scooted around the bed, kneeling down beside Tiluk, taking her hand gingerly—the little whale rested there. "Miles," she looked at him, then at Tiluk, searching their faces for something. Then she just stared into Miles' eyes, for about a thousand years in his one heartbeat, and he felt her recognize him, he felt himself respond. He knew this girl. "I'm so glad you're here," she whispered simply.

Suddenly everything washed through him and exhaustion flooded his bones.

He'd made it. He was where he was supposed to be. Right now. Finally. He was so tired. So tired. He blinked again and squeezed her hand. That was enough for now.

Just then the doctor whisked into the room, all business and focus. "Terra," she said with a smile as she glanced down at the chart. "You decided to come back to us." The boys stood up and everyone but Claire backed up to stand by Dave, making way for the doctor as she pulled out her stethoscope, listened to Terra's heart beat and breathing, checked all the instruments again, and said, "How are you feeling?"

"Ready to leave," Terra replied, glancing at her mother. "I've got friends I need to see at home."

The doctor smiled and chuckled as she put the stethoscope back around her neck, and sat down in the chair next to Terra, focusing now on her pupils with her little pinprick of light flashlight. "How does your belly feel?

Any nausea?"

Terra shook her head no. "No, I'm fine. Really."

"Terra, you let the doctor decide when you're fine," grumbled Bill. "You thought you needed to see your 'friends' out on Harrowing Straight, too, and look where that got you," he said reprovingly.

Terra looked at Miles and Tiluk, her eyes grinning at them, "Yeah, you're right Dad. That is true."

The doctor smiled at Bill, "Terra's vitals are great. She looks good, her color is back, and all her reflexives are functioning well. I want to check her once more in an hour, but then if everything still looks normal, you are all free to go." She caught everyone else with her quick, efficient eye, and said,

"Having you all here helped this young lady get home. And that means a lot."

The words "free to go," hooked in Miles mind, they started repeating, and, as if replacing the drumbeats, *wake up wake up wake up,* now he heard, *free to go free to go free to go,* and he saw his whale trapped in that horrible concrete jail. He sat down on the couch next to geezer Dave. Dude, he was sooo tired. Doodle. Miles suddenly felt a sharp twinge of longing, he missed his little sister. And then he thought of the whale and *his* little sister, the one he didn't even know about... the whale, he'd *felt* him: *Tulku.* Tiluk was really Tulku... Tiluk, Tulku, Tiluk, Tulku. He was so tired. *I'm just going to rest my head here for a second,* he thought as he let himself lean against geezer Dave's comfy flannel shirt, the pleasing aroma of tobacco and cedar filling his senses.

The doctor peered at Terra over the clipboard as she marked notes on her vitals. "Your face is going to hurt. I'm sending you home with some painkillers, and you'll need to leave that ridiculous contraption on your face for ten days. If you are pain free by then you can go ahead and take it off. Your nose should mend just fine. Someone was watching over you out there..."

Miles heard Terra say something to the doctor about the whales saving her life as he began to zone, his head and eyes were so heavy, he couldn't move. Then the doctor was gone, and he heard her say, "Oh my gosh, Fierce!?" Tiluk jumped up from the couch, rousing him.

"Fierce is fine Terra," Tiluk said, kneeling down next to her again, his hand interlocking with hers. "He's fine. Jason's been taking care of him. He's probably a little cooped up and antsy by now, but he's fine."

Miles saw Terra's eyes go soft, and she looked over at him again, her stare holding his as if she were trying to say something to him without words. All he could hear was *free to go free to go free to go.* He felt so zoomy, as if a thick ball of invisible cotton surrounded him and all he wanted was to surrender to it. But her eyes, they pierced through the thickness, and held him. Her mind reading his. *Free to go free to go free to go.*

Terra tore her eyes away from Miles. The doctor was gone. She looked around the room at everyone, then down at the ancient whale carving in her hand...the carving that no one had really explained yet. She spoke firmly. "I need to see the whales."

Miles couldn't resist, he felt himself succumbing, like a leaden anchor someone threw over the side of a boat, falling, falling, down, so heavy, towards bottom. He'd been awake for so many hours, more than a whole day.

And the trips to OceanLand in the middle of the nights before that, and the nightmares, and…and…the whale. Voices shimmered above him, the light dappling the surface of the water, he, beneath, so heavy, barely hearing them.

"Granny…took me back in time," Terra's flicker of light, he felt it penetrating through the thick, dark, heavy water. "Tiluk was there….he told the prophecy…of his great teacher Tulku. Tulku is Tiluk. Tulku is Tiluk. Tiluk is Tulku." The light flickered and brightened; a revelation. He tried to ascend, but the anchor was so heavy, the flannel so warm against his cheek.

Then dark shadowed the light and another voice flickered, angry. "Terra… just dreaming. You were not talking to whales." Miles shook his head against the dark, the voice was wrong; he knew it as surely as he knew Tulku was his brother. That they were linked. He tried to ascend, but felt even heavier, the flannel so warm, so comforting, the raven's heart beating strong beneath.

The light flamed brighter, pushing back the dark, he so far beneath it all, but anchoring it somehow. *Instrumental*, he heard the word in his mind again. Then her bright light voice, "Great Ages Past…first whale dreamers.

The bond. Between greatest minds on Earth." Peace radiated across him, so heavy, the raven's heart shushing him. Shushing. He expanded into the water, he became the water, the anchor was gone, and he spread outwards, into everything.

"But then, the Great Sadness…whale dreamers disappeared…. fire-tool cultures grew…so much to tell you…sleeping-fire energy… population…. hoarding, violence, greed, fear…shrinking resources… heating planets…. guns, steel, machines… and the pools of captivity!! They are so horrible!!! But they are just a symptom…humans dominating and destroying each other and the Earth…and their brothers and sisters…*Until now*…the whales know this…they have communicated with others…always happens with those like us…universal law… other worlds…some survive their Great Sadness, some do not…but there is great hope for humans…many pathways…whale dreamers will return...that is the prophecy...whale dreamers and a great force for harmony...the end of the Great Sadness is the beginning of some-thing more beautiful than we can imagine..."

Miles felt a brilliant shaft of light hurtle downwards into his sleep, Terra's strength finding him. Then the weight of water, the peace, overtook him, more light flickered above him, the voices mingling, no more anger, but wonder, awe. The light and the dark were one and the same. They were one and the same. The raven's wing wrapped around him, drew him close. The raven's heart beating warm and strong beneath him, sustaining him. They were all together, this was right. He was here.

The awed light, the voices, "How can she know these things? What is going on? ...What does she mean, 'until now?'"

The raven speaking, changing everything. "Your daughter is a whale dreamer."

REUNION

TERRA LET HER FATHER carry her up to her yurt once they were home from the hospital much later that night. "It's pitch black out here sea squirt," Bill said as he reached into the back seat. "Let me just get you up to bed safely, okay?"

"Okay Dad, if you insist." She *was* kind of tired, and he was right. It was one of those moonless nights of complete darkness beneath the grove of cedar and fir trees.

"Good night sweetie," Claire and Maggie said in unison. Both the moms got out of the back seat right behind her, then reached for her as Bill pulled her up into his arms like a princess, and kissed the top of her head, avoiding the bandaging on her face. "It's good to have you home, honey," Claire said, then kissed her once more before turning to Maggie and the two moms walked towards the house arm in arm.

Raven Dave's beat up old car, so covered in rust you couldn't tell what color it was, pulled up just then, and Miles, Tiluk and Joseph piled out in the dim light from the house. Claire and Maggie had turned on the porch light for them.

"Look what you found," Joseph said to Bill with a grin, eyeing Terra in Bill's arms. "The sleeping beauty."

Terra knew better than to resist Joseph's good-hearted teasing, so she rolled her eyes and said, "Yep, that's right. Here I am…the damsel in distress."

Miles, whom they'd finally had to awaken from his stupor at the last minute before leaving the hospital, stood next to Joseph and Tiluk. "You are about the last person in the world I'd consider a damsel in distress, Terra." She felt her face get hot. Then Bill's grip tightened around her as Raven Dave stepped close to her, his body puffed up and his voice raised in indignation, "You are no damsel in distress, Terra. *You* are a *whale dreamer*."

He turned, and shuffled back to his car shaking his head and grumbling to himself in disgust about how the idea of damsels in distress had nearly murdered the great feminine.

"Claim your power, so that others may do the same," he called from the driver's seat, his window open. "Honor those who've given their lives to keep the people connected to the Earth Mother during the rise of the fire-tool cultures. Honor them by being who you are…for it is their time to rise again."

Then he spit out the window, shoved a cigarette in his mouth, and drove off in a spray of gravel.

Bill stared after the car's tail lights, mouth hanging open at Dave's little speech, trying to integrate everything that had happened in the last 24 hours. Then, as if he'd made some kind of decision, he looked at Joseph with a new kind of respect and said, "All right everybody, say good night. I'm taking the whale dreamer to her sleeping quarters now."

"'Night Lewis," Tiluk said. "You have some things to tell me about tomorrow." Tiluk yanked gently on her braid, conveying his care and curiosity in that one gesture. She knew he understood he'd been involved in her journey somehow, he just hadn't heard whole shebang.

"While we take Fierce to hunt…" she felt how close Miles was standing to her, giving off an almost protective energy, and found herself wishing he was even closer, "with Miles."

"Terra," Miles leaned in near her ear, and she felt her cheeks grow warm underneath the thing on her face. "I'm really glad you woke up."

"Better take the sea squirt up to her yurt before these boys keep her up talking all night," Joseph intervened, stepping to Terra, and laying a gentle kiss on her forehead above her bandages. "You've done well, Terra. Get some sleep."

"Joseph," Terra reached for him, and held his shoulder. "The whales…" "Tomorrow, sea squirt. They're waiting for you."

"Good night people." Bill turned towards Terra's yurt, his arms tiring. "This kid is not two years old anymore, and I'm not 27 either. The princess is off to her castle now."

"Oh Dad," Terra nestled her face into the crook of his neck as he walked with her in his arms. "Ouch!" She'd gotten her nose too close to his shoulder, and the pain shot across her face and down her throat.

"Just like the doctor said, huh honey?"

He held her tight as he managed to open the door and turn on the light. Then in one sweeping motion he pulled back the covers and squirrelled

Terra gently into bed. "I wouldn't bother with changing out of your hospital clothes tonight, sweetheart," Bill said, referring to the gown the nurse had suggested she wear home. "What with that thing on your face. Just get some rest."

"Dad?" Terra asked as she snuggled under her covers, one hand finding the carving in her pocket, the other pulling the covers up underneath her chin. She sensed a change in him. "Are you still mad at Dave?"

Bill's shoulders slumped, and he sat heavily down on her bed, taking her free hand. He drew a long breath. "I was never mad at him, Terra." He gently ran one hand up over her forehead, and down the long length of her hair.

Then he took the elastic band off her braid, and began to unwrap her tresses, a gesture typically reserved only for her mother. "I was worried about you." "Oh." She looked closely at her father's face, and saw a weight that hadn't been there before. "I didn't mean to scare you, Dad."

"I'm sorry I couldn't hear you at first, sweetheart. And I'm sorry for how I treated Dave. I was so worried about you. We didn't know how injured you were, and I didn't know if you were going to come back to us." He stopped the unraveling for a moment and looked up, away from her, into the dark-ness beyond the yurt's window.

"It was just so much to take in…I've been a scientist all my life, and this… this…" He drew his hands over his face and rubbed his both eyes. They were pink with exhaustion. "This is just so hard to believe."

He finished unweaving her hair, and spread it out on her pillow. "I'm all about the evidence. And I have to admit, you've given me a lot to think about today."

Terra looked at him and realized it had been her dad who'd sat with her all that time when she'd been out cold as Joseph and Tiluk drove to the airport, before the moms showed up with Miles. No wonder he looked so haggard and vulnerable. She felt an overwhelming urge to comfort him, he looked shattered. Terra reached for her father's hand, and he took it, then lifted it to his lips and kissed her palm tenderly. "I love you sweetheart," his voice thick and dark.

"It's okay, Dad. I love you, too. Thank you for believing me." She pulled out the whale carving. "Here," she said, wrapping his hands around it. "She's the reason I wanted you to trust me. Her," Terra looked into her dad's eyes, "...and *all* the orca. This connection is happening because they can help us. And we can help them."

Bill looked down at the carving, his first chance to hold and examine it. He rolled the burnished form between his fingers, seeing the worn cracks, the rubbed and darkened wood. There was no doubt it was extremely old.

He glanced at her, a flicker of adult camaraderie dancing across his features.

"It really is the same carving you made of the new calf?" "Yes."

"Which means, it really had to have gone back in time..." "Yes."

"Which means..."

"That part of me went back, too." Terra looked carefully at her father. "And you returned with things I can't explain," his voice thick with wonder. Terra was changed, and after she'd woken up, everyone, including her dad, noticed it. What's more, as she'd told her story at the hospital earlier, she began to realize that when she merged with Granny during her coma, she'd become privy to the whale's databanks of wisdom. Her mind had absorbed some of it, even things they hadn't actually focused on. Like the Council—the matriarch leaders of the main pods that make up the Northern

Residents off Vancouver Island and the Southern Residents of the Salish Sea.

Like Granny, there were leaders of each of these other pods, and despite large distances that often separated them, the chief leaders made decisions, worked together, and held governance over their huge combined area of home waters and food resources. Granny hadn't specifically shared this with Terra, but as she talked, she'd recalled it, like it was something she'd known all along. Her parents had gone electric when she'd told them, their scientist minds working overtime. "Think of what this could mean!" she'd heard her mom whisper to Maggie. "A whale Council would show systematic governance...something we thought only humans were capable of!" Only Joseph was not surprised. He'd just smiled.

Or the orca graveyard: she'd recalled that, too. Granny's reverent knowledge of the sacred place where Salish Sea whales take their dead. The specifics of this place were so secret, so sanctified, that even Terra couldn't access the exact location. Burying one's dead was once believed to be a uniquely "human" endeavor—until now.

Her dad had opened a door between them, but she was hesitant. "Now that we're linking up again," Terra said, "the orca and people, I mean…" She wavered. "Well, it's just that Granny gave me other knowledge I forgot until just now." She grew quiet.

"What do you remember honey?" her dad asked. "It's okay, you can tell me…I won't doubt your experience again." He sighed and looked down at the carving in his hands. "*Really.*" He looked back up at her, asking for her trust, the stress-pink exhaustion of his eyes was turning to simple fatigue. He was letting go of his denial and feeling the unconscious relief of acceptance.

Terra closed her eyes for a moment, letting the words filter back up through her. As the world had gone dark after she'd watched Tiluk and the shaman and the tribe all those thousands of years ago while she was linked with Granny and Tulku and the calf, and as she'd flashed outwards into everything, feeling at one with the universe, Granny's last words had come to her as she'd left the brilliant circle of whale-human connection, just before she'd started to wake up in the hospital room. Then, clear as a bell, right there in her yurt as she looked inward trying to recall the message, it was as if Granny was there again, saying it to her once more:

As a whale dreamer linked to Tulku, the Great Protector, and to my great granddaughter, the next Keeper of Life, you'll find an unexpected force for harmony unfolding around you.

Her eyes flew open. Her dad was looking right into them, and felt her surprise. "What is it sweetheart?"

"Wow, Dad. It's just…" Terra bit her lip. Suddenly, with instant clarity, she knew what she had to do. The message made everything so clear. She'd received the words but also a powerful vision. It was so obvious! But she wasn't going to tell her dad. Not yet.

"It's just that Granny said things would be…easier…Now that we've made contact."

Bill chuckled at this, his face relaxing even more, and said, "Well that's good news. Easy sounds great to me." Terra could practically see her dad's thoughts scatter from her accident to the death at OceanLand to the pod's cries when they heard Tiluk on the live feed, to the overarching concern they all had for the wild whales' survival and the planet in general. "Yeah, easy would be a nice change." He looked at Terra, and pulled her carefully into a strong hug, "Come here you…I'm glad you came back." They hugged, silent.

When her dad finally let go he put the whale tenderly back into her hands and wrapped her fingers around it. "Sweet dreams," he said meaningfully, giving her a light kiss on the top of her head, careful to avoid her sore face. He stood, put another log into her woodstove against the cool damp outside, and walked to the yurt's door, turning back to her with fond bewilderment.

"I have no idea what's going on here, Terra. But I know enough to pay attention to the evidence. And to you."

"Good night Dad." "'Night sweetie."

Terra turned out her light, lay on her back with the whale tucked between her fingers, and pitched headlong into a chasm of slumber—the potent, dead-to-the-world kind of restorative sleep her body and spirit craved after so many days of questions, learning, shock, and awe. When she awoke, fifteen uninterrupted hours later, she was in exactly the same position. The whale still nestled in her hands. There'd been no dreams.

Terra sat up gingerly, her face hurt even more this morning. She reached for her two-way. "Tiluk, you there?"

"We're here," Tiluk's voice crackled through immediately as though he'd been waiting for her. "You slept well. We've been taking turns checking on you, but your mom wouldn't let us wake you up."

Us. Miles. *Miles*! Terra blushed. "Meet me at the mews in ten. Bring Miles. Over."

"Good. We have things to tell you. Over."

Terra stared at her two-way for a second, curious. "Things to tell you." What things? Hadn't there already been enough "things" to last for, oh, another five thousand years? She managed to get out of the hospital gown and pull on her clothes, careful to choose shirts and a sweater she could button up the front since nothing would fit down over her head with this contraption on her face. Then she put the whale carving in her pocket. *Well, I've got things to tell them, too.* She thought, recalling her vision from last night, the one she got when she'd recalled Granny's parting words about a force for harmony, the one she hadn't mentioned to her dad. *And I know exactly what we need to do.* She thought for a second about the message she'd heard from The Others, about ending the Great Sadness. *I might not know how to do that, at least not yet, but I do know a few other things.* Terra's experience of traveling beyond her body had changed her. She'd awoken with a conviction of her interconnection with everything. The ancient ways were real to her now. But she hadn't tried to talk to anyone about that yet...

Fierce started squawking when he saw her walking to the mews, as if he'd been waiting forever for her to show up. She hadn't seen him three whole days. "Shhh, I know beauty. I know." She pulled on the leather glove, stepped in, and didn't even have time to raise her arm before the bird descended on top of her head, flapping madly, still squawking.

As soon as she stepped inside the mews, Terra was hit by the terrible pool confining the whales. This was Fierce's version. Her stomach clenched against this realization, and she sat down heavily, tuning in to how Fierce must have felt in her absence. She knew it wasn't as bad for him as for the whales, with those terrible walls echoing a constant clatter of noise and the harsh, glaring light, and the other whales who fought, and the total lack of any way to swim in the open ocean...the total lack of any way to do much of *anything*. But still. It hit her that her beloved Fierce had been trapped in here while she'd been gone. It hit her that he was here at all.

Swallowing hard, she let the bird tell her all about it. He flapped and squawked and even bent down and plucked wisps of her hair up with his beak, yanking. He couldn't contain himself, frustrated as he'd been by his confinement.

"I know," she crooned again. "I know Fierce. Let's go take care of that right now." She stood up. The bird finally calmed down and stepped onto her shoulder, leaving the top of her head. He was still holding a length of hair tight in his beak and he refused to let go; as if by pinioning her tresses, he was reminding her not to leave him alone again.

"Who *are* you?" a hushed voice breathed nearby. Terra turned around, and there was Miles standing next to Tiluk at the door of the mews. They'd walked up silently behind her, watching Fierce's reaction. His face was rapt, looking at her and Fierce. *Miles.*

Terra stepped out of the mews, to Miles. She took in his angular face, his shock of light brown hair, trimmed neat and clean, and the glint of his radiant blue eyes flashing at her. He was so familiar. She felt a blush sweep her face as she stood in front of Miles, Fierce on her shoulder, peering into his eyes, the metal contraption covering her nose and cheeks, forgotten.

"Somehow, I think you already know." Her long brown hair, loose today, glinted in the greenish light of the conifers standing around them. Miles' face reflected his abject wonder, seeing Terra standing there with a kestrel on her shoulder, her hair in his beak, her ease in this grand cathedral of natural beauty almost overwhelming him. The rightness of her, of this place, of this boy Tiluk, was so different than what he was used to at home. He caught himself wondering what Florida would be like if it had been allowed to stay itself, like this place. *Aria…* he wished she were here to see this.

Terra looked to Tiluk who stood shoulder to shoulder with Miles, then back at Miles. "I think you are part of the prophecy, too, Miles," she said seriously. Then, recalling how she'd seen Tiluk—the boy dreamer—during her journey back in time, she said, "Come on you two, we have a lot to talk about." Wordless, she and Tiluk took Miles to their boulder den, each boy walking on either side of Terra, somehow both protective and deferential at the same time. *Like male orca*, Terra smiled to herself. Miles' face registered awe, as they walked into the den surrounded by the grove of silent giants, the moss covered rocks strewn beneath. Then, there in the den, as they all sat down together on the large moss-covered rock where she and Tiluk had spent so much of their childhood, she flung Fierce up from her hand, saying "Go!" They watched as Fierce hurtled into the dark woods, intent on a kill.

"Free as a bird," Terra whispered to herself as she watched him fly away.

"Terra," Tiluk said simply, "Tell me."

And she did. She hadn't told everyone in the hospital yesterday about Tiluk being the boy dreamer...she'd glossed over that part, sensing it would be too unbelievable for them to handle, especially her dad. She also had the strong sense this was something to keep between her, Miles, and Tiluk. And maybe Joseph and Raven Dave. But first she had to tell Tiluk.

"It was you but it wasn't you. You were in a different body. And it was like you knew I'd be coming, you were so powerful. And you called me and Granny back, and made sure I was there to hear the message from The

Others...and to hear Tulku give the prophecy." He stared at her, a flicker of recognition in his eyes.

She went on. "It was like we'd been partners in lifetimes before that... whale dreamers together. Like you've always have been my brother, and we've always been whale dreamers."

Tiluk just stared at her. Silent.

"You know, it was Tiluk who was drumming in the hospital room while you were out, Terra," Miles said softly. "He was drumming here, while you were meeting him...there."

"There's that, and there's the fact that Miles and I dreamed together last night," Tiluk said quietly.

She looked at them and shivered. Could this really be happening?

Her life had flipped over.

"We dreamt with Tulku last night," said Miles, his voice strong, as if all of a sudden in their circle of three, he was laying claim to his own somersaulted existence. "He called us…" Miles nodded to Tiluk. "Both of us."

"We both had the same dream Terra," said Tiluk gently. "It's already happening."

"And the calf was there. She was with her brother. Tulku knows his sister." Miles continued. "Because of your help linking Granny and the calf and Tulku, he can reach the dream world without Granny's help anymore. He can leave that bloody pool and find us and his sister in the dream world."

He stared at Tiluk, their eyes linked, their bond already so strong, and a hint of—*Was it joy?* wondered Terra—crossed his face.

"I got to meet him there…" Miles' voice caught. "He thanked me. For the music. For the live feed. For the call from his mother and family." He swiped his jacket sleeve quickly over his eyes, blinking hard. *Miles.* Terra resisted the urge to wrap her arms around him. Miles looked down for a moment before looking back up at Terra, their eyes catching and sharing much more than words.

Tiluk spoke. "I recognized him, too, Lewis. You're right. We've been dreamers together."

Terra nodded, not surprised to hear Tiluk's immediate acceptance of all this. As if he'd been waiting his entire life for it to finally happen. She leaned into him, the familiarity of him—the trust, their bond—made clear.

Miles went on. "And let me tell you, those two? Tulku and the calf? They've got some serious clout in the dream place!"

"They have big medicine together, that's for sure," added Tiluk. "They gave us her name…" Miles said. Suddenly, Terra knew it, too. As one, the three of them—Terra, Tiluk, and Miles—whispered in unison, "*Harmony.*"

Just then, Fierce landed heavily on Terra's shoulder with a partially dis-membered ground squirrel. He squawked and grabbed a lock of Terra's hair, yanking it sharply. It was as if he was saying, "See? I can still remember how to hunt, but don't you dare leave me alone for so long, ever again!"

The trio burst out laughing. Then Terra crooned, "Don't worry Fierce, I know, beauty," as she reached up and gently lifted the bird off her shoulder, bringing him down onto her wrist, so he could settle into his meal on her lap and she didn't have to worry about squirrel parts dribbling down her shirt.

"Speaking of Harmony," Terra stared for one long moment at Fierce tucking into his meal, then back up at the boys, "we have some planning to do." Then she told them about last night, and the vision she'd had when she remembered those incredible words that Granny had left her with:

As a whale dreamer linked to Tulku, the Great Protector, and my great grand-daughter, the next Keeper of Life, you'll find an unexpected force for harmony unfolding around you.

"It's just like your first dream, Lewis," Tiluk breathed, a little spellbound at Granny's powerful words.

Miles caught it, too. "This is amazing. She's basically telling you the whales have your back, and they're going to be helping from the dream place." It *was* just like her first dream, now that she thought of it. That first dream when Granny had summoned her and told Terra she was being given a mission to save Granny's family with help from the new calf and her brother. The brother that Terra never even knew existed until the killing at OceanLand.

Tulku... Harmony...Granny...

"I need to see them," she said, glancing down at Fierce. "Right now." Miles looked at her, seeing a power he didn't quite understand, but one that made him want to bask in its glow: to shine it back, to behold it, to help unleash it. "Let's go whale dreamer." His radiant blue stare pierced her, and the heat of her blush warmed the air around them.

"Come," Tiluk stood, taking Fierce as Terra and Miles got up, shaking off the intense moment. "I'll get my flute. You get your drum, Terra."

"And I'll get my z-phone," Miles added. The three of them linked arms and headed back down to the yurts.

"After we see the whales, I want to finish making our plans, okay?" Terra reminded them of the vision she'd started to share.

"Whatever you say, Lewis. There's a reason those whales follow the female leaders...smart whales know the Keepers of Life have everyone's best interests at heart." Tiluk spoke more words in that one breath than she'd heard him say since she'd come home from the hospital. "*I'll* follow you." "I am so in with that!" Miles added. "After the whales, planning time it is, Earth girl. We'll brainstorm." Terra took note of Miles' additional term of affection. *Whale dreamer...Earth girl.* She felt a flash of heat somewhere in the pit of her stomach.

Tiluk dropped Fierce off at the mews, the three parted ways to gather their instruments, and a few minutes later they all convened down at the dock in the midday sun—it was one of those perfect Puget Sound summer days, when the light is fast and bright, everywhere the trees are glittering dark emeralds, and the water is a sheen of milky black calm reflecting the clear expanse of sky.

Miles was 100 percent awestruck. "My God," he said to no one as they sat down next to each other on the dock, he, swiveling his head back and forth like a barn owl, looking one way, then another, eyes blinking in the bright sunshine. "How can it be this beautiful? My God..." he said again.

"Miles look," Terra nudged him with her elbow in the soft spot under his ribcage, a little jolt of electricity hitting her at the contact. He followed her stare to the dorsal fins hanging in shadow at the far side of the cove. "Look..."

"Holy cow..." he breathed, overwhelmed. "There they are."

Then Tiluk was piping out the first phrase of Dueling Banjos, that awe-some question. Miles' face broke out in a smile warmer than Terra had ever seen. Tiluk remembered what Miles had done for their whale, and was hon-oring Miles by playing the same song.

Miles answered boldly. His xylophone rang out loud and bright on the crisp summer air. Terra started up on the drum, and they all took off. *Took off!* The boys zoomed up and down the phrases, faster and faster—dueling each other—their feisty, playful duo threading alongside Terra's brisk drum beats. The three sealed something right then and there, the music linking them forever.

WHOOOSH, CRASH!! Granny's huge body erupted up, way up, all the way out of the water in full body breach, just a few yards from the dock.

The explosion of frigid water sprayed over them, splattering the entire dock, the waves pushing so hard the dock moved a little. Less than a second later, Granny's enormous head appeared next to Terra: she rose up out of the water in a four-foot spyhop so that their eyes were level with one another, her black skin glinting in the bright sunshine, her white eye-patches the size of enormous snowballs. Terra felt their link instantly. Granny was welcoming her home. In Granny's eyes she saw everything she'd experienced on her journey, and she knew without doubt that Granny had been with her, had taken her back in time, had linked her with Tiluk, Tulku, and the calf. It was all there in Granny's ancient, wise eyes.

"Bloody freaking helicopters," Miles uttered under his breath. He put his xylophone down on the dock behind him, water dripping from his hair down his face, and stared in disbelief.

"Miles, say hello to Granny," Terra said quietly, setting aside her drum, not looking away from the whale's stare.

Miles gaped, speechless. Then Granny dropped below the water and instantly resurfaced right in front of Miles. He went rigid and stopped breathing in the shadow of her colossal bulk. Terra looked from Granny to Miles, and saw his cheek quivering. Granny was intentionally making eye contact with Miles, giving him her full and mighty presence. It was over-whelming him. Then a second giant head popped up next to Granny's.

Tiluk expelled a loud breath of surprise. "Oh. Wow…" he said quietly. "Miles, this is Wendy…Tulku's mother."

Tiluk put his arm around Miles' shoulder, as if to steady them both. "I think she wants to thank you," Tiluk's voice had gone reverent with wonder. "Wendy has never approached anyone before. Ever."

The quiver in Miles' cheek gave way like a dam, and tears started rolling down his cheeks. Something that had been held back ever since his parents' divorce, ruptured. He still couldn't speak. Instead, he put his hands together in prayer pose and leaned towards Wendy, dipping his head down towards her, deferential. When he looked up again, straightening tall from his seated position, he'd reclaimed his voice. "Whatever I can do, Wendy, I'll do it. Tulku is my brother now."

Wendy dropped underwater and swam off just as another great spray of water came hurling at them from a few feet away.

Harmony. In playful greeting, the calf swiped them with her tail again, blasting all three kids with another wave of water. A smile broke across Miles' face through the tears and salt water.

"Which makes *you* my sister, little one," Miles called out to the calf as she swam off at top speed after her mother.

Granny slid back down into the water and rolled onto her side, taking a moment to make eye contact with each of the three kids. First Terra, then Miles, then Tiluk, as she coasted by them alongside the dock.

"Time to fish!" Terra felt the impulse powerfully in her belly, it was much more than words—it was an experience of eager, hungry joy. Somehow

Granny zinged her with it. Then she zoomed off at top speed, leading the whole rest of the pod out to Haro Strait for the first time since Terra's accident...since they'd begun their vigil.

"Holy smokes," Terra murmured. "She just told me they're off to find fish.

I *felt* it...like I was one of them!"

"Terra, you're linked with her now," Tiluk offered, his voice still shaky.

Even steady, mystical Tiluk was grappling with what they'd just experienced. "You'll be able to feel that direct connection more and more often, even while you're awake. It's part of being a dreamer. I talked to my dad."

Miles stood up suddenly, with urgency, wiping his face with his sleeves. "Come on you two. I can't stand this. Tulku should be here with his family." He reached out to pull Terra up from her seat on the dock. "Let's go make those plans of yours, whale dreamer."

MATRIARCHS

"WHO'S THAT TAPPING on my chamber door," joked Maggie as she walked to the entry to answer the brisk knock they'd all heard.

"'Tis the Raven?" Terra asked with a giggle. They were all expecting Raven Dave—the kids had asked him to join them while they made their plans. Actually, they'd made plans *for* him. After they'd come up from the dock and their amazing experience with the whales, Miles hadn't been able to sit still. He kept walking to the window, peering out at the cove, coming back to Terra and Tiluk, sitting down, getting up again. Talking at high speed, offering ideas while they brainstormed. Terra, on the other hand, had suddenly been overcome by fatigue. Her muscles were sore, her face hurt, and she felt glued to the couch.

Within moments after returning from the dock, they'd all agreed to call Dave. Miles whipped out his cell phone and placed the call, "Hey Dave. It's Miles. We're planning a ceremony." Miles held Terra's eyes. "Yeah, for Terra and Tiluk's 14th birthday and the calf's naming ritual."

"You got it. We're combining the two. Can you come over and give us some input?"

"Uh-huh. Right. It's going to be on the summer solstice, in three days." "Okay."

Miles snapped his phone shut. "He's on his way," Miles said, frowning a little. "I got the impression he'd been waiting for my call."

Joseph peered at Miles meaningfully. "Chances are good that Dave knew you'd be calling…especially now that Terra's made the link with the whales." Tiluk looked over at Joseph from his spot on the couch next to Terra. "Hey papa bear, speaking of knowing things. Can Miles use your marimbas?"

Joseph had a set of old marimbas that he'd used in tribal ceremonies over the years. It was a set handed down from his grandfather, who'd received the marimbas by trading a totem pole he'd made—with orca, ravens, and bears—with another tribal elder who'd been visiting from Belize. He'd been in a traveling marimba group and he'd shared music, dance, food and stories with Joseph's grandfather's family. The native people across both continents had found ways to stay connected over the years since the whites commandeered the great land.

Joseph's face wrinkled in pleasure. "Miles, if there is an instrument on this Earth that is more meant for you than marimbas, I'll eat my drum."

When Miles raised his eyebrows in curiosity, they explained what marimbas are to Miles—essentially, they consist of a giant, stand-up xylophone made of hollow wood or gourds with wooden keys laid across, but with *way* more oomph than any xylophone. Then Claire had glanced at Miles with a big smile, and said, "I have a feeling about this marimba thing Miles…" Now he couldn't wait to try them out.

But first thing's first. Next they'd worked out a few more details and zipped off an email to the Florida journalist, Tim Sinclair, inviting him up to San Juan Island to report on their ceremony. They'd heard back immediately. "Got your proposal. I'll be there. Do you mind if Joanna Burns, former OceanLand trainer, comes, too?" No. They didn't. Actually, that sounded great.

Then, Maggie made hot cocoa while everyone waited for Dave to show up. Miles finally calmed down and sat next to Terra, Tiluk on her other side. Even Claire and Bill, settled on the other couch across from the kids, had decided not to work that day. As Claire said after the kids had come up from visiting the whales, "It's the kind of day to stay home and be together, sweet-heart. Besides, we want to get to know Miles a little better." She'd smiled at

Miles then, and he nodded over his hot cocoa, still basically astonished— and kind of embarrassed—by this family and his luck at finding them. Only

Gwen and Jason were missing. They'd gone out on the boat, tracking some of the other Southern Residents, and watching for Granny's pod to resume their normal fishing activities.

When the knock on the door finally came, Maggie jumped up to answer it, making the crack about the tapping on the chamber door. But it wasn't Raven Dave who stepped into the entry.

It was Jane Goodall.

"Terra, you have visitors," Maggie said mischievously. Maggie had kept the J Squad posted during Terra's ordeal in the hospital. She'd also filled them in on the meeting she and Claire had had with OceanLand officials, along with the proposal for Tiluk's retirement to Blackfish Cove. But no one expected them to visit—except Maggie, who had gotten the call and was in on the big surprise.

Terra's parents saw her first, and their faces registered a mixture of open shock and delight. Terra could tell by their reaction that it definitely wasn't

Dave who'd come in.

She turned carefully around, favoring her sore muscles and aching body, to peer back towards the door, and there was her biggest hero *ever*, Jane Goodall, standing there smiling at her. *Jane Goodall!!* She was exactly like

Terra knew she would be: tall and trim, her blond hair pulled back in a ponytail, her face wizened with kindness.

"Hello Terra, it is so lovely to meet you." Terra's mind went blank, as if her systems had been jolted by an electric shock. "We heard about what happened from Maggie, and we decided we needed to come see you and these whales," she said as Janet Carson stepped through the door. Terra's eyes bugged out, still speechless. *The J Squad! In her living room!* The two women smiled at each other as if they were best friends, a sense of glee between them. They'd surprised her.

Before she knew it, Jane Goodall came right over and, with a quick smile for the boys, knelt down in front of her and took her hands, looking into her eyes, ignoring the tape and brace covering most of her face. Terra had to remind herself to shut her wide-open mouth.

"We're so happy to hear you're okay," Jane said. "You must have been so upset about what you'd learned about Korky and how she'd lost her calf and how she tried to break through the walls of her pool. Especially after everything you'd just found out about Tiluk and his captive life...and Dusky's death." She reached up and squeezed Terra's shoulder. "That is a lot of sadness to learn about all at once. It's too much sadness. Especially when you love the whales like you do."

Terra stared into Jane's eyes, she could hardly believe this was happening. And Jane Goodall—*Jane Goodall!!*—understood her. "I want you to know you aren't alone, Terra," she went on. "I would have paddled into the Strait, too." Jane looked over at Terra's parents for the first time, their pleasure was palpable. Jane met Claire's eyes, a considered, meaningful look in her expression. Then she turned back to Terra and said seriously, "That force is what drives my entire life."

Jane examined the contraption covering Terra's broken nose and the heavy bruising that had bloomed on the parts of her cheeks and forehead that were visible, then reached up and cupped her head, almost exactly the way Joseph always did, and added, "Let's work together to find a safer and more productive place for your wonderful energy, okay?" Terra could only nod, still 100 percent mute, her throat tight.

Then Jane stood up, slowly straightening her slender body, and smiled at Tiluk and Miles "Hello boys…I hear you are big part of this team, too." Miles was still so flabbergasted that his mouth hung open. Terra nudged him. He quickly slammed it shut and smiled awkwardly— in full blush—into the face of a woman he considered to be one of the most famous people in the world.

Tiluk, meanwhile, stood up, saying a quiet, unruffled hello before drawing Jane further into the room to the large windows, to show her Blackfish Cove and to see if the whales had returned from their foraging. Jane put her arm around Tiluk's shoulders as if they'd known each other forever, and together they looked out at the Cove. The whales were still gone.

After watching with Tiluk for a few moments, Jane turned from the window towards Terra, and with the same ripple of wisdom Terra had felt coming from Granny, she said, "We want to hear everything."

Maggie made hot tea and cocoa. And Raven Dave finally showed up.

The two women, Jane and Janet, sat down with them all and Terra chronicled her experience once again. She passed the whale carving to the women, who took long turns staring at it, rubbing the primeval wood. Miles noticed that Dave still smelled like tobacco, but there was no spitting today. Terra recounted the whole story with occasional interruptions and questions, first from Tiluk, who told about the Morse Endeavor and how the whales spelled out "Very bad" after Terra's accident. Then from the J Squad, especially when she got to the part about the seeing Tulku and Granny in the dream world, and the horrible pool of captivity, and then The Others and the Great Sadness, and the details she'd learned about how some worlds survive their Great Sadness and others don't—at which point, Jane Goodall stopped her, and asked serious and specific questions about what she'd learned. She wanted to know more about The Fallacy, and about the history of peace Granny had described from the Great Ages Past. The way she paid such close attention, then caught eyes with Janet Carson, made Miles shiver. He was so relieved the J Squad was here, it was obvious they understood about Tulku, and could help them do something. Then the kids told their plans for the ceremony, including their idea for Dave's role, the exciting news that Tim Sinclair would be here to record it all, and that a former OceanLand trainer was coming with him.

At the end, after all the questions, there was a long stretch of silence. Finally, Janet Carson said quietly, her voice thick. "It looks like we have some things to do…"

"Yes," came Jane Goodall's soft reply. "It's even more than we could have hoped for…I didn't expect this in my lifetime." She trailed off, staring out the large windows, fingering the carving once more before returning it to

Terra. "Are the whales back, yet?"

Tiluk walked quickly to the windows and scanned. "They're back. They're at the far side of the cove. Looks like they're playing. Harmony has kelp across her dorsal fin and her sisters are chasing her." He was smiling.

Jane stood up, filled with sudden purpose, and said, "It would mean a lot to me to meet Granny. Would anyone mind if I go out there alone?"

Terra sensed that everyone had the same vision at that moment: Jane Goodall, the most beloved and compassionate Keeper of Life on the planet, was to meet Granny, perhaps the oldest, wisest and most respected orca on Earth. Miles breathed out, *"Shite-sa,"* so quietly next to her, she was sure she was the only one to hear him. Tiluk walked over to Jane, helped her to her feet, and led her out the glass door, pointing to the dock.

"This meeting is happening because of you, Terra. Remember what I said, whale dreamer," Raven Dave spoke firmly. *Claim your power.* Yeah, she knew what he was talking about. But wow, even after everything she'd experienced, it was hard to believe this was happening. If she could have picked one person in the world to meet Granny, one person who might understand the whale's tremendous memory banks, spiritual power, and magnificence, one person who might be able to believe in the value of her dream and *do* something about it, it would have been Jane Goodall. And here she was, and Terra hadn't even known she was coming.

Then she recalled Granny's words. *You'll find an unexpected force for harmony unfolding around you.*

"The Great Feminine lives in these wise matriarchs. They are the great Keepers of Life," Dave continued. "Whether the rest of us let them lead, and *protect* them while they do it, is the only question now. That's what The Others tried to tell you, Terra. It is the Keepers of Life on other worlds— the Keepers and those still allied with Life—who lead those worlds out of their Great Sadness. They are the ones who stand for unity first. They stand for their sons and daughters. They stand to stop the rising tides of sadness, anger, hate, violence, greed, and ignorance brought on by the Great Sadness. They stand for their children's future."

"It is no accident that Jane and Janet are here." His shoulders broadened and his black eyes glittered at Janet, who dipped her head in respect. "But all Keepers of Life, here and on the other worlds where a Great Sadness arises, need help and protection after so many years of strife and conflict.

We cannot survive the Great Sadness without those who would stand with the matriarchs…and those who would stand with the great circle of Life."

Dave stood suddenly, tall and dark, emanating a rippling field of energy.

Joseph joined him at the window to watch. Terra caught a glimmer of the shaman she'd seen on her journey. *Dave? Could it be?*

"As a whale dreamer, you are among those who will guide us," he said, his black eyes piercing Terra's brown ones. "As you know, too many of us on Earth have forgotten the circle in our desperate hungers. We need you and those like you."

Miles reached for Terra at Dave's words and their fingers wrapped together unconsciously. Claire and Bill stared at Dave as if he was speaking in tongues. They were nodding, though, won over by his strange but powerful words. Tiluk listened from the window, nodding, and watching as Jane Goodall descended the long stairs to the dock.

"When we stand with the unity of all Life, the ancient ways grow strong," Joseph said quietly as he moved next to his son. Tiluk straightened up, stretching tall between his father and the shaman in silence. He'd grown nearly to Joseph's height, Terra noticed with surprise.

"Terra, Granny is coming to the dock," Tiluk spoke. "Jane is kneeling down and Granny is spyhopping up in front of her." He turned and looked at the rest of them. "She's acting like she already knows Jane."

"Now that the link is open," Dave gave Terra a pointed look, "Granny can recognize Jane's power and leadership."

"They are kindred souls," Joseph added as Terra and Miles came to the window, Janet and her parents joining them. And they were all watching this moment together. The hydrophone, as always, was turned on. They heard Granny's exhalation as they saw her drop down and blow mist all over Jane.

"She's raising her pectoral fin up next to the dock," breathed Claire. "Granny must really recognize her wisdom and compassion somehow. I've never seen her solicit human contact before. I wish Gwen and Jason could see it, too."

"Honey, look, I just noticed that their boat is anchored at the mouth of the cove. I think you've got your wish," Bill whispered.

Jane reached out and rubbed Granny's fin as she laid herself flat on the dock, stretching out over the water, maintaining the contact with Granny as the whale slid the length of her body alongside, letting Jane slowly caress and scratch her all the way down to her tail flukes. Then she sat up, and they could see her take out her hanky, and wipe her cheeks and eyes. "This has to be one of the biggest moments of her life," murmured Janet Carson. "Right up there with first contact with the chimps."

"Only better," Miles said, thinking of what the whales had already taught

Terra. And the promise of that learning.

"You're right Miles," Janet said appreciatively. "And maybe, just maybe, we're ready to receive the whales' wisdom."

"It's time. The signs are everywhere. We *are* ready," Joseph said calmly. "The transition is upon us," added Dave. "And Tulku's freedom will be one of many joyous events in our first steps forward."

"Oh look, it's Harmony!" Terra let go of Miles and clapped her hands together. The calf erupted in a clumsy little breach, right next to the dock, full of mischief. She drenched Jane, who rocked backwards, her peals of laughter carrying all the way up to the house.

Then, as Jane wiped her face off again with her hanky, Granny turned downwards. She lifted her great tail up above the dock, and slammed it down, soaking Jane once more. But she didn't stop, and when Tiluk realized what was happening, he moved to stand next to Terra, putting his arm around his chosen sister, both of them listening to the hydrophone, waiting to decode the message. They listened, watching Jane receive a baptism of whale-human communion, splash upon splash upon splash. They waited as the whale coded her tail slaps, and their listening held all the hours, weeks, and months of their Morse Endeavor, the persistent tapping to the whales they'd done together years before as hopeful and innocent young children. And suddenly, now, here they were.

As they listened to Granny's message, her head instinctively found the cradle of Tiluk's neck and shoulder. *Brother.* The flush of recognition hit her, the value of this boy to her life, and in that moment her heart ached for the other Tiluk, *Tulku*, and all he'd lost. She slipped her arm around Miles' waist, pulling him close on her other side, feeling gratitude for what he'd begun to restore to Tulku.

Finally, the whale stopped her tail slaps, and Jane, who'd knelt without moving throughout Granny's coded message and who was now totally saturated by seawater—her hair dripping, her sweater clinging to her—slowly stood and stared up towards the house, a question on her face. Tiluk let go of Terra, stepped through the door to the deck outside, cupped his hands to his mouth and hollered, "She said…'Very Glad!'"

Janet, head of NOAA, and the other member of J Squad sucked in her breath, turned quickly, and walked back through the living room. "Excuse me, I need to make a call."

PROMISES TO KEEP

"IT'S TIM AND JOANNA!" Terra exclaimed to Tiluk and Miles when she heard the car pulling to a stop at the end of their long driveway two days later. She still couldn't believe it. First the Jane Squad. Now this. Tim Sinclair unfolded his tall, sturdy frame from behind the wheel, stood up and stretched, looking way above his head to the towering tips of the cedars and firs, and breathed out a long, unbroken sigh.

Without turning to look at Joanna, whose pale blond hair was draping down her shoulders as she got out and looked up, similarly absorbed by the forest's dark glory, he said quietly, "Dorothy, we're not in Kansas anymore." "My thoughts exactly, Tim," Joanna murmured. "I can't believe we're here." Miles stepped forward, grabbed Tim's hand and started shaking it. "It sure isn't Florida, is it? I'm Miles. The one who saw it happen."

Tim turned his focus to Miles over their strong handshake, his face some-how registering respect, warmth and disgust all at once, and said, "Well then Miles, you and I have some things to talk about, don't we?"

"Terra…" Joanna peered over at her, taking in the face mask and Fierce sitting on her shoulder. Tiluk sensed Terra's daze, and pulled her over to

Joanna's side of the car, leaving Tim and Miles to talk. Joanna reached for both of Terra's hands, clasping them gently, taking in her appearance with consternation and fondness. "Thanks for sending Tim the ExplOrca proposal. And thanks for starting the Blackfish Cove Facebook page. You're making links that are going to make a huge difference for the whales." She trailed off, obviously thinking.

Terra returned Joanna's squeeze, their hands clasped, thinking.

Joanna. Her name was Joanna. She was part of the J Squad, too, and Terra got that little jolt of coincidence that was becoming more familiar each day. Terra knew Joanna had spent a decade of her life working with Tulku (although she knew Joanna thought of him as Tiluk, or maybe Shantu), teaching him to perform tricks and stunts for thousands of people, watching his day-to-day life unfold in that tiny, confined tank. And that she'd quit. And that now she worked all the time to teach as many people as she could, the truth. Granny's words came back to her again, about that unexpected force for harmony. Here were two people—Tim a well-respected journalist, and Joanna, an OceanLand trainer who'd quit her job over the horrors she'd witnessed—right here in her backyard. Ready to do whatever it took to help. *Granny,* Terra heard her-self say silently. *Granny, it's happening. I promised, and now it's happening.* She couldn't shake the feeling that Granny already knew. That somehow she was helping, too. That this is what Granny had planned from the beginning. From that very first dream. Tiluk nudged her, bringing her back from her reverie.

"We're really glad you're here Joanna," Tiluk said. "I'm Tiluk."

Joanna's eyes widened in surprised recognition. She'd only known one other Tiluk, and he was definitely not human.

"Our parents named him after our whale…both our moms were pregnant with us when he was kidnapped," Terra said simply, coming out of her daze.

"They named him Tiluk so they'd never forget what happened, and never stop working to fix it."

Joanna's hand went involuntarily to her mouth, staring at the two of them with deepening understanding.

"I didn't know," she whispered, grappling with her almost permanent heartsickness over all the years she'd spent with Tiluk the whale, trapped and immobilized away from his family, while this boy grew up free and nurtured by his. "I'm honored to meet you both."

"Well, just wait 'til you meet Wendy and Granny…" Tiluk uttered seriously.

"I wouldn't miss a chance like that for anything, Tiluk," Joanna said, smiling and grasping his hand with a firm shake.

"You won't have to wait long. Our folks are getting the big boat ready to take you guys out. We're just up here to get you settled before we take you down to the dock."

"Let's do it then," said Tim as he strode purposefully over to meet them, grabbing Terra's then Tiluk's hands, his shadowed eyes intent with purpose. "We have a lot to do today!"

He wasn't kidding, either, Terra had thought to herself a dozen times as the day went by. She'd noticed the flurry—the hustle and bustle of what was happening now that everyone was here. With Miles, Dave, and the J Squad, and now Tim and Joanna all here, suddenly it was as if something had tilted. As if the arc of their journey got forever bent towards where she knew they needed to go. It was the only way she could explain it. She knew Tiluk felt it, too. Everyone here had a purpose, and each one was just as significant as Terra's dreaming. The group was greater than the sum of its parts...with Granny and her family central to that mysterious equation.

By the time they'd all sat down to eat dinner together that night, gathered around her mother's beloved table, they'd become a team. It hadn't taken long. When Tim filmed Joanna's first response to seeing the wild whales—

Tulku's mother and grandmother and great grandmother—foraging for wild salmon out in Haro Strait, she'd just stared, tears sliding down her cheeks, shoulders shaking with built-up grief, and Joseph had put his arm around her. She'd been unable to speak. And Tim had quietly filmed her, the former

OceanLand trainer weeping with Tulku's family in the background, their dorsal fins and blows aligned in foraging formation. They were chasing the fish. When Wendy breached after they'd feasted on the salmon, Joanna's face lit up, and she'd turned to Terra, eyebrows raised.

"It's his mom," Terra had said simply.

Joanna had wiped her face dry, and spoke out towards to whales, her voice edged with steel, "We're going to fix this." Then she'd turned to Gwen and Jason—who had been pointing out all the whales by name, pinpointing their foraging patterns, and keeping up a running dialogue of what they were seeing—and added with respect, "I sure do wish I could've picked your career path instead of getting sucked into OceanLand's mess."

After the boat trip, they'd spent the whole rest of the day doing inter-views with Tim. He filmed each of the kids in turn, taking quite a while with Miles, as he told the terrible story of seeing Dusky Dey lose her life. Terra noticed how gentle Tim had been, checking with Miles, careful about bringing up the horror he'd had to witness. But Miles had shrugged at Tim, saying, "Seriously? I need to tell you about this. Other people need to hear it. I'm just glad I can talk to you about it."

Then Tim made a point to tape Terra and Tiluk, as well as the adults, about the live feed and how the trapped whale had reacted when he'd heard his mother's calls for the first time, and how the entire pod had started to vocalize his signature whistle, and how mother and son had sung together.

He also got Miles on tape, telling how Tiluk had rammed his head against the gate over and over again after he'd heard his mother's calls. Claire gave Tim a copy of the whole recording so he could splice it into his report. And he taped Joanna's reaction as they'd played her the recording of the live feed— the moments when the whale "Shantu" she'd worked with for so many years heard his mother for the first time in 14 years, and Wendy's response. Tim caught the way Joanna broke down crying for the second time that day, as she'd listened to their duet. Finally, Tim asked Terra to tell about her accident, and got Joseph on tape explaining how the whales had saved her life.

"This is what our ancient stories tell us," Joseph had said into the lens, as he sat on the dock with Blackfish Cove appearing behind him, a few dorsal fins near the far side. "Once, the orca and the people were partners and worked together. During the recent domination of the oceans—the terrible whaling and shootings and captures—the whales learned not to trust the people. But now," he looked away from the lens, staring at Terra—Tim panned to her face, capturing the expression between Joseph and his chosen daughter, before the two of them turned and looked at the whales on the other side of the cove.

"For the first time in many years, they are learning to trust some of us again."

Tim had lingered on Joseph's wise face, then swept the camera all around Blackfish Cove, slowly, capturing the lovely, deep beauty of the place, panning at last down towards the dark, almost black water—the whales' home.

"We must live up to their trust," Joseph's words hung against that last shot.

When Tim had finished up all his interviews for the day, Terra, impressed by his obsessive focus, asked him point-blank why he was so committed.

He'd just shrugged as he put away his video camera, and gave her that serious, disturbed look of his. "Once you learn about what's really going on for those whales, you can never go back."

Now it was dinner time, and they were all squeezed around the table together passing plates of food with a familiarity and fondness that had settled over them, united by their singular goal. As they chatted, Terra realized that Joanna had joined Tim for the trip to Blackfish Cove because they both stayed pretty tight with each other when it came to tracking what was going on with the captive whales at OceanLand—she had a direct interest since she'd worked with them for so long. They'd both gone a little bananas when Terra had emailed ExplOrca's proposal to retire Tulku. So when Tim got the invite, it had been a no brainer for Joanna to join him up here.

"Besides, I needed to see the wild whales," she said to everyone at the table. "For so many years as a trainer, I truly believed they were getting everything they needed with us. I really thought we could give them that.

And OceanLand teaches all its trainers and staff to believe it," she said, dis-gust in her voice. She hung her head, overcome by emotion for a moment. "I was so wrong. Seeing them here, in their true home? I won't rest until every last dolphin or whale in captivity is free to go home…or at least to true retirement in a sea pen. All of these animals work until they die. And their work is just brutal, with no hope of ever swimming free again. Almost every single one of the animals still in captivity today could be returned to the wild tomorrow." She took a breath and spit out, "Money is the only reason they aren't." She caught Jane Goodall smiling gently at her, com-passion radiating from her features. Joanna added, "We humans made a terrible mistake."

Jane's smile broadened and she said, "It's only a mistake if you don't learn from it."

"Speaking of which, Tim, I want to thank you for agreeing not to include the Morse coding by these whales in your story," Janet Carson said over the steaming hot plates of fresh asparagus from their garden and hollandaise sauce that Gwen and Jason had whipped up with eggs from the chickens. Janet and Jane had insisted on doing the salad, and together they'd browsed the garden collecting baby lettuce, spinach, carrots, green onions, and radishes. Terra couldn't resist snapping a candid picture from the deck of the two women, baskets in hand, bending over together in the dirt, taking joy in the harvest. Two women who'd already changed the world for the better. Two women who bent every single day under the weight of the Great Sadness, but who stood up anyway. She knew she'd treasure that photo forever.

Tim put down his fork, pensive with a hint of outrage beneath his words. "We've spent a long, long time on this planet doing all the taking. It's time for us to start giving back. There's no way I'd leak something like the whales' Morse coding in a world where the corporate military establishment still holds it acceptable to use dolphins as bomb carriers and spies, or to test their deafening sonar in oceans filled with animals who's hearing is way more sensitive than the nerves under your fingernails. Then there's the underwater sounds used for finding more buried oil—which is pure insanity at this point anyway! Those sounds are louder than rocket blasts and can travel for hundreds of miles. They're 100 times louder than a jet engine. *A hundred times*! It's no wonder we've got more and more mass strandings of whales and dolphins all over the world. These animals beach themselves, trying to escape the noise, their eyes and blowholes leaking blood. We are killing ocean life with sound, not to mention overfishing, and oil. *We* are doing this!"

He shoved back his chair, and very nearly glared at Janet Carson, the head of NOAA. "You know it firsthand. The oceans are dying. Period. I'm here to perform CPR, not just on these captive whales, but on all the degraded systems on this planet…not to mention climate change." He turned to the other adults. "Maybe this story you've given me will help people decide to stand up and take action, too. If they don't, I'm pretty sure this entire planet is going the way of the dinosaurs."

"Sucks to be a well-educated journalist, doesn't it Tim?" observed Jason, his shaggy, sun-bleached locks falling across his handsome face. Jason had found an ally in his deep frustration. "Kind of like it sucks to be studying a bunch of wild whales who are about to go extinct on our watch."

"Stop it!" Joseph brought his fist down hard on the table and spoke firmly, a sharp edge in his voice. "Stop it right now. You two are indulging in despair. That kind of thinking will kill this planet faster than anything else. Faster, even, than climate change."

"Come on Joseph," Tim came right back at him, his voice raised. "Give me a break! These are facts. And they are piling up every day, worse and worse. It's reality!"

"It's a choice," Joseph raised his hand, palm towards Tim in the universal signal for *slow down*. He took a breath, calmer. "It's a choice to ignore the bigger reality. At your own and the planet's expense."

"What the hell are you talking about? There *is* no bigger reality!" Tim spit out. He was fuming. But now Terra knew what Joseph was doing, and she watched curiously. Miles and Tiluk took her cue, and sat quietly on either side of her, observing.

"You are a storyteller, Tim. A journalist by trade, but a storyteller by calling. You know what can happen when people hear a good story."

Tim just shrugged, still pissed.

"Right now, you are telling the worst story we've ever heard in the his-tory of civilization: *The planet is dying, and it's all our fault*. Think about that, Tim…" Joseph smiled at Tim and raised his eyebrows. "Are you going to rally global passion and support with that story?"

"You're going to trigger a whole string of suicides is what you're going to do," said Gwen, engrossed by what Joseph was getting at.

"And that's happening, all over the world. Right now." Joseph replied. "People are as trapped in this brutal story as those whales are trapped in their pools." He waited a second, letting his words hang in the air. "There are other versions of it, too: GMOs are taking over the world. Cancer is epidemic.

War is necessary for peace. The natural world is gone forever." "Corporations are evil," piped in Bill, who was fascinated by the discussion, one he would have dismissed in scorn just days ago, but, just days ago, he'd been changed by his daughter. He added, "The media serves the money, and not our best interests."

"This is a scary time to raise a child," chimed in Claire.

"Bullies, bigots, and haters are horrible people," said Maggie quietly. "Women are the weaker sex," added Jane Goodall with a sly grin.

Tim was nodding, seeing something he hadn't before. Joseph asked,

"What happens to people when they believe those stories as reality?"

"It breaks them. Then they either fight against it with everything they've got, or they shut down and hide from it all." Tim was mulling things over, rubbing his chin. "Those stories might be true, but they are massively dis-empowering, threatening, and disturbing."

"But *are* they true, Tim? How do you know they're really true?" Joseph shifted back in his chair, and wrapped his arm around Jane who leaned into Joseph in response. "Do you think for one minute, this brave soul allowed stories like that to keep her from seeing a *bigger* reality... one that was both more true *and* more wonderful?"

Terra felt a warm glow rising from somewhere in her solar plexus. Under the table she reached outwards with both hands, found Miles and Tiluk's fingers, and intertwined her hands with theirs. *She* knew the bigger reality.

"The bigger reality is that we are on the verge of a great awakening: as a global human family we're about to realize that *we are all one. We are all connected!* And *that* is the most exciting time to be alive, ever!" exclaimed Terra. She clasped her friends' hands hard, feeling the joy of her journey—the grid of light—suddenly fill her every cell.

"We *have* been changing the planet and hurting ourselves and so many others..." Terra's voice rang out as she straightened in her seat. "Because we forgot the truth while we had our global population explosion, and all the greed, war, suffering, and violence that came with it. That's ending now. It has to, one way or another. The Fallacy is over."

Tim's mouth went slack in astonishment at this 13-year-old girl recapitulating, in one a sentence, what humans had fought and died over since the rise of Western civilization, while her parents stared at her like she was Joan of Arc. Gwen's eyes went wide, and Jason was scowling. But Joseph and Jane were smiling at her, nodding.

She took a breath, and spoke to Tim directly. "The only reason your story is so harsh, is that too many people forgot our connection to everything else. And it makes total sense that so many people *would* forget during our population explosion and the desperate hunt for resources that came with it." "What do you mean by The Fallacy," he asked quietly, as if that one point would clarify everything, as if the answer might change him forever, as if Terra was no longer a girl but a prophet, wise beyond her years.

"It's what can happen when highly-social-smarty-pants like human beings who can make and use tools release HUGE amounts of energy—like with fossil fuels or agriculture—early in their evolutionary history. Some populations explode with all that unleashed energy. And some of those populations fight to dominate and take over all the other populations, both human and non-human. It happens on every planet with intelligent, collaborative toolmakers. But that's just a blip on their evolutionary journey. Not every culture makes that mistake." Terra glanced at Joseph, the look on her face saying what everyone already knew. That *his* native culture had not tried to dominate others. "Don't you see? *That's* The Fallacy." She looked at

Tim with pointed confidence, trusting him to get it. "The big mistake these populations make is being addicted to the awful idea that the domination of resources, other people, and animals, is their natural behavior."

"But it's not!" Terra laughed out loud. "It's not at all! They're natural behavior is empathy! And if they get a grip and see their true interconnection with everything else, they move to their next evolutionary stage: global peace and harmony! Just like the whales did millions of years ago."

Tim's mouth dropped further open, his face sheet-white as he tried to wrap his mind around what he was hearing, and who he was hearing it from.

"It's actually pretty simple." Terra shrugged and looked at Jane Goodall.

"You didn't forget though, did you?"

Jane's eyes wrinkled in a smile. "No sweetheart, I didn't. I was lucky to have a mother who supported my romping and roaming all over the out-doors, and through all the books in the public library. I never learned that I *wasn't* connected to everything. Everything, every one, every animal, was my friend. The chimps knew that about me from the very beginning."

"So," Tim interjected…his mind aflame, "Are you saying that once people see that when we trap the whales, we're also trapping ourselves, that we'll spontaneously set them free? Or, at least, as free as they can be in harmony with their own highest good?"

"That, my friend, is *exactly* what she's saying." Joseph nodded, looked around the table, and winked at Terra.

"And," Tim went on, "are you also saying that when we 'wake up,' as you say, to realizing that we are truly connected to everything, that we'll also spontaneously create permanent peace and restore a healthy and thriving planet, despite all the suffering and the harmful changes?"

Joseph stayed silent, and turned to Jane Goodall. She answered Tim as if she had treasure to share, her voice calm but bright with genuine wonder. "Even after all I've learned about what stressed-out, wounded, and desperate humans are capable of…especially in the face of that toxic notion of domination, and the war and hoarding that go with it…" She looked down into her lap, her hands clasped there, blinking for a moment. "The good, the creativity, the collaboration, the support, the generosity, the solutions we find…the *love*…well, we humans are, in my humble opinion, among the most extraordinary creatures ever to evolve on Earth." She took another breath. "When human beings unleash their natural empathy," she looked around the table at each of them, and Terra felt the air get still, "they tap into an exceptional capacity for social change. You just need to look at history to see what happens then." Jane looked at Joseph meaningfully. "All we need now is some wisdom."

"The ancient stories tell that when we gain that wisdom," Joseph added, "a new era of great peace and joy will arise on this planet. The dawn of a new age for Earth's global family. It will be unlike anything we've ever imagined before."

"And speaking of wisdom Terra," said Jane, looking pointedly at her. "I think you need to consider that the whales know a lot more than Morse code. My strong suspicion is that by your fierce passion to teach them the code, they actually picked up on your thoughts. It seems to me that you and your 'Morse Endeavor' may well have opened a kind of *thought bridge* between you and the whales."

Terra looked at Jane, dumbfounded. *Of course! That's it!* It had to be!

That's how come Granny had been able to reach out to her for that very first dream, and it explained everything about her journey, and the electrified link she felt with Granny that began with the jolt she'd felt down on the dock the other day. Granny's zing to her: *Time to fish!* And how Terra had felt it as though it was her own thought in her own body.

She looked at Jane, their eyes held, and she knew this wise, wise woman knew more than she could ever hope to know… just like the whales did.

"You need to give yourself credit, my dear," said Jane, almost as if reading her thoughts now. "Your and your friends' empathy with these whales has given us all an opportunity the likes of which I could only hope for before. If the whales have wisdom to share, we may be ready to receive it thanks to your powerful urge to connect with them, and to understand them on their own terms."

Terra recalled Granny's words, *It is your drive to connect that attunes you to us.* They were saying almost the same thing. *Whoa.*

Miles gripped Terra's hand harder; she'd almost forgotten that she or either of the boys was even there. She'd gotten so pulled in by Joseph and

Jane's words that she'd nearly lost herself. Now Miles brought her back with a jolt of hope, his emotion coursed right through their interlocked fingers, and she turned to meet sparks in his radiant blue eyes. He had a look of rapture on his face.

"Do you think it's really possible, Terra?" Miles asked her, his voice tinged with wonder. "Can we really have that kind of life on Earth, where everyone is living in harmony and there is actual peace? No more bullying? No more school shootings? No more ugly divorces?"

Miles' mind was going a thousand miles a minute, his capacity to track Terra's thinking was uncanny, and he surprised her when he zeroed in on her learning and asked, "Do you think these are all just symptoms of our population explosion and the horrible ways people have learned to be with each other and the planet? Just because this screwed-up worldview made everyone so crazy and obsessed for such a long time?"

Tim was choking up. The conversation had pricked a hardbound core of gloom inside him, and he was visibly moved. "And if we wake up to our interconnection to everything, we could actually create a world where we don't have say goodbye to the whales and the polar bears and the tigers and the elephants and the lions? Or the rest of the great apes? Or the rainforests and everything in them? Or so many children of oppression?" His voice cracked, and went low as his face twisted. "A world where we stabilize the climate? And move past war, starvation, pollution, and extinction, once and for all?"

"We're already creating it, Tim, don't you see that?" Terra knew he didn't expect an answer, but she replied anyway. "The very fact that you and Joanna," she glanced at Janet and Jane, "and the J Squad are here, proves that we are doing it. People around the world are doing it right now! It's the first time in history that we've gone global, and the shift is already happening...

It's still hard to notice, because it's so easy to see all the terrible stuff..." She sat back and raised her hands, still clasped with the two boys, so their fists were raised. "But it's happening!"

Terra let go of the boys' hands as she reconsidered the "thought bridge" that Jane had just mentioned. "We are luckier than some, because the whales have great wisdom to help us," she added matter-of-factly. "Up until now, they haven't been able to share it."

Miles turned in his seat to face the rest of the group while reaching his arm around Terra, pulling her towards him. His touch igniting a fire that shot up from her toes to light off a blaze beneath her face mask, the hurt in her crushed bones suddenly flooded by warmth. "But up until now, they haven't had this awesome whale dreamer!"

"Whale dreamer?" Tim and Joanna asked in unison.

And that's when they told about Terra's journey, and she got out her whale carving, which both Tim and Joanna gawked over, absolutely stunned. She was learning...*notice the force for harmony and go with that flow*. When Miles spilled the beans, it was obvious that telling her story was exactly the next step. But she hadn't stopped with that. No way! She'd also told about the boys sharing their dream with Tulku and Harmony...that her friends were also whale dreamers, and that there would be more dreamers to come. By the end of the night and their revelations, Tim's face—before, so rippled by frustration and despair—had gone slack and open.

When they'd finally headed to bed it was after midnight. But Joanna found her out in the dark beneath the shadowy cedars and firs as she'd headed to her yurt. "Terra, Tim probably can't speak to you about this because he's got to be such a rational, by-the-books journalist. But listen. What you said in there? What you and Joseph and Jane explained tonight? I think you just changed the man's life. I know you changed mine. You've given me a whole new way to see what's happening on this planet right now," she stopped, and Terra sensed Joanna's relief and gratitude.

"Just…" Joanna impulsively grabbed her and hugged her hard, careful of her face. "Thank you, Terra."

FIERCE HARMONY

TERRA HAD ONLY SEEN Joseph dance in his full regalia on a few occasions. Every time, it had filled her with a sense of mystery, as if his heritage and native dancing could connect her to something precious that she didn't even know she thirsted for, like a turtle egg buried in mud awaiting the rains, the signal to hatch. Today—June 21st, the summer solstice, the longest day of the year and the day the Earth marks its great journey around the sun—the mystery deepened into something different. She finally knew her purpose and understood her role: to not only bear witness to the dance, but to drum it to life…to foster her dreams. The rains had come.

But this time it wasn't just Joseph dancing. This time he danced with the shaman, Raven Dave. They were all here circled together on the dock, sitting around the two men who danced and chanted in their face-paint and ceremonial garb: the parents, Jason and Gwen, the J Squad, Joanna, Miles on the marimbas, and Tiluk playing his flute. And Fierce. He was here, perched on her shoulder while she drummed, holding a lock of her hair in his beak…a fixation he'd adopted ever since her absence. His new, slightly neurotic habit grated on her. It reminded her of what he didn't have.

She looked at Dave's bird, a large, black raven who sat quietly perched on the bottom railing of the stairs, as if overseeing them all. None of them had known Dave had a bird until he'd shown up with him this morning. Or, more like, the bird had shown up on his own. Dave had stepped from his rickety rust bucket of a car and started to pull all his gear out from the back seat, handing his leather-fringed leggings to Miles, his raven-feathered headdress to Tiluk, and his long wooden staff, to Terra, saying, "Be careful with that, whale dreamer," when Terra had ducked as a huge black shape swooped down over her head and landed on a large branch behind her. Fierce had started squawking madly from his mews.

"Holy smokes, what's up with that crazy raven?" she asked not expecting an answer as she stared at the bird, who stared right back and cocked his head.

"He's with me," Dave shrugged, nonchalant. "Just ignore him, and help me get this stuff inside."

The three kids ogled Dave over the way he was acting like this striking black raven was no big deal. They all looked at each other, then at Dave's shuffling form as he walked into the house, ignoring the bird. Then Tiluk peered up into the branch, nodded, and said, "Greetings brother Raven," before following Dave inside; Miles and Terra walking behind, each dip-ping their heads at the bird as they passed beneath his large black body hovering above them on the branch. The way he stared at her had made Terra nervous.

Now, sitting here on the dock with Fierce on her shoulder, and that huge raven acting like he was supervising everything, like he knew some-thing no one else could know, she wasn't nervous anymore. She'd never felt more certain in all her life. She'd realized he was part of the vision she'd had, the vision she'd brainstormed and planned out with the boys, the vision she'd known the moment those words had come back to her from Granny:

You'll find an unexpected force for harmony unfolding around you.

The *vision* being this ceremony. And even though she hadn't known about the raven before, right after he showed up she realized that he was part of that unexpected force. She was beginning to understand from Granny's message that once she claimed her power and followed her instincts, helpful things would start to happen that she couldn't predict. Like the J Squad showing up. Like Tim dropping everything to come up here…and Joanna coming, too. Like last night's dinner conversation and the way Tim had looked when she put her ancient whale carving into his hands—as if she'd given him a newborn baby. And like her inspiration for how to end this ceremony. That was new…and it was all because of Dave's raven. A raven she hadn't known existed until this morning.

The drumming was working. Everyone in the circle had gone into a quiet reverie, absorbing the magical dance of Joseph and Dave. Their chanting, the quiet shuffle of their feet, and their ageless attire magnified the music somehow. Dave with his fringed leggings and raven-feathers draping from his head down his back, the feathers mingling with his long gray hair, his full black sleeves adorned with raven feathers, too, so when he raised his arms, he had wings. And Joseph with his buckskin boots and fringed native cloak, both painted with ornate totemic art. Orca, ravens, and wolves dancing with him, the fringe stretching almost from his waist to below his knees, shimmering and waving back and forth like a meadow of sea grass.

Watching them dance, Terra glanced at Tim. After their talk last night, she had to remind herself he was a reporter for The Orlando Weekly and her heart skipped a beat, knowing how instrumental he could be to their dreams…to Granny's family. He was set up on the far side of the dock, near where they kept their kayaks tethered. From his vantage, he was filming their entire circle of people, the dancers, and the raven. After double checking with him earlier, she knew if the whales decided to partake in this ceremony, that his wide angle lens would capture them, too.

Watching Tim, her rising hope reminded her of what else had shown up out of the blue. This morning, before Raven Dave and that huge crazy raven showed up…there was The Letter. Granny was right! Things really were happening, and *fast*. As if the force Granny told her about was real. While everyone had been piled around the table, eating breakfast, and making last minute plans for the ceremony—Terra double checking with Tim about where the best camera location would be, Miles and Joseph figuring out how to get the huge set of marimbas down that long flight of stairs to the dock, and Tiluk talking with the J Squad about whether they wanted drums or rattles for the ceremony—the FedEx truck had pulled up outside.

Claire went out to meet the truck, none of them thinking twice about the delivery since ExplOrca got stuff via FedEx all the time. But then, moments later, the iron dinner bell was clanging. Terra's pulse skyrocketed, and she saw Tiluk's look of panic. What was going on?

They all hurried outside, and there was Claire, holding an unopened letter. From OceanLand. All of them—the grad students, the J Squad,

Tim with his camera, Joanna, and the parents—gathered around Claire as she read it out loud in the yard behind the house, the yurts tucked nearby and the majestic cedar and Douglas fir trees standing with them, as if listening in the hushed quiet.

OceanLand
Marine Mammal Team
Orlando, Florida
June 20, 2013

ExplOrca
Attn: Dr.'s Claire Lewis and Maggie Ravenwood
Friday Harbor, San Juan Island, Washington

Dear Dr.'s Ravenwood and Lewis,

We are writing to affirm that we are taking your recent proposal for Tiluk's retirement into full consideration. Although this would be a highly unusual move for OceanLand, we have come to see the potential value for him, as well as our audiences, in this action. For many years, we at OceanLand have maintained that captivity for these whales was an acceptable part of the immense educational value we see in audiences witnessing their intelligence, biology, and athleticism up close. But after losing Dusky Dey, the third person to die in Tiluk's tank, we are seriously re-evaluating our earlier stance. We at OceanLand are heartbroken by her death, and are reassessing the health and stress level of all our captive marine mammals, especially the killer whales. We know Tiluk loved Dusky, and the fact that he killed her tells us far too much about his state of mind and his stress level. Also, re: your taped recording of Tiluk and his mother, you'd have to be heartless to ignore how devastating it is for these whales to be separated from their families. Further, we know that whales killing trainers is not good for our company's bottom-line. We need to consider alternatives for the sake of our shareholders.

When the star of *Free Willy*, Keiko, was actually freed into his native waters of Iceland, many in the captivity industry, including those of us at OceanLand, claimed that he died an earlier than necessary death after a long and sad decline in a frightening, isolated world. But we are coming to see that this may be the furthest thing from the truth. After his careful reintroduction to the wild, Keiko did, indeed, find other whales and socialized with them. It is likely he spent a great deal of time traveling in his natal waters, searching for fish, and living the natural life of an orca, before his death—which may well have been hastened by the many prior years he'd spent in captivity. We mention Keiko here, because his was a kind of test case, and we are taking all that was learned from Keiko into consideration as we evaluate your proposal for Tiluk's retirement, including the exemplary large pre-retirement facility that was built for Keiko in Newport, Oregon's Aquarium, not far from where you are now.

Should OceanLand decide to move forward with a more serious consideration of retiring Tiluk to Blackfish Cove, we would work closely with ExplOrca on all facets of this project. We are sending this letter to alert you to that likelihood.

Sincerely,
The Marine Mammal Team
OceanLand, Orlando

Claire sank to the grass halfway through, her voice shaking, unable to finish reading the letter and Joseph took over. When he finished, Tiluk whooped at the top of his lungs, the cry of a successful warrior. Terra had never heard anything like it before. Quiet Tiluk erupting. He went to the dinner bell and started ringing it with all his strength, his face split open by a ray of light, his wide smile and dancing eyes riveting all the rest of them… and they all started hugging each other and crying and jumping up and down with one another, in disbelieving joy. In the midst of all the revelry, even the trees shimmered a more brilliant green as a startling cast of sunlight broke through the upper branches.

Terra saw Maggie look pointedly at Janet—the head of NOAA—in the middle of it all, a question on her face, and Janet shrugged her shoulders with a small grin, catching Jane Goodall's eyes.

"Sometimes a phone call can tip the balance," she said softly.

But before Terra could ask Janet for more detail, Miles caught her hand and twirled her around, picking her up and spinning her carefully in his arms, alert to her wounded face and bruises. He set her down at last, hugged her hard, and whispered in her ear, "I'm so glad I found you, Miss Terra Incognita Lewis."

"I'm so glad I found you too, Miles," she whispered now as they all sat in their circle on the dock, Tim running the camera, and that crazy raven looking down his beak at everyone. No one heard her, of course, but still. She *was* glad she'd found Miles. Very glad. He'd already changed her life for the better. All their lives, really. Whales included. She knew him. She didn't know how, and maybe it didn't matter, but she did. Once they made eye-contact that first time in the hospital, she just knew. And it was huge, the knowing. So huge, she hadn't even begun to wrap her mind around what it meant. She looked at him now as he drummed, lost in the music he made with the marimbas. Tiluk's hunch was right, the marimbas were meant for Miles. He *was* the music as it welled up from inside him and shot out through the mallets, keys, and pipes. She looked at him, and she trusted him and the hugeness of their connection, even if she didn't understand it, and she trusted the whole thing…the whole experience…the ancient ways. She trusted it all. She'd felt it all. The oneness. It gave her hope that everything would really be okay.

Miles looked up at her then, his shocking blue eyes pinned right to hers, and her heart tingled. This was it. It was time. Her vision. Made real.

She looked to Tiluk, who nodded. He was ready. Together the three of them quieted their music, the drumming slowed and softened, the flute and marimbas moving their tones to resolution. The rest of the circle followed suit, everyone else had drums or rattles, and they all slowed and subsided following the kids' lead. Joseph and Dave slowed their chanting and rhythmic footsteps, and as they did, they met one another in the center of the circle, face to face. The spectacle was breathtaking….and it was exactly what Terra had seen in her mind's eye the other night when she'd had the idea for this ceremony. Only now it was much more than that. And Tim was going to share it all with an audience. On TV. *Maybe*, Terra thought, *OceanLand will even use this very same video the day they announce that they've decided to retire "Shantu" to his rightful home and his family here in Blackfish Cove.*

And maybe this story will remind people of how connected they are to the whales. She reflected on the thing she'd told Tim, on tape, just before they started the ceremony. "Because when you see how much these animals love their family, the way mothers and sons and daughters stay together for their entire lives, how they swim for a hundred miles every day, how they use language to communicate, and have their own communities and cultures…well, you can never go back to seeing a whale in a tank without it breaking something inside your own heart. And that is proof, right there, that what happens to the whales, happens to us."

But here, now, something else was going on. Something very different.

Her heart was growing. Stretching past its former boundaries, widening in a way that almost ached because it was so unfamiliar. She caught Tiluk watching her again, his warmth steadying her, his presence still a marvel and a mystery. Who was this boy, and how had he managed to call her back in time? How did his partnership with Tulku fit into all this? *Brother*. But she was awakening to something far more potent than their simple earthbound closeness. That was it… the stretching in her heart was her soul. It was expanding. Making room for more than she'd ever thought possible. Before.

As Dave and Joseph stopped their dancing, facing one another, they called out in unison, "AHO!"

And everyone in the circle responded, "AHO!"

Dave reached down to pick up the staff waiting at his feet. As he stood, the raven took a dive off his perch and swooped over the people in the circle, taking one full circuit around everyone's heads before landing on Dave's staff. Fierce squawked and fluttered on her shoulder as he watched the raven go by. *Whoa.* Terra shot Miles and Tiluk a look than checked to see that Tim had caught that. He was standing next to his camera, gaping at the raven.

Yep, he got it.

Uh-oh. Terra saw Harmony coming towards Tim from behind, and before she could do anything to alert him, the calf had side-swiped him, camera and all, with a tail-push. A big wave of water sprayed all over him. Tim had the presence of mind to zip the camera around to catch the calf hanging in the water below him, eyeing him up on the dock as the rest of the group erupted in laughter at her unexpected appearance and antics. *Well, I guess the whales are going to participate then,* Terra thought to herself with a smile.

Good. The drumming and music had worked just as she'd hoped. The whales knew to come find them.

As if on cue, a loud exhalation sounded just below the dock next to their large circle of people. Tim swung the camera back around just in time to see Granny's immense head surface above the dock in a spyhop. She was only a few feet away from Terra, and her form eclipsed Terra altogether.

The whale was a backdrop against Terra and Fierce, the camera lens filled by a small girl sitting cross-legged in front of the mammoth face of Granny, a wild whale. Fierce squawked again, getting more agitated, and hopped around to face Granny, still squawking. Granny turned, just a little, and blew a huge expulsion of wet air right at Terra and Fierce, spraying the rest of the group, too.

"Greetings ancient mother," Raven Dave turned to face Granny with a chuckle, while the rest of the group tried to stop laughing. "We are grateful that you joined us."

Granny tipped her rostrum upwards in a quick nod, then slid back down underwater, next to the dock. Harmony glided in next to her great grand-mother, and rolled sideways, trying to see the humans sitting above her.

"Greetings young one," said Joseph with a smile and wink at Terra. "It seems you are a bit of a sea squirt like your sister, Terra," he said, grinning at Tim who was still dripping wet and trying to dry himself unobtrusively with a handkerchief while manning the video camera.

The two men—Raven Dave with his staff and the huge raven, and Joseph—stepped towards the edge of the dock so that they faced the whales, with the rest of the group circled around behind them like a small audience around a stage. Only this stage had whales *and* people, acting together with no set script. Each in their own worlds…yet linked by a timeless primal bond long overlooked and, in too many cases, profoundly abused.

"CRRR-UCK! CRRR-UCK!" The raven's voice hit Terra in the chest with a thump. She hadn't heard him before, he was so loud!

This time it was Harmony who spyhopped to face the calling raven. She nosed her head upwards, her eye tilting to see the bird. The raven called again, and Harmony blew, her misty exhalation directed right at him.

"CRRR-UCK! CRRR-UCK!" The bird took off and swooped down, aiming straight for the young whale, then angled out over Blackfish Cove and flew skywards, up and up, before plunging down in a dramatic spinning fall, only to twist away from the water at the last second and fly back to Dave, landing on the staff once again with a rush of wind from his wings. By now, Fierce had forgotten all about Terra's hair and was hopping madly on her shoulder, squawking in his much quieter voice, at the raven...who completely ignored him. Instead, the raven glared haughtily down at Harmony after his show-off-display, and cocked his head at her, as if to say, "Well? How was that?"

Harmony dove and disappeared. The group grew quiet, wondering if she had something more in store for them. Granny remained at the dock, rolled sideways, staring up at Dave's raven, unmistakably making eye con-tact with the large black bird. *She almost acts like she knows that raven,* Terra thought to herself as she tried to calm Fierce down a little. Which wasn't exactly working. She'd had to reach up and grab his jesses and hold tight to keep him from flying off after the raven's aerial display. "Easy, Fierce," she murmured. "Easy, beauty."

Then, all of a sudden, Harmony popped up and jerked her head towards the dock, letting go of a huge salmon so that it came to rest at Joseph and

Dave's feet. Wendy was with her now, as if they'd been in cahoots on this little feat. The group gasped. The whales were *food sharing...*a clear sign of powerful intelligence, empathy, and the special knack to build group cohesion. A capacity that Terra knew had only evolved in highly sentient, self-aware and social creatures like humans, the other great apes like the chimps and bonobos, lions, wolves, elephants, and a few others. But these whales were doing it *between* species. *That* might even be new to science,

Terra realized. She looked at her mother, whom she knew would be the most stunned by this behavior. Claire was white. *Please, Mom, don't hyper-ventilate right now*, Terra thought as she checked on Tim and his camera.

Tim had moved way beyond amazement. He had the look of someone who'd given up and was just compelled to keep up with what was happening…Joanna's words came back to her. "I think you just changed the man's life."

She noticed that Jane and Janet had scooted very close together as they sat watching the scene unfold, spellbound. Everyone else in the circle was captivated, too. Gwen and Jason, too, were snuggled together in awe. This had to be the biggest day of their career, and they'd already thought that had happened with the live feed. *Wild whales choosing to engage with a human ceremony!* Terra couldn't have hoped for it to go better than this. She never even dreamed that Harmony would bring food. And Tim was getting it all on tape! As Joseph reached down to pick up the large fish from the dock, the raven screamed and jumped down onto the fish, covering it with his immense wings, turning his large, broad back against Joseph's outstretched hand as if to say, "MINE! She gave the fish to me! *I'm* the one who flew a somersault for the whale, not you, silly human!"

Joseph stepped quickly backwards, deferring to the raven, as everyone broke out in laughter once again, and Dave grumbled, "Damn bird has a mind of his own."

Fierce finally settled. He sat on Terra's forearm, staring hard at the raven, who was now gorging on the salmon, ripping hunks of meat from the carcass, tossing back his head, swallowing the chunks eagerly. And Harmony lingered watching the raven as he gorged himself. Granny and Wendy stayed with the calf, all of them clustered below the raven, Dave, and Joseph. The rest of the pod, including the calf's uncle, Big Jake, stayed further out, across the cove. Now Terra knew that Jake was essential to the girls' ability to engage with them here. He was guarding the mouth of the cove, giving his mother and grandmother and niece peace of mind. Eve, too, stayed further out across the cove. Just then, Terra caught a glimpse of her dorsal fin, and she wondered if Eve understood what was happening with her grandchildren, Harmony and Tulku. She hoped Tim would remember to sweep the cove, and capture the rest of the pod on film.

She took a deep breath. Now it was their turn. It was time. She stood with Fierce and handed him off to her dad for a few minutes. Then Tiluk and Miles got up, and Tiluk handed her the large kelp frond she'd man-aged to get when she was out in her kayak yesterday while the whales were off foraging. She and the boys walked to Joseph and Dave and stood before them facing the whales, but giving the raven a wide enough berth that he didn't jab any of them with that huge beak of his. "We don't want your fish, brother," she said to him quietly. He ignored them, intent on his meal.

The three whales hanging below the dock were only a few feet away from her and the boys now. She stood and watched them for a few seconds, and they waited, expectant. She kept the kelp hidden behind her back. This ceremony was the perfect way to mark the start of her and Tiluk's active journey with the whales, and the beginning of their adulthood. Together they'd bridged something enormous, and she didn't even understand it yet.

But she knew she was no little girl anymore. She was a whale dreamer. And so were Tiluk and Miles.

Then Joseph and Raven Dave raised their arms upwards, and Joseph spoke to the calf, his voice steady and strong, his leather fringe and native garb a testament to the ancient truths he spoke.

"Welcome to the world, little one. Welcome to the family who will shelter you and love you and teach you all the songs of your family. Welcome to the sea and the land that will provide for you. Welcome to the people who will sing new songs with you." He swept his arms around, reaching towards the circle of people gathered behind him on the dock. "Welcome to your Granny, who will guide you together with these whale dreamers as you restore the bond..." He looked with gravity and respect at the three young adults, then put his arms around them as if presenting them officially to the whales. "The young people and the Blackfish are allies once more, and together you will help ignite the Earth's great transition to harmony. Together you are a blessing upon our Earth." He stopped for a moment, letting the stillness fill them. Then he looked intently into each of the kids' eyes: first Terra, then Miles, then his son Tiluk. "Bring your dreams and blessings to the world...and to each other. They are more powerful than you know."

Shivering at his words, Terra reached behind her for the kelp in accordance with her vision, and the three kids unfurled it to its full length, nearly ten feet long. Then they draped it down over the dock, so that it hung just above Harmony's back, and gave it to her. It was their own offering, a blessing not of food, but of play and joy. Harmony recognized it instantly, and scooted her back around to catch the kelp so it rode in front of her dorsal fin. Then she took off at top speed, making a large circle around the cove, as if to show off her gift to the rest of the pod, and her uncle Jake and grandma Eve. A minute later, she reappeared below them, the kelp still draped over her dorsal fin, and spurted a mouthful of water right at Terra.

"THANKS! I LOVE TOYS!" Terra felt the zing in her belly from Harmony and gasped...their bond was ignited. *A thought bridge.* She looked at Joseph... his wise gaze told her he knew. He was right. And so was Jane. There was a kind of power rising here that she couldn't explain, but that she somehow understood and trusted more than anything else.

Then Raven Dave called out, "And even though he can't be with us physically *yet*, welcome to your great brother Tulku, who loves you across lifetimes."

At these words, a grand wind rushed up across the cove, hitting them all like a miniature gale. The wind raised everyone's hair up and off their shoulders, and just as quickly set it down again. *Tulku.* Terra knew he was here, dreaming with them right now. *Tulku. Welcome brother.* She turned around quickly, and saw by everyone's round eyes and expressions that they all felt him, too. Miles grabbed her hand, sucking in his breath. "It's him, I feel him," he whispered.

"I know, Miles. He's here," she said softly. Miles looked at her then, his face a beam of open wonder. "How is this possible?" he breathed so no else could hear him, his stare consuming her. And she knew suddenly that he was not talking about the whale anymore, but about their connection.

Then Raven Dave and Joseph moved up to the edge of the dock with the kids. They knelt down before the calf, reached over the dock, and swept water up with their hands, sprinkling it over her. "Welcome to Earth young Harmony," they said in unison, as the calf nudged her face upwards towards them, the kelp still dangling off her back. Her mother and great grandmother on either side of her.

Terra stood up. This was the part she'd envisioned just this morning. The conclusion to their ceremony. She walked to Jane Goodall, reaching into her pocket. As she knelt down in front of the great Keeper of Life, she was suddenly back in the ceremony on the beach of this exact cove 5,000 years ago and she put a hand down on the dock to steady herself, dizzy with what was happening. *We've been waiting for you*, Granny zinged her, as if to remind her that this mystical parallel she felt was no coincidence. Taking a deep breath, she pulled out the ancient whale carving. The relic that had been as much a part of that ancient ceremony as it was now, and held it up before Jane, speaking clearly so Tim's camera could pick up her voice and everyone else could hear her.

"We are whale dreamers, here to join with the Blackfish and heal the Great Sadness. Many others are coming. We might not know how to do it yet, but we know the force for harmony will guide us." Terra took Jane's hand, opened it, and placed the little burnished whale carving into her palm, closing both their fingers around it. "She is for you: A reminder of what is possible, of what we can all do together, humans and others." Terra closed her eyes and swallowed, feeling a weight of reverence and gratitude bloom that made it hard to speak. She opened her eyes, tears sliding down her cheeks, and looked into Jane's gentle face. "Thank you for all you've done as a Keeper of Life. You've kept hope alive during the Great Sadness. The dreamers and those allied with the circle of Life want to thank you." Her voice went quiet, and what came out was a whisper that only Jane could hear. "We wouldn't stand a chance now without all you've done."

Jane smiled her tender, compassionate smile, and blinked quickly in response to Terra's gift. She was speechless and simply nodded, receiving the whale with a small bow. The others in the circle were wiping their faces; all were deeply moved and had forgotten Tim and his camera entirely.

Then Terra stood up, wiping her own eyes, went to her father and reached for Fierce. Bill took her hand before she could turn back, and could barely get his words out for the tightness in his voice, "It's an honor to be your father, Terra. Thank you for being who you are."

"Oh Dad, don't make me cry again!" She leaned over to hug her dad and held tight for a moment, feeling that almost painful expansion of her heart once again. Her soul rising up. Fierce squawked at the disturbance.

He'd finally fallen asleep on Bill's arm and he was annoyed. "Come on you. Let's go take care of that," she said softly to the agitated bird.

Terra turned and walked back to edge of the dock as the boys rose and stepped back to the marimba and flute. She hadn't told them, or anyone, what she was about to do, and she sensed their support and curiosity. She'd only asked them to play.

"CRR-UCK? CR-UCK?" called out the raven, a question in his voice. He flew up from the fish to resume his perch on Dave's staff, stared right at Fierce, then shook his large head and ruffled his neck feathers until they stood out in a black cloud around his neck. "CRR-UCK?" he asked again.

Fierce cocked his head at the raven, then peered up at Terra. He squawked, grabbed her braid with his beak, and yanked. *Yes, he was telling her it was okay.* It was the right thing to do. He deserved to have a choice.

She began humming. Tiluk pulled his flute from its sheath and began to play the same song while Miles gently touched the tune to life on the marimbas. It was the tune she hadn't been able to shake. Ever since she'd woken up this morning, it hung there. *Imagine.* She wondered if John Lennon had known the oneness like she did. He must have. This song was all about unity.

Terra kept humming while everyone in the circle murmured as they recognized the tune. Then her voice opened and she was singing. Some of the adults began singing the words with her. Words they all knew by heart. Now even Tim got hit once more with the meaning of it all, and she saw him wipe his eyes as he stood behind his camera, pointing it at her. She looked up into the vast blue sky above, then back down at Fierce. The voices behind her mingled, strengthening.

As her voice rang out, the words claiming her role as a dreamer, Terra turned around and looked once more to Miles and Tiluk, her soul linking with theirs. Knowing that there were other dreamers right here with her, and those arising in other places around the world, just as Tulku had foretold in The Prophecy. And she noticed that all the adults had stood as if drawn by one mind, threading their arms around one another's waists in a semi-circle behind her. Quietly singing. Then she turned back towards Harmony and knelt down on the dock, tenderly removing the leather jesses from Fierce's legs. *Yes, the other dreamers would join them.* The huge black raven screeched from behind her and leapt off the staff, swooping over her head and out to the center of the cove, calling loudly. Dry-eyed and clear, with a rising chorus of voices behind her, Terra stood up, looked down at Harmony and sent her a crisp vision of Tulku swimming wild by her side. In that instant she was one with them, with everything. Then she raised her arm out over the whales and cast Fierce to the sky. He was free.

THE WHALE DREAMERS

Terra Incognita & The Great Transition: Book Two

Coming Earth Day 2017

A LETTER TO READERS

Dear reader,

One night, early in the summer of 2012, I had a dream. In it, a wise matriarchal killer whale slid up out of her black waters onto a sunny, pebbly beach beside me and my sons. We were on the Pacific Northwest coast, and the dream felt more real than life. The whale gazed into our eyes, and the joy my kids and I felt in her presence was indescribable. Somehow, I knew she had a message, though, at the time, I didn't understand what it was.

Less than five months later, through a series of fortuitous events—especially my "accidentally" stumbling across the newly-released book *Death at SeaWorld* by David Kirby— I'd finished the first draft of this novel. Many years earlier, I'd had the idea for this book: knew its title, characters, and set-ting. But it wasn't until the dream, then Kirby's book, that the story ignited.

Most of the fictionalized facts described in *The Blackfish Prophecy* are inspired by actual events. Almost every news story you've read in these pages came direct from real life…right down to the ripped open jaw on one captive whale, Miles' dream of being dragged around his tank and almost drowned by a frustrated killer whale, and a distraught mother orca cracking the walls of her tank as she stared at the stuffed orca toys in the gift shop after the death of her calf. Miles' character was inspired by a 10-year-old boy named Bobby who went to a "Dine With Shamu" event at SeaWorld to celebrate his birthday, then witnessed Dawn Brancheau's gruesome death in Tilikum's tank.

In this story the whale, Tiluk, is inspired by two real whales: Tilikum at SeaWorld and Lolita (also known as Tokitae) at the Miami Seaquarium. Tilikum's story is detailed exceptionally well in David Kirby's *Death at SeaWorld*, in Tim Zimmerman's *Outside* article, "Killer in the Pool," and in Gabriela Cowperthwaite's breakthrough documentary, *Blackfish*.

Tokitae has been captive at the Miami Seaquarium for all the years of my life; she was kidnapped from her family in Penn Cove before I was born in 1971. The capture industry took or killed 58 wild whales from the Southern Resident population reducing their population by nearly half. Tokitae is the last living member of the Southern Residents trapped during the capture era of the mid-60s and early-70s. Ocean Sun, Tokitae's 80+-year-old mother, lives to this day in the Salish Sea. The two would surely recognize each other if they had the chance to reunite.

Granny (J-2) is a real whale, the matriarchal leader of J pod and of the Southern Resident Killer Whale community made up of J, K, and L pods. Though I used Granny's name and likeness (the image on the cover of this book is based on the real Granny), she is a fictional portrayal of an actual whale who, as with all cetaceans, is far more complex a being than any human could ever imagine, let alone capture in words.

There is one significant break with history in these pages. In this novel, the capture era continues well into the 1990s so that my characters can give con-temporary accounts of their experience. In truth, the capture era in the United States ended in the mid-1970s thanks to the Marine Mammal Protection Act of 1972. As an author of fiction-inspired-by-fact, I'm comfortable with the rift: the capture era, though it ended in the United States more than 40 years ago, impacts and affects every member of the Southern Resident Killer Whales to this day. The traumas remain and have kept the whales from ever visiting

Penn Cove again. Since 2005, the SRKW population has been listed as officially endangered—at risk of extinction—with close to half their pre-capture numbers, maybe less. This not only a result of the capture industry, but of dwindling salmon runs, serious pollution, and other challenges.

A number of remarkable things transpired during the creation of this book. First, a dedicated group of people—led by Orca Network and others— crafted a detailed, science-based proposal to retire Tokitae from the Miami Seaquarium.

Because of their efforts, and the signatures and letters of nearly 20,000 people, on February 4 2015, NOAA Fisheries announced that Lolita/ Tokitae was to be officially recognized as a member of the endangered Southern Resident Killer Whale community, giving legal teeth to that proposal and, with fierce additional efforts, a real chance that she could return home. There is even a sea cove in the Salish Sea designated for her possible retirement.

Then *Blackfish* happened. I was editing this book when I first saw the trailer in the spring of 2013 just before it went to Sundance. I can still recall watching it over and over again with a dizzying, electrifying sense of what was to come…and of what that movie would mean.

Next, J-50 was born. When I drafted this story in 2012 there were 77 members of the Southern Resident Killer Whale community. Besides the fact that it is tough to keep track of how many whales there are at any one time, there was also a recent spate of deaths. Tracking these whales is only possible thanks to the tireless work of the real life orca researchers at The Center for Whale Research and Orca Network; especially Dr. Ken Balcomb and Howard Garrett who, along with their teams, have spent much of their lives following, photographing and identifying the individuals of J, K, and L pods. But at the time I drafted this book, there had been no new or surviving calves in years, and many who watched the whales wondered if we might be seeing signs of their imminent extinction.

But on December 30 2014, people saw a new calf, J-50, swimming alongside J-16, Slick, possibly the oldest known killer whale to give birth. Slick, as it turned out, was the same age as Wendy in this story, and had given birth to a female calf. In celebration of Slick and her new baby Scarlet, I gave Wendy and Harmony the same numeric classifications, J-16 and J-50. And although the real J-50 was the 78th whale to appear in the population (not the 80th as in this story), she heralded a prophetic shift: Since Scarlet's birth, nine more calves have been born to the Southern Residents. Eight of these appear to be thriving. (Sadly as this book went to press the Center for Whale Research announced that the most recent newborn, J55, was missing and presumed dead.) At this writing, the total number of Southern Resident Killer Whales stands at 84 individuals; 85 if you count Tokitae as I and many others do.

[On a related note: The whale Tiluk in this book is labelled J-22. Although a J-pod whale with that classification lives wild with her family (J-22, a female known as Oreo) Tiluk's numeric classification was otherwise inspired.]

As this book went into production, I came across three exceptionally relevant authors: Robert Moss and his active dream work, Dr. Riane Eisler and her foundational work on domination versus partnership culture, and Dr. Larry Dossey and his review of universal consciousness. Through Moss's books and a workshop, I discovered that an ancient and powerful lineage of shamanic dreaming exists across most indigenous cultures. Via Eisler's extraordinary vision arose a swift assurance that The Fallacy is real and we are experiencing the last gasps of it now, that it is a blip in human history, and that it can be left behind. And in a chance workshop with Dossey who explained the evidence for "One Mind," I sat in stunned silence, having had a first-hand experience of what he described. Perhaps more than any other synchronistic coincidences that occurred since my first orca dream, these affirmed my experience of this story: that it was meant to be told.

My experience of this book is that it wrote itself. The fictionalization of Dr.

Goodall poured out alongside the rest of this narrative. Over the months following that first draft, I watched the real Jane Goodall's active involvement in the plight of captive cetaceans the world over with awed wonder. It is my great hope that she feels some of the world's gratitude for her and her pivotal life's work through reading this story.

Finally, it became clear that the Blackfish Effect, as it's come to be known, is one small but vital (and viral) part of something happening on this planet that is much, much bigger. That in some mystical, remarkable, new-to-the-world emergence, the Great Transition is happening in real life, right now. And that many thousands of people around the world are dedicating their lives to the greatest social transition in human history. Once, a few years ago while wearing my science writing hat, I had the good fortune to meet Bill McKibben—one of the key human change agents of this epic transition. With that serious, intense looks of his, he asked me pointedly after we were introduced, "And what are *you* doing to help?" His question never strays from my soul…it is a question for all of us.

So, if there is one thing you take away from this story, let it be an honoring of yourself as a blessing upon the Earth. You live in the most electrifying, unprecedented era in the history of humanity. This is the time when we decide. As Pope Francis says: *To change everything, we need everyone.*

Your dreams create and heal the future. May they be sweet…and filled with harmony.

Rachel Clark
From the Salish Sea watershed
Spring 2016

ACKNOWLEDGMENTS

For his instrumental role in illuminating the nexus between the captive and wild whales, and corporate tyranny, I'm forever indebted to David Kirby, author of the landmark *Death at SeaWorld: Shamu and the Dark Side of Killer Whales in Captivity*. This book wouldn't exist without his. He also happens to be a brilliant editor. Thanks to David's exceptional eye for structure, craft, and language, this book is a more highly evolved animal.

Likewise, the incredible stories in the pages of David's book wouldn't exist without the heroism of The Superpod, a group named in honor of the phenomenon of numerous pods of wild killer whales coming together to socialize and play. By their tremendous inspiration and much more, the

Superpod helped guide me all along the way. Thank you Dr. Naomi Rose, Dr.

Jeff Ventre, Samantha Berg, Dr. John Jett, Carol Ray, Elizabeth Batt, Heather Murphy, Kyra Laughlin, David Neiwert, Lara Padgett, Kim Ventre, Debbie Blalock, Sandy McElhaney, Colleen Gorman, Jeff Friedman, Howard Garrett,

Dr. Ken Balcomb, Dr. Ingrid Visser, Eric Hoyt, Dr. Giles Zissou, Ric O'Barry, Tim Zimmerman, David Kirby, Gabriela Cowperthwaite and so many others.

Dawn and Tilikum came to me through a book. But they've come to many thousands more people because of the gripping, visionary movie *Blackfish*. For his role in breaking the story in *Outside* magazine's "Killer in the Pool" and for her prescient decision to grab a video camera in hopes of answering "Why?," Tim Zimmerman and Gabriela Cowperthwaite have my endless gratitude, and an ocean of appreciation from a rising tide of people who now know the truth—in the permanent, life-changing way that is a hallmark of exceptional filmmaking.

Closer to home, my family pod—by blood and by choice—sustained and helped with a flood of riches. Susan Dente Ross, my first adult reader and first (likewise brilliant) editor, appeared out of nowhere at the perfect moment to offer unexpected gusto, candid critique, and a pivotal friendship.

My mother-in-law, Susan Caudill, mother (and librarian) Elyse Cregar, and friend Sandi Klingler—each avid, passionate readers—were among my very first test cases. Their memorable responses told me this book might have something to offer. Thank you to all my early readers: Chris Caudill, Debbie Berkana, Maryanne Lysett, Kimberly Vincent, Tammy and Mike Bonney,

Brian Koepke, Heather Murphy, Kyra Laughlin, my "Great Mother" in-law,

Patricia Caudill, and especially to my first young adult readers Avery, Isabel,

Forest, Semolina, Sawyer, and Jared. Thanks also to Mr. Pierce's 2015 7-8 crew, who wouldn't let me stop reading. If I've forgotten any one of you, please forgive me.

I wrote *The Blackfish Prophecy* for my sons, for all the children of their generation, and for those of the future. My very first reader was my then 12-year-old son Avery…who, with his esteem for primal skills, inspired the first scene of this book. But I was unprepared for his response. He holed up in his room for three days emerging only for meals and school. When he finished, he came to me beaming, and in a moment I'll never forget, burst out, "Mom, can we move to San Juan Island?" My younger son will get a copy soon. But at the time I first wrote it, his heart was too tender for this book. Nevertheless,

Keenan heard the stories I told while I was writing and took action. He's been a devout vegetarian ever since I finished the first draft. Boys, you help remind me that every step we take into "deep nature connection" helps shift this planet to Harmony. Because your eyes reflect the future, you teach me not only of what's possible, but of what's right.

More than anyone else, Chris Caudill saw this book born. As he'd done with the birth of our two sons, he stood by my side offering steadfast encouragement, loving support, and peaceful shelter. Thank you Chris… your constant curiosity about the story and where it was going helped keep it alive and breathing. Your instrumental, generous, and inspired parenting throughout this journey is a touchstone for all of us. And in the midst of it all, you heroically safeguard the salmon.

Our hometown pod… *You're family, all of you.* Not only is there a book because of you, but our lives are enriched beyond measure by your company.

Everyone at Palouse Prairie School for Expeditionary Learning and Twin Eagles Wilderness School, you've changed our boys'—and our own—lives. We're so grateful for the emergent models you so generously share of deep nature connection with peaks of human social bonds, empathic love, wise mentoring, self-discovery, creativity, and collaboration that are the hall-marks of the Great Transition.

Mom, thank you for books. Thank you letting me read *Pet Sematary* over your shoulder when I was little, even though it scared the sleep out of me. Thank you for feeding my *Black Stallion* dreams with actual horses. And thank you for inspiring a passion for literature that changed the fabric of my life. I'm so glad you love this one.

Dad, thank you for connecting us to the Earth. You woke us at 4 am with

"Rise and shine girls" to get us out paddling, catching fish, pitching tents, and caring for ponies and chickens years before I ever heard the word computer. And Linda thank you for everything—the trips, the family time, the sunsets with ice cream, Boggle—and for supporting Dad's dreams.

Beautiful Tamara, sister of heart and blood. Your intensely creative spirit inspired me from the days you first called forth Sparkle and painted unicorns, gnomes and rainbows on the walls. This book is for Rose, too. Imagine.

There's one more human family to thank: the book production crew. When friend and author Paula Marie Coomer first suggested Booktrope, I almost couldn't believe my ears. Here was the kind of publishing house and model that demonstrated the collaborative, transformative, empathic, and highly creative human endeavor I'd dreamt about emerging with the Great Transition. Thanks to everyone on the visionary Booktrope team: you've given *The Blackfish Prophecy* a prophetic home.

Special thanks to Katherine Fye Sears, Ken Shear, Jennifer Gilbert, Jesse James, Adam Bodendieck, Lydia Thomas, Babs Hightower, Paula Marie Coomer, Rachel Thompson, Kate Burkett, and the crew I have yet to meet.

Maggie Dallen, thank you. Steady, reliable, fast, and excellent…you're a fantastic proofer and writer, and it's a sweet bonus that you also love the whales. Karen Savory, our "accidentally" finding each other is one of the great synchronicities of this journey. Your block prints are beyond my wildest orca dreams. Susan Marie Andersson, your design work on this project speaks for itself. Further, you bring a depth of orca knowledge that has made all the difference, and helped give the world a beautiful celebration of the real Granny on the cover. And what can I say Jodi Thompson? Your prowess as book manager is beyond definitive. Having you aboard is meant-to-be.

One more very special thanks to Dr. Jane Goodall (and the intrepid Jacob Petersen, Outreach Coordinator for the Jane Goodall Institute). While I wrote, the real Dr. Goodall— instrumental hero of Life—had no idea a fiction arose interweaving her name and inspiration with a crusading team of teens and whales. It is among my most humbling moments that she graciously and generously agreed not only to read the book, but to then give it her blessing… and her brilliant idea of thought transference.

Finally, *Hy'shka* to the whales. We hear you. The dreamers aren't just coming, they're already here.

FURTHER RESOURCES

You can find additional information at www.blackfishprophecy.com. Thankfully, resources related to the Blackfish Effect and the Great Transition are erupting the world over, and a comprehensive list is impossible. For starters though, check out the following:

Books

Death at SeaWorld: Shamu and the Dark Side of Killer Whales in Captivity, David Kirby, 2012, St Martin's Press.

Beneath the Surface: Killer Whales, SeaWorld, and the Truth Behind Blackfish, John Hargrove, 2015, Palgrave Macmillan.

Of Orcas and Men: What Killer Whales Can Teach Us, David Neiwert, 2015, The Overlook Press.

Puget Sound Whales for Sale: The Fight to End Orca Hunting, Sandra Pollard, 2014, History Press.

Beyond Words: What Animals Think and Feel, Carl Safina, 2015, Henry Holt and Co.

War of the Whales: A True Story, Joshua Horwitz, 2014, Simon & Schuster.

Blessed Unrest: How the Largest Social Movement in History is Restoring Grace, Justice, and Beauty to the World, Paul Hawken, 2007, The Penguin Group.

The Green Boat: Reviving Ourselves in Our Capsized Culture, Dr. Mary Pipher, 2013, Riverhead Books.

Rewilding Our Hearts: Building Pathways of Compassion and Coexistence, Marc

Bekoff, 2014, New World Library.

Brainstorm: The Power and Purpose of the Teenage Brain, Dr. Daniel J Siegel, 2015, Tarcher.

One Mind: How Our Individual Mind Is Part of a Greater Consciousness and Why It Matters, Dr. Larry Dossey, 2013, Hay House.

The Great Transition: Shifting From Fossil Fuels to Solar and Wind Energy, Lester R. Brown, 2015, W.W. Norton & Company.

Thank God for Evolution: How the Marriage of Science and Religion Will Transform Your Life and Our World, Michael Dowd, 2008, Viking.

This Changes Everything: Capitalism vs The Climate, Naomi Klein, 2015, Simon & Schuster.

Merchants of Doubt: How a Handful of Scientists Obscured the Truth on Issues from Tobacco Smoke to Global Warming, Naomi Oreskes & Eric Conway, 2010, Bloomsbury Press.

Laudato Si: On Care for Our Common Home, Encyclical by Pope Francis, 2015,

Our Sunday Visitor. Available online at: w2.vatican.va/content/francesco/en/encyclicals/documents/papa-francesco_20150524_enciclica-laudato-si.html

Half the Sky: Turning Oppression into Opportunity for Women Worldwide, Nicholas D. Kristof and Sheryl WuDunn, 2009, Knopf, and by the same authors, *A Path Appears: Transforming Lives, Creating Opportunity*, 2014, Knopf.

The Jane Effect: Celebrating Jane Goodall, Dale Peterson and Marc Bekoff (editors), 2015, Trinity University Press.

Books by Robert Moss. A few suggestions: *Dreaming the Soul Back*

Home: Shamanic Dreaming for Healing and Becoming Whole, 2012, New World Library; *Active Dreaming: Journeying Beyond Self-Limitation to a Life of Wild Freedom*, 2011, New World Library; *Conscious Dreaming: A Spiritual Path for Everyday Life*, 1996, Harmony.

Books by Dr. Riane Eisler. Especially, *The Chalice and the Blade: Our History, Our Future*, 1987, Harper Collins; *Tomorrow's Children: A Blueprint for Partnership Education in the 21ˢᵗ Century*, 2000, Basic Books; *The Real Wealth of Nations: Creating a Caring Economics*, 2007, Berrett-Koehler Publishers.

Books by Bill McKibben, such as, *Deep Economy: The Wealth of Communities & the Durable Future*, 2007, Times Books; *Eaarth: Making a Life on a Tough New Planet*, 2010, Times Books; *Oil and Honey: The Education of an Unlikely Activist*, 2013, Times Books.

Books by Dr. Jane Goodall, including, *Reason For Hope: A Spiritual Journey*,

1999, Grand Central Publishing; *Hope for Animals and Their World: How Endangered Species Are Being Rescued from the Brink*, 2009, Grand Central Publishing; *Seeds of Hope: Wisdom and Wonder from the World of Plants* (with Gail Hudson), 2013, Grand Central Publishing.

Web

Center for Whale Research (www.whaleresearch.com)
Orca Salmon Alliance (www.orcasalmonalliance.org)
OrcaNetwork (www.orcanetwork.org)
Voice of the Orcas (voiceoftheorcas.blogspot.com)
The Whale Museum (www.whalemuseum.org)
YoOceans! (www.yooceans.org)
SeaWorld Fact Check (www.seaworldfactcheck.com)
Tilikum & Co (sites.google.com/site/tilikumandco)
Jane Goodall Institute (www.janegoodall.org)
Earth Guardians: #GenerationRyse (www.earthguardians.org)
Global Oneness Summit (www.globalonenesssummit.org)
The Big History Project (www.bighistoryproject.com)
A Path Appears (www.apathappears.org)

350.org (www.350.org)
Children's Trust (www.ourchildrenstrust.org)
Citizens Climate Lobby (www.citizensclimatelobby.org)
This Changes Everything (www.thischangeseverything.org)
Climate Mobilization (www.theclimatemobilization.org)
Union of Concerned Scientists (www.ucsusa.org)
The Great Transition Initiative (www.greattransition.org)
The Work of Byron Katie (www.thework.com/en)

Film

Blackfish (www.blackfishmovie.com)
Racing Extinction (www.racingextinction.com)
Lolita: Slave to Entertainment (www.slavetoentertainment.com)
A Day in the Life of Lolita (www.danielazarian.com/portfolio/lolita-visser)
The Whale (www.thewhalemovie.com)
DamNation (www.damnationfilm.com)
The Shift Movie (www.theshiftmovie.com)
I Am (www.iamthedoc.com)
Unity (www.nationearth.com/films)
This Changes Everything (www.thefilm.thischangeseverything.org)
Merchants of Doubt (www.sonyclassics.com/merchantsofdoubt)
A Path Appears (www.apathappears.org/film)
Women and Girls Lead (www.womenandgirlslead.org)
Illuminating Our Common Home (www.ourcommonhome.world)

Lightning Source UK Ltd.
Milton Keynes UK
UKOW02f1321140916

282963UK00005B/145/P